D0029269

CAPITOL SCANDAL

Sarah Gregory

A SIGNET BOOK

SIGNET
Published by New American Library, a division of
Penguin Putnam Inc., 375 Hudson Street,
New York, New York 10014, U.S.A.
Penguin Books Ltd, 27 Wrights Lane,
London W8 5TZ, England
Penguin Books Australia Ltd, Ringwood,
Victoria, Australia
Penguin Books Canada Ltd, 10 Alcorn Avenue,
Toronto, Ontario, Canada M4V 3B2
Penguin Books (N.Z.) Ltd, 182–190 Wairau Road,
Auckland 10, New Zealand

Penguin Books Ltd, Registered Offices:
Harmondsworth, Middlesex, England

Published by Signet, an imprint of New American Library,
a division of Penguin Putnam Inc.

First Printing, December 1999
10 9 8 7 6 5 4 3 2 1

 REGISTERED TRADEMARK—MARCA REGISTRADA

Printed in the United States of America

PUBLISHER'S NOTE
This is a work of fiction. Names, characters, places, and incidents are either the product of the author's imagination or are used fictitiously, and any resemblance to actual persons, living or dead, business establishments, events, or locales is entirely coincidental.

Prologue

Joggers in the nation's capital fall into two categories, political and passionate. Political runners are less than dedicated, their regimen limited to an occasional tour of the loop around the mall, where they hope to see the President working out. On most days the Man is nowhere in sight, the result being that political runners accumulate stone bruises and muscle pulls while watching other unnotable joggers pass by in the opposite direction. Their gaits are best described as the Congressional Waddle or the Presidential Prance.

Washington runners of the lean and mean variety shun the mall in favor of Rock Creek Park, which features fifteen miles of wooded trails winding all the way into Maryland. Such was the case with Roger Derr and Barbara Peterman, who left their BMW near the P Street Bridge at 4 A.M. one early December Sunday, and set out on their morning trot in twenty degrees. The couple lived together in Georgetown. Both held master's degrees in engineering and both were into designing computer chips. Roger had competed in one New York City Marathon and Barbara was determined to enter the women's division the following year. They wore reflecting white insulated jogging suits. Battery-operated lanterns were molded into the crowns of their soft leather headgear.

The park didn't open until seven, so the lovers planned to avoid the main entrance and catch the trail a quarter mile in. Stretching, loosening up, lifting first one knee and then the other, their breaths fogging as they stepped carefully over patches of ice, the couple used wooden steps to negotiate the steep incline alongside the bridge. They touched each other a lot. As they neared level ground, a man in evening clothes came out of the woods.

So much did the unexpected meeting startle the joggers that they later disagreed in their descriptions of the man; Barbara insisted that the stranger wore a tux even though Roger was just as certain that he had on a dark formal suit. Both agreed that the encounter seemed to rattle the stranger as much as it did them, and that as he passed them by without a word he averted his face. He was breathing heavily, as if from exertion. Leaves and twigs clung to his jacket and were tangled in his hair. He quickened his pace, running up the embankment, slipping once in his formal shoes, reached the pavement, and melted into the darkness on P Street. In seconds a starter chugged, an engine caught and raced, and headlights stabbed the night as a car drove away. Roger and Barbara jogged in place for a moment, debating whether to continue. Their dedication to running won out, and the couple trotted on in among the trees.

The lovers' jaunt was a short one, for them at any rate, an eight-mile jog along the banks of Rock Creek to the zoo and back again. The exhilaration of near-top-speed running drove the meeting with the stranger from their minds. As they neared their original starting point they watched for the crooked stick which Roger had left upright in the ground, marking the shortest route through the woods to their car. Sunrise was a couple of hours away. Roger was a few strides in the lead. His bobbing head lantern illuminated the knobby stick. He made a quick left turn and charged off among the trees. "Race you," he called out playfully.

Barbara accepted the challenge, shrieking in delight, ignoring the small branches tugging at her clothing as she zigged and zagged her way through the woods. At the center of the couple's relationship was a hot competitiveness, usually culminating in frenzied lovemaking. Barbara grimaced, lust building within her, her breath coming in ragged gasps as Roger's lantern bobbed and weaved ahead of her. This morning she would show him something new, would mount him right there in the BMW at the edge of P Street, would ride him into submission until, writhing in pleasure, he would beg her to stop. You are in for it, Mr. Derr, she thought as the uneven ground jarred her from head to toe. Barbara Peterman, M.E. from North Carolina, once known as Miss Conservative all over the freaking campus, is about to fuck your brains out of your . . .

Fifty yards short of the clearing where the wooden steps led up to P Street, Barbara Peterman's foot struck something solid. She fell headlong.

The sleeve of her jogging suit scraped rough bark,

skinning her arm without tearing the cloth, but otherwise she wasn't injured. Prone on the ground, her nose buried in frozen leaves, icy frost melting and soaking into her clothing, Barbara felt nothing so much as dumb. How could she be so stupid? She rolled over quickly and sat up, using a thumb and forefinger to aim her lantern toward whatever had tripped her.

The beam illuminated a smooth-shaven leg bent at the knee, and a slender foot with painted toenails. Shivers parading up and down her backbone, Barbara hoisted herself upright. The body over which she stood was that of a young woman, wearing a backless and sleeveless sequined cocktail dress. The girl's skirt was bunched around her waist; she wore no pantyhose or underwear. Her skin in the light from the lantern showed a yellowish tint, rapidly turning blue. She had short dark hair and her neck was bent at an odd angle. A branch had fallen over her upper torso, partially obscuring her face. Barbara bent from the waist and moved the branch aside. There were two silver dollar-sized holes in the dead woman's head, one through her cheekbone and the other through her forehead. Both wounds oozed blood and grayish matter.

Barbara Peterman's scream split the frosty silence, followed by the sound of her retching as she vomited on the ground. Roger Derr heard her as he jogged in place near the road, and quickly retraced his steps to stand beside his lover. He stared dumbfounded at the spectacle on the ground, placing a comforting arm around Barbara's shoulders. He never suspected that before she made the grisly discovery, he'd been in for a mind-blowing lay.

1

On the last day of October, Sharon Hays flew home to Texas from California. In five short days she'd become a celebrity, clearing one of America's best-known actresses, Darla Cowan, from murder charges in a hearing televised around the globe. The attention made Sharon nervous. When fellow travelers on the 747 shot glances in her direction, then averted their gazes and whispered among themselves, she felt like hiding under her seat.

Sharon's newfound fame had her torn. Part of her wanted to take the limelight, appear on *Leno,* give every interview requested, take all the high-profile cases that were certain to be offered. But she was a single mother with a daughter to raise, and Melanie's critical teenage years lay dead ahead. Sharon pictured Melanie taking dope, staying out all night, giving in to a succession of eager boys as her mom flitted blithely around the country. The image made Sharon want to stick her head in the sand up to her shoulders, and never leave Texas again.

Washington, D.C.

The D.C. metropolitan police detectives assigned to investigate the corpse in Rock Creek Park were named

Virginia Toledo and Isaac Brown, and as partners were a study in opposites. Ginny Toledo, small and olive-complexioned, held a degree in English from American University. She'd signed on with the police department seven years earlier because nighttime work allowed her to pursue her master's during the day, but tuition funds had waned shortly thereafter and she'd taken the detective's exam out of necessity. She was married to a Virginia highway patrolman and lived on just the other side of Arlington, and had long since abandoned her dream of becoming a teacher. She did, however, carry a small tape player in the unmarked detectives' sedan, and listened to audio books en route to and from crime scenes while her partner suffered in silence.

Isaac Brown had been to college as well, though he didn't have a degree. A six-foot-four, two-hundred-and-ninety-pound black man, he'd been an all-ACC offensive lineman at the University of Maryland. He'd skipped his senior season, opting for the pro draft, and the Seattle Seahawks had picked him in the third round. A training camp knee injury had ended his pro career before it had gotten off the ground, and he'd migrated into police work twelve years ago. Now thirty-three, Detective Brown continued to pump iron with a passion, and his massive neck and sloping shoulders turned a lot of female heads. He'd learned police procedure from the ground up, beginning his career as a guard in the metropolitan jail, and subscribed to the kickin'-ass-and-takin'-names theory of law enforcement. Many cops called him Ram-Bro. Ginny Toledo, properly brought up and politically cor-

rect, considered the nickname racist and referred to
her partner as Ike. Detective Brown didn't act as if he
cared either way; Ram-Bro, Ike, all the same to him.

The detectives questioned Barbara Peterman and
Roger Derr without learning a great deal; the lovers'
description of the man they'd seen was sketchy at best,
though they did agree to drop by headquarters the
following day to look at photos. Toledo and Brown
then supervised the uniforms' securing of the crime
scene, waited for the medical examiner to pronounce
the victim dead, printed the corpse, and bagged its
hands, and stayed with the body until the meat wagon
hauled it downtown to the morgue. This task com-
pleted, the detectives filled out report forms and called
it a day.

The *Washington Post* run a one-column story about
the unidentified corpse on Page Two of its Metro section, and the story produced a positive ID around ten
o'clock the following morning. The identifying party
was named Melissa Rudolph, a curvy twenty-year-old
student living in Arlington, who appeared at police
headquarters with the newspaper folded and tucked
underneath her arm. Though she wore jeans with
holes worn in the knees, dirty white sneakers, and a
frayed man's shirt with the tail out, her hair and
makeup were perfectly fixed. She had pretty soft features and had retained some baby fat in her cheeks.
When the morgue attendant pulled the shroud aside,
Miss Rudolph murmured tearfully, "Gee."

A half hour later, Detectives Toledo and Brown
interviewed Miss Rudolph in a small office adjacent
to the squad room. Her hands trembling as she sipped

canned Dr Pepper through a straw, Miss Rudolph told the detectives that the victim was her roommate, Courtney Lee.

"How long since you've seen her?" Brown asked. He spoke in a pleasant rumbling basso.

"Saturday afternoon." Melissa Rudolph's voice was soft, an educated Texas twang.

"What time?"

"Around two. Wow, I can't believe this."

"How long had you and Miss Lee been living together?"

"Just since school started. August. But I've known Courtney since first grade."

The detectives exchanged a look. Toledo said, "In Texas?"

"How did you . . . ?" Miss Rudolph showed a sad smile. "Oh, yeah, my accent. Yes, Baytown." She pronounced "accent" as "ack-say-yent," as if the word had three syllables.

Brown kept his tone sympathetic. "You young ladies came up here to go to college?"

Miss Rudolph set down her drink and twisted her fingers together. "Oh, no. This is my junior year, but Courtney just moved here. She's been going to S.M.U."

"In Dallas?"

Miss Rudolph nodded vacantly.

Brown glanced at the tape recorder. "The machine won't record a nod, miss."

"I'm sorry. S.M.U.'s in Dallas, yes."

"She was a transfer student?"

Miss Rudolph quickly shook her head. "Courtney

is taking, *was* taking a year off. She's been interning for a congressman. I should tell you, her dad and Mattie Ruth Benedict are close."

Brown lifted her eyebrows. "*Senator* Benedict?"

"Yes, sir."

Brown looked at Toledo as if to say, Oh, Christ. Mattie Ruth Benedict (D-Tx) was the current Senate Minority Leader and one of the president's main legislative supporters, the previous midterm election having placed the Democratic Prez in the hands of a Republican Congress. Mattie Ruth's Texas-twanged rally speech at the most recent Democratic Convention had wowed 'em across the country, and had solidified her reputation as a no-nonsense, acid-tongued but regal lady. Her husband Paul, a former U. of Texas law professor and now a power in a corporate firm, was a leader in the fight against Big Tobacco. Mattie Ruth had one son, Will John Benedict, a junior congressman in his first term. Hardly a day passed when Mattie Ruth, Will John, or Paul Benedict wasn't mentioned in the D.C. social pages. Metro police hated cases where public officials became involved; often the red tape choked the investigation beyond repair.

Toledo's interest picked up. "It's been our experience that interns, what interns we've come in contact with, are generally children of party supporters. Donators . . ."

And hell raisers, Brown thought. When he'd worn a uniform he'd busted a few interns, mainly during parties after neighbors had phoned in noise complaints. Daddy always made bail. A call from a senate or congressional aide to the U.S. Attorney generally caused the charges to disappear. D.C. cops now considered such arrests a waste of time, and usually let the offenders off with warnings.

"You couldn't expect anyone to live on Courtney's pay." Miss Rudolph's nose wrinkled. "Six hundred or something."

Rents in the area where Melissa Rudolph lived were twice that figure. "Supplemented with funds from home?" Toledo said.

Miss Rudolph nodded. "Courtney's daddy and my daddy are partners."

"In what?"

"A law firm, Rudolph, Lee & Stickelmeyer. Mr. Stickelmeyer isn't in the office much. He's a state senator in Austin."

Toledo's features softened. "Would you care to notify the next of kin? Normally we do that, when it's someone local, but . . ."

Miss Rudolph sniffled, about to cry. "I couldn't face Mr. Lee. I'd prefer not to."

Detective Brown straightened in a businesslike posture. "When you saw your roommate on Saturday, was it at your apartment?"

"I was just leaving. My boyfriend's at Annapolis, and he had liberty."

"We'd like to visit your place and go over Miss Lee's things," Brown said.

Miss Rudolph shrugged, a sad but pretty gesture. "Just let me know when."

"When you spoke with her," Brown said, "did she indicate she was going out?"

"She borrowed my dress."

"A sequined cocktail dress?"

"Yes, sir."

"I have to tell you, miss. It's what she was wearing when she . . ."

"I know. It said so in the paper."

"That's right," Brown said, "it did. The dress is evidence. You understand that?"

"I wouldn't dream of wearing it anyway, sir, after what happened."

"It will be in our property room. Did she tell you where she was going?"

There was the barest flicker of Miss Rudolph's lashes, a slight aversion to her gaze. "I'm not sure."

Brown exchanged a glance with Toledo, then leaned forward to rest his forearms on his thighs. "We sympathize this is a shock to you. but this is a murder investigation. To withhold anything from us would be a mistake." Toledo's look at Brown was disapproving. He acted as if he didn't notice.

Miss Rudolph hugged herself, trembling. "I wouldn't want to get anyone in trouble."

"Someone's already in trouble. Miss Lee. She's dead."

Miss Rudolph watched her lap. "Courtney went to a lot of parties."

Unblinking, his expression stoic, Brown said, "Parties where drugs were present?"

Miss Rudolph looked away. "I don't know anything about . . ."

"Miss Rudolph," Toledo cut in, "we're not the narcotics bureau. We're looking into a homicide. But we find where drugs are a factor it give us certain options, where to point the investigation." She smiled. "Only the killer has anything to fear from us. Drugs would be incidental."

Some of the tension left Miss Rudolph's look, but not all. "She didn't go, like, I'm doing good dope here or doing it there. But a couple of times she brought some home."

"From the parties?" Brown asked.

"Yes, sir."

"Who threw these parties, miss?"

"Gee, Courtney was into older people. Those she met at work."

"At the congressman's office?" Brown's jaw was set.

"There and . . . You know, people she met around the Capitol Building."

Brown ignored a sharp look from Toledo and bored on in. "What people?"

"Specifically?"

Brown expelled air. "I've got to tell you, Miss Rudolph, you sound evasive. This is probably your first encounter with law enforcement. But this is serious business."

"I got stopped a few times in high school," Miss Rudolph said.

"Back in Baytown? Where everyone knew your father?"

She showed a half smile. "He's pretty well known."

"This isn't Baytown, miss, and we deal every day with people a whole lot more famous than your father. Obstruction of justice isn't funny."

She seemed confused. "Obstruction of . . ."

"It's where you know who's selling dope, committing murder or whatever, the police ask you and you feed them a line of shit."

"Ike," Toledo said softly but urgently. Brown held up a hand and waited for an answer.

Miss Rudolph shifted uncomfortably. "Would anyone know who told you?"

"Not just if you told us where she was going," Brown said. "But if you witnessed something, and later had to testify, that would be different."

Pretty gray eyes watched the corner of the room. Finally the coed told them, "Courtney was seeing a married guy. A guy like, pretty old."

Brown shrugged. "How old is pretty old?"

"Thirty-five at least."

"What's his name?"

"Benedict."

"Mattie Ruth Benedict's son? The congressman?"

She nodded. "Will John Benedict. She's interning in his office. If this gets out back home it will be *so* not cool . . ."

"Will John Benedict gave the party?" Brown asked.

"I don't know who gave the party. But that's who Courtney's like, been seeing." Miss Rudolph frowned anxiously. "Mattie Ruth doesn't know. Will you tell her?"

Brown's jaws clicked together. Toledo leaned nearer the girl, nodded, and said tenderly, "Under the circumstances, we have to."

A tear ran down Miss Rudolph's cheek. "Daddy was right."

"Fathers often are," Toledo said. "Why, what did he tell you?"

"It wasn't just Courtney who wanted to be an intern. I did, too. Daddy wouldn't hear of it. He told me, any man turning his daughter loose with that Washington crowd was just throwing her to the wolves. I told Courtney what he said, and then Daddy and Mr. Lee had this big fight over it. Nearly broke up their partnership." Her look was pleading. "Look, Courtney wasn't *bad* or anything."

Brown's scowl disappeared, replaced by a look of understanding. "Someone was. Thanks, Miss Rudolph. Your cooperation is the first step toward finding out who."

Any investigation involving the Capitol Hill crowd was a hot potato within the department, so Brown and Toledo reported to their shift commander as soon as Melissa Rudolph left the building. The shift commander was a young lieutenant named Morgan Reece, who covered his butt by calling the brass upstairs. The duty clerk punched him through to the Chief of Detectives, who canceled his lunch appointment and met with Toledo, Brown, and Reece during the noon hour. The C of D's was Howard Morganthal, a granite-faced man with steel-gray hair. He was a former Secret Service agent who'd guarded the President, and often appeared on the evening news. He listened carefully as the detectives detailed their progress up to now, then got right to the point. "What have we told the press?"

Shift Commander Reece handed the ball off. "I'll let you answer that one, Mrs. Toledo. Save us having to repeat ourselves."

Toledo crossed her legs and folded her hands. "As

of now, zilch. They ran the usual unidentified body piece this morning."

"From now on," Morganthal said, "everything on this case comes through me. What's your next step?"

Toledo now deferred to Detective Brown. The huge black man sat at ease. "To get the guy in here for questioning," Brown said.

Morganthal swiveled his chair to look out the window, at traffic rolling by on Pennsylvania Avenue, at men and women pouring out of the lobby over at the Justice Building, hunching their shoulders against the cold, tiny snowflakes swirling down like confetti. "What guy is that?" Morganthal said.

"The boyfriend. Congressman Whoever."

Morganthal jabbed his finger in the air. "Not at this point. Not Mattie Ruth Benedict's son, no way. At the most, you call his office and make an appointment."

Brown looked at Toledo, who lowered her gaze. Brown leaned forward. "Begging respect, sir, but giving him time to get his story straight, that's not our priority."

"If you call him in," Morganthal said, "he won't come. He'll send his lawyer. Then you'll have no story, period, straight or otherwise. If he does talk to you, you say up front it's a murder investigation, give the decedent's name and why you believe Congressman Benedict has information you need. If he plays solid citizen and opens up, more the better. If he stonewalls, turns you over to a bunch of aides, that's when you start waiving subpoenas. This is not Willie Dickwagger from the Southeast Sector. This is a guy whose profession is ducking issues." He rubbed his eyes, and pinched the bridge of his nose between a thumb and forefinger. "Damn these politicians. If they could learn to keep it zipped, there'd be a helluva lot less trouble in the world."

The C of D's kept his back turned as Shift Commander Reece and Detectives Brown and Toledo looked at each other. Toledo got up and walked over to the window. Her hair was short and flipped up in back. "Not just politicians, sir," she finally said. "You could make that statement about any number of men."

Detective Toledo called Congressman Will John Benedict's office in the Russell Building while Brown tried to reach the victim's family. The black policeman obtained the number for Rudolph, Lee & Stickelmeyer, Attorneys, through Baytown, Texas information, but Courtney Lee's father wasn't in. He wasn't expected back until the following Monday. Brown asked if he could call Mr. Lee at his residence.

"Sorry, sir," the switchboard operator told him, "but I'm not authorized to give out Mr. Lee's home number."

Brown left his name, number, and extension, then hung up and looked at Detective Toledo. Their desks butted up so that Brown and Toledo faced each other. The pretty female cop looked concerned. "That's odd," she said.

Brown tilted his chair and folded his arms.

Toledo dumped a package of Sweet'n Low into a Styrofoam cup of coffee, and reached for a plastic stir stick. "Benedict's in. Won't talk to anyone, but he's in. I left my number."

Brown spread his hands. "What's odd about that? Politicians don't talk to anybody they don't know."

"What's odd is that he's in in the first place. Congress isn't in session. They're in the ten-week break after Thanksgiving, until the day after the State of the Union address, end of January. Most of them leave town, go back home to spend the holidays with their families and constituents." Toledo finished stirring, sucked the end of the stirrer, and dropped the plastic stick into the wastebasket. "Drum up campaign funds. Merry Christmas and fork over, bud."

"Unless they've got something going around here," Brown said. "Such as some poontang."

Toledo blinked. "How delicate. What's the area code for Baytown, Texas?"

Brown gave her the area code, and Toledo called Congressman Benedict's office in Texas after getting the number from information. She winked at her partner as she listened to a series of rings over the line. Her chin lifted as she said, "Yes. This is Annie Proux with the *Houston Chronicle*. I was wondering if it would be possible to set up an interview with the congressman and his wife. A series I'm doing, how our representatives are spending the holidays." She listened, sipping coffee as she did. She said, "Well when will he . . . ? I see. And Mrs. Benedict, is she in town so she'll be available to . . . ? Thank you. No, I'll call back. I'm in and out of the office, so my number wouldn't help you much. Thanks." She hung up, thoughtfully drumming her fingers. "The Honorable Will John Benedict has been spending the holidays back home, but came to Washington last Friday and won't return to Texas until this Thursday."

"Leaving his old lady in Bumfuck, Egypt over the weekend?" Brown asked.

"Baytown, Texas."

"What's the difference?"

"He came to Washington alone," Toledo said.

"Hey, Ginny, when you left your number at his Washington office. You tell 'em you were the heat?"

Toledo nodded, one corner of her mouth tightening.

Brown pointed a finger. "Lay you odds he doesn't call you back. You might hear from his lawyer. Him, no way."

Toledo pushed her chair back and stood. She lifted her handbag by its strap. "My thinking exactly." She took a couple of paces toward the exit, then stopped and turned. "You coming, or what?" she asked Detective Brown.

Two hours later, Brown and Toledo were parked on South Capitol Street in between the Rayburn and Longworth Buildings. Straight ahead on the Capitol lawn, trees had an eerie look as snow piled on leafless branches. The detectives had been sitting there since making the ten-minute drive over from headquarters. Brown started the engine occasionally so that the heater would warm the car's interior. Detective Toledo was listening to an audiocassette of *Cold Mountain* by Charles Frazier. Detective Brown suffered in silence.

Brown held the House of Representatives' pictorial directory in his lap, open to the B's. Will John Benedict was a white guy with soft cheeks and a double chin, and with a shock of blondish hair swept down over his forehead. Brown closed the book and laid it aside, and looked across the street just as Congressman Benedict came out of the Longworth Building.

Or pranced out, actually, wearing a gray collarless sweatshirt, sweatpants, and blue running shoes, jogging in place, lifting his hand and offering political smiles to pedestrians who hurried past on the sidewalk. As the congressman broke into a loping gallop, headed north toward Independence Avenue, Brown turned and said to the couple in the backseat, "There's our man. You recognize him?"

Roger Derr and Barbara Peterman had agreed to sit with the detectives during lunch hour, and had grown more and more antsy as time went by. On two occasions they'd threatened to leave, but Brown had talked them into staying by promising to put in a word with the couples' supervisors. Roger and Barbara were dressed in business suits and topcoats. His suit was navy blue. Hers was gray with a skirt which stopped three inches above her knee. Both topcoats were beige London Fogs.

Roger watched the congressman's fast-retreating backside. "It's the guy."

Barbara was less than certain. "I don't think so, Roger. The man the other night was shorter. A bit broader as well, I think, though a cumberbund can deceive you as to someone's build."

Roger's smile was tight. "He wasn't wearing a cumberbund, sweetie. He had on a suit."

Barbara's tone showed just a hint of exasperation. "A cumberbund, darling. A bow tie and studs."

Roger dropped all pretense of being lovey-dovey. "It was a *suit,* Barb. A fucking Armani."

Barbara folded her arms and looked the other way, toward the Capitol. "A tux, you asshole. What are you, blind?"

Detective Brown wondered how the couple's upcoming wedding would go. He exchanged a meaningful look with Detective Toledo. Both cops got out, walked forward, and met in front of the auto's hood.

Isaac Brown's breath fogged the air. "I don't think they'll be very good witnesses."

"At least for sure *she* won't be," Toledo said. "What do we tell the C of D's?"

Brown glanced toward the backseat, where Roger Derr and Barbara Peterson seemed ready to square off and come to blows. "I think the guy shows more perception," Brown said. "His ID of the suspect is plenty good enough for me, Ginny."

"I'd like to have her more positive," Toledo said. "So what do you think?"

Brown shrugged as Will John Benedict rounded the corner and vanished behind a building. "Appears the congressman's been naughty."

Toledo chewed her lower lip. "Looks that way," she said.

As soon as his meeting with Brown, Toledo, and their shift commander was over, Chief of Detectives Howard Morganthal looked a number up in his Rolodex. He called and made an appointment. Then he speed-dialed his wife and told her he was working late, attending a meeting with the Commission on Violent Crime. Finally he told his assistant that he was knocking off for the day, checked his Buick Electra out of the police garage, drove southwest out of the city, and crossed the Theodore Roosevelt Bridge into Virginia.

A half hour later he passed under a wrought-iron arch and cruised down a blacktop lined with cherry trees. White wood three-rail fences marked off polo fields, horse and dairy barns. Landscape rolled gently into the distance. The snow fell heavily now, and soon the whiteness would blanket the ground. Forecasters had predicted a bitch of a winter. Straight ahead loomed a Colonial house with tall white pillars.

He parked in a circular drive and climbed up onto a wide brick porch. His hands were deep in his overcoat pockets and his shoulders were hunched. He pressed a button, and a maid in a starched uniform answered the door. Morganthal told her, "Harry Fry to see Ms. Carboneau. She's expecting me." The maid nodded, took Morganthal's coat, and hustled off to the rear of the house after telling him to wait in the entry hall.

The C of D's strolled past a six-foot grandfather clock, breakfronts with pewter cups and crystal goblets stacked inside, and paused at the foot of a carpeted staircase. On the wall hung a cluster of large gilt picture frames. Inside the frames were blowups of Rita Carboneau's books. Each had been a huge bestseller, and each dust jacket had the author's name across the top in letters larger than the title. On a mahogany counter below the frames stood copies of the books themselves. They were unauthorized biographies of three movie stars, one talk show host, and one former President of the United States. Rita Carboneau was known—behind her back, never to her face—as the Duchess of Dirt, and the *New York Times* review of her latest book had appeared under the headline, IF YOU CAN'T SAY SOMETHING NICE, SIT HERE NEXT TO RITA. Her syndicated twice-weekly column appeared in two hundred newspapers. She credited most of her tidbits to "anonymous sources," though she'd acknowledged input from a Secret Service Agent known as "Harry Fry" for her graphic descriptions of the ex-President's sexual conquests. Only after consultation with the publisher's lawyers had she confessed that "Harry Fry" was a pseudonym.

Howard Morganthal's salary as C of D's was eighty-six thousand dollars a year. The payments on his Georgetown condo were five thousand dollars a month. His wife was the current president of the Junior League, his daughter a freshman at Duke and a Tri-Delt pledge. Enough said; Morganthal's legitimate income didn't stretch very far. He turned from the literary shrine as Rita Carboneau bubbled into the room.

The face was ageless—though her books had been published over a twenty-five-year period, making her fifty if she was a day—and the dye job on her short raven hair was undetectable. Her waist was trim. Her blue silk lounging outfit molded around firm thighs and tented over upturned breasts enhanced with silicone. As she took Morganthal's hands and allowed him to kiss first one cheek and then the other, expensive jewelry clinked. The aroma of Enigma wafted up Morganthal's nostrils. She led the way into a den with a stone fireplace above which oil paintings hung. At her direction Morganthal occupied a leather chair. Rita Carboneau sat on a chintz sofa and curled up her legs. The maid brought apricot brandy in tiny stemmed glasses, and set the drinks on a teakwood coffee table. Rita Carboneau sipped. "It's been too long. Why have you been such a stranger, Harry?"

"Howard."

Carboneau cut her eyes toward the maid's retreating backside, and imperceptibly shook her head.

"Harry is a nickname," Morganthal said, watching the maid as well. He tweaked Carboneau a bit by saying, "Kitty Kelley's latest is all the rage."

She wriggled testily. "Yes, *The Royals*. Have you read it?"

"I don't have much time to read." Morganthal held his glass in both hands with his elbows on his armrests.

"Don't bother with *The Royals*. It's crap. I could have done much better." Her eyes widened. "What brings you here?"

"A murder case."

Carboneau shrugged. "Washington is the murder capital of the world."

"This murder is going to grab a lot of headlines, once the news gets out."

"A lot of murders grab headlines." She seemed nonchalant. For the information on the ex-President's extracurricular fucking, Rita Carboneau had paid Morganthal twenty-five thousand dollars. Since then he'd learned that the sum was a pittance, and that she'd forked over three times that amount for information on a certain movie star. On this occasion,

Howard Morganthal would use fancier footwork at the bargaining table.

"Our suspect is high profile," Morganthal said.

One plucked eyebrow arched. "Is the President involved?"

"Not yet."

"Damn."

Morganthal set down his brandy and hitched around in his chair. "This could be bigger than the President."

"Oh, come on, Howard." Carboneau gave a shoofly wave. "Nothing's that big."

"We have a young half-naked woman. A grisly butchering. Sex, infidelity . . ."

"So far you haven't shown me a book. A magazine article, perhaps." Carboneau touched her hair.

"A family that's a household name."

"The Kennedys? Hah. They've been done to death." Her voice lowered an octave. "Besides, how can you offer me an exclusive?"

"I've already arranged it," Morganthal said. "My detectives . . . Everything flows through me. Everyone will have the general news, of course. But inside info?"

Carboneau's mouth twisted sensuously in a look of lust. "Is it Teddy?"

"Not the Kennedys. Not them at all."

Carboneau's breath quickened. "Give, Howard. I'm not going to blow you for the information, if that's what you . . ."

Morganthal assumed a crafty posture. "For this you might."

She sat stiffly erect. "Nice seeing you, Howard."

His eyes widened. "Must I call Kitty Kelley?"

"She's out of the country."

Morganthal sat back and regarded her thoughtfully. "It's the Benedicts, Rita."

Carboneau was obviously shocked. "Mattie Ruth?"

"Her kin."

"Christ, Howard. Paul?"

Now it was Morganthal's turn to look puzzled.

"Paul's her husband," Carboneau said. "He's known around town as Bull One."

"Bull?"

"God, Howard, you are out of the loop. Just mention the nickname to any number of women. Paul Benedict is hung like, unbelievably." Carboneau's eyes grew big and round.

Morganthal's curiosity got the best of him. "Are you speaking from experience?"

Carboneau put her feet on the floor, then crossed her legs. "None of your fucking business. Come on, Howard, is it Paul?"

Morganthal had a knowing look. Rita Carboneau would claim personal knowledge of anything inside the Beltway, including some mover and shaker's dick size. The C of D's felt slimy, just talking to this woman. "Not Paul," Morganthal said.

Carboneau was incredulous. "It can't be the wuss."

"Wuss?"

"The congressman, Mattie Ruth's son. Will John Benedict. That guy can't even spell sex. Rumor is, he won't even touch his wife that way."

"Our evidence thus far says you're wrong," Morganthal said.

Carboneau opened a drawer and pulled out a pack of Virginia Slims. She unwrapped the cellophane ribbon. "Christ, Will John Benedict? Christ, Christ, Christ, Christ, Christ." She popped a cigarette into her mouth, and paused with her thumb on the flint wheel of a Bic disposable. "Let's talk turkey, Howard," she said. "If it's really the Benedicts, and you can really supply information exclusive to me—and those are pretty big ifs, by the way—then there might be something we can do."

2

On the second Tuesday in December, Sharon Hays used part of her fee in the Darla Cowan case to buy a car. She settled on a three-year-old Buick Skylark, two-tone blue with twenty-eight thousand miles on the odometer, and paid sixty-eight hundred bucks after haggling with the used car manager at Don Snell Buick for a couple of weeks. She'd agreed on the price the previous Friday, but had spent the weekend agonizing over trading in her dented old Volvo. The Volvo had been her transportation for eight long years, the car in which her daughter Melanie had grown into teenhood. As the salesman drove the heap to the rear of the lot, Sharon stood beside her shiny late-model Skylark and wiped away a tear.

She rode to downtown Dallas in comfort, listening to a stereo system with no static in the speakers for a change, yet continued to pine for the Volvo. To hell with it, she thought, it was a piece of junk. She stopped by AAA Bail Bonds to drop off a check and pick up bail documents for two of her clients, a burglar named LaTarrance Williams and a drunk driver named Willis Clay. She then proceeded to the Lew

Sterrett Justice Center adjacent to the Crowley Courts
Building, both mammoth structures on river bottom land
west of downtown. She parked in the courts building lot
and hustled over to the jail in muggy seventy-eight degrees under an overcast sky. Nowhere else but Texas
did one sweat profusely in the middle of December.
God, wasn't winter *ever* going to come? She entered
through double doors and stood at the bail release
desk. The lone attending sheriff's deputy was at the
back of the office with his feet up, watching television.
Sharon flopped her briefcase onto the counter with a
bang and loudly cleared her throat. The deputy didn't
seem to hear. She *harumph*-ed a second time.

The deputy looked at her over his shoulder. He was
in his early twenties and wore a thin mustache along
with wire-framed glasses. Sharon knew the guy by
sight, but couldn't recall his name. "A minute, okay?"
he said. "It's the Benedict deal." He squinted at her.
"Oh, it's you, Miss Hays." He got up and walked
quickly in her direction. The metal tag above his
pocket identified him as Deputy Kinsolving.

The sound on the TV was too low for Sharon to
hear, but the picture told her all she needed to know.
It was the daily White House press conference, and
the attending newsies would be firing questions about
the Chief Executive's position on the looming murder
investigation targeting Will John Benedict. No one
had charged Will John with a crime, but the leaks to
the media had already convicted him in the public eye.
Last night Jay Leno's monologue had consisted of one
joke after another about the case, none of which
Sharon thought were very funny. The press conference

vanished from view, replaced by a head and shoulders shot of Will John alongside a photo of what's-her-name, the victim. Poor Mattie Ruth, Sharon thought. As the deputy approached she said, "That's about all you can get on TV. I've gotten sick of the whole thing." She also thought that the media was really feeding at the bottom by speculating on the dead girl's sexual history. The supermarket tabloids were having a blast. Yesterday's *Inquisitor* had featured a college student on the cover, his lips parted as if in shock, and the caption had read, "Courtney's college lover: Whipped cream her specialty." The kid looked like a moron, and Sharon wondered how much the tabloid had paid him. Every time she heard Will John Benedict's name mentioned, Sharon had twinges of guilt that she hadn't felt since law school. She rolled her eyes at the TV, unfolded the bail bonds, and spread them out on the counter. "Could you let these little guys out for me, please? They tell me they don't like your crossbar hotel very much."

The deputy spun the papers around so that he could read the prisoners' names. "I got to tell you, Miss Hays, this is developing a lot of respect for you."

Sharon leaned over the counter and looked down at the bail bonds. "Excuse me? Taking care of these two characters is developing respect?"

The deputy waved a hand as if batting mosquitoes. "That you still take the time for cases like these. Most lawyers, when they get famous, they don't have time for the little guy no more."

Sharon blushed in spite of herself. "Come on, I'm not that famous. Had my fifteen minutes like everyone else in the world, but hey. Six months from now, no one will remember my name."

"Those people remembered you." The deputy jerked his thumb in the direction of the TV set. "You knew those Benedicts, huh?"

Sharon frowned in puzzlement as she looked at the television. A commercial was in progress, the adorable Chihuahua saying, "*Yo quiero* Taco Bell." Sharon said to Deputy Kinsolving, "Yes, as a matter of fact. Paul Benedict taught me in law school in Austin, back when Mattie Ruth was State Comptroller. Will John was in my law school class. But how did you . . . ?" She trailed off as the commercial ended and her own picture appeared on the screen.

It was footage she'd seen umpteen times before, her hair disheveled and her clothing askew as she led Darla Cowan down the Los Angeles Criminal Courts Building steps on the day of Darla's release from custody. If they had to splash her image all over hell and gone, at least they could have chosen a more flattering pose. The picture changed, now showing Russell Black as he stood before a bank of microphones, and Sharon recognized this footage as well. It was Russ's press conference on the day of Midge Rathermore's acquittal, two years ago. Now Mattie Ruth Benedict's photo appeared, her grayish hair perfectly fixed, her features firm, in her eyes the look of eagles. Sharon blinked. What was going on?

She pointed to the rear and said to the deputy, "Could you pump up the volume on that?" As he turned, however, another commercial came on, and

Sharon said, "Never mind. You have any idea why they were showing mine and Russ's pictures?"

The deputy looked incredulous. "You don't know?"

"I've been running all morning," Sharon said. "Haven't seen the TV news or read the paper."

The deputy grinned. "I think you're just bein' modest, Miss Hays. It's been all over every channel. Accordin' to the paper, and accordin' to Mattie Ruth Benedict's news conference last night, if Will John Benedict gets indicted you and Russell Black are defendin' the guy."

Sharon hastily posted her bail bonds and then hurried from the jail. Normally she would have waited for her clients' release and told both of them to come to her office tomorrow, but her curiosity was bursting at the seams. LaTarrance Williams and Willis Clay would have to fend for themselves.

She drove the mile and a half in stop-and-go traffic, drumming her fingers impatiently at every delay, and pulled into the parking garage across from her office at a few minutes before 11 A.M. The parking garage was a converted gas station across from the back of the George Allen Courts Building, which was the former criminal courthouse but now served as the arena for civil suits and probate matters. Sharon's office was catty-cornered from the Allen Building. She killed her engine, grabbed her belongings, hustled out of the lot and through the crosswalk. Andy Wade waited in front of her building along with a still photographer and a man in shirtsleeves toting a minicam. Andy was the court beat reporter for the *Dallas Morning News* and Sharon's best friend in the media, but this morning she hadn't the time even for him. "Not now, Andy," she said as she approached. The minicam operator aimed his lens at her and the photographer's camera flashed.

"You don't have a comment?" Wade had a pen and steno pad ready. He wore a pale blue shirt and black tie without a coat, and his stomach pooched out over his belt.

Sharon paused with one foot up on the step. The office was a walk-up with a sign on the door reading, RUSSELL BLACK, LAWYER, with SHARON J. HAYS, ASSOCIATE in smaller letters underneath. Sharon said, "A comment on what?"

Wade wrote something down. He wore thick glasses in plastic frames. "Does that mean that Mattie Ruth Benedict *hasn't* retained you?"

Sharon shifted her briefcase from one hand to the other and glanced toward the office entry. "What did Russ tell you?"

"The same as he always tells me. No comment. I'd think he would trust me by now, Miss Hays."

Sharon secretly agreed with the reporter; Andy Wade had been instrumental in helping her and Black free an innocent man, Raymond Burnside, from the death house. Russ was unpredictable and always had been. Sharon said, "I suppose you've got another no-comment, then. From me."

"Even more than Russell Black," Wade said, "I'd expect cooperation from you." His eyes were downcast and he looked as if his feelings were terribly hurt.

Which they weren't, Sharon knew; Andy's skin was

as thick as a crocodile's. He wanted something, anything, to put in the paper, and if it took playing on her sympathy to get her to talk he wasn't above it. Sharon ascended to the second step and turned around. "Once and for all. You know as much as I do. I first learned that we might have something to do with the case about fifteen minutes ago, over at the jail. Since I don't know beans about what's going on, how can I make a comment?" She leaned impulsively over and kissed the reporter's cheek. "Love ya, Mr. Wade," she said. "But for now, that's all you're getting from me."

Sharon swept in through the reception area, which contained a desk but no receptionist, and made a bee-line for Russ's door. Light showed through the crack at the bottom. She entered without knocking to find Black on the phone. A console TV sat against the wall. Sharon turned on the set, muted the volume, and fiddled with the channel changer until she tuned in CNN. Clips of Mattie Ruth Benedict appeared, the handsome senator at the podium as she addressed the Democratic National Convention. Sharon sat in one of Russ's visitor's chairs and testily crossed her legs.

Black finished his conversation and dropped the receiver into its cradle. "Travel agencies aren't worth shootin'. Man'd do better makin' his own reservations."

Sharon glanced at the TV, which now showed Will John Benedict shoving his way through a gang of media people as he tried to enter his office. Will John had an angry determined look, and Sharon wondered if he'd toughened any in the last . . . oh, ten years or so since she'd seen him. The ordeal in store for him was

going to require more than just being a nice guy, and
Sharon felt a surge of pity. Will John Benedict's problem
had always been that he was *too* nice; people who'd
never been through the judicial process couldn't imagine
the pain and humiliation. Sharon said to Black, "Hi,
boss. Have you neglected to fill me in on something?"

Black tilted his chair and intertwined his fingers behind his head. "I suppose I have. We might have a
new case."

"So I hear. From a deputy over at the jail, who heard
it on television. The TV people in turn got *their* information from Mattie Ruth Benedict's press conference.
Andy Wade was waiting for me outside the office,
meaning everybody in the country knows what's happening except me. So I thought I'd check with you."

Black looked apologetic. He had blunt honest features and a square chin, and Sharon thought her boss
and mentor resembled nothing so much as an old-time
western lawman. His down-home country-boy manner
shielded a legal mind second to none. Russell Black
at fifty was *the* premier criminal defense attorney in
the Dallas area, not to mention one of the best in the
country, and that Mattie Ruth Benedict wanted Russ
to defend her son would come as a surprise to no one.
Black said, "I was gettin' around to tellin' you. Mattie
Ruth didn' call me until yesterday afternoon, after
you'd gone home. She sends her regards. I didn' know
that you knew her."

"I knew the whole Benedict family when I was in
law school. One of the restaurants where I worked
was a political hangout where Mattie Ruth and Will
John were regulars. The father, Paul Benedict, was

one of my profs." Sharon decided she'd better leave it at that. Her dark hair was short, with bangs in front. She had deep brown eyes, and wore a conservative gray courtroom suit along with matching spike heels. She looked away. "I wish you'd asked before you committed me on something that big, Russ."

"Me and Paul Benedict go a whole lot further back than when you were in law school." On the wall behind Black's desk were his framed law degree—University of Houston, Class of '69—and a photo of himself, wearing jeans, standing behind a steaming pot at the Terlingua Chili Cookoff.

Sharon frowned. "You've never mentioned you were close with the Benedicts."

Russ showed a guarded look which was rare for him. "Close in a business sense. Personal's different. My first year practicin' law, Paul and I collaborated on a case. Kept in touch ever since. I know he taught in Austin several years. I should have realized it was during the time when you were in school down there."

"I had him for Torts." Sharon hesitated, then decided that to say more about Paul Benedict would be a mistake considering Russ's obvious respect for the man. "I don't think I should get involved in defending Will John," she said.

Black stroked his cheek as he looked her over. "Mind tellin' me why?"

Sharon inhaled through her nose, and quickly decided on, "Christmas is on us, for one thing. I promised Melanie we'd spend time together," which was as good a spur-of-the-moment lie as she could come up with.

"And part of doing what we do is in bein' prepared

for anything at any time. Criminal defense work dudn recognize the normal holidays. Your daughter understands that. Besides, nobody said anything about missin' Christmas. We won't really have much to do until—and if—Will John's indicted. That won't happen till January if it happens at all. Until then you're talking a week in D.C., no more than that."

"They'll indict him, Russ," Sharon said. "If they weren't going to, they wouldn't be leaking all that information to CNN." She pointed to the TV screen.

"Leaks are one thing," Black said, "but this is a new wrinkle, even on me. Using that gossip columnist to break the story."

"Rita Carboneau is a whole lot more than just a gossip columnist. She's a"—Sharon drew a pair of quotation marks in the air with her fingers—"Washington insider, which means the public thinks she knows things even if she doesn't. It's through her that they've gotten the Bull One nickname before the media. Nothing's been said about the size of Will John's penis, they're leaving it up to public imagination, but the larger minds among us are tuned in to Jerry Springer and believe, like father like son, you know? Will John Benedict is going to be faced with defending himself while the world laughs behind his back and wonders how far his dong hangs down. He doesn't deserve that, boss."

Black looked out the window across Jackson Street. He was the easiest man to embarrass that Sharon had ever met, a trait which she found endearing. "You'd best get accustomed to the subject," Sharon said. "If you handle the case, it's going to come up over and over."

"I know it," Black said resignedly. "It's just going to take some gettin' used to. What's a nice guy doin' in Washington to begin with? One reason I need you, you can deal with this kind of thing better than I can."

"How flattering. So I'm a woman who doesn't mind talking about penis sizes in public, eh?" Sharon grinned. Her smile faded as she looked down, then back up. "I wasn't kidding. I don't think I should get involved."

Black sized her up. "If you shouldn't, it's for some reason other than what you've said. Something you're not tellin' me."

Sharon smoothed her skirt, measuring her words. She said, "There are thousands of things I haven't told you, most of which I'm never going to tell anyone. Let it suffice to say, the Benedicts likely wouldn't want me involved, either."

"Mattie Ruth Benedict specifically asked for you. Fact o' the bidness, I got the idea the main reason she called was because, one, she knows me, but mainly because you're my associate. You got me playin' second fiddle, young lady."

Sharon permitted herself a grim smile. "Mattie Ruth would feel that way. It's the Benedict men who'd just as soon they never saw me again."

"Which one is that?" Black said. "Every time I turn around, a different man jumps outta your past."

Sharon felt a surge of amusement. Two years ago when they'd defended Midge Rathermore, she'd had previous ties to the prosecutor *and* the main investigator. She doubted if Russ would ever get over it. "I'll say this much," she said. "There was never anything romantic between me and Will John Benedict. Or Paul

Benedict, either." She wondered if she should cross her fingers. No, she thought, the thing with Will John was strictly a one-way affair. And as for Paul Benedict . . . Sharon hugged herself as a tremor ran through her. Mattie Ruth's image was front and center on the TV screen. After all this time, Sharon still felt uncomfortable facing Paul Benedict's wife or even a picture of her. She decided she'd better change the subject. Switching to what she hoped was a professional tone, she said, "In D.C. you'll be dealing exclusively with the feds, you know."

"So I'm told. There's no local D.A. in the District of Columbia, and even the police are on the federal payroll. All indictments are in federal court, with the United States Attorney for the District of Columbia representin' the people. D.C. inmates with long sentences do them in federal lockup."

"And all trials conducted under federal rules," Sharon said. "The federal rules of evidence are quite a bit different from state court, Russ. You'll have your work cut out for you."

"Which is what I got my assistant for, keepin' up with the law and the rules of court." Black read something from his notepad. "We got a reservation on American at seven A.M. in the morning, into Reagan National. There's a later flight but it goes to Dulles, out in the boonies."

"Russ . . ."

"I know, short notice. You'll have to arrange for your daughter's care."

"That's no problem and you know it. All I have to do is call Sheila." Sharon tried hard, but couldn't keep her eyes from misting. "I shouldn't get involved in any case where I'm representing any of the Benedicts. Please don't ask me why. But I shouldn't."

He studied her. He assumed a hurt look. "I'm not going to pry, Sharon, but at the same time I'm dependent on my assistant. You're my right arm. I can't be trying any case, particularly one to hell and gone away from Texas, without your help."

She went through a range of emotion in a flash, opposing forces tugging at her from both sides. She owed her career to Russell Black. At the same time, any contact with the Benedicts might be more than she could bear. Not to mention that she could never be objective when it came to Will John or any of his family, which could damage her effectiveness as a lawyer. She expelled a sigh as she made up her mind. "Of course I won't desert you, boss, I owe you too much. I'll go to D.C. with you, and give it hell on the preliminary investigation. Just don't be surprised if I have to bow out if it comes down to a trial." Her lashes lowered as she watched her lap. "It's all I can say, and believe me, I wish I could tell you more. But my misgivings are so serious that you wouldn't believe."

Sharon decided that if she was going to leave town in the morning, she'd better knock off for the day in order to pack and take care of some things. She cranked up her Skylark and drove to East Dallas with a LeAnn Rimes tape vibrating the car's interior and her insides twisting like a nest of boas. She turned onto her street and drove between old restored houses with winter-dead lawns, and had pulled halfway into her drive when a thought occurred to her. She applied the brakes with a tiny squeak of rubber.

She backed out and toured the block and a half to the Winston place, parked behind Sheila's Pontiac wagon, went up on the porch, and rang the doorbell. Sheila answered wearing ironed slacks and a fresh blouse. Her glasses hung from a chain around her neck. The attire was about as formal as Sheila got, which meant that she had a patient.

Sharon said, "Sorry to butt in. Call me when you're done, will you?" She turned to leave.

Sheila followed her out. "We're almost finished now. Why don't you wait in the living room?"

Sharon felt her nerve slipping. "I'd be in the way."

"Nonsense. I've already made plans to keep Melanie, if that's what you want to see me about."

Sharon's forehead wrinkled in puzzlement.

Sheila tilted her head. "After watching the news, I assumed you were headed for Washington. Was I wrong?"

Sharon relaxed. God love Sheila to death. "No," Sharon said. "I'm catching a seven a.m."

"So, really, if that's all you wanted, it's taken care of. But if it's something else . . ."

Sharon expelled air through her nose. "There is a little more."

Sheila watched Sharon intently. The woman shared a sort of ESP, mental telepathy which was nothing less than spooky. Sheila said, "I think you'd better come in and wait. The lady in my office only thinks she's got problems. From looking at you, kid, I believe you're troubled for real."

*   *   *

Sharon sat in Sheila's parlor beside a sweet-smelling pine hung with tinsel and ornaments, and read an article in *Psychiatry Journal* on how to deal with children in single-parent families. Sheila had handed her the magazine—with the pages of the article clipped—on her way in to finish up with her patient. According to the MD author, it was essential for the child to maintain a relationship with the absentee father, a subject on which Sharon and Sheila had gone around and around for several years. Sheila wanted to help, Sharon thought, but every single-parent kid didn't have Rob Stanley for a father.

As Sheila's patient, a well-groomed woman in her sixties, paid by check and exited through the front door, Sharon dropped the magazine on an end table. She then followed Sheila to her office adjoining the kitchen and had a seat.

The office was ultraprofessional with tasteful beige walls and muted lighting, complete with a psychiatrist's couch and a bookcase full of medical volumes. Sheila had moved her practice into her home several years ago. She didn't solicit business, handling only enough patients to pay the bills, leaving plenty of time to raise her daughter Trish. She folded her hands on top of her desk. "For a woman who's just snared the biggest case in America, you seem awfully uptight. What's wrong?"

Sharon had made up her mind to open up all the way. "Plenty."

"Having to do with the case?"

"Having to do with who we're going to represent.

Mattie Ruth Benedict didn't hire me, she contacted Russ. If she'd of talked to me I would have declined, but now that Russ has accepted I can't desert him. I'm afraid I'll need counseling to get through this. It's why I wanted to see you alone."

Sheila leaned back, and rested her chin thoughtfully on her lightly clenched fist. "You want my professional help?"

Sharon nodded. "With all the confidentiality the relationship carries. With a retainer to make things official."

"Yeah, okay." Sheila took out a pad and pen. "Give me a dollar. I'll write you a receipt."

"I'm not looking for a price break. I'd want to pay your regular rate."

Sheila gave a gentle laugh. "For you, my regular rate is a dollar. I consider you a special customer."

Sharon felt guilty, but fished a dollar from her purse. Sheila tucked the bill inside her desk and scribbled a receipt. She tore the receipt from the pad. "So give."

"You're familiar with the Benedicts?" Sharon said.

Sheila lifted, then dropped her shoulders. "What I've read. Texas's number one political family."

"Made so by careful planning. Mattie Ruth worked in the State Comptroller's office to put Paul Benedict through law school. By the time he'd gotten his LLD she was first assistant. The Comptroller died in the middle of his term and she became acting, and the Democrats sort of drafted her into running in the next election. She served four terms, all while her husband taught at U.T. Law. I had him for Torts, let's see, about a year before Mattie Ruth ran for the Senate."

"The husband," Sheila said, "Paul Benedict. According to what one reads, he's the driving force behind the entire family."

"Yes," Sharon said bitterly. "Aside from being the asshole of the century."

"Uh-oh." Sheila looked concerned. "You don't get your claws out very often. I may not like what I'm about to hear."

"When I was a first-year law student," Sharon said, "and Melanie was about nine months old, I went to work at Nacho Louie's, a bar-slash-restaurant just off Sixth Street in downtown Austin. Mattie Ruth and her son were every-night regulars, though I only saw Paul Benedict in the restaurant occasionally. If you can imagine a typical Texas political hangout, Nacho Louie's was it. We were only a few blocks from the State Capitol, and all those state reps are aces at letting their hair down. Drink like freaking fishes, Sheila. A lot of good-ol'-boy backslapping and political bullshit, tempered with a fair helping of graft exchange at the darker tables. Mattie Ruth held court at the Benedicts' special table, and if you listened with only one ear you'd think it was a Ma Kettle comedy routine. But if you cut through all the B.S., Mattie Ruth used her contacts at Nacho Louie's in setting up her U.S. Senate campaign like the oldest of pros. For herself *and* Will John. Forget the public image, Sheil. Deep down, Mattie Ruth Benedict is about as cornpone as Jackie O. Will John was a law student back then, but his mother was already building his network of connections. The truth is that he isn't particularly brilliant. He's the kind of nice-nice guy that's easy to manipulate, and don't think people didn't take full advantage." Sharon lowered her lashes. "I went out with Will John a few times. It would've been better for both of us if I hadn't."

Sheila lifted her glasses and sucked on an earpiece. She didn't say anything.

"He was a good-enough-looking guy," Sharon said, "but, God, the hang-ups. Complex piled on inferiority complex. If you've ever felt trapped in a relationship you'll know what I'm talking about. Solicitous, God. Flowers delivered to me at the restaurant about every day, little gifts at my apartment. The times we went out, the most expensive places in town."

Sheila seemed incredulous. "That's your idea of a bad relationship? Like, mind if I cut in?"

Sharon laughed. "Sounds like a slice of heaven, doesn't it? It didn't work, Sheil. Don't ask me why. It was, this guy doing everything for me, but . . . The bells just weren't ringing, you know? He was just too damned sweet to me, it was yes, Sharon this, and, yes, Sharon that. The quote, modern woman unquote, won't admit it, but things haven't changed that much since the caveman. Women simply don't want to feel totally in control. We don't want someone on a leash, and that's where the relationship with Will John was headed.

"The week before I cut things off with him, I didn't sleep a wink. It was like putting your pet to sleep, crass as it sounds. I rehearsed all these speeches over and over, but in the long run there wasn't any way to let him down gently. I hurt him, Sheil. I felt like Simona Legree." Sharon softened her gaze. "In light of what's been on the news lately, many women would feel that I shouldn't have terminated the relationship without first getting a look at what was in his pants."

Sheila bent nearer. "Is it really that big? God, those news stories . . ."

"I don't have the slightest idea, but every woman in America is likely wondering at the moment the same thing you are, even if they'd never admit it at the dinner table. I'll tell you something. In spite of his public image, Will John Benedict is scared to death of women. The times we were together he never tried anything, though you could tell he was dying to but couldn't get up the nerve. It was like I was Polly on a Pedestal. I didn't want that. No woman would.

"When I finally got up the nerve to end it," Sharon said, "things became even worse. He kept calling, making these sick-eyes at me around the restaurant, the whole bit. Never in my life have I felt so freaking guilty. Even today when I see him on television, I want to apologize to his image on the screen. And I didn't do a damned thing wrong. A slice of life I'd as soon have not experienced."

"Sounds to me," Sheila said, "like a guy who can't have a normal relationship with a woman. You run into them. I won't bore you with medical jargon, but trust me that it goes back to the man's relationship with his own mother." She frowned. "Isn't Will John Benedict married?"

Sharon nodded. "Yeah. No kids, though." She sighed. "Cassandra Mason. Cas was in undergrad, about three years younger, a campus beauty, sorority queen, you name it. She's from one of Austin's First Families. There's a street, a tributary of the Colorado River, and a town in the Hill Country named after her grandfather. Masonville, Texas. It's as if Mattie Ruth drew up Politician's Wife Requirements and Cas Benedict stepped directly off the page. Cas is not one of my favorite people, either, and the feeling's mutual.

"She had designs on Will John before, during, and after the time I went with him. I didn't know that, but I never could have convinced anyone that I didn't. It was like anyone who didn't know Will John was Cas's property, then they must be from Mars as famous as she was around the Student Union. Well *I* didn't know who she was, and to hell with her. I never was in the loop when I was in law school. I went to class, to work, and to pick up my daughter, and I didn't know the campus big wheels from Sister Sue.

"I'd never even heard of Cas Mason," Sharon said, "until one night shortly after I'd ended things with Will John, when Cas and two of her cohorts came into the restaurant and sat at my station like a reincarnation of the Stepford Wives. It was while I was serving them drinks that she looked me over and said, 'Sharon Hays, right?' or something to that effect, and I nearly dropped my tray in surprise that she knew my name. Then she told me, 'So you're the little waitress,' and I answered, 'I suppose that I am,' without having the slightest idea what she was talking about. She said, 'Well, I just wanted a look at you.' That was the extent of the conversation, and it was later before one of the other restaurant workers clued me in as to who she was. At the time I was like, So what? In fact I was glad, hoping Will John could find someone to take his mind off of me, you know? I don't mind telling you that with Cas Mason despising my insides and Will John's father as my Torts prof, I was between a rock and a hard place for a while there. I'm told Cas goes ballistic at the mention of my name even today, but what can I do about it?''

"Did Paul Benedict know at the time that you and Will John were dating?" Sheila asked. Her degree from Yale hung in a frame behind her, alongside her sheepskin from medical school.

"Yes. But that's something else I wasn't aware of. Stupid me, right? During the times we were together, Will John never mentioned his father."

Sheila rubbed her cheek. "I don't see what's so devastating here. This was years and years ago."

"That sounds odd coming from a psychiatrist," Sharon said. "Hang-ups are hang-ups, and stay with us for life. Frankly I think his family was a large part of Will John's problem. They made him feel inferior. He had an all-star lawyer father and a mother who was about to become one of the most politically powerful women in America. Will John didn't fit the mold, and you can bet that his current congressional career is a result of Momma's and Daddy's pushing. He struck me like nothing so much as a lost puppy dog. I've never been so glad to get anything over with in my life."

Sheila fiddled with her ballpoint pen. "You haven't told me anything which should be a barrier against you defending the guy. If you never had any kind of sexual relationship, well . . .''

Sharon looked away. "Will John and I didn't. Will John isn't my problem. My misgivings in taking the case have to do with Paul Benedict," she said.

Sheila looked at the ceiling, her pretty chocolate-colored features slack with concern. "Sharon, you didn't have an affair with your married law school professor, did you? After ditching his son?"

Sharon felt a surge of anger. "An affair. An *affair*?"

"That sort of thing happens more than people realize," Sheila said. "It's just that you're not the type, unless you've changed over the years more than I think you have."

Sharon squeezed her own leg as tears stung her eyes. "This has been a secret forever, Sheil. I've never told anyone."

"Under the circumstances," Sheila said, "that's understandable."

"You're not getting it," Sharon said. "I never had an affair with Paul Benedict." She took a deep breath and let it out slowly. "I've tried to shut this out of my mind for about ten years now. But Paul Benedict tried to rape me. I don't mean, tried to seduce, that I could have handled gracefully. I mean, tried to rape, as in brutally. He damned near put me in the hospital." She watched her lap for a moment, then slowly looked up. "This has to remain between us, Sheila. When you hear the whole story, you'll understand why."

3

Sharon told Sheila that one would just have to've been there, to understand Paul Benedict's impact on the U.T. Law School and its student body. He was the most powerful speaker she'd ever heard, and the only professor in captivity who could teach a Tuesday–Thursday 8 A.M. class and keep everybody awake for an hour and a half. His steel gray hair and cobalt blue eyes kept female students in a quivering lather, and other faculty members were in a constant jealous snit over the number of times he was published and appointed to President's Councils. The money for Mattie Ruth's senatorial campaign had come from Paul Benedict's connections on Capitol Hill, and points east and west around the globe.

A college campus is about as busy a rumor mill as there is, and the U. of Texas at Austin was no exception. Sharon heard gossip about Paul Benedict and several of his female students long before she laid eyes on the man. Call Sharon Jenifer Hays Miss Naive; she'd discounted the rumors as wishful thinking on the part of the women telling the tales.

And besides, she'd had no time to speculate on Prof

Benedict's conquests among the student body even if
she'd been of a mind to. Her first year in law school
she'd been running scared, terrified of not making her
grades, flunking out. She thought it amazing what a
fistful of student loans and a daughter to support
would do for one's study habits; she wouldn't have cut
Paul Benedict's class if he'd been a hunchback and
stumped around like Igor. It was Sharon the student
and Paul the professor, period. If he'd sent out any
vibes, either they were awfully weak or she was too
caught up in causes of action and punitive damages to
notice. In fact it would've shocked her to learn that
he even knew her name.

Her job at Nacho Louie's was considered a plum
among the working class. Waiting on the older political crowd translated to super tips and fewer guys rubbing up against the waitresses while fumbling for their
billfolds, which was more the case in the college hang-
outs farther on down Austin's Sixth Street. Not that
those state senators and reps were above a little fanny-
patting, but at least they were more subtle about it.

Nacho Louie's was in a stucco building with the
inside walls plastered to look like adobe. The restaurant featured rustic wooden tables with candles burn-
ing in little piñatas, and an elevated island bar area
with seating for thirty. The menu was a hundred percent Tex-Mex, and like most really trendy Austin restaurants the decor was much better than the food. But
Nacho Louie's did whip up a bitch of a margarita,
with two-for-one specials most nights, and after a few
shots of tequila, Sharon thought, who could taste anything anyway?

She worked a lot of split shifts, and the incident which was to change her life forever occurred one evening when she was to get off at six and return at nine to work until closing. It had been about a week since her last contact with Will John Benedict, and when one of the busboys came to her and said that Mr. Benedict was waiting, she thought seriously about ducking out the back but changed her mind. If she scorned Will John he was likely to cause a scene; the Benedicts had enough stroke around town that such a scene could cost Sharon her job. In the long run she decided to see him. She gritted her teeth and hurried past the bar for the table. She was so intent on rehearsing her lines, what she was going to say to let Will John down as easily as possible, that she had reached the table before she realized that its occupant wasn't Will John Benedict at all. Professor Paul Benedict lifted his chin, smiled at her, and pushed back a chair for her to sit.

Talk about in awe; Sharon couldn't have been more stunned if her guest had been Sean Connery in person. Her knees turned to rubber and she fell into her chair. Twin reflections of the candle-lit piñata shined in the lenses of his glasses, whose frames cast shadows on his temples like devil's horns. He gave a palm-up gesture and said in his melodic basso, "Miss Hays. Something to drink?"

She was barely able to squeak, "No, thank you," and somehow managed to keep from melting under the table.

"Oh?" he said. "Surely a margarita. They're excellent here." One thing about Paul Benedict, he didn't put on any phony Ah'm-from-Texas accents like his wife; he was educated at Princeton and wanted the world to know it. Of course, Sharon thought, he isn't running for office in Texas, either. If he was he might suddenly become the reincarnations of Jett Rink like the rest of the Austin political crowd.

Sharon said, "Well I don't know if I should drink while I'm on duty, Professor. I don't get off for—"

"Call me Paul," he interrupted. "And I'll call you Sharon if it isn't too presumptuous. And I have influence with your employer."

And with that he signaled toward the bar area and, splat, splat, the bartender sets two 'ritas on the table as if he'd had them waiting in the wings. Which in light of later events he probably had, but at the time Sharon was too preoccupied to notice. Paul Benedict studied her as if she were a lab specimen. She felt as if every eye in the room was on her. She had a quick gulp of margarita to calm her nerves.

He sampled his own drink, put down the glass, and said, "You have my son in quite an uproar."

She collected what thoughts she could. "I didn't intend for that to happen, Professor."

"Paul."

"Paul. Listen, I want you to understand I don't . . ." She trailed off as he held up a silencing finger.

"Not that I can't easily see why he's attracted," he said. His tone wasn't particularly wolfish and she blushed over the compliment. He then said, "I'm not in the habit of apologizing for my son's behavior, but in this case I should."

Later Sharon would realize that he'd set her up perfectly. He pronounced the words with just the right amount of poor-me in his voice, so that she couldn't help but feel sorry for him. She reached across the table and put her hand on his arm. "No offense taken," she said. "Will John hasn't really done anything wrong, and even if he had, it isn't your fault."

He lowered his head as if in shame. "But I feel responsible. His attitude toward women is really getting to be a point of concern. He seems to constantly feel he's falling in love, over and over, and when the young woman rebuffs him he just won't take no for an answer. I've really come to my wits' end."

"I don't think it's going to be any more of a problem where I'm concerned," Sharon said. "I haven't seen him in a while." If she'd had time to think, she would've wondered how Paul Benedict knew that Will John had been going out with her at all. But right then, right there in Nacho Louie's, all she could see was a man she looked up to and respected like, too much for words, all broken up over the way his son had been acting.

"I know it's over for you," he said. "But there might be a way you can help me keep the same thing from happening again. I feel so out of line in asking you, but . . ."

She bent nearer the table like Carole Concerned. "No, no, anything to help. It's just that I probably don't have anything that significant to tell you, but if you want to . . ."

He made a show of peering around the restaurant area. "I feel out of place talking here," he told her.

She looked around as well, as if searching for the enemy.

"Where I'm so well-known," he said. "In the company of one of my law students. Innocent as the circumstances might be, people will interpret it the way they want to."

In retrospect, Sharon thought the whole thing unbelievably slick. After all, she didn't just fall off a load of hay. She'd lived in New York, acting, so it wasn't as if she'd never heard a line before. It absolutely never occurred to her that Paul Benedict had any motive other than concern for his son. He was, for God's sake, her Torts prof.

The next thing she knew they were in the parking lot and he was holding the car door open for her. He drove a Lincoln, one of the big mothers. She felt really safe and secure, sinking down in leather cushions as they left Nacho Louie's. She actually racked her brain for insight into Will John's character, trying to help the kindly professor with his problem. In the history of the world, she would later think, never had a woman been more freaking dumb.

Sharon had been talking for nearly an hour, and needed desperately to catch her breath. She left Sheila seated behind her desk and went into the kitchen. The passage of time hadn't helped; just talking about the incident with Paul Benedict tied her insides into knots. Sheila kept Pepsi in the fridge. Sharon selected a blue, red, and white can, popped the tab, and rolled the frosty metal across her forehead. She carried the drink back into the office and offered Sheila half. Sheila declined. Sharon sat down and took a swig. "The rest of this is pretty difficult to tell," she said.

Sheila remained stoic, in her psychiatrist's mode. "How does telling about it make you feel?"

"Angry. Disgusted with myself."

"Just with yourself?"

"I have a lot of hate for Paul Benedict," Sharon said. "But I have myself to blame for getting in that situation at all. I should have known better. I did know better. Brand the scarlet letter on my forehead, Sheil. Hester Primm had nothing on me."

Once Paul Benedict had driven Sharon away from Nacho Louie's it was as if Will John and his problems had never existed. She waited for him to bring up the subject of his errant son as he left downtown and headed north on Mo-Pac—the local nickname for Loop 1 in Austin, which runs along the same route as the old Missouri–Pacific Railroad and leads out into the Hill Country. Driving north on Mo-Pac is a sensation not quite real; one minute you're in the bustle of downtown Austin, then once you enter the freeway you're out in the boonies like, immediately. Rolling hills stretch on both sides of the highway as far as the eye can see. Country roads twist here and there through the forests. It's easy to get lost in the Hill Country, as Sharon was soon to learn.

At first she was so wide-eyed and openmouthed in the company of the U. of Texas's demigod of a law school prof that it never occurred to her to ask where they were going. Even after he left the freeway proper and angled off to the west along a two-laned blacktop,

Sharon was so caught up in small talk that she barely noticed that they'd left civilization. Mostly he went on and on about causes of action—which was the subject of the week in Torts class—and Sharon asked a couple of scholarly questions along the way. It was only when he left the blacktop and rattled along on a gravel road that she became the slightest bit uneasy. And even then she wasn't particularly frightened. He pulled into a little turnaround and stopped with the nose of his Lincoln pointing off a steep drop-off. And there she was, Sharon was later to reflect, Sharon Jenifer Dumass Hays sitting there like a moron expecting Paul Benedict to launch into a discourse about his and Sharon's strategy for saving Will John from himself. Night had fallen. The air was clear of smog and the stars twinkled over the lights of downtown Austin in the distance. Paul Benedict killed the engine and turned halfway toward her with his elbow hooked over the seat back.

They sat in silence for a count of ten. Finally she said, intending to break the ice, "You know, Will John's really one of the nicest people I've ever met, and it's not his fault that I don't have any, what you'd call feelings for him. I've never felt in any danger from him, Professor. It's just that he's awfully persistent, and time will heal that."

Paul Benedict seemed deep in thought, and nothing could have prepared Sharon for what was coming. He looked straight at her and said, "A complaint I hear over and over about my son is that he has some odd sexual ideas."

Later, during her time as a Dallas prosecutor,

Sharon was to learn a lot about the psychology of weirdos. Though some nuts are subtler than others, with each and every psycho there is a time when the mood changes. When the guy switches from a fairly normal topic to sex, and the end result in each case is the same. When Paul Benedict started talking about his son's sexual habits, it was as if Sharon had been stabbed in the back with an icicle. Chills up her spine, the whole bit. She looked away from him as she answered, "I wouldn't know about that, Professor."

"Paul," he said in a coaxing tone. "Paul. Nothing we discuss will go any further, Sharon. I want you to feel that you can open up completely."

She'd never been so nervous in her life. She said, "I am opening up. It's just that there never were any . . . Look, I think it's probably time for me to—"

"Most of these young women have complained," he went on as if she hadn't even spoken, "that Will John doesn't really want to participate in the act itself, that he'd rather watch the woman . . . ah, how can I put it delicately? Arouse herself. It's perfectly understandable, of course, that a healthy young woman wants a partner in such activities. Every one of us has our own preference as to, position say, but none of us particularly wants to go it alone." He laughed then, the creepiest sound she'd ever heard.

She hugged herself, shivering. She tried, "Listen, I have to be back at work in—"

"How do *you* like it, Sharon?" He spoke with sudden intensity. Each word was like a separate slap in her face. His breath quickened and his gaze riveted on her like a madman's. For just an instant she was

too frightened to move, and when she finally got un-
tracked she reached for the door handle. Her thoughts
were a jumble. Get out, she told herself, jump out of
this freaking car and make a run for it. Before she
could move he bent near her, slid his hand up under
her skirt and palmed her mound.

Just like that, and just that quickly. One instant they
were sitting there in the moonlight, the next she felt
his fingers work up her thigh and into her crotch. He
made guttural sounds, like growls. She grabbed his
forearm and thrashed around in the front seat, trying
to get away from him, but he was strong as a bear.
Tears streamed down her cheeks and there were
noises coming out of her mouth—screams, she later
supposed—but all to no avail. In desperation she
slapped him across the face as hard as she could.

There wasn't room in the front seat for her to wind
up and land a haymaker, but her palm landed solidly
on his cheek and stung her hand. His grip loosened
between her legs and she squirmed frantically away
from him. He yelled, more in anger than in pain,
reached across the seat, grabbed her hair, and yanked
her toward him. Then he doubled up his fist and
punched her in the jaw.

It wasn't any glancing blow. Her head snapped
backward and she blacked out for a few seconds.
When she came to he had her pinned against the passenger door, trying to yank her panty hose down. She
was acutely aware of his hands as they stretched the
nylon waistband and pulled downward. Her jaw
throbbed and her face was swelling. His weight was
against her chest and shoulders and the door handle

dug into her back and hurt like the blazes. Up to that point she'd been terrified, but now she got mad as hell, and she was pretty sure it was the anger that saved her. She had only one thought, that this bastard was *not* going to get her pants off and get into her, not while there was breath in her body.

As he twisted and grunted around on top of her, the side of his neck was a fraction of an inch from her lips. And right there in the front seat of his fancy Lincoln Town Car, Sharon Hays sank her teeth into Professor Paul Benedict's throat like a vampire. She clamped her jaws together and twisted her head to one side, and felt the flesh tear as warm salty liquid ran across her tongue. Even as frightened as she was, his yell of pain was music to her ears. She hated him enough to kill him. If she'd had a gun she would have used it.

He squirmed backward off of her, clutching his throat, and blood seeped between his fingers in the moonlight. She didn't hesitate. She reached behind her, yanked upward on the door handle, rolled out of the car and hit the ground running. He screamed, *"Bitch"* at the top of his lungs, scrambled across the seat, and came after her.

In her confusion she headed straight for the drop-off. When she turned to face him she stood on the ledge of the fifty-foot cliff. Jump, she told herself. Before this son of a bitch touches you again, just step off into space and . . .

He was in a crouch, panting. She feinted in one direction, then tried to run around him on the opposite side.

Sharon was in pretty good shape, and in running shoes she was sure she would have made it, but the restaurant's working uniform included three-quarter-inch heels. One of her shoes caught in a crevice. She pitched sideways, turning her ankle. Sudden pain blinded her. She went down on all fours on rock and gravel, skinning her knees and ripping her panty hose to shreds.

He grabbed her shoulder, rolled her over on her back, and fell on top of her. His full weight came down as he landed across her thigh. She heard a tiny *snap,* and agony shot up her leg like a thousand razor blades.

He hit her three times in rapid succession across her nose and mouth. Blood gushed from her lip and dripped on the ground. Her vision blurred; she was groggy, passing out. She watched through a haze as he drew back his fist to punch her again. His teeth were bared like the madman's in a horror movie. Without warning, something stopped him cold.

It was like watching a man wake up from a trance. His hand froze in midair. His lips relaxed, and in place of the loonish grin there was now a look of puzzlement. He looked at his doubled-up fist as if he'd never seen it before, then slowly lowered his arm.

He came to his feet, and backed away with his hands out in a defensive posture. "Miss Hays, I . . ." He covered his face and began to sob.

He babbled apologies. He didn't know what had come over him. He begged her not to think badly of him. *Think badly of him?* Sharon thought. Jesus Christ, if she'd have had a gun or knife she would have . . .

She had a single purpose, to get the hell away from there before he lost it again. She somehow managed to rise and wiped her sleeve across her face. The sleeve showed smears of blood. Anger shoved her fear aside. She stepped toward him. "Get away from me, you bastard." Her screams echoed in the stillness.

He backpedaled as if the castle ghost were after him. "Please, Miss Hays, I didn't mean . . ."

"Shut up! Shut the absolute fuck up, you insane asshole. You back away and stay as far from me as possible." Later she would suppose that she sounded as crazy as he did.

And back up he did, all the way to the edge of the drop-off and stood there shivering. She kept her gaze riveted on him as she carefully groped the side of the car and felt her way around to the driver's side. The keys were in the ignition. She fell in behind the wheel, slammed the door and thunked the door locks down. She switched on the lights and the beams illuminated him. He never moved, just stood there watching her. Her leg burned like fire and her nose throbbed; she wouldn't learn for two more days that her septum was crushed.

Somehow she managed to start the car, back up, turn around, and drive away. He stood stock-still. If he'd taken so much as a step in her direction, she would have thrown the lever into drive, stomped on the gas, and run the bastard down.

Sharon drove back to downtown Austin in a state of near hysteria, sobbing loudly, wiping tears away with the back of her hand. She should go directly to

the police. But what about her job? At the moment
her income from Nacho Louie's was the only thing
between her and living on a street corner. And Melanie, God, what about her? It was almost eight, and
Sharon was scheduled to return to work at nine. During her afternoon shift Melanie stayed at a day-care
center, and during Sharon's hours off she was to de-
liver the baby to a woman who kept Melanie while
Sharon worked at night. Seeing to her daughter's care
was more important than anything. More important
than reporting a beating and attempted rape? Sharon
thought. You bet it is. Turning Paul Benedict in to
the police would have to wait.

She parked the Lincoln in the restaurant lot beside
her ancient Ford, climbed into her car and looked in
the rearview. God, she looked like the victim in a
horror movie. She couldn't pick up her daughter in
that condition, no way. She got out, ran inside Nacho
Louie's with her breath whistling between her teeth,
and went in the ladies' room to scrub the blood away.
When she'd finished, her nose and one side of her face
were grotesquely swollen, but at least the bleeding
had stopped. The bodice of her waitress's uniform was
soaked in blood. She'd have to stop by her garage
apartment to change before she picked up Melanie.
She dried her face with a paper towel, left the restroom,
and walked toward the exit as calmly as she could.
The restaurant manager stopped her in the foyer.

His name was Ray, a man in his forties, and up
until that moment he'd never acted as if he knew she
was alive. The bartender at Nacho Louie's bossed the
waitresses, and Sharon had never spoken to the man-

ager that she could recall. Normally, in fact, the manager wasn't there at night. His voice showed concern. "Sharon, are you all right?"

"Fine. I'm . . . fine. Look I'm late picking my daughter up." She tried to go around him and out the door.

He put his hand on her arm. His tone intensified. "I want to make sure you don't do anything foolish."

She gaped in surprise. Foolish? She'd already been foolish, leaving with that madman to begin with. She said hesitantly, "Excuse me?"

He leaned closer and lowered his voice, "Foolish, Sharon. It would be foolish for you to tell anyone what happened."

Sharon stood in the restaurant foyer with blood pounding in her swollen lip and fractured nose, and wondered how the manager of this freaking restaurant could possibly know where she'd been or what had happened to her. Had Paul Benedict made it to a phone and called the guy? Or did this sort of thing happen so often that the restaurant manager knew what to say without being told? She'd heard rumors that Mattie Ruth Benedict was a major stockholder in the restaurant. Sharon continued to gape. She was beginning to feel like a moron.

He held the exit door open for her. "We're giving you the night off with pay," he said. "After you've slept on it, call me in the morning. Before you talk to anyone about what happened to you tonight, talk to me." Then he handed her a business card containing his office and home telephone numbers. She went into the parking lot with her feet dragging. She felt numb, terminally so.

*   *   *

Somehow Sharon made it to the day care and picked up Melanie without alarming any of the staff, though a few did double takes when they looked at her. She told them she'd fallen at work, and though they seemed dubious they refrained from commenting.

She took the baby home and put her to bed, then sat on her couch and stared at the phone. She looked up Police Emergency in the directory and punched two or three numbers into the dial, then hung up in frustration. Finally she went to bed, tossing around and kicking the covers to death until daylight. She might have slept in the wee hours, she wasn't really sure.

In the morning her face throbbed and she couldn't inhale through her nose without whimpering in pain. She cut class and stayed in bed, moving only when Melanie raised the roof with her cries of hunger. Around midmorning the restaurant manager called. "I've been expecting to hear from you," he said.

She lay back on her pillow with the receiver clamped against her ear. "Why is that?"

"You said you were going to call."

This was her boss and she desperately needed the job, but at the moment she didn't care. "No, I didn't, Ray."

"I thought that was our agreement."

"You misinterpreted, then. You told me to call. I didn't say I was going to do anything of the kind."

After a moment's pause he said, "Oh. Well, have you thought about our conversation?"

"Quite a bit. Next to nearly getting raped and having the hell beaten out of me, our conversation is uppermost on my mind."

"Well it should be. Have you called the police?"

"Not yet."

"Well are you going to?"

"About the attack, I haven't made up my mind. About you bugging me, I won't report you unless you call again. Good-bye, Ray."

"Dammit, don't you hang up."

Sharon held the phone and didn't say anything.

"You don't want to get the cops involved in this," Ray said. "Think of your job."

Sharon's grip tightened on the receiver. "Think what of my job? Are you threatening me?"

"I didn't say that."

"No, you merely intimated. Here's the situation in a nutshell. As far as the job goes, you can take it and you-know-what. I don't know what grip Paul Benedict holds over the management of Nacho Louie's and don't care. Prof Benedict deserves jail for what he did to me last night. A lot of jail. But I have my daughter to think about, and how it would affect her for me to go public. That's the only thing that will influence my decision, not you, not my job, or anything else other than Melanie's welfare. So fuck you, Ray. And if you should run across Professor Benedict in your travels, that goes double for him."

Later that day, Sharon went over to the university's add-drop office with Melanie in her arms, and picked up a permission slip to withdraw from Torts class. No matter her decision about reporting the incident to the police, she wasn't about to sit daily in a classroom where Paul Benedict was the prof. The lady in the office told her that the semester was too far along for her to drop the course without a penalty, to which Sharon said fine, give me an F or something. The woman said that Sharon could only withdraw from the course with the permission of her faculty advisor. Sharon said fine, and left the add-drop office near the point of hysteria.

Her advisor was a woman named Diane Lutz who taught Criminal Law, and who punctuated each spoken sentence by smacking her lips at the end. She laid the drop slip on her desk and watched the piece of paper as if it were a rattler about to strike. Finally she said, "This is a required course, Miss Hays, it wouldn't be advisable to drop at this time."

Sharon was ready to scream. She didn't care about the consequences, she just wanted out of that freaking class, and if Lutz the Smacker wouldn't approve the drop slip she'd quit attending and take a failing grade. Which would end her quest to be a lawyer, but any sort of levelheaded thinking was beyond her by then. Lutz told her to take a day to think it over. Sharon snatched up her paperwork and stalked out of the office.

On the drive to her apartment in northwest Austin, Sharon made up her mind to call the police. To hell with Diane Lutz, to hell with law school, and in particular to hell with Professor Paul Benedict. She parked on gravel, unstrapped Melanie from her car seat, and ascended the steps with the baby riding her hip. A man waited on the landing outside her door.

She'd never seen this guy before. He was a short, bald, sweaty type, wearing an expensive suit that hung from his body like an off-the-rack from JC Penney. He produced a business card. Sharon shifted Melanie from one hip to the other as she read. Apparently the stranger was David Matusek, a lawyer from a firm downtown. Sharon tilted her head in curiosity. He asked if he could have a chat with her.

After what she'd been through the past twenty-four hours, she supposed that one more lunatic in her life couldn't make any difference, so she told Mr. Matusek to come inside. She carried Melanie to the back and put the child down in her crib. When she returned to the kitchen the lawyer was seated at a rickety table that Sharon had bought in a garage sale. He'd taken a sheath of papers from his briefcase and was reading them over. Sharon sat across from him and waited.

Finally he laid the papers aside, took off his glasses, and sucked on an earpiece. "I think first I should deal with your reluctance. Read this." His voice was calm, his manner businesslike. He pushed the stack of paper over in front of her.

Her blood boiled as she read over what amounted to a contract between Sharon Hays and the man who'd tried to rape her. If she signed the document she was agreeing that Dr. Paul Benedict, Professor Emeritus and all that crap, had never laid a land on her or tried to. That whatever recent injuries she'd sustained resulted from a fall she'd taken while Professor Benedict was counseling her regarding her recent breakup with his son. That she'd willingly accompanied Professor Benedict out in the woods for this so-called session, that she'd tripped over a rock and fallen halfway down a ravine, and that Professor Benedict had jumped on a white horse and rescued her. That while Professor Benedict was in no way responsible for her injuries, out of concern for her condition he agreed to pay for any medical treatment she might need in return for her signature on the release included at the bottom of the document. The papers were fresh off the press, likely dictated by Paul Benedict himself that morning in his lawyer's office.

She gave the papers back to the guy. "Go fuck yourself, sir," she said. She thought that if nothing else, since the incident with Professor Benedict she was becoming adept at telling people where to go and what to do to themselves.

Attorney Matusek seemed amused. He said, smiling, "Somehow, Miss Hays, I thought that would be your attitude. So I think we should now discuss the alternatives. Do you know that Professor Benedict's wife plans to run for the U.S. Senate in the future?"

She blinked warily at the guy. "Which affects me how?"

"Oh, it could have a very positive effect," he said, "on anyone who expects to practice law in this state. Don't ever discount a lawyer's political connections."

"And don't discount the effect it could have on an election," Sharon said, "if the candidate's husband is sitting in jail for assault."

Matusek wasn't fazed in the slightest. "Yes, that could be unfortunate. Not to mention the problems it could cause for a law student, being on the wrong side of an important faculty member."

Sharon bit her lip. There was nothing which scared her more than not getting through law school. She'd gambled her life on the chance. She said, with less conviction, "He deserves to go to jail for what he did."

"I'm sure you feel that way. But I'm not here to argue morality. I'm here to offer compromise."

"I'm not accepting any compromise, sir. If this guy thinks he can go around injuring women, brutalizing them, and then getting off with paying their hospital bills—"

"You haven't heard everything, Miss Hays. May I finish?"

Sharon stared at him. She hated Paul Benedict, and the mere fact that this lawyer was Benedict's representative caused her to despise the lawyer as well.

Matusek favored her with an oily smile. "There are benefits to you that aren't in writing. Before you send me on my merry way, it would behoove you to listen. The unspoken benefits will make what's happened to you worth your while, and then some."

Sheila gaped in amazement. "Good Lord, you didn't sign the freaking thing."

"The discussion with this lawyer," Sharon said, "went on for an hour or more. Sure, I could file a complaint, after which it would be my word against one of the most distinguished profs in the state. I'd never practiced criminal law back then, of course, but I can tell you from my experience as a prosecutor that the D.A. probably wouldn't have listened to me. I left the restaurant with the guy of my own free will, right? Plus if I did try to make something out of the situation, I could expect not to be in school the following semester under any circumstances. Paul Benedict could have arranged that with one phone call. And the alternatives. Jesus, Sheila, the alternatives.

"If I was a good sport and kept my mouth shut," Sharon said, "I would find my life to be quite a bit easier. Not only could I get treatment for my injuries gratis, I could be guaranteed special consideration when things like grades were handed out, and my job could become very lucrative. I'd only wait on special customers, translating to big tippers, and I could pretty well set my own hours without consulting management. I could fight city hall, in other words, or I could sell out for a mess of pottage."

Sharon rotated her chair and watched the far wall, letting her gaze rest on an aerial photo of downtown Dallas and a print of happy children at play. When she turned back, Sharon's features were relaxed in an expression of resignation. "I signed it, Sheil," she said. "God help me, right there at my kitchen table, I signed what was left of my dignity away."

Sharon was unable to look Sheila in the eye. She watched the far wall as she said, "Once I'd committed to prostituting myself, I suppose there have been worse trade-offs. The best eye, ear, and nose specialist in Austin straightened my septum and, hell, my nose looks better now than it did. My job became a piece of cake. I doubled my income while working about half as many hours. Paul and Mattie Ruth Benedict became my best customers in the restaurant. They'd sit at my station at least once a week, maybe more, and the tips he'd leave were gigantic. Every time I accepted money from Paul or Mattie Ruth, my flesh would crawl.

"It was a month or two before Will John Benedict and I were on speaking terms again, but I got enough out of our conversation to know he was completely in the dark as to what had gone on. Will John's a mouse, Sheila. The years haven't changed that. If he's guilty of this murder he's accused of, this is a completely different guy from the one I know.

"I did draw the line once," Sharon said, "right at the end of that semester. I completely butchered my Torts final and knew it, yet when grades came out I had an A in the course. I went to see Paul Benedict in his office, it was the only time I had a conversation with him after the . . . you know, the incident. I told him I wasn't accepting a grade I hadn't earned, and if he didn't correct the record I was going public with what I knew about him. The meeting required more nerve than I ever thought I was capable of. Just being in the same room alone with that bastard made my throat constrict.

"And, you know what? Keep in mind that he was the predator and I was his victim. I've seen guys in prison who, when confronted with victims or families of victims, have such feelings of guilt that they withdraw into themselves like schizos. Not this guy, not Mr. Paul Asshole Benedict, no sirree. He acted like he *enjoyed* seeing me, and even suggested that I go to dinner with him some evening. I ended the meeting by going into hysterics, telling him that if my grade wasn't changed within twenty-four hours I was headed straight for the newspapers. After I left his office I went home, and don't think I went out in public again for a week or so.

"Which is how I wound up with a C in Torts, and considering the pressure I was under that semester it's a miracle I passed the course at all. I spent the summer in a state of shock, and had no intention of returning to school the next fall. I couldn't look in the mirror without curling my lip in disgust with myself, and Jesus Christ, I hadn't done anything wrong to begin with.

"The only reason I did finish law school," Sharon said, "was that summer, there was an announcement in the paper that Professor Paul Benedict, distinguished motherfucker that he was, was resigning his post at U.T. Law School to run his wife's political campaign. Mattie Ruth won in a landslide and the Benedicts moved their act to Washington. If she'd lost, if he'd returned to the law school staff, I'm sure I would've dropped out. More than likely I'd still be waiting tables. I couldn't bear the thought of living in the same town with the guy, much less seeing him on campus every day. Criminals I can deal with, Sheila, do all the time, murderers . . . But what drives someone like Paul Benedict is beyond me." Sharon lapsed into silence.

Sheila pulled a pad and pen from her desk and wrote something down. She laid the pen aside and thoughtfully pinched her chin. "Is that all?"

Sharon put her elbow on her armrest and rested her cheek on her lightly clenched fist. "All that comes to mind."

"When you came in here," Sheila said, "you told me that you wanted my professional help. I'm not sure what you're asking. You've concluded your monologue by asking what makes people like Paul Benedict tick. Earlier on I thought you wanted my advice as to how to cope with this situation you're in. Which is it?"

Sharon rubbed her eyebrow. "A little of both."

"Analyzing Paul Benedict is easy," Sheila said. "Power. Power and its privileges." She tore the top page from her pad. "There are sociopaths, and then there are sociopaths. Most wind up in prison, I won't bore you with that rhetoric, but there is a second sociopathic type. Both men and women fall into this category, though it's a rarity for the subject to be female. From the cradle to the grave, this person is totally self-absorbed. There's disagreement as to the cause, but the symptoms are the same in every case.

"This guy," Sheila said, "is normally quite successful financially, but is incapable of love. He'll take a wife and then abuse and cheat on her. He gives nothing of himself to his children, other than to throw money at them to keep them out of his way. He's persuasive, which explains why so many of these, let's call them power freaks for want of a better term, turn to politics. They crave power the same way a Hatcher Street bum craves crack cocaine.

"This type personality is similar to a serial killer, believe it or not, in that he doesn't see other people as human beings, only means to whatever end our psycho has in mind. Your Jeffrey Dahmers regard their victims no differently than you'd regard a herd of beef cattle. Ditto with our power freak, though he considers himself civilized and would stop short of feasting on your bones. A lot of these congressional types look on the women under them as just another possession, and feel that taking every woman they meet to bed is a privilege just like getting special service when they go to a restaurant. I had a patient once who used to sleep with a U.S. Senator. She was eaten up with the glamour, but admitted in therapy that the sex was purely bim-bam-thank-you-ma'am. Once he'd gotten his jollies he was through with her. Her gratification was of no consequence to him.''

Sheila fell silent for a count of ten. She pushed the piece of paper across her desk. Sharon picked up the page and read off the names of two periodicals.

Sheila said, "They're articles you should bone up on when you have the time. Your violent criminals are one thing, they can be locked up, but our power freak is different even though his mind-set is practically the same." She thoughtfully massaged her forehead. "My advice to you would be not to get involved in this. Period."

"That isn't an option," Sharon said. "I've promised Russ."

"Well, then," Sheila said, "if you're going to take Will John Benedict's case come hell or high water, there are things you should be aware of. Not the least of which is that your power freak, when he's rebuffed, is capable of anything. I think you're right that Will John is just his father's underling dupe. Children of these guys are often so dominated that they lack independent thought. It's likely that Will John places all women on a pedestal and didn't just pick you out

for special treatment. Probably that's the reason Paul
Benedict turned violent; he wanted to show his kid
the real way to handle this wench. Five'll get you ten
that Will John got a blow-by-blow, leaving out the
part where you left the old man out in the boonies,
the second the old man got home. The trait isn't ge-
netic, Sharon, it's a learned response. If Paul Benedict
is one of these weirdos, and from what you've told
me there's a ninety-nine percent chance that he is,
then it's likely his son's flaws are the result of Daddy's
dominance. Be careful, Sharon. If you're bound and
determined to do this, watch your backside every step
of the way."

4

Sharon went home to pack while Sheila picked up the girls at St. Thomas Episcopal. Sharon stepped into her house, hurried past the old Spanish-style sofa which was the centerpiece of her den, went into her bedroom closet and hauled out her only respectable piece of traveling luggage. It was a really nifty leather-and-knit piece, whose umpty-jillion compartments folded neatly into a two-by-three-by-two tetragon complete with rollers and a retractable handle. In a few minutes she'd stripped her closet bare, laying her entire wardrobe out on the bed. She wrinkled her nose.

Though she was far from a clothes horse, Sharon prided herself in keeping her ensembles up-to-date, and the fact was that her four presentable courtroom suits—including the navy blue that she now wore—needed replacing. She'd bought the outfits while she was with the D.A.'s office, and she'd now been in practice with Russell Black for three whole years. As she stowed the suits and matching shoes into her luggage, she made a mental note that some serious shopping was in order when she returned from D.C. She then added two pair of jeans, khaki slacks, and a number of blouses, white Nikes, and some brown casual pumps. After thinking for a minute, she also packed a strapless and backless sequined cocktail dress because, what the hell, one never knew. Finally she stuffed in a warm coat along with a waist-length mink she'd inherited from her mother, the only fur that she had. She'd checked the weather reports, and D.C. was going to be cold. After tossing in Jockey for Her panties and white, beige, and navy bras, she folded up her luggage, snapped the snaps and zipped the zippers, pulled up on the handle and clicked it into place, and finally rolled the loaded-down suitcase into the corner. She changed into raggedy cutoffs and an oversized T whose front displayed a cartoon of Snoopy over the caption, "Get Met. It pays," and went into the backyard.

Commander loped up, trotting along beside her, rearing and trying to lick her face, as she went behind the house and filled the shepherd's water dish. She muttered, "Holy shit, Commander. Down. *Down,* dammit . . ." while she filled a large plastic bowl with Kibbles'N Bits. There was a ten-gallon washtub in the garage that she considered filling with dog food as well, then changed her mind. With Melanie remaining in Dallas there was no need; Melanie adored the shepherd, and would make sure that Commander didn't starve.

The feeding and watering accomplished, Sharon sat on her redwood deck and played fetch with Commander for a while. A crooked hickory branch was the prize, and Commander was terrible at the game.

Oh, he'd charge after the stick as if on a Holy Crusade, pouncing on and crushing the wood between his teeth, but instead of laying his prize at his master's feet he'd then roll onto his back and wait for Sharon to come to him. God, retrieving the stick from Commander required a freaking tug-o'-war. The most exasperating dog Sharon had ever known, but the most lovable as well. After fifteen minutes of the game, she gave up. She scratched Commander between the ears. She had a sudden mental image, a picture of Professor Paul Benedict, his teeth bared in a look of insanity as he'd snaked his hand up inside her skirt in the front seat of his Lincoln ten years ago. She buried her face in the shepherd's fur and repressed a sob. "Watch the ranch, old pard, okay?" she said, then went in the house while Commander sat on his haunches with his head cocked in curiosity.

Sharon's list of things to do clicked through her mind as she called the post office to have mail delivery halted for a week, then punched in the number for the *Dallas Morning News* subscription service to suspend delivery of her morning paper. She programmed the VCR a week in advance to record her favorite shows— *NYPD Blue, Law & Order, Homicide* and, God help her, *Minions of Justice: The Streets,* starring Melanie's father in the flesh—then removed clean sheets from the dryer and headed for Melanie's room to drop the linens on the bed. On the way through the den she stopped in her tracks. She sighed, let the laundry slide to the carpet, and sank down in a chair.

Last week she and Sheila had picked out identical

Christmas pines, and her own six-foot green tree now sat in its stand beside the home entertainment center. The bowl at the base of the stand was filled with water, and a few needles had drifted to the carpet. Earlier during her psychiatry session she'd noticed that Sheila's tree was already decorated—beautifully and tastefully, of course, which was Sheila's normal way of doing things—and she felt a twinge of guilt as she looked at a stack of boxes containing gold and silver spheres, Stay-brite lights, plastic angels and chiming Santas. On the day they'd brought home the tree, Sharon and Melanie had hauled the boxes down from the attic with great enthusiasm. Every day they'd intended to hang the decorations, but something—courtroom appearances, after-hours briefings at the library, the Nativity pageant at Melanie's school—had always interfered. Now, if she stayed in D.C. for a week, she wouldn't return home until the day before Christmas Eve.

Her jaw set in determination, Sharon carried the laundry into Melanie's room and dumped the sheets on the bed, then returned to the den. Muttering, chiding herself, she opened her breakfront cabinet and withdrew her sterling silver punch bowl.

Melanie Hays wallowed in gloom as she rode home in the backseat of Sheila Winston's station wagon. When Melanie and Trish had come out of the school, both fourteen year olds walking in grown-up, cool-princess strides, Melanie had known immediately that something was wrong. It was *so* not with-it that Sheila was waiting across the street to pick them up. Just that morning Melanie's mom had promised to drive her home in the new car—okay, so it wasn't *completely* new, but the shiny blue Skylark was to be the first really pimp ride in the Hays household since Melanie had been alive. Melanie about died on the days when her mom drove carpool, when she had to climb into the dented old Volvo while the other kids' mothers—or, in many cases, their mothers' chauffeurs—arrived in Caddys or Mercedes, some of them even pulling to the curb in Porsches or Jags. And now, on the day of all days when Melanie wouldn't have to hide down in the seat as Mom drove her away from school, old Mommyroo had to break her word. On seeing Sheila Winston's station wagon, Melanie had hung her head in shame. To die, she'd thought. To absolutely freaking die.

Not that Melanie hadn't grown accustomed to people breaking their word. *Duh*-uh, hello. Daddypoop was an ace at flaking out. Other kids thought it was a Big Fucking Deal—shortened to B.F.D. among the adolescent crowd—that Melanie's father was a television star, but Melanie had Rob Stanley marked down as just another B.F. liar. Only two months ago she'd flown with her mom to California and her dad had taken her to the studio. Which Melanie supposed was okay, meeting Jerry Seinfeld and whatnot, but now she was certain that the whole Daddy-of-the-Decade bit had been an act. He'd promised to write, but to date hadn't said hello, good-bye, kiss my A. or F.U. in the way of a letter, and Melanie was now certain that Rob Stanley didn't give a S. about his child. So what else was new? Melanie should have realized that he didn't care about her when he hadn't come around for the first eleven years of her so-called existence. And now, to top things off, it turned out that her mom was a B.F. liar as well.

And that part sort of hurt, not that Melanie was going to allow her disappointment to show. Her mom had always been there for her, since birth. But that was before Mom had gone to California to be the lawyer for a famous movie actress, and in the process had gotten on television and become a B.F.D. in her own right. Only six weeks earlier Melanie's periods had begun and her mom had seen her gently through the trauma, but in Melanie's adolescent mind six weeks might as well have been six years. Mom was now a B.F.D. just like good old Dad, and B.F.D.'s had no time for their kids. And, Melanie thought as Sheila Winston explained that she was to stay at the Winston's while Mom flew off to Washington, the next step beyond becoming a B.F.D. was to be a B.F. liar as well. All of Mom's promises about Christmas shopping, about spending the holidays together in this state of euphoria, all of that was a B.F. lie.

Sheila steered into the Hays driveway, cut the engine, and watched Melanie expectantly over the seat back. Melanie offered Sheila a smile of innocence. "Be right back," she said, and reached for the door handle as Trish moved her legs aside to give her room. Melanie threw Trish a confident wink, climbed over her best friend in this world, and trotted across the lawn toward her front door. The sparkling Buick Skylark sat in the drive, but Melanie averted her gaze from the car. So it's a car, B.F.D., she thought as she hopped up on the front porch and reached for the door handle.

Melanie hoped that Mom was in the backyard with the dog, so that she could grab her things and haul A. without saying good-bye, but that wasn't to be. Sharon was in fact in the den, wearing a goofy Met Life T as if she was trying to be a kid, standing on a stepladder and stretching to her full height in order to affix the star to the top of the tree. Oh, goody, Melanie thought as tears stung her eyes, Christmas. Santa Claus. B.F.D. In spite of her bitterness she couldn't help but notice that her mom was pretty without makeup, wearing her grodies, and couldn't help remembering that, not so long ago, she'd been proud that Mom and she looked more like sisters than mother and daughter. Now, however, Melanie resented her mom's leggy good looks just as she resented the fact that Sharon was leaving town. Mom *looked* like a B.F.D., *acted* like a B.F.D., *was* a B.F.D., and a B.F. liar along with the rest of the adults in the world.

Sharon turned on the stepladder, lightly touching pine branches to steady herself, her expression softening as she gazed at her daughter, and stepped smoothly down onto the carpet, barefoot. She took a long stride toward Melanie and opened her arms. "Hi, sweetheart," she said.

Melanie allowed a brief hug, a short smacky kiss to the cheek, then stepped around her mother and walked quickly toward her room. "I've got to hurry, Mom. Sheila's waiting for me."

"Mrs. Winston," Sharon said, though her tone wasn't as reproachful as it normally was whenever Melanie called Sheila by her first name.

"Well, whoever. I've got to go."

"Melanie . . ."

Melanie stopped near the step-up entrance to the hallway, and turned around.

"I've fixed punch." Sharon pointed to the sterling silver bowl where it sat on the dining table. The bowl was three-quarters full of frothy pink liquid, with lumps of green sherbet floating on the surface.

Melanie wrinkled her nose. "No, thanks," she said, and hustled on down the corridor.

Sharon followed, reaching Melanie's room and pausing in the doorway as Melanie flopped her overnight case on the bed and opened the lid. "I thought we'd decorate the tree," Sharon said.

Melanie opened a drawer and turned around with panties bunched in her fist. "I don't have time. I told you, Sheila's waiting."

"Trish and Mrs. Winston are invited." Sharon kept her tone cheerful, though her voice broke slightly at the end.

Melanie dropped the panties into the overnight case and walked to her closet. "You don't have to do that."

Sharon came into the room. "But I want to."

Melanie was inside the closet, rasping through the hangers. "Well I don't."

Sharon near the dresser. "Melanie."

Melanie came out, folding over a pair of jeans. "Chill, Mom. Just chill, will you?"

Sharon's voice quivered in sudden anger. "No. I won't chill. What's wrong with you?"

Melanie dropped the jeans in on top of the panties, and retreated once more inside the closet. "You don't want to know."

Sharon rested her lightly clenched fists on her hips. "Yes, I do. You're my daughter."

"Am I? *Am I,* Mom?"

"Yes, you are. And as long as you live in my house . . . Don't be like this, Melanie."

"Like what?"

"You know."

Melanie stopped in the doorway and sighed. "You can make me, Mom. You can force me, and we'll have Sheila and Trish in here and decorate like mad and drink punch and pretend we're all like, totally delirious. But that won't change anything. You're leaving town. I'm staying here. It's okay, Mom, I like it that way."

"I have to earn a living."

"Oh? By screwing up Christmas?" Melanie stepped toward the bed.

Sharon blocked her daughter's path. "I'll be home before Christmas."

"Don't bother." Melanie tried to step around her mother, but Sharon moved to the side and stood her ground. Melanie lowered her head. "It's okay, Mom. Really it is. You have your Christmas, I'll have mine. Now. Will you please move? Just chill, Mom. I told you, Sheila's waiting outside."

Sharon reached out as if to grab her daughter and give her a shaking, then lowered her hands. "My leaving can't be helped, and I think you know that. If it wasn't important I wouldn't be going." She moved aside. "But have it your way."

Melanie tilted her chin. Her eyes were moist. "Cool, Mom. And I will have it my way. From now on, that's just what I intend to do."

Sharon watched her daughter leave, sashaying down the sidewalk with a drawstring bag slung over her shoulder, climbing into Sheila's station wagon and slamming the door without so much as a glance back over her shoulder. As the wagon backed out of the driveway, Sharon leaned her forehead against the doorjamb. It was all she could do to keep from running into the yard and calling out to Melanie, begging her little girl not to be angry with her.

Making the right choices in rearing a child on her own was an impossible task; good sense told her not to give in to Melanie's tantrums, to be the adult and display an outward veneer of calm, but doing so ripped her emotions to shreds. She took a deep breath, backed away from the door and steadied herself. Then she returned to the den, gazing helplessly at the Christmas tree for a moment. Finally she sobbed in frustration, hefted the punchbowl and carried it into the kitchen, and dumped the entire concoction out in the sink. She stood as if in a trance, watching the thick pinkish liquid glug down the drain.

5

Russell Black didn't have much to say on the early-bird flight to Washington, and Sharon thought it just as well. There was an ache in her throat which would have made conversation difficult, a painful lump which tightened each time she thought of Melanie. Mother-daughter spats had become more and more common as Melanie moved into teenhood, little skirmishes that always ended with the two of them making up, but yesterday had been entirely different. The fourteen year old had been awfully transparent, using sass to cover what was really troubling her. Melanie was feeling neglected, and—*dammit*, Sharon thought—had a right to. After her daughter had gone to Sheila's, Sharon had tossed and turned until 2 A.M., and several times had nearly called Russ and canceled the trip. She felt ripped in two, half of her wanting to tend to business, the other half wanting to say to hell with practicing law and become a full-time mother. Which she couldn't afford, of course, not for long. As the American jetliner floated over the snow-covered landscape and began its descent into Reagan National, the White House, Treasury Building, and the Capitol were visible below like architects' miniatures. Sharon had never been to the nation's capital. She touched the cold glass of the jetliner's window, and wished with all her heart that she hadn't come.

Sharon adjusted her shoulder bag strap and switched her topcoat from one arm to the other as Russell Black trailed her up the accordion walkway and into the terminal. She did a sharp column-right, passed a bank of telephones, the men's and women's restrooms, a row of concourse gift shops, and finally reached the security station. Boarding passengers dumped carry-ons onto the conveyor belt, then dropped keys and change onto trays before stepping through the metal-detectors. One man in an overcoat spread his arms in a sheepish posture as a guard ran a hand-held detector over his shoes and clothing. Sharon hustled on, setting her game face, telling herself that her problems at home weren't going to interfere with business, no way. She had a sudden sensation of being alone in the crowded airport, and stopped and turned. Russ had hung back a good twenty paces and was looking around with a puzzled look on his face.

Sharon retraced her steps and stood before the older lawyer. "What is it, boss?" she said.

Black shrugged and moved forward. Sharon fell in step beside him. Black said, "Guess I was assumin' too much. We didn' really talk about it on the phone, but I thought Mattie Ruth might be waiting for us. Idn like her, to let out-of-town visitors fend for themselves." The pair moved past the security stations and on into the massive airport lobby.

Sharon let her gaze rest on a Starbuck's coffee shop across the way. "Not in her current circumstance, Russ. With the publicity? I doubt Mattie Ruth Benedict can set foot in public without a gang of newsies and paparazzi on her trail."

They continued on, with Black playing the gentleman as always, herding Sharon along in front of him as if he were her escort. Sharon stepped on a large gold medallion that was painted on the floor, and stopped dead in her tracks. Russ bumped her gently from behind.

Directly in front of the lawyers from Texas was a picture window five stories high and the length of several football fields. Visible through the glass was the edge of a runway and, further in the distance, a river which had to be a couple of miles wide. Snowdrifts padded the riverbank, and bleak icy whiteness covered the tree branches along the runway. On the other side of the river, the dome on Capitol Hill towered over the city.

Sharon drew breath. "Will you look at that. Like a picture book on your coffee table."

Black stepped up beside her, lugging her briefcase, and viewed the panorama with his face expressionless. "I've seen it before," he said. "Ol' George had an arm on him."

Sharon blinked. "Who?"

"Washington. Throwin' that dollar across the Potomac." Black stepped toward the baggage claim area, then stopped and turned. "Just looking at the width of that river tells you the story idn true, can't be, but there's a lesson to be learned. S'pect old George had him a press secretary. Wadn the first fish story to come out of the District of Columbia, and wadn the last by the longest shot imaginable. Keep that in mind, Sharon. You have to check out everything people tell you in this town."

Sharon said, "Right there." She pointed to her luggage as it thumped from the conveyor belt onto the carousel. The skycap hopped to, rolling his cart up next to the carousel and readying himself to grab the suitcase as it passed. Russell Black's two large bags were already on the cart. Sharon had put on her smooth beige topcoat in anticipation of going out into the cold, and now stood back with her hands thrust deep into fur-lined pockets. A flight from Chicago had landed at the same time as the plane from Dallas; the baggage claim area was wall-to-wall humanity, well-dressed men and women pumping change into slots to rent luggage dollies, or picking out bags for a skycap to schlep as Sharon had done. She looked through the crowd toward the exit doors. A man stood beyond the railing holding a white pasteboard sign above his head. Sharon tugged on Russ Black's sleeve and pointed in the stranger's direction. Black turned.

The guy holding the sign stood among a gang of limo and taxi drivers, but no way was he one of them. He dressed like someone in authority and probably was, a big man with polished shoes. His overcoat was open to reveal a white shirt and an expensive patterned tie looped into a square knot. The coat looked like a Ralph Lauren, conservative gray in color, a thousand dollars off the rack if it was a dime. He had iron gray hair clipped and barbered, a strikingly handsome man around fifty years old. BLACK/HAYS was lettered on the sign in bold strokes with a Marks-a-Lot. Russ slipped the skycap a five-dollar bill and led Sharon over toward the well-dressed stranger. As he neared the railing, Black said, "I think we're the ones you're looking for."

The man looked a bit sheepish as he folded the sign over twice, then jammed the whole mess into a garbage container. He came over and extended his hand. "It was the only way I knew to get your attention. Leonard Smith, Mr. Black. Porter, Ragsdale & Jones. I recognize Miss Hays from her pictures on TV and in the newspapers."

Black gripped and shook, then lowered his arm to his side. "Russ. Nobody's called me Mr. Black since law school."

"Yeah, well." Leonard Smith beckoned to Sharon's skycap, who now had all of Sharon's and Russ's luggage loaded onto his cart and stood expectantly by the conveyor. "I have a car waiting," Smith said. The skycap rolled the cart toward the exit, readying ticket envelopes and claim checks for the security guard's inspection.

Sharon had kept a deadpan look when Leonard Smith had mentioned the name of his law firm, but now permitted her upper lip to twitch a bit. Porter, Ragsdale & Jones was a humongous Dallas outfit with over two hundred lawyers on the payroll, and with branches in Washington, New York, and, let's see, Sharon thought, maybe Los Angeles as well. She'd heard that Porter, Ragsdale & Jones's D.C. operation was more into lobbying than practicing law. She wasn't surprised that Mattie Ruth Benedict had picked attorneys with Texas roots as her local Washington counsel, though Leonard Smith was certainly no Texan. He had an eastern accent, not quite the clipped Manhattanspeak that Sharon recalled from her acting years, but very close. If she had to guess as to Smith's origin, she'd say New Jersey. The vanilla Anglo surname could easily be a pseudonym; the practice of changing one's name for political purposes was common in Washington. Smith's manner was as brusque and businesslike as Russ Black's was laid-back. Though he was obviously doing his best not to show it, Russ was bristling; he had no use for big civil firms and even less for attorneys who dabbled in politics. As she fell into step alongside Black and followed the Washington lawyer out of the terminal, Sharon suspected that Russell Black and Leonard Smith weren't going to get along.

The cold was invigorating. Tiny snowflakes peppered Sharon's cheeks in a series of icy stings. She walked carefully but quickly, following Leonard Smith toward a shiny black Mercedes which waited near the curb, moving aside to give the skycap room to roll the luggage to the rear of the car. Russ's breath fogged as he supervised the skycap's loading of the bags into the trunk. Leonard Smith held the front seat door for her, and Sharon ducked her head to climb inside. Her high-heeled patent leather shoe sank down into a puddle, and freezing water sloshed around her toes and the ball of her foot. As she stepped onto the Mercedes's floorboard, she sneezed.

*   *   *

Sharon sat in front on plush leather cushions while
Russ hunkered close behind her, breathing down her
neck. Leonard Smith kept up a flow of tour-guide dialogue, pointing across the Boundary Channel and Jef-
ferson Davis Highway toward the Tomb of the
Unknown Soldier, then giving a brick-by-brick description of the Lincoln Memorial, which lay dead
ahead as they rolled over the Arlington Memorial
Bridge. Never once did he mention Mattie Ruth, Will
John Benedict, or the pending murder charges, and
Sharon was pretty sure that the omission was intentional. As a political animal, Smith would know on
which side his bread was buttered, and he wouldn't
dare discuss the Benedict family problems without a
herd of advisors present. Never having seen the famous D.C. landmarks, Sharon was fascinated, but
from the way that Russ shifted around behind her she
could tell that the older lawyer had had it up to here
with the travelogue. She wondered for how long Russ
would be able to keep his mouth shut. He breathed
rapidly through his nose. He's about to erupt, Sharon
thought, and mentally crossed her fingers.

Leonard Smith was saying, "The Grand Foyer is the
size of three football fields, and you don't want to
miss the Israeli Lounge. Stunning paintings of Old
Testament scenes." He gestured to his right, toward
the massive rectangular whiteness of the Kennedy
Center for the Performing Arts. An overhead sign said
that they were on the Rock Creek and Potomac Parkway, headed north, and that the next right turn would
take them to the Watergate Complex. On their left, a
sliver of snow-covered land a couple of miles long lay

in the middle of the Potomac. Sharon mentally dialed up an undergraduate D.C. history course she'd taken as an elective. Roosevelt Island, she thought, and near its northern rim was a monument to Teddy himself, Rough Rider uniform and all.

Sharon looked over a stirring quote from JFK, which was carved into the Kennedy Center wall. "It's fantastic," she said.

"The tour is worthwhile," Smith said. "Would you like to—?"

"Takin' awfully long to get where we're goin', idn it?" Black tersely interrupted. Sharon inhaled a shallow breath and held it. Russ said, "Last time I was here we drove downtown in fifteen minutes or so."

Smith kept a bland expression, though his leather-gloved hands tightened their grip on the steering wheel. "There are shorter routes, over the Key Bridge onto M Street, but I thought I'd give you the cook's tour." He smiled and waved expansively. "We can take a detour here and go right in front of the Watergate Complex. It's mainly famous for the break-in, of course, but did you know they have apartments which are—?"

"Mr. Smith." Russ's tone held a soft edge. "And don't think I'm bein' rude, because that idn my nature. But we're here on business. I can tell that you're only playing host, an' that you're not supposed to be talking about anything approachin' the nature of what we're here for. I'm not sure *why* you're not discussing it, but I understand you got your orders. But Mattie Ruth Benedict's who we need to be seeing, as soon as we can. Assuming we're successful with what we're here to do, we'll be glad to see the sights on the way *outta* town, but not just now." Black sat back with an air of finality. "For now, sir, just get us where we're goin'. If I want a tour guide, the Smithsonian furnishes all of those I'll ever need."

Leonard Smith shed Russ's outburst like water off a duck's back, and showed a pleasant but businesslike demeanor as he discontinued the tour and pointed the Mercedes's nose downtown. They'd taken a really roundabout path from the airport, and Smith had to double back a couple of times in order to reach the hotel. Mattie Ruth Benedict had made the sleeping arrangements in a pattern of secrecy; the State Plaza wasn't a hotel where the media would expect Will John Benedict's pricey defense team to stay. It was a stone-and-glass front, twin-towered structure on E Street. Across the way stood a huge building that, according to Leonard Smith, housed the State Department, and the city map in Sharon's purse told her that they were on the opposite side of town from the courts and Capitol Building. Mattie Ruth's choice of hotels was a long way from dumb; on this get-acquainted trip, she and Russ would be more effective without a gang of reporters dogging their steps. The time for press conferences was later, when and if Will John came under indictment. Smith pulled his Mercedes up to the hotel entry, where Sharon and Russ dropped off their luggage and obtained card keys to their rooms, then headed for Smith's office.

During the ten-minute drive the Washington lawyer mentioned that Porter, Ragsdale, & Jones officed in Foggy Bottom, and his tone of voice indicated that

anyone who'd never heard of Foggy Bottom was likely
a cretin. Sharon assumed that the location was trendy
as all get-out, and managed to act impressed even as
she looked up Foggy Bottom in her *Frommer's Washington Tour Guide*. The Foggy Bottom area was west of
the White House, and so named because of the mist
that used to linger when D.C. was largely wilderness.
But now the haze in Foggy Bottom blended with the
rest of the downtown smog. After a ten-minute drive
they slowed in front of a beautiful refurbished building
that had to be a hundred years old. To Leonard Smith's
credit, he hadn't taken any additional detours.

They parked underground, crossed under the street
through a tunnel, and entered the building. Sharon
and Russ followed Smith to the elevators, and the trio
rode to the ninth and topmost floor. On exiting they
passed an antique oval receptionist's desk, where a
chic-looking young woman routed calls as she peered
at a monitor. She chanted in a singsong monotone,
"Porter *Rags*-dale," listened and said, "One moment,
ple-as," and then expertly swiveled her mouse to click
on the caller's extension. The name of the law firm
was in carved mahogany letters, and a door behind
the receptionist led to a medium-sized conference
room with a picture window. Smith deposited the
Texas attorneys inside, then excused himself and disappeared down the hall. Sharon discarded her coat,
shoulder bag, and satchel in a chair, and stood before
the window with her arms folded. Her view was straight
down Pennsylvania Avenue. She had distant glimpses
of the Executive Office Building and the snow-covered

White House lawn, places she'd dreamed of visiting all of her life.

Behind her, Black said, "You think I was too short with him, dontcha?"

She turned around. Russ was seated at the table, which had a rustic sheenless top and legs like varnished tree stumps. He'd shed his overcoat. Sharon gave him an inquiring look.

"That guy." Black pointed at the door where Smith had exited. "You think I was tough on him when I shouldn'a been."

Sharon lowered her lashes. "I thought it was out of character."

"Well you're right. It *was* out of character, and it won't be the last time you'll see me that way while we're working on this case. You keep playin' Good Lawyer and I'll be the heavy. But take it from me, I've been here before. This is Washington, D.C. If you let people here think you're swallowin' their line of bull, then bull is all you'll get from them."

They cooled their heels for twenty minutes—which, Sharon was to later reflect, was the exact amount of time that Leonard Smith was supposed to have delayed their arrival while giving the cook's tour of the city—before Smith returned with three men. The men were dressed like peas in a pod, in dark suits, snow-white shirts, fifty-dollar ties, and black-laced shoes polished like mirrors. Sharon turned from the window as the foursome entered. One had sparse gray hair, the bearing and demeanor of a man twenty years younger than he obviously was, and seemed to be in charge.

He smiled at her and gestured palm-up toward the table. "Sit. Please," he said. Sharon obeyed, sinking down into a chair alongside her coat, purse, and satchel. Black had been sprawled out with his ankle resting on his knee, but now placed both feet on the floor.

All four newcomers remained standing. "Let me do the honors," Gray-hair said. "I'm Boots York, Managing Partner of our Washington office. Leonard Smith you already know. This"—he pointed at the youngest man in the group, a sandy-haired blonde who looked late thirties, early forties at the most—"is Mack Taylor, head of our trials division. Mack did two years with the Boston prosecutor's office before he came on board, which qualifies him as the only member of our firm with any criminal experience."

Mack Taylor raised a hand in greeting as Sharon nodded and smiled and Black folded his hands. Boots York and Mack Taylor, Sharon thought, mentally rolling her eyes. Good old Boots and good old Mack. She'd bet that there wasn't an attorney whose name ended in "stein" or "berg,"—or in "ino" or "witz," for that matter—in the entire firm. There would be a couple of token females and a Harvard-educated African-American or two, but that would be the extent of the mix. She looked expectantly toward the remaining newcomer, who was a handsome black with kinky hair receding from his forehead. He was dressed in conservative gray and had an intelligent, authoritative air. Now this guy is no token, Sharon thought. All four men were slim and erect, like cutouts from a fitness center ad.

"And this," York continued, indicating the black guy, "is Wallace Burns." He nodded toward Russ.

"Your reputation proceeds you, Mr. Black. Our pleasure." Then he beamed at Sharon, an expression more like a leer than a welcoming smile. "Ah," he said, "and the famous Miss Hays. It's an honor to meet you in person. I seldom miss your husband's television show."

There were five seconds of silence as Sharon's forehead tightened and her eyebrow arched. York's companions exchanged nervous glances. Taylor, the blond man, started to say something, then closed his mouth. Sharon thought, of all the phoniness. York was a typical stuffed shirt, so wrapped up in himself that he paid little or no attention to what went on in the rest of the world, and one of his cohorts had likely told him of Sharon's connection to the star of *Minions of Justice* on the way down the hall to the meeting. The idea of Boots York sitting around in his undershirt, slurping beer along with America's blue-collar crowd while Rob cleaned the bad guys' clocks—and then screwed all the rookie female officers and widows of victims as an encore—was laughable. Stuffed-shirtlike, York had been listening with half an ear while his underlings thumbnailed Sharon's bio, and now had managed to bungle his entry. Sharon fumed. She was conscious of Russell Black on her left. The Good Lawyer role doesn't fit me, old boss, she thought.

York looked around at his companions. He said, "Didn't you say she was . . . ?"

Sharon gave her sweetest put-down smile. "Rob Stanley and I were never married, Mr. York. We lived together, and he made me pregnant."

York's expression froze, like that of a man who'd

just realized that his fly was open. He rapidly cleared his throat and gestured to his companions. "Be seated, gentlemen." All four sat as one, with the table between them and the Texas lawyers like a line in the dirt. Avoiding eye contact with Sharon, York said, "You're set up to meet with Mattie Ruth Benedict at two o'clock. In the meantime we thought we'd bring you up to snuff on what we've done in a preliminary vein."

Rob Stanley's wife my ass, Sharon thought. "We'd appreciate that," she said, then watched Wallace Burns, the authoritative-looking black man, as she continued, "I didn't catch your position with the firm, Mr. Burns." She'd decided she'd better inquire before Russ did. Mystery men attending meetings bugged Sharon no end, and Burns's unexplained presence would send Black into orbit.

Burns had large white teeth, which he showed in a grin. "I'm just observing."

York took the floor before Sharon could speak again. "I'll briefly touch on the cons, then we'll emphasize the pros," York said. "Congressman Benedict was having an affair with the girl. It's common knowledge. You won't be able to get around that. They have witnesses out of our control."

Sharon was incredulous, that the guy would come right out and say such a thing. *Whose* control? she thought. Oh, *that* control.

York went on. "We think we should take the position, *have* to take the position that, okay, Will John Benedict confesses his weakness, are you with me there? The public accepts apology. Mrs. Benedict will stand firmly by his side. A family in a united front will make the affair problem go away."

Black said evenly, "In the eyes o' the public, maybe. The eyes of the jury, that's a different matter."

"The public *is* the jury, Mr. Black." York looked around at his cohorts, who nodded agreement.

Black's features tightened in an expression that Sharon recognized. It was the same look she'd seen on occasions when Russ had dressed her down when she'd disagreed with him on trial strategy. Sharon mentally winced in anticipation as Black said to Boots York, "The call I got was from Mattie Ruth Benedict. Any particular reason why we're meetin' with you guys?"

York seemed unperturbed. He laughed without humor. "Let's call us the advance guard. Senator Benedict wanted us to fill you in on the legal status of the case."

"Which will be a big help," Black said, "as long as you don't become a backseat driver." He turned to Sharon. "Miss Hays, you got any questions of these folks about what they've been up to?"

Sharon was ready. She whipped out a legal pad and pen, opened the pad on the table, and prepared to take notes. "Have you gentlemen looked at any physical evidence? The media's put out a lot of hints, but until one sees evidence in person . . ."

The Washington lawyers exchanged looks that gave Sharon an almost irresistible urge to giggle. They'd expected to brush the visitors from Texas aside like so many houseflies, but were about to learn the hard way that intimidating Russell Black was impossible. Black sat unmoving. Sharon swept the other lawyers with an expectant gaze. "I'm sorry," she said. "Should I repeat my question?"

Finally York said, "That's Mack's bailiwick."

Mack Taylor leaned forward. With his razored hair and manicured nails, the blondish man fit the big-firm image as if a cookie cutter had stamped him out and he'd just dropped off the conveyor belt. "They have a few hair samples," he said. "Some skin recovered from under the victim's nails. Certain fibers, trace evidence . . ."

Sharon offered a tiny smile. "That information was in the papers. But have you seen any of those items in person?"

Taylor seemed to deflate. "I confess that I haven't."

"So." Sharon made a note. "Our first order of business is a trip to the forensics lab. My job, boss, which I'll tend to first thing in the morning." She returned her attention to Taylor. "Any clue as yet who's going to prosecute?" She was taking Will John's indictment for granted, and hoped the Washington lawyers didn't waste a lot of time with what-if-this-is-a-false-alarm speculation.

"Why, Gregory Campisi, I'd think," Taylor said.

Sharon had never heard the name, and looked to Russ. Black said, "Idn he the United States Attorney?"

Taylor looked surprised, as if Gregory Campisi's name were a household word and Russell Black had been living in a vacuum if he didn't know the answer to his own question. "Right," Taylor said. "Appointed at the beginning of the presidential term."

"And a guy you'd expect to hog the glory in a high-profile case," Black said. "But I think that Miss Hays was askin' is, who's prosecutin'?"

Sharon waited for an answer. Receiving none, she said in a feigned helpful tone, "Who's doing the grunt work, you know? I'm sure Mr. Campisi isn't going to personally make trips to the law library, interview the witnesses . . ." While having minorities on the payroll wouldn't be in keeping with the image of this white-collar law firm, the appointment of an Italian-American to the U.S. Attorney's post would fit right in with eastern politics. She recalled that in South Dakota, near the Sioux Reservation, the presidential appointee was named Harold Standing Rock.

Taylor's smile was uncertain. "If you need the AUSDA's name, I can give Greg a buzz."

Sharon was puzzled for an instant. Greg who? Then it came to her. Greg *Campisi,* you dodo, she thought, the U.S. Attorney guy. Big-wheel lawyers such as the ones across the table always pretended to be on a first-name basis with everyone important, even if they'd never met the guy. If the subject of the conversation had been the president of the United States, Taylor likely would have said that he'd give *Bill* a buzz. Sharon said, "That won't be necessary, the people at forensics will know." She pretended to make a note, but actually wrote down, "These guys don't know phooey," tilting her pad so that Russ could read. "Let's see," Sharon said, "you don't know what evidence they have, and you don't know who's prosecuting." She folded over her legal pad. "That's all I have, boss."

"Yeah," Black said, then mumbled, "Yeah," again

before saying, "Nice to meet you guys." He put both hands on the table and started to rise.

York held out a restraining hand. "Wait. There's more."

Black relaxed, looking slightly bored.

York glanced to his left. "Wally?"

The handsome black man, Wallace Burns, leaned into the discussion as the others sat respectfully back. Sharon blinked in curiosity, getting it, realizing that Wallace Burns was the man with the real stroke around here, and that the delay in getting from the airport to the office had been a ploy, a stall to enable Burns to arrive on the scene before the meeting began. Burns took the floor. "Mr. Black, we defer to your knowledge of criminal law, but you should defer to ours where the territory's concerned. There are ways to do things in sane society. Unfortunately those methods seldom work in Washington. And face it, there are other factors to consider than Will John Benedict."

Russ hesitated in obvious surprise. Finally he said, "What factors?"

"The affair with the intern is something we can deal with in time," Burns said. "We're working on that over at our shop. A bigger problem is going to be the embarrassing business with . . ." He cut a glance at Sharon, then looked quickly away.

She felt a twinge of amusement. "It's quite all right, sir," she said. "If they can discuss the size of a man's penis on national television, far be it from me to shy daintily away from the subject. My observation is two-fold. First, it's Will John's father who's become the laughingstock, not him. And second, no one can possibly look dumber than all those network anchors pronouncing the word. I picture this dialogue coach going"—she made her tones round and clear, shades of her off-Broadway days—" 'pee. Pee. *Pee*-nis.' " Russ looked embarrassed while the Washington lawyers wiped grins away.

"Yes, then . . ." Burns cleared his throat. "I'm sure you can see, the girl's death is serious enough in itself. But the . . . organ size attributed to Paul rubs off on Will John. It throws a cartoonish pallor over the entire mess. Ridicule hurts us more in ways than extramarital affairs or suspicions of murder."

Black's tone sharpened. "I got to ask. Who's 'us'?"

York, Smith, and Taylor exchanged looks. Wallace Burns watched Russell Black, two men in a sizing-up mode.

"You're not with this law firm, right?" Black said. "You're talkin' about your shop, indicatin' it's someplace other than here. You a lawyer, Mr. Burns?"

"I'm licensed, a member of the bar." Burns gave a casual wave. "I don't practice much. Currently I'm a consultant." His skin was dark, the color of bittersweet chocolate.

"Excuse me," Black cut in, leaning more over the table. "Don't think we're not glad to know you. But before we launch into any long-winded discussion, we need to know exactly what your function is." His grin was tight, a bit less than friendly. "For all we know, you're the prosecutor."

Burns pyramided his fingers underneath his chin. "Rest assured I'm on your side, Mr. Black."

Black didn't give an inch. "Nice to know. But so's my daughter. I got to know what your interest in this meetin' is before we go any further."

Burns and Russell Black locked gazes while the other three men swapped nervous glances. Sharon kept her expression mild but inquisitive.

Finally York said, "Wally's from another firm."

"That's somewhat enlightenin'," Black said. "Which one?"

There were five seconds of silence before Wallace Burns said, with an air of confidentiality, "Waters and Johnson. We're up in Belle Chasse."

How nice, Sharon thought. Waters, Johnson . . . God, they sound more like fugitives' aliases than names for politically connected lawyers. She suppressed a grin.

Russ's chin lifted a fraction. "That *Mitchell* Johnson?"

York leaned back. Leonard Smith and Mack Taylor remained motionless. Wallace Burns cleared his throat before saying, "Yes."

Sharon was confused. "Is Mitchell Johnson someone you know, boss?" A Martindale-Hubbell legal directory sat on a table in the corner, and Sharon wondered if she needed a program in order to identify the players here.

Black never took his gaze away from Burns. "Know of," Black said. "I've seen him on television, makin' the nine-hole turn at Congressional. Mitchell Johnson's the one drivin' the golf cart."

Sharon got it. She pictured the president before a bank of microphones, wearing a golf shirt, explaining his position on the crisis in Iran or the war on drugs while a pale-skinned guy waited impatiently in the background, chomping at the bit to go on to the back nine. She said merely, "Oh."

" 'Oh' is right." Black placed his elbows on his armrests and intertwined his fingers in front of his midsection. "Mattie Ruth Benedict know about this?"

York's features tightened into a defensive scowl. "Of course. On a matter this delicate, we wouldn't make a move without consulting her."

"No, I mean about him." Black pointed across the table at Wallace Burns. "Does she know about him sittin' in?"

York cleared his throat. Burns nervously tugged on his lapel. No one said anything.

"About what I thought." Black reached for his coat, which he'd tossed over an adjacent chair back. "Okay, gentlemen, rules are: Mattie Ruth called us about representin' her son on potential criminal charges. That's what we'll do, represent Will John Benedict. Which dudn include progress reports to the Democratic Party about defense strategy, or helping out with any press relations. Gettin' votes is your business. Defending against criminal charges is ours. Whatever Will John or his mother wants to tell you is up to them, but you're not getting anything more from us." He glared at York. "You say we're to meet with Mattie Ruth at two o'clock?"

York turned his palms up. "That's the schedule."

Black stood and lifted his overcoat. "We'll be there, then. Good day to youall."

Sharon stood as well, the backs of her knees bumping her chair and pushing it back.

"It's imperative I keep the Party up-to-date," Burns said. "You wouldn't believe how critical all of this is."

"What's important to you," Black said, "idn necessarily important to us." He took a long stride toward the door.

York looked at Leonard Smith, who took his cue and got up from his seat. "I'll drop you," he said.

"Appreciate the offer," Black said. "But if it's all the same, we'll take a cab." He turned on his heel and left the room.

Sharon snatched up her belongings and followed after Black. She'd reached the threshold, the oval desk, and the receptionist visible through the doorway, when Burns called out, "Miss Hays."

Russ gave her an impatient look from near the hallway exit. She smiled diplomatically, raised one finger in Black's direction, then stepped back inside the conference room. "Yes?" she said.

Burns glanced around at his companions. He was obviously searching for words. He said, "We watched you on television in the Darla Cowan hearings. Quite impressive."

Sharon didn't feel particularly flattered. She moved her topcoat from one forearm to the other, and adjusted the strap on her shoulder bag.

Burns smirked conspiratorily, and lowered his voice. "But if I may offer a word to the wise, homespun only plays well on politicians. Being quaint and rustic won't go over with the courts in this town."

Sharon glanced quickly over her shoulder toward the reception area. "You mean Russ?"

Burns nodded. "I'm sure it's fine in Texas, but . . ." He spread his hands, palms up.

Sharon stiffened in reflex. "Where he's performing in front of a jury of hicks?"

Burns looked down. York put a hand on Burns's arm and interjected, "I'm sure Wally didn't mean—"

"Oh, I'm sure he did, sir." She took a step closer to the conference table. "I did quite a bit of time in New York."

Burns smiled. "So we're heard. Onstage."

Sharon nodded angrily. "Where the eastern idea of Texans is a series of corny caricatures. I had to reinvent myself, take diction lessons to change my accent in order to conform with the artsy-fartsy Manhattan ideas, because I knew no one would consider me for a serious role until I did. Thank God Russ doesn't have to put on any airs."

She paused to allow her words to sink in, shifting her weight from one foot to the other. "We're not all straight from *The Best Little Whorehouse,* gentlemen. J. R. Ewing was a figment of a Hollywood scriptwriter's imagination. And for your information, Russell Black knows more law than the lot of you combined, not to mention the eleven consecutive acquittals on his record. And I . . ." She closed her mouth. Sweet Christ, why was she always losing it at the wrong time? She hugged her coat to her chest, getting a hold on her emotions. "Sorry for the outburst, folks," she said. "And good day to you. I'm sure that before this is over, we'll all be talking again."

6

Sharon watched through the backseat window as the taxi cruised down Independence Avenue and passed the Capitol Building. It was snowing for real, large cottony flakes, which stuck to the sidewalks and melted on the taxi's engine-warmed hood. A surge of patriotism flowed through her as she bent sideways to peer up at the Capitol dome and thought of God, Patrick Henry, John Hancock, Abe Lincoln, Davy Crockett, young and handsome JFK, names she'd studied in history class. She pictured senators and representatives scurrying through the corridors or hotly debating issues on the floor, their jaw muscles bulging as they fought for the public good. Then another image came to her, those same senators and reps groping their privates as they peered up dresses worn by female pages and interns. The awestruck feeling left her. She turned away from the window toward Russell Black, who silently read that day's *Washington Post* story about the murdered girl and Will John Benedict. Today's "shocking" revelation came from a woman who, while walking her rottweiler in the snow, claimed to have seen Will John and Courtney Lee arguing on a street corner three nights before the crime. Sharon sighed and leaned back against the cushions. It was stifling inside the cab. She considered asking the driver to turn down the heater, then changed her mind. Visible beneath the clicking meter, the dashboard clock showed a quarter till two.

A block and a half past the Capitol the cabbie pulled to the curb in front of two buildings connected by walkways, the easternmost of which had narrow two-story windows. On the facade facing the street were artistic drawings of working men, their muscles straining as they toiled, their eyes shaded under the brims of their hard hats.

The driver slid the partition aside and turned around. "Hart Building on the left," he said in a tourist-info monotone, "Dirksen Building on the right, that's where your senator's at. If she ain't, try the Russell Building back there." He pointed a block behind them. "All kinda senators wandering around them buildings. That'll be nine-fifty." He held out his hand. Black deposited a ten and a couple of singles, which the driver looked over without enthusiasm, then held the door for Sharon as they alighted in the cold. The taxi's wheels spun in slush as it fishtailed out into traffic. An inch of snow covered the sidewalk as Black escorted Sharon toward the Dirksen Building. She was freezing. She wished that she'd brought her galoshes.

They were in luck. The Dirksen Building's lobby receptionist directed them to Mattie Ruth's office, and they rode up in the elevator. Black pinched his reddened nose as the doors rumbled open.

Fine minutes later they waited in leather armchairs

while Mattie Ruth Benedict's assistant went in to announce their arrival. The Stars 'n Stripes hung from a pole in one corner of the reception area, with the Lone Star flag of Texas drooping alongside. A floor-to-ceiling bookcase exhibited Texas Almanacs, U.S. and Texas history books, along with doorstop-sized bios of LBJ, Sam Rayburn, Stephen F. Austin, and Dwight D. Eisenhower. At various locations around the room hung photos of Mattie Ruth in action, addressing the Senate, striding purposefully across the Capitol lawn, on the deck of a yacht along with Barbara Bush and Jackie O. One of the photos showed the greeting line at a White House reception. Sharon blinked as she zeroed in on Senator Benedict shaking hands with Hillary Clinton while the Chief Executive chatted with the president of China. Prominent in the background stood Paul Benedict himself, dressed in a tux, his steel gray hair perfectly combed, his cobalt blue eyes fierce, his jaw jutted out. Sharon's upper lip curled.

Mattie Ruth's assistant, an attractive thirtyish woman with jet black hair, returned to say, "The senator will see you now." Black nodded, stood, and hurried past the reception desk. Sharon started to follow. She had a sinking sensation in the pit of her stomach and her knees turned to jelly, and for just an instant she feared she would faint dead away.

The meeting with the Washington lawyers plus thoughts of problems at home with Melanie had temporarily shoved the Benedict family to the back of her mind. Now the past rushed upon her, the awful night ten years ago in the Austin foothills and, even worse, her choice to sweep the attempted rape under the rug while accepting what amounted to a bribe. She should have turned the bastard in. Of course she should have. Would give anything if she'd told Paul Benedict's lawyer where to put his freaking contract, and picked up the phone and called the police, right then and there. She pictured the scene as it should have been, Sharon Hays fearlessly pointing her finger at Paul Benedict from the witness stand. Like her ages-ago dreams of stage and movie stardom, a fantasy that never was and never would be.

Oddly enough she dreaded facing Mattie Ruth even more than seeing Will John or, God forbid, Paul Benedict himself, because a face-to-face meeting with Mattie Ruth would intensify the feelings of guilt that Sharon had harbored for all these years. Christ, the guy had beaten the hell out of her and tried to yank her panties down, yet she couldn't help feeling that she was somehow at fault. When she'd been a prosecutor she'd listened to countless stories from rape victims who, blameless as they were, wondered if they'd done something to provoke the attack. She recalled one young woman, raped and sodomized at seventeen, who two years later was afraid to appear in a bathing suit and wore severely cut clothing that hid her body. Sharon's phobia had never reached those proportions, but then the rape hadn't been successful, had it? Had Paul Benedict been able to finish the job, Sharon wondered what her feelings would have been today. Of all the people I'd hoped never to see again, Sharon thought. She straightened, catching the look of alarm from the senator's assistant as she continued on her way. "I'm fine," she said over her shoulder. "Just a sinking spell. Jet lag." Then she firmed her posture, took a deep breath, and went on in to say hello to the senator from Texas. She'd as soon have taken a beating.

She hadn't anticipated seeing Will John so soon, and stood by and locked gazes with the tortured congressman while his mother gave hug-hugs to Russ and kissed him on the cheek. Will John Benedict was seated on a sofa across the room, looking alone and very afraid. He'd been a soft-faced young man as a law student and had aged rapidly, his jowls thickening and drooping. Sharon tried to offer a helpful smile. As she did, Mattie Ruth turned to her and extended both hands. "Let me look at you, Sharon Hays. This is a helluva long way from Nacho Louie's. Paul always said you were one of his top students, and danged if time hasn't proved him right. I told him last night you were coming, and he couldn't believe it."

Sharon's smile felt frozen on her face. I'll just bet he couldn't, she thought. She endured a cheeks-touching routine with Mattie Ruth, the odor of makeup wafting up her nostrils, though her gaze never left Will John Benedict. She said without looking at Mattie Ruth, "You've come a long way yourself, Mrs. Benedict."

"Mattie Ruth. Come on, come on, take a load off." The senator gestured toward a love seat and pair of armchairs, then sat behind her desk. Her voice was an octave higher and her down-home accent a couple of shades thinner than when she'd wowed the nation during the Democratic convention, but her rural Texas upbringing was evident. Mattie Ruth had an educated manner and finishing school bearing, yet tempered the sophisticated package with charm straight from Bug Tussle, U.S.A. The senator was a graduate of Baylor U., a good-looking charismatic woman, a campaign manager's dream. Sharon didn't think Mattie Ruth had aged ten years' worth since she'd last seen her, though there was more gray in her hair. Sharon wondered if the wool was completely over Mattie Ruth's eyes where her husband was concerned, or if political ambition had caused her to stick her head in the sand and ignore the obvious. Neither scenario was flattering to Mattie Ruth. In the first situation she looked a fool; in the second she'd given away her self-esteem. Fame and power aside, Sharon wouldn't trade places with Mattie Ruth Benedict for all the tea in China. No, Miss Sharon-on-a-Pedestal, she thought, you wouldn't do such a thing. But you would sell your mortal soul for a mess of pottage, which is what you did after Paul Benedict tried to rape you. She forced a smile as guilt surged through her in waves.

Sharon accepted the invitation to sit.

The senator was tall and elegant in a wool business suit and high heels. Her hair was done in soft curls. Her corneas were gray like the streaks in her hair, and there were tiny worry lines around her eyes. Though Mattie Ruth seemed gracious and composed, her hands trembled. She gave Russ a weary smile. "How was your trip?"

Russ exhaled as if he was at the point of exhaustion. "Tirin'." He extended a hand in the direction of the sofa. Will John got up, limply gripped Russ's hand, then sank back down. Russ said, "Been a long time, son. Wish the circumstances were different."

"Hope the flight wasn't too early for you," Mattie Ruth interrupted. "We told the press you'd be comin' in around three this afternoon. I expect in about an hour there'll be cameras all over Reagan National. How's the little daughter, Russell?"

"She's twenty-three and a college graduate."

"No." Mattie Ruth's tone was incredulous.

"We're not gettin' any younger, Mattie," Black said. He shared a brief laugh with Mattie Ruth, then resignedly cleared his throat. "Hate to get right to the point, but . . ."

Mattie Ruth looked down at her lap, then slowly raised her chin. "Not as much as I hate your havin' to bring it up." She seemed to brace herself. "Will John's ready to fight the fight, Russell. My boy didn' do this. He told me face to face."

Will John looked down at his knees. His thick razored hair was parted on the right, JFK style, the modern candidate's appearance being more important come election time than his stand on the issues. He wore a light gray suit. This man is thirty-five years old, Sharon thought, and his mother is still doing the talking for him. She restrained her pity, and looked back to the senator.

Russ's expression turned serious. "It's good to know he didn'. We'll be talkin' about that today, among other things. Not the least of which is the meetin' we just had with your local lawyers."

Mattie Ruth's tone was dismissive and offhanded. "That was Paul's idea, a lawyer-to-lawyer meeting before Will John saw you. Boots York was speaking as a lawyer. I'm talkin' as a mother. You should know the difference."

" 'Course I know the difference," Black said. "And that part's okay. But what about the guy that was speakin' as a Democrat?"

Mattie Ruth watched him. Her head tilted inquisitively.

"You know Wallace Burns?" Black asked.

"Wally was there?" The senator's surprise was genuine.

"He was the main ramrod. The whole idea was to keep the Party up-to-date with what's goin' on. You know I can't stand politics, Mattie. How'd you let 'em send that guy?"

Mattie Ruth's expression of surprise dissolved into a political mask, an impersonal, guarded smile. "I'll have to ask Boots about that." Which she really didn't have to, Sharon knew; five would get ten that Boots York had called Mattie Ruth within minutes of the Texas lawyers' departure, filling the senator in on every detail of the meeting. Worried and frightened as Mattie Ruth might seem in private, every speck of hesitancy would disappear the moment she stood before the cameras. Sharon had known actresses with the same chameleonlike quality; there was, in fact, little to choose between the psyches of politicians and those of movie stars.

Black's mouth tightened. "If that's the way you want to leave it, then we'll leave it that way. But sendin' a political consultant to a meeting that was supposed to be about defending a murder case, that wadn right.

You know it and I know it. Dammit, Mattie. We both know who's paying my fee. But I can't talk about the case to anybody except my client, no matter where my money's coming from."

Mattie Ruth's eyebrows lifted. "He can account for his whereabouts every moment of that night. I'm not sayin' my son is a saint, Russell, but he's no murderer."

Black paused, then kept his tone gently firm as he said, "We need to hear that from him, Mattie. In private. Conversations between you and Will John are admissible in court, so it's best you don't have any more talks with him about the murder. If it was Paul under investigation you'd have husband-wife privilege. The privilege dudn extend to your child."

The senator's mouth trembled. "I had to know, so I asked him."

Black expelled a long breath and seemed deep in thought. He glanced at Will John, then finally said to Mattie Ruth, "Why'd you have to know?"

"Because I'm his mother, dammit."

"That's what I'm getting at. Whether he did it or didn' do it, he's not gonna lose your support. So why ask?"

"He could lose his father's support. As of now Paul's with him, but you know Paul."

Will John sat stoically on the couch. Sharon couldn't believe it, Mattie Ruth discussing a full-grown man as if he were a baby, right there in front of the guy.

Black crossed his legs and intertwined his fingers over his knee. "Oh, yeah, I forgot about Paul. To him guilt or innocence would make a difference."

Sharon was stunned, both by the matter-of-factness

in Russ's tone and the bluntness of his statement. Up to this moment Russ had acted as if Paul Benedict had hung the moon. So you don't think my old Torts prof is perfect, eh, boss? Sharon thought. Well, before this case is put to bed I may have a story to tell you. She couldn't imagine anyone turning their back on their own child, murder charges or no. But if anyone could, she thought, Paul Benedict is certainly the man.

Mattie Ruth nodded agreement. "Paul has an agenda the size of Houston over punishin' the guilty. The guilty being his own flesh and blood wouldn't matter. He'd throw Will John to the dogs if he thought he did this."

Christ, Sharon thought. *Paul Benedict* has a thing about punishing the guilty? What about his own freaking punishment? Jesus, *God* . . .

"Mattie," Black said, "you want to help all you can, that's understandable. So for now, dealin' with your husband is your number one assignment. Keep Paul on our side, at least until this is over. Above everything, you and Paul have got to show a unified front. Where's he now?"

"On the coast, in a tobacco lawsuit."

"That has to change," Black said. "He should be here by morning. The damn liberal press has got to see Will John's folks standin' behind him."

Mattie Ruth leaned back in her chair. Her eyes were damp. "I'll call him. I can't promise he'll come."

"If worse comes to worse, tell him that if he dudn put in an appearance in forty-eight hours, he'll be dealing with me." Black winked. "That may put the fear o' God into him."

The senator watched the veteran lawyer. Her smile was sad. "It might at that," she said.

"Get him here, Mattie. Me and Miss Hays got plenty to do without fieldin' questions as to why Will John's daddy's not here to back him up."

"He'll have the tobacco suit as an excuse, if he wants to use it."

"Bull. A crisis like this will get him a continuance from any civil judge in captivity. As a last resort, tell him I'm willin' to fry him in the press over his lack of interest. We need him." Black looked to Sharon for reinforcement. "Right, Miss Hays?"

Sweet Jesus and all the angels, Sharon thought. Now she was supposed to pretend that having Paul Benedict on the scene meant the world to her. She should have leveled with Russ back in Dallas, bowed her neck, and refused to get involved in this mess. She said softly, "Right, boss."

Black checked his watch. "I'm still on Texas time. But we need an hour or two with our client. Your office okay?" He looked toward the exit. Outside on the windowsill, two pigeons pecked around in the snow.

Mattie Ruth opened a drawer, dropped some pencils and pens inside, and started to rise. "Suppose we'd better retire to my anteroom."

"Not you, Mattie." Russ's folksy manner dissolved. "Just me and Miss Hays and our client."

Will John showed a sheepish look. He wouldn't cross his mother if his life depended on it, Sharon thought.

Mattie Ruth seemed determined. "There's nothin'

you can discuss that Will John wouldn't want me to hear."

Russ expelled a long sigh. "Maybe. But there's things *I* might not want you in on."

The senator showed a flash of anger. "Anything involving my son is my business, Russell."

"Forget he's your son, then. He's our client. No outsiders, period, including you."

The senator and the veteran lawyer locked gazes for a count of three. Mattie Ruth gave in first. "Keep me up-to-date."

"That'll be up to Will John, whatever he wants you to know." Black's expression softened. "You got to trust me, Mattie, it's better this way. Get on the phone to your husband, you hear?" He turned to Sharon and extended a hand toward the rear exit from the office. "Miss Hays," Black said. Will John got up from the sofa and trudged resignedly to the door.

Sharon hefted her satchel and shoulder bag, and stood. She said politely, "Nice to see you again, Senator."

Mattie Ruth seemed at first not to hear. She spoke to Black in a commanding tone. "Don't you dare let me down on this, Russell." Her gaze shifted to Sharon, an appraising look. "The pleasure's mine, Sharon," Mattie Ruth said in a dismissive tone.

Sharon didn't have time to feel miffed as she turned and left through the senator's rear exit. She'd made up her mind to be ready; ghosts of the worst months of her life were about to leap at her from all directions, and she simply had to keep her cool. Her expression firm and businesslike, Sharon drew a tiny breath. She followed her congressman/client out of the room, doing her best to forget that she despised his father more than anyone else in the world.

Sharon might not have recognized Will John Benedict if she'd accidentally bumped into him. God, he looked so old, and she had to remind herself that Will John was within a year either way the same age as she. Sharon considered his affair with an intern/coed, and wondered how on earth the girl could have been attracted. While Sharon might not've recognized the man himself she'd have certainly recalled his expression, the uncertainty about the eyes as if he'd never made his own decisions in life. Which he hadn't very often; between his mother, his father—and now Cassandra (Marry-for-political-clout) Mason née Benedict—Sharon suspected that it took a village to pick out which tie Will John was going to wear. In the far-distant past Sharon had pitied Will John, but at least in law school he'd seemed like a live human being. The man who now sat in the senator's anteroom across from Sharon and Russell Black seemed more like a drawing, an artist's conception of a campaign billboard ad.

The smaller office had a cozier atmosphere, with couches and chairs encircling an antique wood coffee table. In the corner was a big screen TV and VCR, set up alongside a mock fireplace with papier-mâché logs. As soon as the attorneys had settled into their seats, Will John said, "Thanks for excluding my mother from this. It's been a long time, Mr. Black." He nodded to Sharon, stood, and offered his hand. "And you. You've become quite a celebrity."

His attitude was businesslike, and she was relieved that he didn't fawn over her; had he shown the same mooning look as when she'd ended their relationship, she didn't know if she could have dealt with him. His grip was cool and firm, and Sharon held on to his hand a second longer than necessary in order to think of a response. Something like, "You're quite well-known yourself" wouldn't be appropriate after the publicity blitz Will John had received over the past week, and any reference to old law school memories might be painful to both of them. She looked to his eyes for a sign, an indication as to whether he felt discomfort in seeing her, but his expression was direct and mild. Finally she opted for, "Hey, great to see you," and let it go at that.

Sharon and Russ occupied cushioned armchairs. Will John sat down on a love seat with springy cushions, with a coffee table between him and the lawyers. "The meeting at Porter, Ragsdale & Jones wasn't my idea," he said. "I want you to know that."

Russ leaned forward, serious. "I never thought it was. Forget them. Every Democrat in Washington will be stickin' his nose into your business. You're suspected of a murder, son. You've got no obligation to the Party or anybody except yourself. Startin' here and now, don't discuss this with anybody, advisors or the Pope of Rome."

"I'll take your advice," the congressman said, "but know this. I haven't murdered anyone. This whole mess is nothing but political mud-slinging, blown entirely out of proportion. No matter what, it can't interfere with business as usual." He glanced quickly at Sharon, then looked away.

"Come on. That's a rehearsed speech," Black said. "Hell's bells, it even sounds rehearsed. An' I'll agree that politics might be part of it, but let me tell you what *idn* mud-slinging. There's a dead girl. Somebody killed her. The evidence, at least what's been in the papers, points to you as that somebody. Prosecutors are no different in Dallas, Washington, or Timbuktu. If they didn' think they had a case they wouldn't be poppin' off. And if you think *we* might interfere with business as usual, a life sentence in the penitentiary will do a damn sight more than that.

"What we have to offer is exactly what your mother's payin' for. The best defense money can buy, from two attorneys who've got no political motives and don't need the publicity. From day one in this, anybody that acts interested in your case has their own horn to blow. We don't. Don't ask for advice anyplace but right here." He jerked his thumb toward his own chest, then pointed at Sharon.

Will John lost it. He cradled his face in his hands. "I've never dealt with anything like this."

"That's true of most folks," Black said.

Will John leaned back, watched his lap for a moment, and then slowly raised his chin. "I suppose we've got a lot to discuss."

Black rested his forearms on his legs, his tie hanging down between his thighs. "You bet. For starters, we need you to tell us everything that happened from the time you first laid eyes on this dead girl until you walked into this room a few minutes ago. Don't leave

anything out. We'll determine what is and idn important later."

Will John's features firmed into an earnest politician's
look. "That young woman may have been reading more
into the relationship than there was. Sometimes these
pages and interns get starry-eyed."

Black and Sharon looked at each other. Black said,
"I think our client's already makin' a mistake, Miss
Hays."

Will John showed puzzlement, which Sharon recognized as more political posturing. Less than half a day
in the nation's capital, she was learning the ropes. She
inhaled and let the congressman have it, as gently as
possible but with both barrels. "What Russ means is,
lying to your attorneys is a foul-up. Look, Will John,
that last statement is beyond corny. The victim's
roommate, her name is . . ." She looked at Black
for help.

Russell Black shrugged his shoulders.

Will John Benedict said, "Melissa. Melissa Rudolph."

"Odd you're so familiar with the name," Sharon
said. "Right, Melissa Rudolph. She's been all over
television with a blow-by-blow of your affair with her
roomie, and she's detailed your comings and goings
to such an extent that I suspect the prosecution's been
writing her script. The Democratic Party's investigated
the allegations, and their spokesman told us earlier
today that the sexual fling existed and there's no way
around it. So don't lie about it, and that goes if we're
your lawyers or someone else is. Lying about your
affair with Courtney Lee will make you look stupid,

and in this instance stupid will translate into guilty as hell with a jury."

"Will John looked as if he'd been lashed with a whip. "Sharon, I . . ."

Sharon softened her attitude. "Russ has known your folks for years, and you and I went to law school together. You look on us differently than someone who just wandered in, and that's understandable. But please don't make the mistake of worrying about what I think, or what Russ thinks. What the jury's going to think is all that matters, from here on in."

The congressman's gaze wavered when Sharon mentioned their time in law school, as if he wondered how much Russ knew about their past connection. She'd been hoping that Will John had developed some backbone in the past ten years or so, and felt disappointment as the congressman stammered and grasped at straws. "If there ever is a jury," he said.

Black cut in. "That kind of talk is even worse than denyin' the affair. Any speculation that this is going away is nothin' but fantasy. Listen to me. Here's what's real. There's goin' to be an indictment and there's goin' to be a trial, and you're about to enter burnin' hell. I know that's tough to swallow, but I'd be derelict if I didn't lay it out for you." He watched the congressman carefully. "The story, son. All of it, and now, or you won't have to worry about us anymore. Miss Hays and me will be on the next thing smokin' back to Texas, if we don't get cooperation from you."

Will John tightly shut his eyes, and massaged his

lids with a thumb and forefinger. "Christ. Cas doesn't even know the whole story."

Black frowned. "That's your wife?"

Will John opened his eyes, visibly sagging like a man facing defeat no matter which way he turned. He said softly, "Sharon knows her. Or did. Sharon, you remember . . . ?"

"Cassandra Mason, yes," she said. "She was in school when we were."

"Oh? She practice law?" Russ's interest picked up.

Will John shook his head. "She never went beyond a bachelor's. When we got married after her graduation, she became a full-time housewife. This is going to kill her."

"She won't die over anything we're going to tell her," Black said. "We're your lawyers, and as such we expect you to start talkin' to us."

Will John drew breath. "Up front, please know it was the intern who made the first advances."

Sharon's mouth tightened. That's what they all say, she thought. Catch a married man screwing around, always the same song. "I don't think who hit on who really matters at this point," Sharon said. "Stick to the facts, what happened. If any spin needs to be put on the facts, let us do it."

The congressman vacantly watched the far corner of the room. "Miss Lee went to work for us when the fall term began. She did filing, a few errands . . . I should never have been alone in the building with her."

"That's a given." Sharon was nettled. "It's also, to be blunt, whiny. If you try to say that this young girl threw herself into your lap uninvited and unzipped your fly, no one's going to believe you. There is no way, given the age difference and the fact that she was a member of your staff, you're going to avoid being looked on as a sexual predator. But we have to paint a scenario where you're not a murderer, no matter how much you took advantage of this inexperienced college girl."

Will John showed an expression of hurt. He looked down. "She had plenty of experience."

If she had more experience than Will John Benedict, Sharon thought, that isn't saying much. She said, "That's something we might be able to use at the appropriate time. Which isn't now. We're not making any progress, so let's try something different. I haven't laid eyes on you in about ten years. People change. Assume I don't know you at all, okay? Assume that for all I know, you were bending interns over your desk right and left." Sharon blinked, thinking. "So, acting under the assumption that I believe you're Horny Harry Harasser, which is the way the police and prosecutors will paint you, I'll ask questions. Make your answers brief. That way we might be through here before nightfall. You see a problem with that, boss?"

Black dug in his inside coat pocket. "Exactly what I was thinkin'." He set a miniature tape recorder on the coffee table and depressed the REC button. Visible through clear plastic, tiny reels began to turn. "Just so we won't worry later about who said what to who."

Will John eyed the tape recorder as if it might fly off the table and hit him between the eyes.

"It's just for our benefit." Sharon sat forward, all business now. "We're your lawyers, and nothing you say here goes beyond this room. Think hard, Congressman. When was the first time you remember meeting Courtney Lee?"

Will John showed a thoughtful look. "I'm sure it was early summer. My secretary gives all new people the cook's tour, and I'm one of the visited landmarks."

"But you don't have an independent recollection?"

"Afraid I don't. She meant nothing to me at first."

"Which wasn't true at the last, right?" Sharon said. "Who's your secretary?"

"Elaine Trowell. The D.C. police have already talked to her."

"Doesn't matter," Sharon said. "We'll be treading a lot of ground that the police have already covered. Would Elaine Trowell have a record of when she might've introduced Courtney Lee to you?"

"She'd have a record of when Miss Lee came on board."

"Courtney," Sharon said. "Courtney. Call her by her first name at all times. Trying to distance yourself from this young woman, especially since everybody in America knows by now that you were screwing her, sounds phony as hell. Now. Would Elaine Trowell have a record of when she introduced Courtney to you?"

Will John's eyes seemed glazed over. "Elaine has a record of everything. She's very efficient."

Sharon made a note. An interview with Elaine Trowell had just become high priority. "Since you don't remember your original introduction," Sharon

said, "what's the first contact with Courtney that you
do recall?"

Will John cleaned his fingernails with a the file extension from a pair of clippers. His hands trembled.
"She was the one delivering my mail. I've since learned
that she took the mail delivery on herself, with no
prompting. As if she was bound and determined to
meet me. I suppose I first noticed her because she
seemed to have a lot of excuses to linger. I remember
once I had to ask her to leave so I could take a call
from the Speaker."

"Gingrich?"

Will John nodded. "Our committee was late with
its report. Nothing catastrophic."

"Would the Speaker recall that incident?"

"I don't know why. We've had a lot of phone conversations, and there wasn't anything memorable
about that particular one."

Sharon scratched through Gingrich's name, which
she'd just written down. So much for Newt, Sharon
thought. "How about someone, anyone, who could
verify that she spent more time in your office than
necessary?"

"Elaine would remember," Will John said. "She
commented on the girl's forwardness."

Which apparently was no worse than your own,
Sharon thought. She said, "Specifically, how was she
forward?"

"She would . . . Most of our interns are really shy
around me, but not this one. She'd say things like,
well, she had no one to show her around Washington

at night, that the college kids were immature, things like that."

Twisted your arm, did she? Sharon thought. "Will John, we simply have to move on with this, so please quit embellishing. Once and for all, and for the umpteenth and last time. Do not, under any circumstances, try to play down your participation in the affair even if you are telling the truth. If you were sitting around reading *Family Values* magazine and Courtney walked up and squeezed your privates, leave that part out. As much as us older broads are in denial from the truth, youth itself is highly seductive. The men on the jury will sympathize if you made a pass, but if you try to say that *she* put the moves on, they'll think you're the biggest bullshitter in captivity. The women are going to roast you no matter what you say, so concentrate on the men. And if I sound rude and uncaring it's because we need the slimmed-down version. You'll have a chance to give an editorial later. I'm assuming your secretary wasn't in your office when the girl was wrapping herself around you, so she couldn't testify to it anyway. Specifically, how was Courtney Lee forward when she was around Elaine Trowell?"

"I believe Elaine said, how did she put it? That Miss Lee didn't take instruction particularly well."

"Which isn't evidence that she was hot for your body, is it?" Sharon said. "Think on this overnight and give us your answer later. We need any witnesses we can find to say that the girl didn't seem averse to the affair even if she didn't initiate it. If we have only your word, that won't get us very far. Now. When was the first time you saw her away from the office? And stop frowning as if you're in thought. Since you were sleeping with her, I'll venture you recall the first time down to the split second."

Will John haughtily sniffed in through his nose. "That certainly wasn't my original intention, to go to bed with her."

"Just answer the questions. If you sampled the girl's goodies you intended to do so. Your intent will be obvious to the jury long before you take the stand in your own defense, so please spare us the 'holier than thou' act. It doesn't wear well."

Will John showed anger that was obviously feigned. "I don't have to sit here and put up with this. Mr. Black . . ."

"Miss Hays is askin' all the right questions," Black said. "And if you think she's bein' tough on you, wait until you see the prosecutor in action. Wild tales about your intentions, even if they were true, make you sound like a liar." Black held up his middle and index fingers, side by side. "Two things when you're facing criminal charges. One, don't lie. Eventually you'll trip up. If you're guilty, keep your mouth shut. If you're not, picture the truth the way it's gonna sound to others. If the truth sounds ridiculous, then spin the truth until it sounds believable. Shouldn' be hard for you, considering your political background." The older lawyer looked at Sharon. "Miss Hays, I think you can go on now."

Sharon tapped her ballpoint against her chin. "I'll repeat. When was the first time you saw Courtney Lee outside the office?"

Will John seemed resigned. "In July."

"Mmm-hmm. Six months ago."

"I'd been in a judiciary committee meeting very late, until after nine. Considering nominees for the federal bench. I came back to the office to go over some things, and Miss Lee, Courtney that is, Courtney was there doing some filing. One thing led to another . . ."

"Who gave Courtney the key to the office? Was it your secretary?" Sharon asked.

Will John seemed at a loss for words.

Sharon chewed her inner lip. "No one is going to believe that your staff gives interns the run of the office, key and all, with all those sensitive documents laying around. So if she was there doing filing at nine o'clock, someone gave her a key to get in. Was it your secretary?"

"Possibly," Will John said hopefully, then lowered his eyes as he said, "It's doubtful."

"Now you're getting it," Sharon said. "Of course your secretary didn't give her a key, and wouldn't have been authorized to do so to begin with. Which leaves you as the only one with that authority. Which means the meeting was prearranged, and if you try to say it wasn't, the prosecution will eat you for lunch. Are things becoming clearer?"

Will John opened, and then closed, his mouth.

Sharon said, "Okay. When she showed up for a little hotsy-totsy after you'd given your wife the standard working-late excuse, where did you two go?"

Will John tried his best to appear angry, but managed only a frightened stare. "Do you have to put it that way?"

"Why not? The prosecution's certainly going to. Where did you go?"

"A place . . . the Green Lantern Bar."

"Which is where?" Sharon said.

"Falls Church."

Sharon leaned back, showing an inquisitive look.

"In Virginia," Will John said.

"Oh? And how far from your office?"

"Ah . . . thirty miles, maybe."

"So you wanted to go where you wouldn't be seen. I'll lay odds you went in separate cars."

Will John looked at her.

"Did you have sex with her that night?" Sharon said.

"Possibly."

"Where?"

"A . . . Holiday Inn, I think."

"It's a step up from Motel 6," Sharon said, "but not much of one. And to ensure that you'd be incognito, I'll bet you had Courtney register and get the room key. God, Will John, forget trying to convince anyone that she was leading you around by the ear and forcing you to have sex with her." She turned to Russ. "What do you think, boss?"

Black thoughtfully watched the congressman, then said with a wry cant to his mouth, "I think this witness is going to require a lotta preppin'."

"Bingo," Sharon said. "Let's discontinue this session until tomorrow afternoon after I have a chance to talk to forensics and chat with the prosecutor. In the meantime, Will John . . . I assume you have a legal pad. Or do your aides do all of the note-taking now?" Sharon couldn't keep the contempt out of her voice. God, pimps, and politicians . . .

"I still take good notes," the congressman said docilely.

"Good you haven't forgotten how. Between now and four o'clock tomorrow afternoon, I want you to write down everything you remember about your affair with Courtney Lee. All the bars you frequented, every motel, backseat, or park bench where you might've engaged in a sex act, oral or otherwise. Don't leave anything out, because tomorrow we're going to discuss the night of the murder. So have your ducks in a row about what you want to say. Should we meet here again, or is there some other place?"

Will John seemed anxious. "I'll have to check my calendar. I may have meetings, appearances . . ."

"Cancel them." Sharon made her tone fierce. "From here on out and until you're either acquitted or headed for prison, nothing takes precedence over meetings with your lawyers. Now. Where can we meet?"

Will John sounded resigned. "My town house." He wrote something on a tiny slip of paper, which he then handed over. "This is the address."

"Good," Sharon said. She put her notes in her satchel as Black hefted his overcoat. Both lawyers stood. Sharon said, "Oh. One more thing."

Will John looked up at her from his seat on the sofa.

Sharon said, "It's about the size of your sex organ."

Will John grimaced like a man watching a horror movie as Black coughed into his cupped hand. The congressman said without much expression, "Do you have to bring that up?"

"You bet. At this point it's the main thing going against you. The tabloids are making you look as if you're Johnny Wadd and the Stallion of Seville rolled into one, and the nation is tumbling in the aisles in laughter. We have to somehow take the humor out of this situation. We don't want the jurors giggling insanely as they pass down a guilty verdict. When this goes to trial, how well you're endowed is inadmissible. No one can force you to drop your pants so that the jury can have a peek or anything, but there will be a lot of forensic evidence. The ME will testify as to the dead girl's internal stretching and bruising, and since the jury will have read all that crap in the tabloids, the prosecution's going to have the size of your penis before them without their actually broaching the subject. We have to combat the image."

Will John folded his hands and averted his gaze.

"More specifically," Sharon said, "the problem lies with the nickname for Dear Old Dad, Bull One. Rita Carboneau's been having a field day with that in her column. She's hinting that you might be Bull Two. Do you know Ms. Carboneau?"

Will John shrugged his shoulders. "I've seen her at parties."

"Since she's your primary attacker, we need every piece of dirt we can dig up on the woman. We've got to discredit her. At the risk of making the tabloids even richer than they are, we have to get the spotlight away from your private parts. Ridiculous as it may sound, we're better off with the public believing you're hung like a church mouse. I suspect you have sources the same as Rita Carboneau."

Will John smiled for the first time since Sharon and Russ had walked into the room. "I may know a few."

"Use them. Anything, anything at all to make Rita Carboneau out a liar when she writes about the Benedict men and their penis sizes. Not fun. Not funny, either. Totally necessary. Unless Mr. Black has something else, we're through for now. Do you, boss?"

"I got nothing more," Black said.

Sharon bent forward and extended her hand across the table. "Very well. Until tomorrow then, Congressman."

Will John stood to shake hands. There were tiny beads of perspiration on his forehead. "Jesus, Sharon. Can we make the future sessions less intense, with the grilling and all?"

"I doubt it. Painful as it might be for you, it's necessary." Sharon had a thought and suddenly grinned, tried to stop herself but couldn't resist saying, "Makes you glad that our little thing back in law school never went further, doesn't it? A lifetime with me might be more than you could bear."

7

Sharon's room at the State Plaza was on the same floor as Russell Black's, but on the opposite end of the corridor. She reached her quarters with a flush in her cheeks after parting company with her boss and mentor outside the elevators. Her nose was dripping and her throat was turning raw. As she slid the card key through the slot she pictured her foot, shoe and all, sinking down into a freezing puddle outside the airport as she'd climbed into Leonard Smith's Mercedes for the ride downtown. As she opened the door to her room, she hacked and cleared her throat.

The room itself was plain but functional, with two queen-sized beds, a TV hooked up to cable—with Spectravision's pay-through-the-nose-for-a-movie as an option, which Sharon thought was a ripoff—a table and four chairs beside the window. The carpet, drapes, and bedspread were green, the padded headboard pale yellow. Her overnight case was on a window seat. She snapped open the catches, rummaged around, located a bottle of Dristan, and shook two pills into her hand as she headed for the bathroom. She had a thought and paused in midstride. The digital bedside clock read 5 P.M. Eastern, which was six o'clock Dallas time. She dry-swallowed the tablets, sat on the mattress, picked up the phone, and called Sheila. No one answered. She left a Callnotes message, then set about unpacking her things.

A half hour later she rasped the shower curtain aside, wrapped her sopping hair in a towel, and stepped out of the tub into a roomful of steam. The mirrors were fogged, the chrome fixtures covered with tiny droplets. She dried herself by the numbers; neck first, shoulders and back, and finally her breasts and stomach, her nipples stiffening and her flesh tingling as the rough cloth massaged her skin. She stood on one foot, steadying herself against the side of the tub as she wiped one leg, then the other. The Dristan had taken effect; she felt much better but really drowsy. As she rubbed down her calf she heard the phone ringing, faint and far away. She threw on a hotel-furnished terrycloth robe, hustled out of the bathroom, picked up the receiver, and said, "Sheila?"

"Sharon Hays?"

The woman on the phone wasn't Sheila; the tone was huskier, the enunciation a bit more nasal. Sharon recognized the voice, and very nearly spoke the caller's name. She had a feeling of dread as she said, "Yes?"

"Hello, Sharon, it's Cas Benedict." The faint Texas drawl was tempered by years in D.C. and points east. The attitude was cold, far from friendly.

Sharon held the phone against her ear and didn't say anything.

After a pause, the voice told her, "Cas Mason. You don't remember . . . ?"

"Of course," Sharon said. "I waited on you at Nacho Louie's. That I could never forget." She verbally kept her distance, at the same time saying that she hadn't forgotten the contempt with which Cas had treated her in the past.

The laugh over the line was humorless, even bitter. "Have you talked to my husband?"

Sharon thought the question odd as all get-out; not only should Will John Benedict's wife have known he'd been visiting with his lawyers, if she hadn't spoken with Will John since that afternoon, how did she know the name of Sharon's hotel? Only one answer was possible: Mattie Ruth. Sharon said, "Yes, earlier. Around two. What can I do for you, Cas?" Her tone was guarded. She waited for a response.

"I thought we could visit," Cas Benedict said.

Sharon lifted, then dropped her shoulders. "Sure. Go ahead."

"No, I mean in person. Someplace where we aren't likely to be seen."

"I don't know as I'd feel comfortable with that. Will John's my client. I don't think it would be kosher to meet with his wife without his knowledge." An ache began in Sharon's sinuses; she had the beginnings of a cold, possibly even the flu. Damn that freezing puddle, she thought.

"I know some things that you'll want to hear." For a woman whose husband's affair with a college girl had become public knowledge, and whose spouse now faced possible murder charges, Cas Benedict's voice was oddly calm.

"I'm sure you do," Sharon said, "and certainly we'll want to interview you. But our meeting should be in daytime with both of Will John's lawyers present. We should have an investigator there as well, in case what you tell us needs follow-up, and Russ—that's Mr. Black, Cas, Will John's other attorney—will likely want to tape-record the session so there'll be no question as to who said what to who."

"I won't speak into a tape recorder."

"There's really no reason not to. It's for your own protection, so no one can put words in your mouth in the future."

"That's not the point. I don't want anyone knowing that the information I'll give you came from me."

Sharon's eyes widened in curiosity. "Not even your husband?"

"*Especially* not my husband."

"Gee, I don't know that I could shield you from my own client. I think he'd have a right to know, since he's married to you. Besides, if you're helping him . . . And as to *testifying* to what you have to say, not even the prosecutor could force you. You'd have husband-wife privilege."

There was venom in Cas Benedict's voice. "No, Sharon. I'll talk to you and you alone, and then hope against hope that you can find a way to use what I tell you without getting me publicly involved. My motive isn't to help my jerk spouse. But as much as I despise Will John at the moment, I suppose I have to come forward. I can give you undisputable proof that

there's no way, no way in hell that Will John could
have murdered that girl. And as for you, like it or
not, I believe you duty to your client includes listening
to me. So please quit beating around the bush. Get a
paper and pen and write these directions down.''

Sharon was furious as she changed into a blouse, vest,
and jeans, and fought her emotions down to a slow burn
as she went downstairs and had the bellman hail her a
cab. She stepped out into the frigid weather before realizing that she hadn't brought a coat, debated, then
ducked on inside the taxi. Her throat was really sore
now, but she didn't have time to return to her room for
something warm. Pneumonia City, Sharon thought. To
make things worse she wore webbed sandals with no
socks, but at least she'd put on pantyhose.

Cas Benedict had set the appointment—or issued
the summons, actually, using the same tone of voice
in which she'd once told Sharon to bring her a vodka
tonic—for seven o'clock. The taxi pulled onto the
slush-laden street. Icy drifts lined the sidewalks on either side. The sky was pitch-black in early wintertime
darkness. Sharon tersely gave the driver the address,
then sat back, folded her arms, and crossed her legs.
Her foot jiggled angrily up and down.

Her past connection to the Benedicts aside, Sharon
would have had a problem with this case under any
circumstances. She'd thrown herself headfirst into defending Darla Cowan because, ditzy as the actress
might be, she was a loyal friend whom Sharon loved
dearly. But *this* freaking cast of characters, God. Not
a single likeable individual in the bunch, like a novel

or movie where there wasn't a player for whom the
audience could root. Will John was a mountain of jelly
and always had been; his mother was a political animal
who'd let her ambition swallow her self-respect; and
Cas Benedict was a spoiled brat without a single endearing quality. And Will John's father . . . Please,
Lord, Sharon thought, let me off of this train.

The taxi cruised east on E Street to the White
House, then turned to the north on 17th. Sharon
looked through the iron fence across the White House
lawn, at the huge Christmas tree twinkling in the Chief
Executive's upstairs window. Silent night, holy night,
Sharon thought, all is calm, and all is total depravity.
As the cab turned the corner and the president's mansion disappeared behind the bulk of the Executive Office Building, Sharon wondered if she'd meet anyone
worth knowing in the entire city of Washington. Somehow she doubted that she would.

The bar was called Beggett's Pub, and gave new
meaning to the term "out-of-the-way." By the time the
taxi had gone through a series of twists and turns somewhere in the vicinity of DuPont Circle and approached
the bar through an alleyway, Sharon was certain that,
map and all, she couldn't have found her way back to
the hotel on a bet. She debated having the driver wait
for her then decided against it, paid the fare and added
a tip, and alighted from the car. On the twenty-foot walk
across the sidewalk to the saloon's walk-up entry, the
cold assaulted her in icy waves of air.

Beggett's Pub was built on two levels, had wooden
floors and walls, and was so dimly lit that Sharon had to

squint in order to see. Behind the bar and around the seating area hung picture after picture of the same pudgy black man—likely the bar owner, Sharon thought—posing with Redskin and Bullet players, golf pros, and two politicians: Dan Quail and John Glenn. Mounted on a platform in one corner was a TV showing an auto race. There were perhaps fifteen customers, all men, hunched over drinks around the bar, and two or three couples sitting close together in booths, drinking beer. There was a dance floor without dancers and a bandstand without a band. Old Bee Gees numbers played over the sound system, and a stairway led up to a balcony which surrounded the room a half level overhead. Sharon climbed the steps and looked around as the jumpy beat of "Stayin' Alive" pounded her eardrums. She spotted Cas Benedict at a table near the rail. Cas wasn't smiling. Sharon approached, nodded to Cas without friendliness, and sat down across from her.

Cas had changed over the years, though the difference was subtle. Her face hadn't aged, but the rah-rah, tennis-anyone look she'd sported in college was gone. In its place was an intelligent sophistication, the light brown hair done in Conservative-Politician's-Wife, I-Fuck-Only-For-Child-Bearing-Purposes, straight-ish bangs. Sharon supposed that Cas's new image was fine for sitting behind her husband on a dias, smiling and applauding on cue, but Sharon thought it a shame for anyone to hide the show-stopping figure that Cas had displayed as a coed. As much as she'd despised Cas after their confrontation in Nacho Louie's, Sharon had always thought the campus queen to be drop-dead gorgeous. She was still beautiful, but the ice-queen look detracted. Even Cas's casual attire appeared overly formal for the barroom setting; she wore a white starched blouse with a navy cardigan sweater. Cas opened her mouth to speak. Sharon waited for her to say something hateful. In the old days Cas had been an expert at the art of the put-down, and Sharon doubted if the woman had changed in that regard.

"I owe you an apology," Cas said. "If nothing else, I'm glad I got to see you again so that I could tell you in person."

The statement took most of the wind out of Sharon's sails. Her forehead tightened in surprise.

"Ten years ago I got word that you'd been sneaking around with my fiancé behind my back," Cas said. "The one time we talked, I suppose I gave the impression that I had it in for you."

Now that, Sharon thought, is the understatement of the freaking month. She said softly, "Apology accepted. You don't have to—"

"The thing was," Cas interrupted, "I thought it was you and only you. I've now figured out, and Will John has confessed to me, that our entire relationship, all thirteen years of it, has just been a series of one trollop after another after another. I know that it wasn't you doing the propositioning, it was him. I'm truly sorry."

The backhanded apology hit Sharon like a slap in the face. So now she was no longer a worthy rival, but just another trollop whose hide hung from Will John Benedict's belt. The smirkiness at the corners of Cas's mouth said that the undisguised insult had been intentional. Sharon told herself to shut out everything except her purpose in being here, but was unable to do so. She sat stiffly erect as the waitress approached, then ordered a Tanqueray and tonic and said to Cas Benedict as the waitress sashayed downstairs, "I'm going to say this one time, Cas. It's what I wanted to say to you a decade ago but was in no position to. Are you listening?"

Cas haughtily inclined her neck, her head set at a looking-down-from-on-high-angle.

"First of all," Sharon said, "that long-ago night in the restaurant you greeted me by saying, 'So you're the little waitress.' I've never forgotten that. Well, you identified me correctly, though I didn't fit in the picture the way you thought. I plead guilty to having to work my way through school, and begrudge not one iota the fact that you didn't have to lift a finger to pay your tuition. That's life and those are the breaks. But read my lips. Will John and I never had anything going, through no fault of his. We went out a few times and that was all, and if I'd known he was pinned to you, dropped to you, or had your name tattooed on his ass or whatever, I never would have dated him. This will come as a shock, but until that night you reamed me out while I was working, I'd never heard of you. Call me uninformed around campus, but that's the truth."

Cas watched with what amounted to a disbelieving pout. Sharon paused to catch her breath, then plunged ahead. "And as for his being a habitual skirt-chaser, that's ridiculous. Not that being a faithful husband is a knock, it's a plus. You say he's owned up to his screwing around, but I'm betting he confessed no such thing to you. Don't try playing the cuckold here, Cas, it won't help the case and it won't improve your image. It's good advice. We don't like each other, but take it anyway.

"Let's hope," Sharon said, "that in fast-forwarding ten years we've grown up a bit, because some silly catfight over what happened when we were both too dumb to know any better can be devastating here. I didn't ask for this case, but now that I've got it I'm going to give it bloody hell. Law school, college, the New Year's Eve we did the town, the day we tore the goalposts down, all that nonsense is history, along with some things that went on with the Benedicts that are too terrible for you to sit in your tower and imagine."

Cas's expression softened. Her lips parted.

Sharon said, "Now. You told me on the phone you had information. I'm listening. To the information and only the information. To nothing about what you think of me, past or present. Is that clear?"

Cas's look was a puzzling mix of sadness and worry. "Sharon, I . . ."

The waitress appeared on Sharon's left, set down a glass of clear bubbly liquid with ice floating on its surface and a lime wedge impaled on the tumbler's edge, marked something down on a pad, and retreated downstairs. Sharon picked up the drink and had a healthy glug. "Stayin' Alive" was finished, and the Bee Gees now sizzled through "Saturday Night Fever" over the sound system. Sharon leaned closer to the table. "This information you're going to give me," she said. "Before you say a word, there's something you should know."

Cas had a look of anxiety. "The things too terrible for me to imagine. Are they—?"

"Nothing about the past. Not one word, I won't listen. But I'm assuming that any information you have about the Lee girl's murder will be in your husband's favor. Remember how you as a source are going to be viewed, since you're married to the suspect, and remember also that the police know that on the night of the killing you were in Texas. So whatever you know, you must know it secondhand, and without some sort of collaboration your information would be hearsay. In other words, in order for us to use you, we'd need backup for what you say." Sharon dug in her purse and retracted a pad and pen. "So now you may talk. I'll interrupt occasionally with a few questions, but for the most part the floor is yours."

Cas's expression changed again. More anxiously, she said, "I do have backup. The problem is, it's from a person I hired."

Sharon's eyebrow arched in interest. "Oh? A private's detective?"

"How would you know that?"

Sharon lifted, then dropped her shoulders. "Your husband was running around. You said you had information from someone you hired. Two plus two."

"I can't say I really *suspected* anything." The ice in Cas's drink was melting. She had a sip and made a face.

"Then it isn't a private detective?"

Cas lowered her gaze as if in shame. "Well it is, but . . ."

Sharon sighed, and laid her pen aside. "I'm going to have to tell you the same as I had to tell your husband. Whatever you do, don't try to lie and don't try to make things sound innocent when they aren't. If you hired a private investigator you had suspicions. No one will believe otherwise."

Cas looked up with intensity. "I was trying to dispel the rumors."

"Which you heard from who?" Sharon asked.

"The word was around. It tends to get around."

"Mmm-hmm." Sharon readied her ballpoint. "What's the investigator's name?"

"He's well-known in town." Cas looked away.

"Oh? I've been getting the impression around here that to be well-known in Washington is to be famous throughout the world."

Cas was hesitant. "He's the best at what he does."

"I don't care if he changes in a phone booth and flies off to Krypton. What's his name?"

Cas fished in a small black purse and popped a printed business card onto the table. She wrapped both hands around her glass, and dully watched the drink as she said, "That's him, there."

Sharon picked up the card. Nothing fancy, just plain black lettering to introduce "Mark C. Potter. Discreet inquiries." There was an office address and a phone number. No logo, nothing to toot the detective's horn.

Cas said, "He handles only special clients."

"Come on," Sharon said. "A lot of private investigators say that. The special client is the one with the special bank account."

"This guy is different. I doubt he could exist in another city."

Sharon laid her pen aside. She was getting it. Mark C. Potter specialized in following politicos around, then reporting to their spouses for a fee resembling the national debt. The wife in turn would file the information away, unable to confront her husband without creating a nasty public scandal. Sharon dispelled a surge of sympathy. Women who, strictly for political purposes, stood by their husbands in the face of publicly acknowledged screwing around turned Sharon's stomach. She said, "What good does it do you to hire this guy?"

Cas looked incredulous. "A wife has to know."

"If you're not going to do anything about it, why?"

Cas looked away, and sniffed a little sniff.

"I'm assuming," Sharon said, "that this detective has information that Will John was somewhere else when the murder happened."

"I'd rather you hear it from him, and then determine a way to use what he has without getting him involved. Or me."

Sharon took some of the edge off her tone, but not all. "Cas, it occurs to me that you'll look better, publicly, if the media knows you weren't running around with your head in the sand. That at least you were hip enough to suspect that something was going on. Look, you have no children to shield from this. Why not preserve your own self-respect?"

"It's not necessarily myself," Cas said with a touch of drama, "that I'm protecting."

Sharon was speechless for an instant. She pictured Mattie Ruth Benedict, and the meeting with the lawyers and the behind-the-scenes operator, Wallace Burns. She said, "Oh. The Democratic Party."

Cas's mouth twisted as she lowered her gaze.

Sharon tried to regain her composure. Jesus double Christ. Mattie Ruth, and now Cas, were more concerned with keeping Will John in office than defending him from murder charges. For it to become public knowledge that the congressman's wife hadn't trusted him would be politically damaging. Sharon resisted the urge to launch into a tirade, took a deep breath, and said, "I can only promise you, if possible we'll keep the guy out of it, and it's a big 'if.' I doubt we can."

"Sharon, this is *so* important . . ."

Sharon slowly shook her head in wonder. "Oh, Jesus. Important to who? The Party? You won't discuss your knowledge of an alibi with your own husband, but you'll clue in Boots York and all those political lawyers."

Cas raised her chin haughtily. "You just don't know this town. Discretion is . . ."

"I may not know this town," Sharon said, "but I do know criminal courtrooms. Very well, and it works this way. In order for evidence to be admissible it has to be presented in a certain manner. If your detective witnessed Will John someplace else at the time of the murder, only the detective can testify to that. Otherwise it would be hearsay. And if we tried to say the detective just accidentally happened to be there as a witness, the prosecution would make fools of us." Sharon glanced once again at the business card. "I'll talk to Mr. Mark C. Potter. Likely I'll have to put him on the stand."

"It could be devastating to my husband's career."

"Not near as devastating as the alternative." Sharon put the business card away. She simply had to get away from this woman before she said something she'd later regret. "Look, Cas, we're both tired. We'll think more clearly with some sleep, or at least I know I will." She smiled, though it took some effort. "It's your party and I'm the guest here. But frankly, I don't feel very well. I could call a cab. But I'd be ever so grateful if you'd offer me a ride."

Cas drove the standard Politician's Wifemobile, a pale blue four-door Chrysler with darkly tinted windows, luxurious but not flashy enough to make the constituents wonder what the congressman did with his campaign funds. The seats were velour, and tugged on Sharon's jeans as she fastened her seatbelt. Cas got in behind the wheel, drove out of the alley and onto streets, which were slick with snow. At various intersections along the way the tires spun and the rear end fishtailed. Sharon gave the name of her hotel. Cas sniffed disdainfully and pointed the Chrysler's nose to the south. The automatic climate control kept the car's interior pleasantly warm.

The women traveled in uncomfortable silence, and Sharon wished that she'd taken a taxi. Relief flooded over her as Cas finally pulled under the awning at the State Plaza. As the doorman tugged on the handle to let her out, she grabbed up her satchel and purse. "Appreciate the lift. I'll call you as soon as I contact this detective." And left it at that, alighting to the curb and stepping toward the entry as the doorman banged the door closed.

She was a couple of strides from the revolving door

when Cas called out behind her, "Sharon? Sharon, wait."

Sharon turned. The Chrysler's electric window slid all the way down as Cas watched her anxiously. Sharon retreated and stood on the curb, sneezing.

Cas seemed hesitant. She said, so softly that Sharon had to bend closer to hear, "You said earlier that . . ."

Sharon moved her satchel in front of her thighs. "Yes?"

"Well, you talked about things with the Benedicts too terrible for me to imagine."

Sharon's jaws clenched. "I told you before. Nothing about the past will I so much as—"

"Did those things have anything to do with Paul?"

Sharon's teeth clicked together.

"Paul Benedict. Will John's . . . father," Cas said.

Sharon said icily, "I know who you mean. Why do you ask?"

Cas measured her. She finally said, "No reason. No reason, really." An electric motor hummed and the window began to rise.

Sharon said urgently, "Cas, dammit, if you know something . . ."

The window halted halfway up. "Nothing to do with right now," Cas said. "Nothing to do with today, and it's you who insists that we not bring up the past. Just forget I mentioned it, all right?" The Chrysler leaped forward, its tires whirling in slush as Cas left the hotel, the dark window closing as Sharon stood alone in the cold.

8

The next morning Sharon went to the offices of the United States Attorney for the District of Columbia, wasted an hour with this assistant and that, and finally learned that the prosecutor heading up the Benedict investigation was named Cedric Hyde. Hyde's office was at 500 Indiana Avenue, a five-block walk from the main USDA headquarters. Sharon wondered why Cedric Hyde was so far removed from the hub of things. She supposed that USDA's dealing with everyday rapes, murders, and robberies in the city of Washington were a step down the food chain from those who chased tax dodgers and politicians, the really dangerous criminals. Sharon went out into forty-degree weather and trudged along. Melting snow dripped and puddled on the sidewalks. Her sinuses throbbed and her face was hot. Likely she was running a temperature. She'd been mainlining Dristan and aspirin tablets to no avail; she felt worse and worse as time went by.

The sooty old building at 500 Indiana was laid out identically to the justice center in every city Sharon had ever visited, with several floors of cramped courtroom space connected to a jail by catwalks. Local D.C. prosecutors officed on the upper levels in rooms the size of broom closets. Sharon's leg brushed the front of Cedric Hyde's gunmetal gray steel desk as she talked to him. Hyde's assistant, a sharp young Oriental named Sally Pong, sat in such close proximity that Sharon could feel breath on her face. Pong smelled pleasantly of wintergreen. She listened in silence as Hyde took the floor. Two thick files sat at Hyde's elbow, more evidence that, in Will John Benedict's case, the prosecution wasn't screwing around.

"Our word is, Russell Black will be representing Mr. Benedict. Will we be meeting him anytime soon?" Hyde was a stoop-shouldered fortyish man with a dark brush mustache. His black hair receded from his forehead, and he was graying at the temples. His question was an intentional put-down, Sharon realized, letting her know that in Cedric Hyde's book she was a second-stringer. Most lifelong prosecutors had chips on their shoulders the size of Sequoia logs; those in it for the money were long gone to private practice by the time they reached Hyde's age. And Hyde, looked down on by his cohorts over at main headquarters, would be more resentful than most AUSDAs. He'd be a whiz on the books, a bore in the courtroom. Though Sally Pong had little to say, her dark intelligent eyes shifted constantly as she listened. During introductions she'd exhibited a well-modulated voice and vibrant posture, and Sharon suspected that when and if the case came to trial, Pong would do most of the talking for the People.

"Russ flew in with me yesterday," Sharon said.

"Today he's in meetings, but he'll be around." Which was so, though Black's morning "meeting" was a breakfast with Mattie Ruth Benedict and he'd made an afternoon appointment with a barber. In truth, Russell Black couldn't stand going over details with opposing lawyers and attended as few preliminary conferences as possible. Sharon wasn't crazy about conversing with the USDA, either, but the further she could stay from Mattie Ruth—and any possible confrontation with the senator's loving husband—so much the better. She offered Cedric Hyde what she hoped was a disarming smile as she said, "The purpose of my visit is, we all know what's been on television and in the newspapers. Our client is very concerned to know what's going on."

Hyde exchanged a look with Pong, who crossed one long leg over the other and smoothed her skirt. Hyde said, fiddling with a paperweight, "We'd like to know the same thing. An interview with your client would be helpful."

Which was a typical prosecutor's request; whether he had zilch to go on or evidence up to here, Hyde would like to see how often he could trip Will John during an interview and get the congressman to change his story. He'd have an investigator present, of course, someone who could testify as to what the suspect had to say, putting spin on the interview to suit the prosecution's purposes. Grilling sessions with suspects caused AUSDAs to lick their chops. "That's a definite possibility," Sharon said, "now that Congressman Benedict has retained counsel." She was putting Hyde on; the police could interview Will John as soon as cows sprouted wings in the barnyard and began laying eggs. An old hand such as Hyde would know that a question-and-answer session with the congressman would never be, of course, but Sharon decided to dangle some bait in the event she could use the interview as a bargaining tool.

Hyde was obviously a serious man, and didn't crack a smile as he said, "Oh? The appearance of a lawyer eliminates interference from the Democratic Party, eh?"

Sharon forced a look of understanding. "Nothing's going to completely do away with that, Mr. Hyde. You know it and I know it. If it's any consolation, we don't like that part of it any more than you do."

"Murder is murder," Hyde said, "regardless if the perp is some guy in the streets or the King of England."

Sharon decided to end the charade. Hyde's contention that this was just another case was as ridiculous as Sharon's own inference that Will John might be available for questioning. "What I'm here for," Sharon said. "is to determine how, if there's any way, we can help each other."

"Of course." Hyde glanced at Pong, who produced a legal pad and prepared to take notes. "You'll be dealing mainly with Sally on this. She's put together the case file." He touched his fingertips together in a dealing attitude. "I'm assuming that we can have blood and saliva samples."

Sharon paused. The prosecutor's request was SOP, and Will John's DNA was available through court order should Sharon refuse. The only question was, how much was Hyde willing to give in order to skirt the formality of going to a judge? She tried the standard defense lawyer's hedge. "I couldn't commit without conferring with my client." And followed with a look as if she weren't accustomed to telling her clients what to do.

Hyde exchanged a glance with Pong. "We'd expect that," he said, "and would look for your answer in the morning."

Sharon's surprise was real. "That soon? My, you're really on the front burner with this one, Mr. Hyde."

"We're not immune to the publicity any more than you are. With the national coverage we have to move one way or the other, and very quickly. If your client's DNA doesn't match, well hey. Been nice doing business with you, you know?"

The conversation was growing less friendly by the minute. Hyde had originally given her the impression that she was interrupting his day, an inference that she had quickly discounted. With possible murder charges against a congressman on his plate, Hyde would have little else to do. So why the deep freeze? Sharon thought. She said, "It's been my experience that sharing makes things go more quickly and smoothly. Look, if you have a photo of Will John Benedict killing the girl, why not show it to me? If you have a slam dunk, sir, why drag it out?"

"It's not our policy to drag things out. We leave that up to defense counsel."

"Which I confess we do occasionally," Sharon said. "But only when we have a clearly guilty client and are stalling the inevitable. So if you have physical evidence, why not give it to me? We'll have it eventually anyway." She couldn't believe this was happening; not even Milton Breyer back in Dallas was this bullheaded when it came to keeping the defense informed. "Unless, of course, you have no evidence. If what's in the newspapers is all wrong . . ."

"I wouldn't count on that," Hyde said, smirking conspiratorially at his assistant.

Sally Pong smiled fleetingly, then looked out the window. Her view was an open area over an alley strewn with garbage. As a youngster on the staff, Pong would be even more hell-bent-for-leather to get a conviction than her superior, but Sharon thought she detected a hair of tension between the two. When she'd been an assistant prosecutor under Milton Breyer, Sharon had despised the man and had taken every opportunity to show him up in the courtroom. She wondered briefly if she could turn conflict between the prosecutors around to her advantage. "I don't suppose you care if I visit with the medical examiner," Sharon said.

"I have no control over the ME's office. Who they want to talk with is up to them. I'll even give you a reference. Ask for Chris Monet." Hyde's look said that if this Monet person gave Sharon the time of day, he'd be shocked down to his toes.

Sharon threw her coat over her arm and started to rise. "Thanks for your cooperation, Mr. Hyde. Or lack of it."

"Don't mention it." Hyde folded his arms and pursed his lips. "Sally, escort Miss Hays out, will you?"

Sharon caught the slightest stiffening in Pong's bearing, as if she didn't like being treated as an usher. Sharon stood. "I'd ask for a courtesy," she said.

Hyde glared at her. "Which is?"

Sharon responded with a tiny shrug. "The usual. If you plan an indictment, we'd like to be notified so that our client could surrender. We wouldn't want him arrested on the House floor."

Hyde examined bitten nails. "We couldn't guarantee that."

Sharon hid her surprise. Not that she'd expected any more; public arrests were one of the government's chief publicity tools. At least Hyde was being up front about it; most prosecutors would lie, promising her the opportunity to surrender her client and then arresting the poor schnook anyway. She said, "Well thanks for your time."

"Don't mention it." Hyde pointed to Sharon and spoke to Pong. "Sally, stick close to this woman. We wouldn't want her wandering around without you nearby to answer any questions she might have."

Sally Pong was difficult to categorize. She was surprisingly tall, an inch or so over Sharon's own five-nine, and moved with an athlete's grace like a dancer or gymnast. Her high Oriental cheekbones were prominent beneath an exterior of soft skin with a complexion to die for. Her dark suit had padded shoulders, accentuating the long legs and trim waistline below. Her voice was strong though well-modulated, her accent eastern chic mixed with a helping of gee-whiz-I-can't-believe-I'm-a-lawyer enthusiasm. Pong was older than she looked; Sharon had assumed she was just out of law school, and barely hid her surprise on learning, on the elevator ride to the parking garage, that Sally Pong had a thirteen-year-old son. In the next breath Pong told her that her boyfriend was a doctor, which meant that she was either divorced or an unwed mother. Sharon acknowledged the possibility that she and Sally Pong could be kindred souls.

And Pong was ambitious. As she steered the four-door government sedan out of the parking garage, she said conversationally, "As one who's experienced it, what's your estimate of the time to spend prosecuting before entering private practice?"

Sharon sat at ease in the passenger seat, her seatbelt loosely about her, her hands folded in her lap. Her satchel lay in the back. "That's a tough question to answer."

Pong was stopped at the end of the drive, watching for a break in the traffic. "I know. If you leave too early in your career, clients will think you're inexperienced. Hang around too long and firms will shy away from hiring you because they think you're too prosecutorially oriented and won't be able to adjust. And let's face it, doubly tough if you're a woman. Plus my ethnicity works against me, I'd have it easier in criminal law if I were black. Not too many Chinese boys in the D.C. jail, you know? It's another strike against me that I'm third generation and can't speak a word of the lingo." She floored the accelerator, centrifugal force pressing Sharon against the door as Pong whipped into the center lane in front of a panel truck. The truck driver slammed on his brakes and angrily honked his horn. Sally Pong smiled as if pleased with herself. "But ballpark anyway, Miss Hays, what's your estimate?"

Sharon's eyes widened slightly as Pong zipped in and out of traffic, changing lanes like a race-car driver. "You can't go by my career," Sharon said. "I wasn't prepared to leave the Dallas County prosecutor when I did. It just . . . happened." She was careful with her words; bringing up the sexual harrassment bit with Milton Breyer would be a waste of breath and could harm her in the long run.

"Things just happening have a lot to do with it," Pong said. "Look at you. The Darla Cowan thing just happened as well, but you took full advantage."

Sharon felt a surge of irritation. "I didn't defend Darla out of any desire to go public."

"Maybe not. But the case did go public and you shined in the spotlight. What wouldn't I give."

"I don't think you can plan for breaks," Sharon said. "If they come, they come."

"Right. Like this one." Pong hit the brakes, whipped into a parallel space behind a minivan, and killed the engine. "It's good you have a couple of high-profile acquittals on your record, because this is a case you won't win."

Pong was baiting. Sharon looked out the window and didn't answer. Confrontation was a total waste of time. Sally Pong would be a tough opponent in the courtroom. She was a single mother with a kid to support, and that alone could make her dangerous. Sharon leaned forward, peering across the street, around the prosecutor. "Are we here?"

"Yes. The three-story building over there." Pong

shoved her door partway open, then paused. "You won't win, Miss Hays." She started to step onto the pavement, watching the cars and trucks whiz past. "Follow me. And watch yourself crossing. Assholes in this town will run over you without batting an eye."

So much for Cedric Hyde's statement that he had no control over the ME's office. Three people waited amid the smell of alcohol and formaldehyde: a slim attractive black woman wearing a coroner's jacket and two Washington police detectives—a tiny Caucasian woman and an enormous black man. The assistant medical examiner was named Chris Monet, and the cops were Ginny Toledo and Isaac Brown. As Sally Pong did the introductions—with a gang of coroners performing autopsies visible through a window in the background—Sharon considered the odds of the detectives' presence being a coincidence. No way, she thought; the instant that Sally Pong had left the USDA's quarters with Sharon in tow, Cedric Hyde had been on the phone. Sharon gave handshakes to one and all, and then followed Monet into a small anteroom with chairs set up around a conference table. As the massive cop sat down, muscles rippled beneath his white dress shirt. He wore a shoulder rig with no pistol.

"As you probably already know," Sharon began, "I represent Congressman Will John Benedict. The congressman is very concerned over the rumors in the newspapers. I'm here to do whatever is necessary to dispel these rumors." Had she been in Texas, Sharon would have referred to Will John merely as "my client," but her short time in D.C. had taught her that reminders of Will John's political status wouldn't be a bad idea. In normal surroundings a suspect's fame added coals to prosecutorial fires. In the Mecca of politics, a suspect being a congressman would make the police dot their *i*'s and cross their *t*'s.

The AME and the cops looked at each other. Detective Ginny Toledo spoke up with authority. "We'd like to end the speculation as well."

Sharon thought that preindictment meetings between defense lawyers and members of investigative teams should be called the Battle of the Bullshitters. The police didn't really want to end the speculation and Sharon didn't really think she could do anything to save Will John from facing charges. To make the situation even more ludicrous, each side understood perfectly that the other was totally full of it. Sharon said, "How can we expedite the matter, then?"

"Simple, really," Toledo said. "Chris Monet here has recovered certain evidence from the victim. Carpet fibers on the clothing, some hair samples, head and pubic, plus some skin under the victim's fingernails. If your client's DNA is a match, it's a slam dunk for us. If it doesn't, we terminate the investigation of your client and begin to pursue other avenues."

Sharon sighed inwardly in exasperation. She'd already heard this line of reasoning over at the prosecutor's office and could have saved herself a trip. She said, "I think the sparring should end now, ladies and gentlemen. If the congressman's DNA matches, it only proves that he was with her. Not that he killed her. Likewise, even if it doesn't match, if you're bound and determined to build a case against Will John Benedict, the lack of physical evidence won't stop you. You'll merely formulate a different plan of attack. You know it and I know it, so could we please cut the verbal jousting and determine whether we can help one another?"

Toledo exchanged a guarded look with Sally Pong. The female cop was attractive and articulate, more like an English teacher than a homicide investigator. She said, "A nonmatch on your client's DNA would certainly give us pause, Miss Hays. We can get samples from Congressman Benedict with or without your assistance, so what are we discussing here?"

Sharon kept her cool. "We are discussing saving you time and effort, not to mention giving our side food for thought as to plea bargaining. You'll have Ms. Monet as an expert witness, to testify as to the physical evidence, and we can send our expert in to refute what she has to say. That's all a given. But if you have evidence other than physical, witnesses and whatnot, your sharing with me now can save immeasurable time. If your evidence is strong enough, hey. We know when we're whipped, and then we'll want to talk mitigating our losses. So if you'll clue me in I'll have a talk with these witnesses. And as you know, this is something I'll be entitled to after indictment, just as you're entitled to a court order for the congressman's DNA. But why go through all that?"

Toledo said nothing. Pong coughed into her cupped hand. Christine Monet fiddled with the lapel of her white coat. Detective Brown flexed his neck muscles. Finally Pong leaned forward and gave Sharon a sideways-angled look. "Any information given to you would be the U.S. Attorney's decision, of course. We won't rule it out. But specifically, what is it that you would like to know?"

Sharon had come prepared. She hauled her laundry list from her satchel, written out on a yellow legal pad. "A list of those you've interviewed, for starters. If any of these witnesses have brought forth anything that could lead to an alternate theory of the crime, we'd like to have that. It's something we can develop on our own, but we're talking saving time here. And as for the victim, she was a healthy young woman. Bloom on the rose and all that, so we assume that an affair with a married congressman wasn't the sum total of the male companionship she enjoyed. If she had other gentleman friends we'd like to know about them." Sharon really didn't expect any answers, at least not here and now, but she was looking for reactions. When she'd asked about other men in Courtney Lee's life, both Toledo and Detective Brown had slightly averted their gazes. She made a mental note that Courtney's boyfriends had just become Number One on the defense's priority list.

Sally Pong remained deadpan. She seemed in thought. Finally she looked directly at Sharon and said, "I don't think we'll be doing any business in those areas with you, Miss Hays. I could lead you on, but I'll show you the courtesy of not doing that. Any physical evidence we have, of course, is yours for the asking."

"Which is?" Sharon asked.

Pong looked at Chris Monet. The assistant medical examiner took the floor with no further prompting. "This murder sort of redefines vicious," Monet said.

"Two gigantic bullet penetrations, nine-millimeter or something similar, one to the temple and the other to the cheek. Both close range, the second with the barrel flush against her head according to the powder burns. Roll her over and it gets even worse. The back of her skull was caved in flush with her ear. She may or may not have been alive when she was shot. The head fracture penetrated the brain cavity and she would have died from it eventually, and since she was killed elsewhere and dragged into the woods, we don't have enough blood flow evidence to determine whether her heart was pumping when the bullets passed through her head. No shell frags or jackets, of course. There are bruise marks at the base of the neck and on the right temple, indicating that whoever did it took several whacks with a bludgeon of some kind. It wasn't a pipe, because the particles clinging to the head wound are sawdust. I'm guessing your standard Louisville Slugger." Monet ignored the no-smoking sign in the corridor, lit a filtered Camel, and wafted a plume toward the ceiling.

Detective Brown sat at ease, his ankle resting on his knee and his shin propped against the ME's desk. Detective Toledo was in a straight-backed posture in a second visitor's chair. Sharon leaned forward. "Have you discounted any possibility that she was raped?"

Monet's lips twitched in amusement as she considered her answer. She had a broad flat nose and piercing, intelligent eyes. She waved her cigarette around. "You are dealing with a first-class fucking here. A rape, I doubt it."

Toledo tilted her head in interest. Brown rested his

cheek on his lightly clenched fist. Pong seemed bored. Sharon played with the catch on her satchel.

"There was both vaginal and rectal penetration," Monet said, "and a slight tearing of both the rectal and vaginal walls, but none of the external or internal abuse we generally associate with rape. Lab analysis . . ." Monet puffed and inhaled. "Lab analysis shows that the slick substance inside and around the vagina and rectum is a prophylactic lubricant. Often rapists don't ejaculate, but the lack of semen present is consistent with the theory that whoever fucked this girl wore a condom. Consensual sex would be my guess, though there was nothing gentle about it. How many rapos take the time to put on a rubber? I mean, come on." Smoke drifted from between her lips and out of her nostrils.

"Unusual," Sharon said. "But not unheard of. I assume you took scrapings from under her fingernails."

Monet nodded agreement. "And found both skin and blood, which is why we're asking for your client's DNA. The clawing could be defensive. But also could be from scratching the bejesus out of someone's back while she squeezed him with her legs. I'd opt for the latter." She paused and smoked some more. She stubbed her cigarette out in an ashtray. "This is more than fantasizing on my part. Wet trees and foliage make for trace evidence out the wazoo, enough fibers to keep the lab busy through Labor Day. Some appear to be expensive carpet fibers. A white smear found on her thigh succumbed to the taste test rather quickly." She sucked her index finger to demonstrate. "It's Redi-Whip, and the faint red stain on its surface turns out to be maraschino cherry juice. Shortly before her death the young lady was someone's vibrant sundae. I doubt it was involuntary."

Monet paused, obviously pleased with herself. She went on, "There was powder residue, inside of and on the exterior of both orifices, front and rear. I won't keep you in suspense. It's cocaine. Same residue in both nostrils. Our girl died high, which blood analysis confirms. A little coke in the right places makes for the ultimate sexual experience." She smiled appreciatively at Detective Brown. "I've heard," Monet said.

Sharon leaned back, took out a ballpoint and chewed on its end. "But the interior damage, the tears in the walls of the vagina and rectum, those don't say the guy forced himself on her?"

Monet seemed thoughtful. "Possible. Not likely. Look, there were no pressure bruises, nothing to indicate her legs were forced apart, no marks on the cheeks of her ass . . ." She gave Brown another once-over, winked, and grinned at him. "Bet me. Someone fucked half of her brains out, then, as if that didn't make her dumb enough, someone beat the rest of them out with a baseball bat. Got no idea if the fucker and the beater are one and the same person, but I'd guess that they aren't. After the performance this girl put on, no way she could have made anybody that mad."

Sharon thought the exchanges between the ME and the muscular cop were a bit less than cute. She sighed in exasperation. "I'm assuming the physical evidence, we can go over it? We'll be entitled eventually no matter what."

Monet smirked. "You're welcome to go over what I have. The whipped cream was pretty well melted, but we've preserved what we could in the icebox."

Pong butted in. "That's my bailiwick, Chris. Miss Hays can see the evidence when and if the court so orders."

Through her anger, Sharon was getting the picture. Cedric Hyde, Sally Pong, and now the police, all were refusing to provide information that the defense normally received without a struggle for the very reasons Sharon had outlined; after all, why go through the time and expense of indictment and trial when any defense lawyer with half a brain, when confronted with overwhelming evidence, would convince their client to cop out in return for a deal? There's only one possible reason for all the stonewalling, Sharon thought, publicity. Someone higher up wanted the case to go to trial, and therefore had dictated that cooperation with Will John Benedict's lawyers was to be nil. So who gave the order? Sharon thought. Cedric Hyde? No way, he wasn't the type. The U.S. Attorney himself? Possibly, but somehow Sharon doubted it. She said, keeping as much testiness out of her tone as possible, "What I'm hearing is, I'll learn nothing from you that hasn't already been in the newspapers. Am I right?"

There were five seconds of silence. Sally Pong said, "I think we can say you're perceptive, Miss Hays."

Sharon glared around at the group. "So I am. Good day to you all." She hefted her shoulder bag and started to rise. She held out a hand in Pong's direction, palm up. "I'll take what you're planning to give me, which will be nothing earth-shattering, of course, but thanks anyway. I suppose our future contact will be in the courtroom, folks. If I have any more questions, I'll read the *Washington Post*. Early edition, right? Anything later than that will be yesterday's news."

9

Sharon accepted what Sally Pong had to offer—a thick fiberboard accordion-style envelope with a tie string—left in a huff, went downstairs, and called a cab. Until the courtroom battle began in earnest she'd had her last contact with Cedric Hyde, Sally Pong, the police, or anyone else connected to the prosecution unless the other side initiated a meeting. She'd made the effort and her conscience was clear. As far as she was concerned, the battle lines were drawn.

On the ride to the hotel, Sharon leaned back in the taxi's overheated passenger compartment and went through the contents of the envelope. There were the usual medical examiner's forms, and Sharon's lips moved as she silently read over the autopsy report. Evidence found at the scene indicated that someone had murdered Courtney at an unknown location and then dumped her body in Rock Creek Park, a situation that created problems in determining cause or time of death. Courtney had suffered massive injuries—blunt trauma to the head along with two gunshot wounds to the face—all of which would have been fatal. With no pooling of blood around the body there was no

way to know if her heart was beating at the time
someone shot her. Likewise, since the frigid temperature in the park would drastically alter the body's
cooling time, the murder could have happened just
about anytime or anywhere. If Courtney had died, say,
in a heated room where it was seventy-five degrees,
and then her killer had moved her to the park, the
temperature change could create a window of opportunity for the murderer of as much as four or five
hours. Her digestive trace was empty, indicating that
she hadn't eaten in about twelve hours before her
death. The inability to pinpoint the time of the murder
created problems; Will John had a great deal more of
his time to account for than Sharon had expected. She
laid the autopsy aside and picked up an envelope of
photos. She softly closed her eyes, mentally steeling
herself.

Crime scene and autopsy pictures were always
tough to deal with, but deal with them she must. The
prosecution would thrust the grisly photos in the jury's
face over and over during trial, and the defense must
carefully plan its demeanor on confronting such gore
in the courtroom. The defendant's lawyers should
show outrage at the treatment of the victim, but at
the same time be incredulous that anyone could think
their client capable of such mayhem. Russ Black's
strategy was to look away when autopsy pictures paraded in front of the jury box, while Sharon's idea of
proper demeanor was to look at the pictures head on,
her gaze full of pity and outrage. She had to get used
to looking at these images of Courtney Lee as she
appeared in death. She took a shallow breath, slid the

first of the pictures from the envelope, and looked it over.

The first picture was Courtney as she'd been in life—furnished by her relatives, no doubt—ready for Cedric Hyde or Sally Pong to hold up for the jury's benefit as Courtney's mother, father, sister, or brother broke down in tears on the witness stand. It was Sharon's first real look at the victim other than the picture that had appeared in *People*, *Time*, and just about every major newspaper in the country. The media had exhibited a gallery shot of Courtney, made up to the gills, wearing an off-the-shoulder formal that showed plenty of cleavage. The photo now in Sharon's hand would have a much larger impact than anything the public had seen up to now.

In this pose Courtney wore very little makeup. She reclined in a porch swing wearing a man's shirt and stitched cutoffs which ended tastefully a couple of inches above her knee, and a Labrador retriever had its head in her lap. This Courtney Lee bloomed with innocence, the girl-and-her-dog shot giving just the right aura of down-home healthy flavor. She had a nice trim shape, though there wasn't the slightest hint of cheesecake in the pose. Her face wasn't as pretty as Sharon had thought after viewing the more glamorous photos of Courtney that had made the media drool. The subject of this picture was a typical all-American girl, not a spiteful or nasty bone in her body, and the jury would fall immediately in love with her. Sharon wondered if there was any way to get Courtney's much-sexier magazine shots in front of the panel. She hated using such a strategy, but those were the rules of the game. So live with it, Sharon thought. She reached inside the envelope and withdrew more photos. Her stomach churned and bile came up in her mouth.

The first picture showed Courtney nude, still in death, face down on the autopsy table, and the beating she'd taken went far beyond brutality. The weapon had been cylindrical, either a pipe or baseball bat, and had left concave indentations where it had cracked, and eventually broken through, the skull. Hair, skin, and bone hung away from the wounds in clusters. There were ugly bruises across Courtney's neck and shoulder blades, indicating that whoever had attacked her had wielded the bludgeon over and over in a rage. Who in God's name could have hated this girl so much? Sharon thought. Not Will John Benedict, no way, he was too much of a coward. Will John's style, if he'd had the nerve to commit murder—which Sharon seriously doubted—would have been a single bullet from behind. She forced her gaze away from the victim's battered head and looked at Courtney's arms. It was as she had expected.

There had been no mention in the press that Courtney had been tied—nothing sinister here, Sharon thought, since it's SOP in criminal investigation to shield details from the media that only the killer could know—but the ligature marks on her wrists were plain as day. The whirly indentations were clearly braided hemp, which Sharon verified by thumbing to one of the laboratory forms inside the envelope. The rope was of a common variety, available in any Home Depot or hardware store, and no remnant had been located anywhere around the body. The murderer's method was a study in contrast; someone had developed a rage intensive enough to inflict a madman's damage, yet had retained the presence of mind to remove evidence in disposing of the corpse. Sharon slowly shook her head in wonderment as she moved on to the next photo. She ground her teeth and forced herself to be clinical. Nonetheless, she winced at the sight.

Same autopsy table, different angle, the body flipped over on its back. The effect was even grislier than the previous picture and, in ways, even more puzzling. The bullet holes in Courtney's temple and cheek were half again the size of silver dollars, completely obliterating the right side of her face. Bone and grayish brain matter showed through the openings. Sharon returned briefly to the first photograph and examined the exit wounds through the left back of the skull, several centimeters away from the bludgeon marks as if the killer had wanted one and all to view his handiwork in its entirety.

His handiwork, Sharon thought, or *her* handiwork? Because of the brutality of the slaying, the police had assumed that the killer was a man. And likely the killer was, but Sharon had pause. She pictured Cassandra Mason Benedict, the hate in her voice as she'd spoken of the murder last night at Beggett's Pub. Cas certainly had motive, though her motive was quite a bit different than one would imagine. The fact that Courtney had been having an affair with Will John wouldn't have driven Cas to murder, but the threat to her husband's political career—and to Cas's time in the spotlight—just might put her over the edge. Con-

venient that Cas's own private eye is a potential alibi
witness for Cas's husband, Sharon thought.

The murderer's methods were senseless. The bullets
would have killed Courtney instantly, so why the vicious beating as an aftermath? Or conversely, after
bludgeoning gaping holes in the victim's skull, why
would someone roll her over and then shoot her in
the face two times?

One killer, or two?

One to beat her senseless, the other to finish her
off with a nine-millimeter. Or one to shoot her, the
other to vent rage on the dead by . . .

Sharon tossed the pictures aside and leaned back as
the cab pulled under the awning at the State Plaza
Hotel. She reassembled the contents of the accordion
file, tied the string, paid the driver, exited the taxi,
and tromped wearily through the slush toward the
hotel entry. A mental picture refused to exit her mind,
the image inside the folder thrust firmly under her
arm, the battered, mutilated corpse of Courtney Lee.

She entered her room. The red light on her phone
blink-blinked, so she picked up the receiver and
punched the numbers to retrieve her messages. There
was a call from Sheila, and Sharon didn't like her best
friend's tone on the recording. The voice was cool and
professional, and someone unfamiliar with Sheila's
moods wouldn't have caught the problem. But Sheila
sounded *overly* professional, as if she was forcing herself to remain calm in order to keep from screaming.
Sharon fought panic as she returned the call, only to
get Sheila's own voice mail and have to leave a call-

back. Christ, what a time for playing phone tag. Something had happened to Melanie. Otherwise, Sheila wouldn't have . . .

There was a note on her bed, a folded piece of paper dead center on the mattress. Sharon unfolded the slip and read, in Russ's familiar scrawl, "Get down to my room, pronto. RB." Sharon sank down and stared vacantly into space. Until she talked to Sheila, until she was certain that her daughter was safe and sound, there was no way that Sharon was going anywhere. What could be wrong? A series of images paraded through her mind, everything from Melanie, pale as a ghost, lying in a hospital bed with tubes running from her nose, to Melanie, helpless and afraid, tied up in the backseat of a car while a lunatic drove her to a lonely spot out in the country. There to savage her, to . . .

You're being a dodo, Sharon Jennifer, she thought. Likely Melanie had merely asked Sheila's permission to go out on a school night, and Sheila was getting the okay from headquarters before giving her answer. Good God, Sharon thought, I'm having Panicked Mother Syndrome. She redialed Sheila's number, got voice mail once again, and told Sheila's recorder that if she wasn't in her room she'd be in Russ's. Then she hustled into the bathroom, checked her makeup, grabbed up her satchel along with the accordion envelope from the ME's office, and took off down the corridor. A knot of dread filled her chest as she thought fleetingly of Melanie. She shook her head, closed her eyes, mentally dialed up Peppier Upbeat Mood, and hurried on.

*   *   *

Russ's entryway was ajar, the bed's footboard and tufted spread visible through the opening, the message being, Come on in, don't bother to knock. At the office back in Dallas he closed his door when he wanted privacy. Sometimes, depending on the urgency of the situation or the mischief in her mood, she might disturb him anyway. Russ barked a lot, seldom bit. As she approached his room, her medium heels sinking into padded carpet with a floral design, his voice carried into the corridor and reached her ears.

Russ was saying, "It's gonna be a long road. You may as well get prepared, and it's absolutely necessary that—"

At first her mentor's words were a faint, faraway sound, then upped in volume and became crystal clear as she paraded down a short entry hall and reached the foot of the bed. She came to a halt as Russ finished, "—through the whole nasty business, both of you show a unified front. Mama an' Daddy got to stand behind him. I already said, I can discuss nothin' with you unless Will John approves. You're a lawyer, Paul, you oughtta understand that."

Sharon stood mute, stunned. She'd known that eventually she'd have to face Paul Benedict—had been steeling herself for the occasion, in fact—but she'd expected more warning. Suddenly there he was, on a sofa beside his wife as Russell Black held court from an easy chair, with a small table in between Russ and Mr. and Mrs. Paul Benedict. And—God, Sharon thought, why does it have to be this way?—where Will John, Mattie Ruth, and Cassandra Mason Benedict had changed noticeably over the years, Paul Benedict didn't look a bit different nor one second older than on the night he'd assaulted her in the wilderness outside Austin. His thick gray hair was in place in just the proper tousled look. There wasn't a line in his forehead, not a single age wrinkle that hadn't been evident ten years ago. His body was trim and he looked in shape. He wore slacks and a sweater over a gold shirt. The same cobalt blue eyes which had mesmerized the female student body on the Austin campus now gazed directly at Sharon without the slightest hint of embarrassment. He even smiled.

Russ paused in his discourse and looked at her.

Mattie Ruth had chosen a black suit and jacket for the occasion, as if she were ready to address the Senate floor. She touched her husband's arm. "Hon, you remember Sharon Hays."

Paul Benedict rose. He said in the same booming showroom voice with which he'd once explained causes of action to the class, "How could I forget? The sharp legal mind and the service at the restaurant. It's been far too long." He stepped toward her and held out his hand.

The moment had arrived. Christ, how could he look so freaking *at ease*? His attitude chilled her more than if he'd snarled in lust or cringed in humiliation. Jesus Christ, as if she were a stick of furniture, a used-up condom or something, an object void of feeling or memory. Oh, yes, I remember you. I beat hell out of you and tried to rape you once, so what time is it? Sharon recalled her conversation with Sheila. A sociopath, Sheila had said, one who saw people as a means to an end and nothing more. Seething inside, feeling sick to her stomach, Sharon forced herself to take his hand. His flesh was dry and his lips curved as if he was amused. Thousands of earthworms crawled and wriggled on her skin. She curtly nodded. "Professor."

The exchange was brief, no more than a couple of seconds. As Paul Benedict returned to sit beside his wife, Russ continued as if he hadn't sensed anything wrong, "I was just explainin' how this case differs from most we handle, in a lot of ways. Take a seat."

Sharon sat in a chair with a springy cushion, and assumed a straight-backed posture. Issues, she thought, legal questions, pure and simple. Concentrate on the matter at hand. She didn't glance in Paul Benedict's direction.

"The fact that we're all previously acquainted makes it sticky," Black said, "but nothin' we can't all handle. I can discuss all aspects, *most* aspects, of the case with you because Will John's given me the green light to. That's his decision. Here's what's my decision, mine and Miss Hays's. Nothin' which transpires directly between us and our client, behind closed doors, is for your consumption. If you want to know anything we discussed, ask your boy. You won't be consulted on any strategy, Paul."

"That's a given," Paul Benedict said. "I'm a civil lawyer, Russ. This is your bailiwick." His tone was humble enough, but Sharon doubted if Paul Benedict's ego would allow him to stay out of the way. She wondered how long it would be before Russ tired of another lawyer's two cents' worth and hit the ceiling.

Black stared at his client's father as if measuring

the man. Finally he said, "I like the words. Know goin' in that there might be a few reality checks before this is over."

Mattie Ruth intervened, leaning forward. "It's your show, Russell."

Russ looked back and forth between the two. "Good for now. With all that outta the way, we got a few minutes before we have to leave for Will John's place. Miss Hays has been out testin' the waters this mornin'." His expression softened as he looked to Sharon. "Surprise us and say the prosecutor's gonna be a teddy bear."

Sharon felt tightness in her neck and shoulders. She wasn't sure she could speak rationally with Paul Benedict seated only a few paces away, but did her best. She kept her gaze riveted on Russell Black, but Paul Benedict's outline was prominent in the periphery of her vision. She cleared her throat. "Just the opposite. I'd be remiss if I didn't tell our client to expect charges any day. They want his samples, for comparison. We have until tomorrow to give an answer. If we refuse, I expect they'll come up with some flimsy probable cause, arrest Will John, and take the samples under a court order while he's in jail. I vote we give them up, though it will only delay the inevitable. Even if the samples don't match, the only answer you're going to get from that ME is that the results are 'inconclusive.' They'll have to dig a little deeper to charge him then, but they'll do it."

There was a minisecond of silence. Paul Benedict said from the sofa, "That bad?"

Sharon couldn't look at him. The best she could

manage was a glance at the carpet about halfway between her and the couch. "Worse," she said.

"Not good, but not surprisin'." Black rested his forearms on his thighs. His solid navy blue tie hung down into his lap. "This prosecutor," he said. "He efficient?"

Sharon crossed her legs, glad for anything to take her attention away from the specter out of her past. "Cedric Hyde. *Comme ci, comme ça,* boss. An old-timer with a grudge, likely knows the lawbooks by heart. His first chair is a woman, Sally Pong. I suspect she's a crackerjack. Cedric Hyde's been around long enough to know he's as far as he's going, careerwise, but she looks on this case as a step up the ladder. Hyde can spot Milton Breyer two knights and a rook in the courtroom, but that doesn't make him formidable. She'll be the main worry."

Russ and Sharon exchanged a look of understanding. Milton Breyer was a Dallas prosecutor whom they both considered to be the clod of clods. "They give you anything at all?" Black asked.

Sharon indicated the folder from the ME, on the floor near her ankle. "A stack of crap that may as well have been copied out of the newspaper. We'll have to file discovery motions out the wazoo, Russ."

Black spread his hands, palms up. "We've filed 'em before."

"Not to the extent that we're going to have to file them in this case. Plus, we're the out-of-towners who've just fallen down the rabbit hole. The brother-in-lawing between the prosecutors and the judges in this city will likely make the Mad Hatter and the

March Hare look sane. Prosecuting a politician makes these folks lick their chops. What I'm saying is, I doubt the courts are going to give us much relief when it comes to ordering them to turn over evidence to us, and I think we can save a lot of time by reinvestigating the case on our own. We need a support staff."

Paul Benedict spoke up, saying, "For investigative purposes, I suppose." He looked to his wife. "What do we have on the dead girl now?"

Mattie Ruth seemed thoughtful. "Nothing that I recall. I'm not sure I even remember her, do you?"

Paul Benedict waved a hand. "All that office help. All those interns running around. I may have seen her. I'm not sure."

Queasiness twisted around in Sharon's midsection. At a time like this, only politicians would consider digging up dirt on a murder victim. So how does this differ from the last election? Sharon thought. They do it to their opponents all the time, so why not the dead girl? The possibility of a smear attack on Courtney Lee had been in the back of Sharon's mind up to now, but came raging to the front of her consciousness. God, she hated this case. Absolutely despised everyone involved. She looked at Russell Black.

Black thoughtfully returned Sharon's gaze. Paul Benedict continued. "Translates to a need for additional funds, I suppose." He took a small notepad from his pocket. "How much are we talking here?"

Sharon managed to look sideways toward the sofa, and found herself watching Mattie Ruth Benedict's knee. Jesus Christ, she couldn't even bring herself to look at the guy. She said, "At least one investigator, possibly two."

Black leaned back, lifted his leg, and rested his ankle on his knee. "Anthony Gear generally works alone."

Sharon thought it over. Anthony Gear was a Dallas private cop, a former FBI agent whom Black employed on a catch-as-catch-can basis. Gear was a gem of an investigator, but also a died-in-the-wool racist and a slob in his personal habits. Not in this town, no way, Sharon thought. She said, "I didn't have Mr. Gear in mind, Russ."

Black scowled in surprise. "Who, then?"

"A British couple, the ones who helped me out in L.A. 'Couple' isn't the right description, actually. They're not husband and wife. They're sort of Darla Cowan's bodyguards. They won't be cheap, but they'll get results."

"Sounds to me," Black said, "like they already got a full-time job."

"They head up an agency. Darla won't mind giving them off, as long as someone can spell them to take their places." Sharon was beginning to like the idea. Working with Lyndon Gray and Mrs. Welton again might be the only pleasant aspect of this whole situation. They were former British Secret Service agents, not to mention that Mrs. Welton was once an L.A. cop as well, and their attitudes and accents knocked Sharon out—all business, but enough humor to make working with them a joy. Not only that, the D.C. crowd wouldn't intimidate Gray and Welton in the slightest, which was half the battle won. Not exactly

John Steed and Emma Peel, but very close. "I'll call them this afternoon," Sharon said. "They'll quote their fee and we'll let you know." She did her best to look at Paul Benedict, but found her gaze instead on the wall above his shoulder.

"Money's no barrier. Consider it done." Paul Benedict made a note and put his pad and pen away. "Are we now ready to go?" He stood and extended a hand in his wife's direction.

Black seemed puzzled. "Go where?"

"Well, you said you were meeting with our boy." Mattie Ruth put a palm-down hand beside either hip and started to hoist herself up.

"We'll stay out of your way," Paul Benedict said. He helped Mattie Ruth to her feet and kissed her cheek. "Besides," he said, "we know the way and can drive you. Escort Russell to the car, Mat, will you? Miss Hays and I will bring up the rear."

Sharon helplessly gripped the arms of her chair. The *bastard*. She couldn't avoid him without making a scene, and well he knew it. The nerve of the . . .

Russ looked perturbed, unsure, as if he didn't want Paul and Mattie Ruth Benedict tagging along but saw no way out. He got up and followed Mattie Ruth out of the room as she conspiratorially gripped his upper arm. Russ paused in the exit, threw Sharon a glance over his shoulder, then went on through. She stood, no one in the room now except her and Paul Benedict. She'd never felt more alone in her life.

She hoisted her belongings, tried to step around him and head for the door. He blocked her path. She looked up at him. She tried to appear brave and unintimidated, but thought she probably looked scared to death.

"I wanted this chance," he said. "A private word."

She forced herself to look directly into eyes of cobalt blue. "Which is?"

"The past. It can get in the way of progress."

Anger surged within her. She stood her ground. "In what way?"

"I can think of a number of examples. For one, you and your client were once close."

"Will John and I had ten dates at the most, professor."

He licked his lips, and suddenly seemed unsure of himself. "And there are matters that you and I should put behind us. I hope you're willing."

She put one foot slightly before the other. "I can see why you would be."

"Everyone has things in their past they're not proud of, Sharon. You as well as I."

"My skeletons don't include criminal behavior." Not entirely true; Sharon had once murdered a man, though no one knew it and no one ever would.

"Which is far removed from present circumstances." He stepped toward the door, smirking. "I confess to a slip, an attraction I couldn't . . ."

"That might be an excuse for an adolescent. An adult college professor is supposed to be beyond the raging hormone stage." She felt as if she had the upper hand, and squared her posture. "All right, you've brought it up. I'm willing to comment."

He stopped and watched her.

Sharon's tone was even. "Ten years ago you rubbed

my face in the dirt. Accepting your bribe hurt my self-esteem more than when you tried to rape me. I'm over it, just an occasional nightmare."

He showed a frown. "That's rather harsh. 'Tried to rape' isn't really the proper . . ."

"Oh, stop. You tried to rape me just like any creep lying in wait out in the alley. You know it and I know it." Sharon worked up an icy glare as she continued. "But there are things worth mentioning here, having to do with the case at hand," Sharon said. "First of all, I didn't want to come here, but couldn't get out of it without embarrassing Russ. I wouldn't do that, ever, so I'm here. I don't at this point think Will John committed the crime, though we'll bust our humps defending him even if we think he did. I simply believe you raised him as too much of a whipping boy for him to commit an act this violent. Know two things, professor. If he's innocent, well and good, you, your wife, and his own wife, can continue to bully him and use him for your own political purposes. But if it turns out he's guilty, you will go through life knowing that fatherly example was a major factor in his downfall. I'm not sure that the latter wouldn't be more personally satisfying to me than winning the case. So what I'm saying is, the more I see of you, the more difficult it's going to be for me to defend your son. Your money will be helpful, even necessary to Will John's chances. But if you want a good defense for him you should stay far in the background, waving your checkbook. In other words . . . oh, hell. Just keep away from me, okay?"

10

"I can't explain or justify my actions. She was so young and fresh. I'm a man, human . . ." Will John Benedict's gaze was desperate as he sought approval where there would be none, no way.

Sharon watched with a bland expression. So you're a man, she thought. You're human. Great. So's everyone. As if every male in this world felt that being horny would explain away any misconduct including murder. When she was a prosecutor she'd come to call such drivel the Hard-on Defense, which she'd heard from rapists, robbers, burglars, you name it, guys who rationalized their crimes by citing the irresistible urge to get laid. *I never wouldda done it if it hadn't been for that woman, Judge.* Christ almighty, Sharon thought.

Russell Black nervously cleared his throat. "The 'why' idn important anymore, son. We need facts. Let us do the justifyin', if any's necessary."

They were in the living room of the congressman's Georgetown condo, which to Sharon's way of thinking was the epitome of, well, a condo in Georgetown. The building was new-built-to-look-old, with a ribbon of down-slanted lawn between the porch and sidewalk. The room where they sat contained antique furniture. A narrow mahogany-banistered staircase led upward from the entry hall. The dark red carpet was patterned with nineteenth-century images, horses pulling carriages and women wearing bustles. The furniture was drop-dead gorgeous, and Sharon felt guilty as her backside indented the cushion of a French Provincial love seat. Cas Benedict, wearing slacks and a ski sweater, had escorted Paul and Mattie Ruth into the kitchen the moment they'd arrived; visible through a hallway opening, daughter-in-law and parents-in-law drank cups of espresso and pretended not to eavesdrop. Cas had given Sharon a nod of acknowledgment, followed by a quick questioning glance whose meaning was clear: Had Sharon spilled the beans about their meeting last night? Sharon had answered with a tiny shake of her head. Russ kept his voice low in order to keep from being heard across the hall, and had cautioned Sharon and Will John to do the same.

Sharon balanced her notepad on her thigh. "Russ is right. You don't have to justify a thing with us. Now, yesterday you told us that you took her to the Green Lantern Bar, in Virginia, and then the two of you went to the Holiday Inn for your first sexual encounter. We have the big picture. We'll need to know who else might've known. Over a six-month period, how many times were you and Courtney Lee, ah, together?" There was a Christmas tree by the window, a live green fir hung with tinsel and shiny blue ornaments. In the fireplace, flames crackled and sizzled, and a log burned in two with a hiss and a shower of sparks. Outside, melting snow *drip-dripp*-ed from tree branches and turned the gutters into icy rushing streams. They'd had their first brush with the media upon their arrival. As Paul Benedict had rounded the corner in his Mercedes, two mobile news units had stood at the curb. Cursing under his breath, with Mattie Ruth watching cautiously for pursuers, the law-professor-turned-high-powered-litigant had whipped down the alley to use the back entrance. To no avail; the newsies had simply walked around the house into the yard and fired questions as they'd exited the carport. Sharon and Russ had no-commented right and left all the way to the back stoop, and Sharon suspected that the State Plaza Hotel's safe-haven status was history. She felt better, though the Dristan had made her drowsy. The ache in her sinuses had receded to a series of nagging throbs. She waited patiently for Will John Benedict to answer her question.

The congressman sagged in defeat. "We were together no more than a dozen times. Always with her initiating."

"Be sure on that point. The prosecution will have your phone records, count on it. You never called her, even one single time?"

Will John looked at the floor. "I suppose I could have returned messages."

Sharon pursed her lips, but wasn't near as exasperated as she tried to appear. All criminal clients, guilty or innocent, lied in order to play down their possible involvement in the crime, and through the years she'd learned to roll with the punches. It was the defense attorney's job to be certain that the clients didn't tell *obvious* untruths, thus giving prosecutors a field day on cross. Sharon asked, "Who else knew you were having an affair? Your parents?" She ignored a sharp look from Russ. Both Paul and Mattie Ruth Benedict had earlier disavowed knowing Courtney Lee. Am I checking out their stories? Sharon thought. You bet your boots I am, old boss; we're representing this guy, and if pointing the finger at his own parents makes for a plausible alternate theory, then that's the way the cookie crumbles. She waited for Will John to reply.

He said quickly, "Of course not. My mother would have died."

What about your father? Sharon thought. She thought that Paul Benedict's response would have been in the area of, Atta boy, hump her one for me. Sharon said, "What about your staff?"

Will John's gaze wavered. "I'm not sure."

One corner of Sharon's mouth tightened. "The girl worked in your office. You can't carry on something like that without creating gossip. Elaine Trowell, your assistant?"

There was a downturned look. "She may have known," Will John Benedict said.

"May have, or did? They'll put pressure on her to testify against you. They have a hammer you wouldn't believe, obstruction of justice charges if she doesn't cooperate, and if she knows anything she'll likely help them. If you used your assistant to run interference, to cover up the affair, you'd best own up to it."

Will John's eyes misted. "You could say Elaine was aware something was going on. If Miss Lee, if *Court-*

ney called or came by, she had orders not to tell any-one. The reason I gave her, we were working on certain projects. Elaine Trowell wasn't born yesterday. Exactly how much she knew, I'm not sure."

"More like it. For our purposes we're assuming the worst, that Ms. Trowell is an incurable gossip and let your whole staff in on what was going on. Okay, moving along. Motel clerks, bartenders . . . ?"

"We went to the Green Lantern a number of times. Courtney was familiar with the place before we . . . That first night, it was her idea to go there."

Sharon chewed her inner cheek. If the Green Lantern in Falls Church had been one of Courtney's regular haunts, she might've made the scene with other gentleman friends. Sharon made a mental note. She said, "So the affair went on for half a year. We may need fill-in details later, but let's move closer, time-wise, to the murder. The newspapers have reported that you'd gone home for the holidays, but came speeding back to D.C. to carry on with Courtney."

"Not true," Will John said sharply, then softened his voice and said more uncertainly, "Not . . . *entirely* true."

"Clarification is all right," Sharon said. "Flat denial is pointless. No one's going to believe that you hot-footed it to Washington during Christmastime to work on your budget. Courtney was from your home district, wasn't she?"

"Yes, Baytown. Is there any way we can de-emphasize that connection?"

Always the politician, Sharon thought. She said, "Not likely. The fact that her father is one of your backers has been splashed all over, and everyone who knows anything understands that that's how intern positions are handed out." She showed a grim smile. "I doubt you'll be asking her father for donations in the future." She thought of something. "Courtney didn't go home for Christmas?"

The congressman expelled breath. "For a few days. If she hadn't . . . Jesus."

Sharon tilted her chin. "Hadn't what?"

"Look, I'd made up my mind to end it. It was just that, damn, every time I did she'd come on to me and I'd weaken. The night before I left Washington for Christmas I told her it was over. Then, the first Sunday we were home, Cas and I went to church and there she was, seated between her parents. During a conversation with her father I had in the foyer after the service she kept watching me as if . . . you know. Then right there in front of her parents, while they weren't looking and Cas was talking to them, Courtney reached out and squeezed my . . . Jesus."

Sharon couldn't help smirking. "I'll bet that put you in the mood to worship," she said. Russ reddened in embarrassment. Sharon asked, "So after that, you felt the urge to contact her?"

"Only to tell her that there wasn't to be a repeat performance of what had happened in church."

"You called her at her parents' home?"

"Ted Lee goes to the church business meeting on Sunday afternoons. I knew he wouldn't be there."

"What about Courtney's mother?"

"She'd gone to a tea."

"Oh?" Sharon said. "How did you know that?"

Will John deflated in guilt. "Because she went with my wife."

By now, Sharon thought, the jurors will be trotting out the hangman's rope. An affair with a college student was bad enough, but Will John being on a first-name basis with Courtney's parents would have the fathers in the courtroom chewing nails. She said, "What did the two of you discuss?"

"Her plans to come back to D.C. She'd told her parents that she had some catching up to do at the office, important enough for her to miss Christmas Day at home. She told me to tell Cas the same thing, come to D.C. and meet her there."

Sharon didn't try to hide her disgust. "Get out. This college girl dreamed that story up on her own?"

"She was resourceful."

"Even if she was, no one's going to believe it. As of now. Nothing about whether it was her plan or your plan. Only that the two of you talked on the phone and agreed to rendezvous back in Washington. Every attempt on your part to lay the blame on Courtney will be counterproductive." Sharon looked to Black, who nodded agreement.

"I'm trying to tell it the way it happened."

Sharon couldn't help sympathizing. Even though everyone in the country would blame Will John for the affair, she didn't doubt that what he was saying was partially true. Men in Will John's position might lust in private over young women, but few had the nerve to make a pass without some encouragement. This was particularly true of man-mouses such as Will John Benedict. Leading guys like Will John around by the crotch is a piece of cake, ladies, Sharon thought, and has been since Adam and Eve. "Just remember what Russ told you yesterday," she said. "Don't tell it the way it *didn't* happen, but tell the portions of the truth that are credible." She leaned back, pensive. "So you returned to D.C., and Cas stayed in Texas. I'm assuming that you at least made a show of coming to the office while you were here."

"Every day."

"Along with members of your staff, who can verify you were there?"

Will John massaged his eyelids. "Everyone was off."

"What about Courtney?"

"She came on the same days as I did."

Sharon watched him. "And signed in and out, I suppose."

"Yes."

"Not good." Sharon peered through the hallway into the kitchen, where Cas Benedict now stood by the window exhibiting her potted plants to her parents-in-law. Sharon lowered her voice an octave. "We're now going to the day of the murder, and we're going into detail. Intimate detail. Don't be embarrassed, and rest assured that I'm not asking because of any voyeuristic streak in my makeup. The police haven't given us the time of day as yet, but I am in possession of the autopsy report. There is going to be physical evidence, body hairs, fluids, and we're assuming that at least a portion of the evidence is going to point to you. We must have a legitimate explanation for every piece of physical evidence they come up with, and in order to do that we need intimate details." She looked briefly at Russ. This was the reason that they'd agreed for Sharon to do the questioning; Russell Black wouldn't be able to broach some of these subjects without cringing. Will John watched Sharon like a man about to mount the gallows.

"She died in a sequined cocktail dress," Sharon said. "The story published in the newspapers, most of which came from her roommate, are that Courtney and you were to attend a party. I've found it curious that, other than what the roommate has to say, the press hasn't come up with the particulars on this gathering, where it occurred or anything else. Care to elaborate?" Sharon smiled. "That's not really a question, Will John, it's an order. Elaborate. I insist. You have no choice other than to do so."

Will John began to perspire. "This gets embarrassing."

"Possibly. But as yet it isn't lethal, which it very likely will be if you don't open up completely."

"There are parties in this town," Will John began, then licked his lips before continuing. "They're secret."

"Obviously. Even Rita Carboneau doesn't seem to know the location. If *that* gossip-monger doesn't know ..."

"It's her existence, the existence of people like her, that keeps it all hush-hush. Lord, if I'd known I'd ever be talking about this . . ."

Sharon watched in silence. Russ Black scooted his chair, tilting back. Cas Benedict's voice drifted in from the other room, something about her plants being her therapy, seeing her through the hard times.

Will John seemed to gather himself. "You hear these rumors the first week you're in Congress. Not that everyone goes, just a chosen few who wouldn't want the word around."

"I assume we're talking members of the House?" Sharon asked.

"A few senators as well. People with good reason not to want their private laundry aired."

"Reasons such as wives?"

"Or husbands, in a few cases. One congresswoman nearly seventy with a twenty-five-year-old escort." Will John seemed to be pleading for acceptance. "Know I never went to these things before Courtney. Never even considered it for my first year in the House. It was all her."

Sharon arched an eyebrow in surprise. "She'd been before?"

"That's the whole idea. Look, it isn't the elected officials who arrange these things. It's their secret lovers."

Sharon glanced at Russ, whose expression was stoic. That congressmen and senators were partners in hanky-pank didn't come as a shock, and Sharon suspected that the secret get-togethers were the only real bipartisan endeavors in the nation's capital. If only Democrats had been involved, the GOP would have blown the whistle to the press long before now and vice-versa. She said, "We're talking some sort of safe hide-away? A lease arrangement?"

Will John nodded. "A house over in Maryland. I honestly don't know if it's rented or bought. Right now there are three women living there."

"Employees of the various elected officials?"

"Yes. Single women."

Sharon watched the Christmas tree, zeroing in on a plastic angel holding a candle. This case was going to be a lid-blower. She pictured committee inquiries, senators hamming it up for the benefit of the viewing audience as they questioned a herd of witnesses. She asked, "How often did these parties occur?"

"No set schedule. When there was a happening, the word sort of drifted around."

"How?"

Will John looked at her.

"Rumors can drift around," Sharon said, "but here we're talking an arranged gathering at a specific time and place. Someone had to get out the invitations, if only by phone."

Will John seemed resigned. "Phones were too dangerous. There was this one page on the floor. She'd distribute the news."

Sharon's lips parted. She looked at Russ, who studied the floor. Sharon said, "God, aren't most of these pages in *high school*?"

"This one was older."

"You mean she was over eighteen."

Will John expelled breath. "Thereabouts."

"No jail bait for you solid citizens, right? How did she distribute the word? A printed invitation, or . . . ?"

Will John assumed a begging tone. "Sharon, if this ever gets out . . ."

"We're only interested in getting *you* out at the moment. Come on, how did she distribute the word?"

Will John toyed with his lapel. "Committee meeting forms."

Sharon leaned back. "How novel."

"It's a fill-in-the-blanks thing. Every member of the House serves on one or more committees. It's a daily ritual that one page assembles the daily log of meetings, fills in the blanks, and distributes copies among the representatives. You know, there will be a meeting of such-and-such at this time or that, at whatever location on whatever date. If a party was scheduled over in Maryland, she'd pass out forms to certain people. The form would identify a Task Force Committee meeting in the Shuttle Room at seven p.m. There is no Task Force Committee, but there are so many committees that someone inadvertently reading the form wouldn't know the difference."

"I don't guess there's such a place as the Shuttle Room."

"Right. But there are so many different rooms . . ."

"I gotcha. As for this particular party, I assume it had to be planned well in advance."

Will John nodded dully. "The final meeting of the fall session, before the break."

"And I suppose, you weren't the only elected official who found an excuse to return to Washington from their homeland during the holidays."

Will John's tone became matter-of-fact. "There was an annual thing, always at this time of year."

Which would fit right in, Sharon thought. Likely the politicians' constituents thought that their representative was missing Christmas at home because of devotion to mother and country. No wonder the Party was so interested in what was going on in this case. "How many people attended this function?" she said.

"A couple of dozen."

"Couples?"

Will John nodded.

"A total of fifty people. We're going to need a list."

Will John's lips trembled. "Christ. Is that necessary?"

"Critical. The time of your coming and going will be a big deal. I don't suppose you know if the police are aware of this haven."

"Not a clue."

"They aren't," Sharon said. "Otherwise it would have already been in the gossip columns. What time did you and Courtney arrive, and what time did you leave?"

"We were there from, oh, eightish, until around midnight."

"I assume these parties are more or less civilized. I mean, no one's doing it on the floor in front of everybody, are they?"

"Of course not." Will John looked indignant.

No one doing it on the floor, Sharon thought. Just all these married men and women standing around, having cocktails, chatting gaily, introducing their stuff-on-the-side to the rest of the depraved. She said, "What about in the bedrooms?"

"There . . . could be some of that."

"More to the point, Courtney's corpse was decorated with whipped cream. Was this any sort of group endeavor during the party?"

"Good Lord, Sharon. You think I'm an exhibitionist? Whatever we did, we did in private."

"Modest," Sharon said, "but in this case unfortunate. You've no idea how helpful it would be to find

DNA other than yours on the body. Did you practice your modesty in one of the bedrooms?"

"Courtney and I were more private than that."

"Oh, I see. You attended this orgy, let everyone else take over the bedrooms, then toddled off to some motel."

"Not always. Not every time we went out, for God's sake. Sometimes we'd just talk, you know."

"About Tolstoy or Shakespeare, no doubt. On this particular evening, since one of you had brought the whipped cream along, I guess this was no occasion for intellect. Where did you go when you left the party?"

Will John's gaze shifted guiltily toward the kitchen. He watched the floor and lowered his voice even more, to a near whisper. "Here," he began, then cleared his throat and said, "We came here."

"Here? To this condo?"

Will John nodded.

"Sweet Jesus and all the angels," Sharon said.

"At the time, it seemed the safest place. No one was here. We'd done this before."

"A safe place for hanky-pank," Sharon said. "Not such a hot spot to commit a murder. The first thing the prosecution will do, at the first hint of probable cause, is get a warrant to search this condo. Clean and vacuum all you want. They'll find evidence that she was here. There were carpet fibers on the body. Five'll get you ten that they connect the fibers to this carpet." She gestured around the room at random.

Russell Black stood, walked over near the Christmas tree, and rubbed the sole of his shoe on the carpet. He lifted his foot and examined the bottom. "Sticks to leather," he said.

"And even better to skin," Sharon said. "Okay, Will John, we need a blow-by-blow. Everything that happened while you and Courtney were here."

"Let's see." Will John looked thoughtfully toward the fireplace. "We had a drink in here."

"Standing, or sitting?"

"I mostly stood, near the tree," Will John said. "Courtney sat on the love seat, right where you are."

Sharon felt a chill. Within hours of being beaten to death and shot in the face, Courtney Lee's fanny rested on the same cushion where Sharon now sat. She shifted uncomfortably. "What then? Straight to the master bedroom?"

"I wouldn't do such a thing in Cas's bed."

"How thoughtful of you. Where, then?"

"The guest room." Will John gestured with his head. "Around the staircase and down the corridor, at the back of the first level."

Sharon followed the congressman's direction, her gaze coming to rest on the open kitchen door. Cas now entertained Mattie Ruth and Paul Benedict with some photos. "Probably wouldn't do to inspect the scene right now," Sharon said. "What's in there?"

"Doubles as a sitting room," Will John said. "There's a daybed."

"A convertible sofa?"

"Yes."

"Which you folded down during playtime?"

The congressman's look showed irritation. "Look, this isn't funny."

"No, it isn't. This next bit will be even less amusing. The girl's autopsy revealed penetration, fore and aft, and there were pubic hairs between her teeth. I need details."

Russ suddenly seemed very interested in an ornament on the tree. Will John stared into space.

"Okay," Sharon said. "By the numbers. Did she perform oral sex on you?"

Will John paled. "She bragged . . . liked to say, it was her specialty."

"I won't inquire as to her competence in that area," Sharon said. "But if she said that to you, likely she said that to others. Other men she was with. It could be important. So, was the guest room also the scene of the whipped cream incident?"

Will John rubbed his forehead. "Yes."

"You licked it off her?"

"Isn't that the way it's usually done?"

"I wouldn't know, Will John. But there will be saliva residue, translating to more nails in your coffin. Was she the only treat, or did she make a sundae of you as well?"

Will John looked ready to throw up. "Both."

"You didn't lick her clean enough. There was enough residue for the coroner to have a taste." Sharon arched an eyebrow. "Penetration after foreplay, or vice versa?"

Will John raised his voice. "My God, how could that possibly matter?" In the brief silence which followed, Cas Benedict closed the kitchen door with a farewell thud.

"It won't, unless you take the stand in your own

defense." Sharon enunciated carefully, wanting her words to sink in. "But if you do you're going to have to tell this in front of twelve tried and true, not to mention a national audience. If you get the events out of sequence, the prosecution will likely have forensic evidence to refute you. The slightest lie that shows up under cross, and you're toast." Sharon gentled her tone. "I'm being this way because it's necessary, Will John. It may take years for you to realize it's for your own good, but it is."

Will John looked to Russell Black. "This is just horrible," the congressman said.

"*Murder* is horrible," Sharon replied as Black shuffled his feet in silence. She switched gears. "Enough of that for now. Between now and when this is over, you should relive every second of that evening. Assume you'll have to tell this story, and tell it exactly right. So moving on. After the sex, what happened then?"

"She . . . sent me on a shopping trip. Those were her words, not mine."

Sharon's forehead tightened. "You went out to buy something?"

"That's right."

"And left her here alone?"

"Yes. Why, is something . . . ?"

Sharon shook her head in wonderment. "It just sounds so unbelievable. You're having a tryst in your own house, then the trystee sends you out for groceries."

"I can't help how it sounds."

"You may well wish you could at some point. You left her in bed?"

"Yes."

"Jesus Christ, weren't you afraid of nosy neighbors or something?"

"I wasn't thinking clearly."

"Obviously." Sharon got up from the love seat, smoothed her skirt in back, and sat back down. "What did you go out to buy?"

Will John's eyes misted. "Drugs."

"Oh, lovely. From a known dealer?"

"I don't know how well he's known. He furnishes for some other members of Congress. I talked to him face-to-face that night, and he'll remember it. I don't know if he has a criminal record, if you're worried about his credibility."

"It doesn't matter. Even if he's never gotten a parking ticket, getting someone to testify that he saw you while he was selling you a load of cocaine, that might be difficult." Sharon paused in thought. "Did you make any other stops while you were out?"

Will John's gaze wavered. "One."

"Where?"

"She wanted some . . . other things."

"I'll warn you, for the umpteenth time," Sharon said. "Beating around the bush is a waste of time. What things?"

"Sex toys. She was spending the night here."

Sharon blinked. "You mean, such as dildos and whatnot?"

"A . . . vibrating penis. A couple of other things. I went to a shop in Maryland. Christ, the last thing she ever said to me was, 'Get me the biggest one they . . .' Jesus."

"So your alibi witnesses, if we can find them, would be a drug dealer and a sex shop employee." Sharon turned toward Russell Black. "I don't think we can afford to put our client on the stand."

Black stepped away from the Christmas tree, hands dejectedly thrust into his pockets. "Might not be the best idea."

"If we can't use an affirmative defense," Sharon said, "then we'll have to take the passive approach. Hope that their evidence won't stand up. I'm just guessing here, but their main witnesses could be a problem for them. Those two joggers. If they could positively identify the guy they saw coming out of the woods, we'd have read that in the paper by now. It's something I'll talk over with Mr. Gray and Mrs. Welton. I'm not sure if we should try to locate this mystery man or hope the prosecution can't. This decision could be a toss-up. Okay, returning to the events of the evening. What did you . . . ?"

Sharon paused. Will John was watching the floor. Sharon said, "What is it?"

Will John inhaled through his nose. "I suppose I should get it out in the open."

"What, you know who the mystery man was? That might not be so bad. If we have to find him, we can."

Will John lifted his chin and looked Sharon in the eyes. "He'll be easy to find," the congressman said. "Look no further."

Sharon was puzzled. "I thought you left her alone in bed. You said, the last thing she told you . . ."

"The last thing she said to me when she was alive. I didn't tell you that I never saw her again." Will John stared helplessly out the window. "I have to use the bathroom. Lord, things are looking bad for me, aren't they?"

Will John left the room and walked slowly down the corridor with his head down. Cas Benedict opened the kitchen door and stuck her head through the opening. Sharon held up a restraining hand, smiling. "We're not finished," she said. "Just taking a break." Cas showed an irritated smirk and pulled back into the kitchen. Sharon said to Russ, "What do you think?"

"I've seen defendants with better stories." Black retreated from the Christmas tree, sat in a rocker, and crossed his legs. "This one sounds so cock-and-bull, it just might be true."

"One would hope a law school graduate has a better imagination, if he's making it all up."

Black frowned. "You keep the pressure on him, young lady. Trip him up if you can."

Sharon changed her position on the love seat. "Don't worry, I will. Know what, old boss? I don't think Will John loves me anymore."

"How much of this have you told your parents and Cas?" Sharon asked.

Will John had just returned from relieving himself, but looked even more uncomfortable than before. He said, "My mother, all of it. I haven't spoken to Dad about anything. Cas I've told very little. She's hard to reason with. I'll be lucky to come through this with my marriage intact."

Sharon didn't think that getting a divorce from Cas-

sandra Mason Benedict would be the most tragic thing
that could happen to Will John, but didn't say so. She
arched her back. "This is going to change your life,
and there's really nothing you can do about it. Let's
go on."

Will John nodded sadly, like a man headed for the
gallows. He exhaled a long, resigned breath. "When I
left Courtney alone in bed, I was gone a couple of
hours. Bought two ounces of cocaine in a bar and
several items in a sex shop."

"I don't suppose we're lucky enough that you have
a dated, time-stamped receipt."

"No. I paid cash."

The congressman had apparently made up his mind
to stick to the facts, and that much was encouraging.
Sharon said, "Write down the name and address of
the bar and the . . . call it an adult bookstore or
something. There'll be enough emphasis on sex in this
case without us adding any. And God help us if we
have to use any of the place's employees as witnesses." She tore a page from her legal pad, laid the
page on the coffee table, produced a ballpoint from
her purse, and placed the pen on top of the paper.

Will John picked up the pen and hesitated. "Now?"

Sharon nodded. "While it's fresh in your mind.
Also, to be frank, so you won't have an opportunity
to look up a couple of names in the phone book,
places you've never really visited in your life, and
claim you went to them. I've told you earlier, I'm
treating this as though I don't believe a word you're
saying. I'm going to verify everything you tell us. The

prosecution will do the same. No one trusts a murder suspect, so you may as well learn to deal with it."

Will John bent his head to write. "I suppose I deserve that last part."

"Indeed you do," Sharon said.

The ballpoint made a scratching noise as Will John wrote something down, stopped to think, then added a few words. He pushed the paper aside. "There. The bartender knows me. The sex shop clerk . . . let's say he's seen me before."

"Ah, a regular," Sharon said. "Nothing like testimony that you were on the peep-show stool every Friday to put the jurors squarely in your corner. Do you remember what you bought?"

"The vibrating . . . thing. Rented a video. Bought a—"

"You don't have to tell me. The main thing, be certain that whatever list you give can be checked out."

Will John scooted around uneasily. "I returned with the goods around two in the morning. Courtney was in bed with the lights out. At first I thought she was asleep, so I got undressed and got in with her. Christ, the sheets were soaked. I turned on the lights. I never would have thought there was that much blood in the world."

"Bloody sheets? Blankets? What did you do with them?"

"I was too stunned to move at first. Then I jumped up and turned on the lights. My . . . *God.* The back of her head was missing. All I could think of was Cas, what she'd think. I panicked. I had to try to cover up what had happened, don't you see?" Will John's look was haunted, wide-eyed, and fearful.

"The prosecution will see it that you had the presence of mind to do away with the evidence. Spare us the theatrics, you may need them later. What did you do then?"

"I . . . got some plastic garbage bags from the kitchen."

Sharon pictured the autopsy photos. "What about her hands?"

Will John frowned in puzzlement. "They looked clean. I put on rubber kitchen gloves, so I don't think I left my fingerprints."

Sharon sighed in exasperation, rolling her eyes in Russ's direction. She said, "What difference does that make? You left your pubic hairs on her body and residue from your mouth in the whipped cream on her leg. Think, now. The autopsy photos showed ligature marks around her wrists. Are you saying her hands weren't tied?"

"Oh." Will John's gaze darted evasively to one side. "That came later."

Sharon was astonished. "What came later?"

"It was me. I bound her wrists."

Sharon leaned back and drew a deep breath. "Why in God's name would you do that?"

"I had to get rid of the body, somewhere. I had the presence of mind to know that sometime, someone would find her. I thought, if her hands were tied, it would look more like the work of . . . a sadist, maybe."

"Which is how you'll be pictured," Sharon said. "Where did you buy the rope?"

"I had it around the house, in the garage. It came from Home Depot."

"That's a plus. The rope's common variety, could have come from anywhere. You'll be hearing about it again. I suppose you had the body in your trunk when you went in to do your shopping."

Will John nodded.

Sharon laid her notepad aside, batoning her pen between her fingers. "Be careful with details. If you don't get everything exactly right, they'll crucify you."

Will John spoke like a man reading a script. "I wrapped her body in plastic, stowed the bloody sheets and blankets in garbage bags."

"What did you do with them?"

Will John shrugged. "Tossed them in a dumpster, en route. I couldn't really pinpoint the location."

"Pray that the police can't, either," Sharon said. "Likely they won't need to, because I suspect that at least a minute quantity of blood seeped through the bedclothes onto the mattress. They'll find it. I assume the same mattress is still on the bed in there."

Will John looked in alarm toward the hallway.

Russell Black leaned sharply forward. "Don't even think about it, son."

Will John gaped at him.

"Disposin' of more evidence is the worst thing you could do right now," Black said. "You can count on, there's somebody watchin' your every move. It'll be better for you if they find the mattress here than someplace you've dumped it. Just leave it alone. It's not a hundred percent they'll even look in your guest room, so as of now, just keep your mouth shut to everybody except me an' Miss Hays."

Will John sagged in defeat.

Sharon asked, "Wasn't she nude when you left her alive in bed?"

"Yes." The congressman's words sounded hollow.

"The corpse in the park wore a cocktail dress. A fact that's been painfully prominent in the news."

"Yes. I put it on her. I felt I had to get rid of any traces of her that might be in the house."

"I've got to tell you, the fact that you weren't too shook up to carefully dress the body and then dispose of her, that isn't going to look good. Eliminates certain defenses for us, such as heat-of-the-moment, which amounts to manslaughter. So you drove her to Rock Creek Park and dragged her off into the woods?" Sharon asked.

Will John nodded dumbly, all the fight gone from him. "Those two joggers."

"As I said, I don't think they can identify you, at least not without coaching from the detectives. Look for the joggers to be positive it was you, when they testify. Odd as it seems, that may be the best thing you have going for you, if we can establish they've changed their stories from what they originally told the police."

"I looked away from them as I passed. Lord, I've never been so scared."

"Now that part I can believe." Sharon picked up her legal pad. Russell Black pinched his pants leg. Sharon said, "Let me make sure I have the story right. You brought the girl here and had sex with her. Then you went out for drugs and vibrating dildos. On your return you found her dead, with blood all over, and your reaction was to dispose of the body."

Will John looked desperate. "It's the truth, I swear, no matter how it sounds." He looked to Black, then at Sharon. "The more I talk the worse it looks," the congressman said. "Do I have a chance here, or are we just kidding ourselves."

Sharon exchanged a look with Black. She dropped her legal pad into her satchel. "Officially, until we interview witnesses and get our investigators on the trail of something, I don't know. And that's what we'll tell your wife and your parents, that we just don't know as yet." Her expression grew deadly serious. "But on the level, Will John. The prosecution makes no noises whatsoever that they're willing to make a plea offer, so that's not a consideration at present. But in the future, any deal, any deal at all, we should consider with an open mind. If we tried to tell the tale you've just given us to a jury, I'm afraid we'd be spinning our wheels."

Paul Benedict said as he looked out the kitchen window, "There's a public function tonight. 'Christmas in Washington,' a television special. Alanis Morissette, Whitney Houston, some groups from the sixties. The President and First Lady. Everyone in the Senate and House who can possibly make it. Everyone inside the Beltway who's anyone. I don't see how Will John can miss it."

Sharon made a face. She couldn't stand Clinton's music, "Somethin's Happenin' Here" and all that crap, songs from the Vietnam era, and Clinton himself being a draft dodger. She wished that Clinton had been a Waylon and Willie fan. She watched her former teacher's back, which was the only way she could look directly at Paul Benedict, with him facing away from her. She and Russ were seated on one side of the breakfast table, with Cas and Mattie Ruth across from them. Will John was at the head of the table, his gaze vacantly off in space.

Russ said, "Easy. Nobody's going to expect him to go to some party with everything he's facin'."

Paul Benedict spun around. "Exactly my point. The image should be confidence, that it's business as usual. Total seclusion will seem a sign of guilt."

"I got to disagree," Black said. "It'll be a sign of a man that's takin' this deadly serious. You want the nation to see a murder suspect out dancin' the Watusi?"

"No. I want the nation to see a respected member of Congress, face-to-face, smiling as an innocent man would smile."

Cas Benedict flipped her hair back over one shoulder. "Besides, I'm going regardless. I'll look ridiculous without my husband."

You would go out, Sharon thought, just to see and be seen. Not many women in your circumstance would have the nerve. But you, yeah. You'll be there with bells on.

Will John watched his wife as if frightened to death of her. "I'll go if you want me to, Cas," he said.

Black bent from the waist and rested his forearms

on the table, speaking to his client. "Your choice, Will John. It can backfire."

Paul Benedict jammed his hands into his pockets and walked forward a couple of steps, toward the table. "He should be there. And I think his attorneys should go with him."

"I can't go along with that reasonin'," Black said. "Aside from the fact that I couldn' enjoy Christmas music with all those politicians hangin' around, what's it goin' to look like? I can see the headline now. THE CONGRESSMAN ACCOMPANIED BY HIS LAWYERS."

Mattie Ruth folded her hands and chimed in, her chin held high. "Oh, hell's bells, Russell, there'll be headlines anyhow. The press already saw you and Sharon, outside here a little while ago, and it's gonna make them thirsty for more. So face 'em. I think the two of you oughtta make some comment."

"I'd be adverse, Mattie. You've had your words twisted by the newspapers enough so's you know it idn a good idea."

Paul Benedict came forward and laid a hand on his wife's shoulder. He looked at Black intently. "Just the newspapers, yeah, if they were the only media present. It's suicide to talk to them. But there'll be television cameras. Everything you say will be documented on videotape. What you say will be what you say."

"Dammit." Black slapped the table with the palm of his hand. "The time to do our talkin' is at trial."

Sharon hesitated. The thought of backing up Paul Benedict gave her the heebies, but . . . "Maybe not in this circumstance, boss," she finally said.

Black exhaled through his nose as he looked at her.

"Ninety-nine percent of the time you'd be right. But if nothing else, the media's going to be interviewing people left and right, for comments. With us there in person, certain ones might not say what they would behind our backs."

Black leaned back and folded his arms. "I just don't like such gatherin's."

"I don't either. But sometimes they're necessary." Sharon ignored Mattie Ruth, Paul Benedict, Will John, and Cas, leaned closer to her mentor and flirtatiously patted Russ's hand. "Besides," she said, "what girl in her right mind would miss a function like that? Especially when she'd be with the handsomest man in town."

11

As Sharon and Russ questioned Will John Benedict at his town house, there was a meeting in progress at 500 Indiana Avenue. What had begun as a two-man chat in Prosecutor Cedric Hyde's cubbyhole had grown into a summit affair. As word spread and additional participants arrived, the crowd first spilled out into the corridor and then adjourned to the second-floor conference room.

The original head-to-head session between Hyde and Gregory Campisi, the duly appointed United States Attorney for the District of Columbia, was somewhat awkward since the two had never met before. Campisi, in fact, had had to get directions to 500 Indiana Avenue just as Sharon Hays had done earlier, and from the same assistant at the main USDA headquarters who'd given Sharon the information. Never in recent memory had two people asked the way to 500 Indiana on the same day. The assistant wondered what in hell was going on over there.

Campisi had decided to visit the low-rent district so that Hyde could bring him up-to-date on the murder investigation involving U.S. Congressman Will John Benedict. The USDA had had numerous media inquiries, and wanted to be certain that his series of no-comments didn't come back to haunt him in the future. During the conference, Campisi asked several questions to which Hyde didn't have the answer. Rather than admit he didn't know his ass from his elbow about the case, Hyde called his second chair, Sally Pong, and told her to sit in.

The summons to Hyde's office caught Pong off guard. Determined not to botch her opportunity to shine in front of the USDA himself, she called in reinforcements from police headquarters, and delayed her arrival at the meeting until Detectives Ginny Toledo and Isaac Brown showed up to go with her. Toledo and Brown had orders to keep Howard Morganthal apprised of all developments, so dutifully informed the C of D's secretary that they were headed for 500 Indiana to help Pong fill Gregory Campisi in on the details of the investigation.

On returning from a discreet lunch with Rita Carboneau, Howard Morganthal hit the ceiling. Christ, now Greg Campisi was sticking his nose in. Like Morganthal, Campisi had his own network of media contacts, and all Morganthal needed was for Campisi to go leaking information to the wrong people. Incensed, Morganthal canceled his afternoon meetings and hustled over to 500 Indiana, arriving just as Cedric Hyde led Gregory Campisi, Sally Pong, Ginny Toledo, and Isaac Brown to the second-floor conference room. Morganthal smirked at Campisi and then fell in step at the rear.

So here they sat, Campisi and Morganthal at opposite ends of the table, Pong and Hyde holding down the side across from Toledo and Brown. One of Pong's two thick file folders lay open in front of her. Toledo had a large folder as well, while Brown had brought along a series of near-indecipherable notes he'd taken on paper napkins and steno pads. It was likely the first meeting in the history of 500 Indiana where one of the participants wore a tux, cumberbund and all. Gregory Campisi's explanation for the formal wear was that he would be too busy to go home and change before attending "Christmas in Washington" at the Kennedy Center that evening. Sticking prominently out of his breast pocket, causing Campisi's underlings to drool, were his tickets to the event. Howard Morganthal had left his own tux back at the office, and was mentally cursing himself for the oversight. "Christmas in Washington" was the social function of the week, and everyone who was anyone would be there. As soon as Campisi had explained his own wearing of the tuxedo, Morganthal had dropped in the information that he was going to Kennedy Center that night as well.

Morganthal touched manicured fingers together. "I think it's time to be talking probable cause." He didn't add that Rita Carboneau was about to hint in her column that an arrest was imminent, a matter which the C of D's had discussed with Carboneau over oysters Rockefeller less than two hours earlier.

Campisi, a dark-complexioned man with a shock of jet black hair, had a dilemma. He was a Democratic appointee. Part of the reason for his visit today was that certain bigwigs, including the President's National Security Advisor, had expressed dismay that Russell

Black and Sharon Hays had said they wouldn't provide the Party any details. Campisi said, "We don't want to jump the gun here."

Morganthal spread his hands, palms up. "What's jumping the gun? We have a witness who saw him leaving the scene of the crime. Anyone else, we'd have locked up days ago."

The cops and AUSDAs swiveled their heads back and forth like spectators at a tennis match.

"Exactly the point," Campisi said. "This isn't just anyone. We are talking charging a member of the House of Representatives."

Morganthal's boss, the chief of the Metropolitan Police Force, owed his job to a group of Republicans. The C of D's exchanged a look with Toledo and Brown, then said, "Which makes us more vulnerable in the public eye. We've already got people calling, accusing us of playing favorites. Detective Toledo, we do have a positive ID, don't we? The . . . stranger in the park, the two joggers . . ."

Ginny Toledo turned to a portion of her file where she'd placed a bookmark. "To be explicit, sir, the man is positive. The woman isn't so sure."

"Is he positive enough to execute an affidavit, that we could take to a judge to get a warrant?"

"It would appear so, Mr. Morganthal. We haven't asked him that direct question."

"If he will, then what's the problem?"

"I don't see that there is one. But didn't we agree that we'd hold off until we could get samples from the suspect, for DNA comparison?"

Morganthal waved a hand. "We might have discussed it. I don't know that we made any agreement with anybody."

"Now hold on here, Howard." Campisi cut in, then directed his words to Cedric Hyde. "Haven't you been in contact with the congressman's lawyers?"

Cedric Hyde's tone was uncertain, like a man's who was in heavier company than he was accustomed to. "Law*yer*, Mr. Campisi. Singular. Miss Hays. Mr. Black didn't see fit to grace us with his presence."

"Rude, perhaps," Campisi said, "but not necessarily sinister. Did you make any agreements with Miss Hays?"

"I didn't. Did you, Sally?" He looked relieved to take the spotlight off himself and place the beam squarely on his assistant.

Pong was ready. She spoke up quickly. "I made no agreement with her. But wasn't there something said while we were all in your office, about when we could get Mr. Benedict's samples?"

Hyde was emphatic. "No way did I promise anything. I told her we'd expect an answer in the morning, but made no promises. In fact, she asked me if we'd keep them advised before we arrested their client, and I told her no. You recall that, don't you?"

"That's right," Pong said. "You did. And once we have the suspect in jail, getting a court order for his samples will be a piece of cake."

Morganthal checked his watch. "If we could get an affidavit executed by the witness in the next hour, we could likely get it to a judge before the day is over." He frowned in thought. If he effected an arrest before Rita Carboneau's column hit the streets, Carboneau would be pissed. He'd have to chance it. He made a mental note that as soon as this meeting was over, he'd have to get Carboneau on the phone.

Campisi took a final, desperate stab. "I'd think before we went off half-cocked, we'd want to get our prosecutors together to be certain we've dotted our *i*'s and crossed our *t*'s. In a legal sense."

Pong spoke brightly up. "We're covered in that regard, sir."

Campisi masked his disappointment. "There's something else to consider. If we get the warrant, go to Benedict's home and he's not there, our suspect will be alerted that we're looking for him. Wouldn't it be better to wait until we're certain where he's going to be at a given time?"

Morganthal zeroed in on the ticket in Campisi's breast pocket. "That's easily taken care of," the C of D's said. "We're certain where he'll be tonight, aren't we?"

The entire group gazed at Morganthal in puzzlement.

"Where everyone who's anyone will be," Morganthal said. "Tell me, Greg. Does buying a ticket entitle you to a guest list?"

All eyes on him, Campisi hid his dejection and unfolded a slip of paper he'd been carrying in his breast pocket. He scanned the list, showing hope, then his mouth turned down in disappointment. "He's on here," the U.S. Attorney said. "Congressman Will John Benedict. Party of four."

12

Sharon and Russ returned to the hotel to clean up and change. As they parted company on their floor outside the elevator, Black wore a glum expression. He absolutely hated social functions. Sharon considered advising her boss that this would be a formal affair, but changed her mind. Russ would dress as he damned well pleased; he'd wear a dark suit, but that would be as far as he'd go. After a quick see-you-in-an-hour, Sharon hustled down the corridor to her room. She wondered about her own motives. Had she insisted on attending "Christmas in Washington" because she thought it would help their client, or was she getting caught up in the whirl? In a place like D.C., getting caught up would be easy to do.

She showered and dressed, wriggling around on the bed like a model in a jeans commercial as she put on her panty hose and, once she'd slithered into her cocktail dress, twirling in front of the mirror to view herself from every possible angle. She stepped into wine-colored suede spike-heeled shoes, shook out her mink jacket, sniffed the fur, and tossed the jacket on the bed. She was glad that the previous summer she'd sprung for the cost of putting the fur in storage; she hadn't worn it in several years, and a couple of seasons ago had hung the mink in her closet and stuffed the pockets with mothballs. She'd finally had the mink cleaned and stored only because, someday when she was gone, she didn't want Melanie to gag from the odor as she received her inheritance from dear old Mom. She took her lone pair of diamond-chip earrings from her overnight case, poked one post through a pieced lobe and fixed the catch, and was tugging down on her other ear when she froze in place. The message light on her phone blinked monotonously. Sharon dropped her hand to her side, loosely holding the pieces of her earring.

Damn, she'd been playing phone tag with Sheila all day. Earlier she'd even left the number for Will John Benedict's condo, in case Sheila's call was an emergency. Either Sheila hadn't gotten the message or she didn't want to discuss anything earth-shattering, since she'd chosen to leave the message at the hotel once again. Sharon picked up the receiver and punched in her voice mail, and sure enough it was Sheila who had called. She hurriedly punched in her best friend's number but missed connections once again. She listened to Sheila's recorded message fifteen hundred miles away, waited for the tone, and briefly licked her lips as she gathered her thoughts.

Finally she said into the mouthpiece, "It's Sharon, babe. I'm going out to . . . well, I'll fill you in on the details later, but it's a tony affair. Suppose we're going to have to spring for cell phones, huh, so we can interrupt each other fifty times a day to chat. Anyway, toodle-oo, but I'll find a pay phone where I am and call you back at exactly ten p.m. That's nine your time. If your phone rings at straight-up nine, it'll be me."

She hung up, affixed her other earring, shrugged into her mink, artfully tousled the front of her hair, scooped up her evening purse, and headed out the door. She paused in the exit and glanced once more at the phone, feeling a slight tremor of dread. No way had anything happened to Melanie, or Sheila would be having her paged all over town. Sharon secured the lock, stepped out into the hall, and softly closed the door.

It was snowing lightly as the taxicab made the curve off New Hampshire Avenue onto Rock Creek Parkway, and neared the majestic entry to Kennedy Center. The mammoth structure literally glowed, flakes drifting down, moisture-formed halos around the sodium lights at the perimeter of the building, the whole scene like a picture on a greeting card. There was a block-long row of taxis and limos waiting to deposit passengers, and the taxi driver braked and got in line. Russell Black watched the proceedings in silence, his nose casting a shadow across his cheek, and Sharon thought her mentor's expression resembled Commander's look when she banished the shepherd to the yard.

She reached over and patted Russ's arm. "It'll be over before you know it, old boss," she said.

Black rested his chin on his lightly clenched fist. "Not near soon enough."

Sharon made her tone nice and cheery. "Come on. It's Christmas in Washington."

"Yeah, right," Black said. "All kind of Santy Clauses running around this city. Keep an eye on me while the show's going on, girl. If you don't poke me every once in a while, I'm liable to snore."

Row after row of portable bars were set up in the lobby, encircling a glistening ceiling-high Christmas tree, with men and women in vests and bow ties pouring highballs, dispensing Evian water, or rattling chrome interlocking cocktail shakers. Russ wasn't the only man not wearing a tux, though he was definitely in the minority. As for the women—holy cannoli, Sharon thought—she didn't think she'd ever seen so many fox and ermine jackets in one room before. She recognized several high-profile senators, chatting in groups of four or five, and one actor whom she'd seen in bit parts and TV commercials. Russ went off to find a Scotch and water for her and a beer for him. She slipped her evening purse into her jacket pocket and waited near a granite pillar.

Most of the crowd was clustered near the main entry, where the First Couple along with their entourage of secret service agents would make their appearance. Formally dressed men and women pretended to sip and visit while shooting surreptitious glances toward the street in search of the White House limo. As Sharon watched, Will John Benedict entered the lobby with Cas on his arm, and with Paul and Mattie Ruth a couple of paces behind him. There was a pause in the hubbub of conversation among the crowd, a lowering of voices as people put their heads together in gossip mode. Sharon turned away. No way, ever again in her life, did she intend to face Paul Benedict without Russell Black as a buffer in between. As she searched the bar area with her gaze, a husky female voice said from behind her, "Well. The famous Miss Hays."

Sharon turned. Rita Carboneau's pictures on her book jackets and in the newspapers missed the mark; the features were the same, the coiffed hair and surgery-enhanced body just as stunning, but the photos were air-brushed and hid much of the toughness in Carboneau's look. The face was wrinkle free, but the glitter in the eyes said, "been there, done that," to every question imaginable. Sharon stood her ground and didn't say anything.

Carboneau was dressed in a silver low-cut sheath with a stole around her shoulders. She said, "The TV pictures don't do you justice, Sharon. I'm Rita Carboneau." She extended her hand. She wore soft white, forearm-length gloves with a diamond bracelet around her right wrist. That bracelet is ten thousand bucks' worth if it's a dime, Sharon thought.

Sharon didn't want to shake this woman's hand, but didn't see that she had any choice. She offered a medium grip. "Your pictures don't do you justice, either, Ms. Carboneau."

Carboneau's smile had a sharklike quality. "Rita. Call me Rita. Please."

Sharon saw no point in putting this woman on. She dropped her hand to her side. "I'd rather not, Ms. Carboneau."

Carboneau arched an eyebrow. Her smile appeared

frozen in place. "Oh? Do I detect a hint of touchiness here?"

Sharon mildly shrugged her shoulders, conscious that all at once she and Carboneau were the center of attention, faces turning toward them from all directions. She wondered fleetingly how this confrontation would play in tomorrow's *Post*. She said, "I think what you detect is a hint of, we both know who's on what side."

Carboneau wore large diamond earrings and a necklace to match. "I'm not on any side, Sharon. What's happening is news."

"Oh, I don't have any problem with the reporting," Sharon said. "It's the slanting that bugs me."

A young man walked up behind Carboneau, a guy around thirty, a hunk with broad shoulders, thick dark hair, and a Cary Grantish cleft in his chin. He carried two stemmed glasses filled with bubbly something-or-other, and offered one to Carboneau. The author took the drink and the guy stood back. Carboneau touched her necklace as she said to Sharon, "Am I getting it right, that it would be pointless for me to ask for an interview?"

Sharon couldn't help laughing, though she thought it to her credit that she held her mirth down to a polite chuckle. "For free?" Sharon said.

Carboneau frowned.

"I've got to tell you," Sharon said, "that it's a bit insulting that you'd ask to talk to me without offering at least your going rate."

Carboneau didn't try to hide her anger. Her voice

trembled. "Would the same go for Russell Black?" She looked beyond Sharon, over her shoulder.

Sharon followed the author's gaze. Russ was on his way, with a highball glass in one hand and a bottle of Heinekin's in the other. Sharon supposed that he'd been gone longer than she'd expected because the bartender couldn't locate any Budweiser on tap. She turned back to Rita Carboneau. "Trying to interview Russ," Sharon said, "would be a bigger waste of time than trying to interview me."

Carboneau tightened her mouth. "Oh? Wouldn't you like to get your client's side of the story before the public?"

"Yes," Sharon said, "but not at the cost. Tell you what, though. How about, tit for tat? You can interview us and we'll interview you at the same time. You can take notes on what we have to say and we'll do the same."

Carboneau moved back a step. The hunk put his arm protectively around her. Carboneau said, "I doubt I'd have any information that would interest you."

"Oh? How about, who you're paying for all this inside information I'm reading in your column? That's something that would help in our client's defense." Sharon smiled at Black as her mentor walked up, and took her drink from Russ's hand. Black eyed the author with a curious scowl. Sharon said, "How about it, Ms. Carboneau? You interested?"

Carboneau breathed in through her nose. She leaned against her escort, then turned to walk away. "Nice meeting you, Sharon," Rita Carboneau said in a dismissive tone.

*   *   *

Paul Benedict tried to maneuver things around so that Sharon would have to sit beside him during the performance. She wasn't imagining things, though his routine was pretty slick. As Sharon followed the Benedict family down the aisle with Russ a step behind her, her former law school prof was in the lead with Mattie Ruth behind him, Cas trailing her mother-in-law, and Will John walking behind his wife with his head down. Mattie Ruth wore a taffeta gown with a full skirt to her ankles, while Cas had on a hugging green cocktail dress that was short enough to show her legs and figure to their best advantage. Congressman's wife or no, Cas had stayed toned and in shape through the years, and Sharon wouldn't have been female if she hadn't drawn a comparison to herself. A tie at worst, she thought with a hint of smugness, though in truth I think I've got her beat. At thirty-five years of age and a shade under five-feet-ten, Sharon Hays could still fit comfortably into a size nine. She thought that strict dieting and twice-a-week morning runs were probably worth the agony. Not bad for a teenager's mom, Sharon thought, if I do say so myself.

Their seats were choice, six across beginning at the aisle and four rows from the front, three behind where Bill and Hillary would sit surrounded by bodyguards. Paul Benedict stood aside to let Mattie Ruth enter the row. Cas waited expectantly in the aisle for him to follow her. The older man said brusquely, "Tell you what. Let's do girl-girl-boy-boy. I need a word with my son." He held out his hand in an usher's pose.

Cas nodded and paraded obediently in to sit beside

her mother-in-law. Will John paused until his father told him, "Go ahead," then edged his way down the row and took the chair alongside Cas. Now Paul Benedict brushed past Sharon as she stood in the aisle, leaving the two end seats for her and Russ. God, just the touch of Paul Benedict's clothing against her skin made her insides wriggle. He sat, and locked gazes with Sharon as he waited for her to take the seat beside him, leaving the aisle position for Russ. Sharon's choices were to sit down beside the man who'd once tried to rape her, or create a scene right here in Kennedy Center in front of God and everybody.

Sharon said to Black, "Listen, boss, you mind if I take the aisle? I've been missing calls from Sheila and might have to get up to use the phone." She blinked apologetically. "Might not look like the most gentlemanly arrangement to the onlookers." She nodded toward the audience at large. "But believe me it's the most practical."

Black hesitated, puzzled. "I guess it won't hurt," he finally said, then plopped down alongside Paul Benedict. Sharon sat on the end, and couldn't help grinning inwardly at Benedict's sigh of disappointment. And the horse you rode in on, you bastard, Sharon thought with a touch of glee.

The show was a knockout, and Sharon jiggled her foot in rhythm as Aretha Franklin, Gladys Knight, and Whitney Houston sang "Silver Bells" in round, with the two rock divas beginning the song and Whitney really belting out the final stanzas, the Washington Philharmonic jazzing up the number in the background.

Three rows in front of Sharon, the President's head bobbed up and down, and the First Lady looked as if she'd like to dance in the aisle. Even the secret service agents seated around the Prez and his missus snapped their fingers. Russell Black watched stoically, his cheek resting on his clenched fist, and Sharon came within an inch of knocking Russ's elbow off the armrest to get his attention. Absently, she checked her watch, then stiffened and sat bolt upright. God, three minutes until ten.

She looked frantically around, holding the watch up to her ear. The timepiece ticked steadily away. Could this show have been going on more than two hours? She couldn't believe it. She'd promised to call Sheila at ten, and this time she wasn't going to be late. Without a word to Russ, she got up and headed for the exit. Leaving in the midst of a performance was a no-no, of course—though, Sharon thought wryly, that hadn't stopped New York crowds from walking out during some of the turkeys in which she'd acted off-Broadway—and she was glad she'd timed her departure during such a rousing number. All the way up the aisle, heads jiggled and fingers popped, and no one seemed to notice the rude young woman in wine-colored shoes as she hustled out of the auditorium. Chalk it up to my being from Texas, folks, Sharon thought, and assume I just don't know any better.

The thick exit door swung closed behind her, muffling the sound from the stage, and the sudden quiet in the lobby was deafening. Two bartenders shot the bull near one of the pillars and a uniformed guard stood just inside the entrance. Sharon's soles whispered on carpet as she skirted the Christmas tree on her way to the bank of phones. She picked up the receiver, punched in zero plus Sheila's number, waited for the gong-prompt and then entered her calling card, and leaned against the wall with the phone jammed between her cheek and shoulder. Through a forest of pillars the main entrance was visible, and something about the guard drew Sharon's attention. This was no security employee; this potbellied guy wore the uniform of the Washington PD. As Sharon watched, three more cops came in from the street to stand with the first policeman. They wore overcoats and gloves. Sharon frowned. Sheila answered on the third ring.

"It's me, babe," Sharon said. "Finally getting together with you."

There were a couple of beats of silence, after which Sheila said in a hushed tone, "Can you talk?"

"Sure, what's . . ." A tremor of dread paraded up Sharon's spine like prickling icicles. "Melanie's all right, isn't she?"

"She's not hurt, if that's what you're asking."

The plastic mouthpiece brushed Sharon's lips. "What's wrong, Sheila?"

"Probably not as much as I'm letting on. It's all part of growing up."

Sharon breathed in as, visible through the glass entrance, three squad cars pulled up to the curb followed by two unmarked sedans. She said to Sheila, "If you don't tell me what's wrong, and right now, I'm going to—"

"I'm not being coy, old girl," Sheila said. "It's just that I don't know the gentlest way to break the news.

I've debated not even telling you, frankly, and the soul-searching I've done over the past twenty-four hours you wouldn't believe."

"Sheila . . ."

"Melanie went out last night. Through the bedroom window. It was just a freak that I know about it. Trish is taking a prescription for a two-day bug she caught last week, nothing serious, but I went in about eleven to be sure she hadn't forgotten her pill. Trish was in bed with a bunch of pillows stuffed under the covers to stimulate Melanie. I'll say this for my little girl, she's no stool pigeon. Took an hour under the heat lamp and a session with the rubber hose, but I finally sweated it out of her."

Sharon turned her back to the Kennedy Center lobby and lowered her head. Sheila's humor was forced, as if she was softening a blow. "Where did Melanie go?" Sharon asked.

"I don't think it's anything earth-shattering," Sheila said. "Think back to your own youth, the tricks you pulled."

"Where did she go, Sheila?" Sharon snapped, then immediately felt remorse. Sheila was only trying to help. Sharon said, more softly, "I can take it, if you're trying to protect me from something."

Sheila exhaled a long slow sigh. "Trish finally confessed that Melanie was out with a boy. An older boy. In a car."

Sharon sagged against the phone stand. She'd done the same thing as a teenager, with an eighteen year old named Buster Long when she was fifteen. He'd taken her to Flagpole Hill, forcibly yanked down her pants, and Sharon had fought for her life to get away from the guy. The incident had scared her so badly that she hadn't dated for a year, and at her age had frightened her even more than the time when Paul Benedict had tried to rape her. She said to Sheila, "Tell me all of it."

Sheila's voice was an emotionless monotone, the psychiatrist in her working overtime as she lapsed into patient-doctor mode. "After Trish told me where Melanie had gone and outlined her escape route, I parked myself on the back porch in a lawn chair. Melanie came scrambling over the fence about five in the morning. She was sobbing, so hysterically that she was halfway across the yard to the bedroom window before she realized I was sitting there.

"I soft-pedaled it as much as possible," Sheila said, "without coming across as a total uncaring adult. I told her all the usual stuff, about how you read in the paper every day, you know, all that. She didn't know I'd seen her crying, and went into Belligerent Teenager Syndrome immediately. She hadn't had a good time, Sharon. It was all she could do to keep from crying some more. I sent her to bed, and we haven't discussed it since."

Sharon slowly turned to face the entrance once more, and watched in curiosity as more policemen poured into Kennedy Center. She said, "Is that all?"

Sheila didn't say anything for a couple of seconds, then answered, "No, it isn't."

Sharon's eyes widened slightly as Sally Pong entered the building with Cedric Hyde close behind her. The two prosecutors were dressed in suits and khaki topcoats. Pong's skirt was a couple of inches above the knee and her makeup was perfectly fixed. Sharon sensed what was going on, but had other things on her mind. She said into the phone, "I didn't think so."

"There was blood in her underwear, Sharon. Oh, don't think I stripped her down, I'm not that uncool, but the poor child is too inexperienced to so much as hide the evidence. She tossed her panties in her laundry basket. I'm sure that in undressing in the dark she didn't even realize they were bloody. I took the girls' things out to wash this morning, and there they were."

Sharon's vision blurred. Oh, Melanie, she thought. My sweet, sweet baby girl. "I'm coming home," she said. She was barely conscious of Pong, Hyde, and three policemen approaching the auditorium entrance. An usher blocked their path. The cops roughly shouldered the usher aside. Pong carried a piece of paper, folded over once. It was a warrant, of course. Hyde followed the policeman inside. Pong's gaze swept the lobby; she spotted Sharon and did a doubletake, then made a beeline for the telephones. Sharon said into the mouthpiece, "It's my fault, Sheila."

"I won't listen to that, as doctor *or* friend. It's curiosity, the same as you had and I had at Melanie's age. It's going to happen sooner or later. We simply have to deal with it."

Sharon watched Sally Pong's approach with an odd detachment. Nothing—including Pong's warrant, absolutely freaking *nothing*—took precedence over what she was hearing from Sheila. Sharon said, "The sex part, probably. But the sneaking out? It's rebellion, Sheil. To my deserting her in the middle of the holidays, to Rob's indifference . . . Jesus Christ, I can't . . ."

Pong sashayed up and held out a stack of paper. There were several copies with their pages stapled. Sharon took one and glanced at it. So they'd convinced a judge to issue a probable cause warrant. Which didn't mean a great deal—most judges dozed cozily through their careers and signed whatever warrants prosecutors thrust in front of them without more than a perfunctory glance—other than to back up what Sharon had suspected all along. That Cedric Hyde hadn't had any intention of waiting until morning for Will John's lawyers to surrender his DNA, and that the prosecution's word wasn't worth two cents. So what else was new? Pong stood expectantly by.

Sharon covered the mouthpiece with her hand and turned her back. Pong was speechless for an instant, then turned on her heel and stalked huffily away. Sharon said to Sheila Winston, "I've got to go. They've just served me with a warrant."

"A warrant for what?"

"My client."

"The congressman?"

"Yeah. It's not a big deal."

"Maybe not to you, Sharon. To the world it will be. This is number one on the national news."

"Screw the world," Sharon said. "I'm coming home."

"Your choice. I won't deny that Melanie could use you right now. But I'm standing by if you— "

"Right now, Sheila. I'm headed straight for the airport. See you in the morning, okay?" She hung up.

The enormity of what had happened to Melanie and what it could do to the rest of her life hit home to Sharon Hays in the mammoth Kennedy Center lobby. The floor shifted beneath her feet and the room spun dizzily around. She leaned against a pillar for support, waited for her head to clear, then stepped forward as the auditorium doors swung open and the cops spilled into the lobby with Will John Benedict in tow.

Will John's expression was one of absolute terror. They'd cuffed his hands behind him and two cops had him between them, one clutching each of his elbows. A gang of reporters had assembled as if by magic; the crowd parted in front of the lawmen and their prisoner and two men hoisted minicams onto their shoulders, pressed buttons, and aimed their lenses. Will John gaped wildly about. His gaze rested on Sharon. "Help me. Please, Sharon, I . . ." The policemen bowed their necks and pushed him firmly on ahead.

Pong and Hyde followed close on the lawmen's heels. Pong stopped in her tracks. "Through with your call, Miss Hays?"

Sharon didn't take the bait. She said merely, "Why, yes."

"Far be it from me to interrupt," Pong said. "But if you're interested, your client will be at the main city jail. The arraignment will be Monday."

Sharon couldn't hide her shock. "Hey, this is Wednesday night. You can't get a bail hearing in the morning?"

"We tried." Pong and Hyde exchanged an open smirk. Pong said, "But you know these court dockets."

Sharon opened, then closed, her mouth. Dirty tricks,

the *dirtiest* of tricks. The law required only that the hearing occur within seven days of the suspect's arrest, but the rule of thumb was that prosecutors showed the defense the courtesy of setting or denying bail at the earliest possible time. Which generally was the following morning. So much for rules of thumb, Sharon thought.

Now Russ Black hurried up, followed by Paul and Mattie Ruth Benedict. One minicam operator trained his machine on the senator. For once she ignored being in the spotlight, dabbing at her eyes with a handkerchief. Her grief was real. Through the open auditorium doors, the orchestra played on. Faint and far away, a strong male tenor voice sang, "Chestnuts Roasting on an Open Fire." The singer sounded like Wayne Newton, and probably was.

Russ leaned close to Sharon. "I think you oughtta go to the jail and hold Will John's hand through the bookin' process. I'll stick with the boy's folks. They're gonna need support."

Sharon permitted herself one glance at Paul Benedict. God, the bastard had lost none of his smugness even with his son under arrest. She steeled herself. What she was about to say was going to hurt. "I can't, boss," she said softly.

Black gaped at her, as if he'd just been punched in the solar plexus.

Sharon continued quickly, afraid she might lost her nerve. "Trouble at home, Russ. So much trouble you wouldn't believe. I've got to catch a plane to Dallas."

Black was incredulous. "You can't, young woman. At a time like this?"

"At a time like this or at any other time. Melanie's . . . don't ask me, Russ. I've got to go." She dropped her gaze and started to walk away.

Black stepped after her. "Well when're you coming back?"

Sharon stopped and turned. Her throat ached. Russell Black meant more to her than anyone in the world except her daughter. She blinked back tears. "I almost didn't come on this trip," she said, "for a number of reasons. One of which is Melanie. I have to straighten out some things. As for coming back, I just don't know. At this moment, I'm not sure if I will."

13

Normally the thought of boarding a flight from D.C. to Dallas while wearing a cocktail dress and fur would have turned Sharon beet-red in embarrassment, but now she had other things on her mind. She ignored the curious glances from passengers and flight attendants, and sat bolt upright at the rear of the business class cabin. She arrived in Dallas without luggage, exited the airport into seventy-degree foggy mist, and boarded a taxi. The cab deposited her in front of Sheila's house at two in the morning, Central Standard Time. She went up the sidewalk with her mink dangling from her fingers and brushing the concrete. She should have been pooped but was wide awake, her adrenaline flowing like white-water rapids.

Sheila wasn't asleep. She answered the doorbell in shortie pajamas with a paperback novel in her hand. The two women embraced in the foyer, then Sheila led Sharon by the hand into the living room and sat her down on the sofa. "I've been studying this situation," Sheila said.

Sharon wasn't in the mood to stall around. "So have I. Where's Melanie?"

"Not until you hear me out."

"I have heard you out, Sheila, over long distance. Look, it's my child. I'm not going to confront her, bawl her out or anything. My little girl needs me. I'm here. So where is she?"

Sheila sank down onto an ottoman. "You've got to give me credit for giving *you* more credit. I know you, and you're not going to fly into her like Mommy Dearest. But, gentle as you're going to be, you can cause serious psychological harm if you aren't careful."

"By giving her the benefit of my own experience? I'd think that would—"

"By not giving her a chance to open up," Sheila said. "By telling her what you know instead of letting her tell you what she wants you to know. Melanie is a whole lot more mature than you give her credit for being, just like Trish is older than I'd like to believe. She's had a sexual experience that's been less than gratifying. If you don't want her to spend the next few years cringing in fright every time a male comes near her, you have to approach the subject in a certain way."

"You're saying I shouldn't even bring up the fact that, oh, by the way, Sheila says you were AWOL the other night?"

"I'm saying more than that. I haven't even told her you were coming. Instead of jerking her out of bed in the middle of the night to demand an explanation of why she sneaked out of the house, pretend in the morning you're only here to surprise her. Trust me, Sharon. She won't be able to keep from asking if you know about the over-the-fence episode. Say that you do, but don't act as if it's all that big of a deal. She'll tell you more, believe me. She wants to know what you think of her, even if she doesn't act as if she does." Sheila got up, came over, and gently touched Sharon on the shoulder. "It's the way I earn my living, and you're more important to me than any freaking patient. What you do in the next twelve hours will affect your relationship with Melanie for the rest of your life. Don't screw it up, Sharon. I'd be less than a friend if I allowed you to."

Sharon listened to Sheila's instructions on how to deal with Melanie for an hour or so, then accepted the invitation to sleep on the couch. She traded her cocktail dress and fur for loaner shorts and T, then tossed and turned on the sofa until after 6 A.M. Finally she abandoned all hope of sleep and went in the kitchen, where Sheila kept her coffee and her bread in the fridge. Sharon fixed a steaming pot and used the popup toaster. She brought in the newspaper and scanned the headlines as she added Half 'N Half to her coffee and spread jam on crispy toasted wheat bread. The *Dallas Morning News* featured Will John Benedict's arrest in Washington in front-page screaming headlines, and fronting the story was a picture of Sharon and Russ conferring as the police led their client out of the Kennedy Center lobby. She scanned the article, found no mention of her leaving town even as the cops toted Will John off to jail, then went on to the Arts and Entertainment section. Mindless drivel, she thought, escapist reading to dodge reality. She was

in the midst of a piece about Matthew McConaughey
when Melanie came in from the bedroom.

First glimpse of her daughter told Sharon all she
needed to know. Melanie never climbed out of bed
this early, never, never, never, and normally had to
be rousted for school with the aid of a howitzer. She
hadn't seen her mother as yet, and entered the kitchen
as if in a trance. The puffiness under Melanie's eyes
said that she hadn't slept a wink, and her expression
was one of total despair. She was bare-legged in panties and a T, and her hair was in pillow-matted clumps.
Her cheeks were streaked with dried tears, and she
was sniffling. There was an empty feeling in the pit of
Sharon's stomach and a sudden ache in her throat. As
Melanie's gaze focused on her mom, the teenager froze
stock-still. She said, "What are you . . . ?"

Sharon forced a smile of greeting and made her
tone cheery and light. "We had a break in the action,
and I thought I'd zip home so we could spend some
time together." She stood from the table and opened
her arms.

Melanie hesitated, then came forward and permitted
a brief hug. She kept her face averted, watching the
opening between the kitchen and den as she said,
"The news last night said the congressman went to
jail."

Sharon exerted her facial muscles and broadened
her grin; feigned happiness required more effort than
she would have believed. "Which leaves little for Mom
to do until his bail hearing," she said, "which isn't
until Monday." She didn't add that she was uncertain
as to whether she'd return for the bond hearing or

have anything else to do with the case. Or practice law any longer, or do anything more to separate herself from her child until Melanie reached adulthood. Sharon chided gently. "Come on, Melanie, be glad to see me. I'm certainly glad to see you."

Melanie's expression remained vacant. "It's just that, it's a surprise is all."

Sharon walked to the fridge, stopped, and turned. "Are you hungry?"

Melanie sat at the breakfast table and folded her hands. "Not really."

"Of course you're not. You just charged into the kitchen at the crack of dawn for the exercise." Sharon opened the refrigerator; cool air wafted from inside and touched her cheek. "How would you like your eggs?"

Melanie's eyes narrowed in suspicion. "Have you been talking to Sheila?"

Sharon faced away from Melanie, bending to look inside the fridge, and allowed her features to twist in sadness. "I called Mrs. Winston last night, to tell her I was coming home, and also said I wanted to surprise you." She kept her tone airy. "Why, is there something that Mrs. Winston should be telling me?" She looked at her daughter over her shoulder.

Melanie hugged herself and stiffened her posture. "So you just flew in from Washington so we could buddy around together. *Sure,* Mom."

Sharon walked thoughtfully and slowly back to the table. She sat catty-cornered from Melanie and leaned close to her. Softly, Sharon said, "Hear me out, Melanie. Christmas is coming, and spending time with you is the most important thing in the world. And that's why I came. Today we can shop, or do anything you want to do."

Melanie's look was doubtful. "It's a school day."

Sharon rested her chin on her lightly clenched fist. "So it is. And a good day for you to play hooky, right?" She glanced toward the front of the house. "Come on, let's go home. Just a mother-daughter day. We haven't had one of those in a while, have we now?"

They crept out of the house without waking Sheila and Trish, and walked the block and a half home in silence, hand in hand. Sharon was barefoot and carried her cocktail dress and jacket over her arm with her shoes dangling from her fingers. Melanie had slipped on jean cutoffs along with blue running shoes, and wore no socks. The sidewalk was damp from the mist, but Sharon ignored the wetness on the soles of her feet. As they turned up their driveway, Sharon put her arm protectively around Melanie's shoulders. Melanie offered a sharp glance and, teenlike, withdrew from her mother for an instant. Then she laid her head softly against Sharon's breastbone and allowed herself to be led. By the time they reached the front door, Melanie was sniffling.

Commander was beside himself. As Sharon and Melanie came out on the porch, the shepherd leaped and whined and did his damnedest to lick both of his masters' faces at once. Something about a dog, Sharon thought, no matter what one's problems, real or imagined, might be, an animal can make things right if only for a little while. Melanie wrapped her arms around Commander's thick neck and buried her face in his fur.

They played keep-away from the shepherd for a few minutes, throwing a tennis ball back and forth between them while Commander darted to and fro with his tongue lolling, his gaze riveted on the ball and his tail thrashing, but Melanie's heart wasn't in the game. Where she normally bubbled with fun at the prospect of playing with Commander, today her movements were listless. Sharon caught the tennis ball, went over and sat on the porch and offered the prize to the shepherd. Commander stretched out on the redwood, let the tennis ball rest between his forepaws, and watched Sharon expectantly. Melanie drooped over and plopped down on the chaise.

Mother and daughter sat in silence, with Commander's panting the only noise on the porch.

Finally, Melanie said, "Mom, did . . . ?" And trailed off, staring vacantly into the yard.

Sharon leaned back in her deck chair and said nothing. Don't inquire, Sheila had told her. Let the child come to you.

Melanie sucked in breath. "You know about the other night, don't you?"

Sheila hadn't covered this particular situation. Sharon winged it. "I'm not sure if I do, sweetheart," she said tenderly. "Which night?"

Melanie showed a hint of petulance. "Oh, Mom, you know. When I left without permission. Come on, Sheila told you all about it."

Sharon thought, Don't lose her. She said, "She mentioned it. We won't let it mess up our time together, unless you want to discuss it."

Melanie blinked, surprised. "I thought you'd bawl me out."

"I'm not happy about you sneaking out, if that's what you mean. But I'm not going to dwell on it. Getting caught wasn't in the plan, huh?" Sharon smiled, as if she saw humor in the incident.

"It's not funny," Melanie snapped.

"I didn't say it was. But Mrs. Winston and I have been teenagers. Let's say, we understand better than you think we do."

Melanie stiffened in interest. "You mean, you snuck out when you were a little . . . when you were my age?"

Sharon didn't feel comfortable confessing the sins of her youth. Not all of them at any rate, not by a long shot. She hesitated before saying, "I may have thought about it. We all make mistakes. Luckily none of mine were terminal."

"What happened to me could have been pretty serious."

"I didn't say it wasn't serious. But you're here, alive and well."

Melanie averted her gaze. "I don't know if I'm well or not."

Sharon closed her mouth and sat forward in a listening attitude.

"I was with a boy," Melanie said.

Sharon continued to watch, not saying anything.

"An older boy," Melanie said. "In a car." She waited

for her mother's reaction, her expression saying, Oh, boy, here it comes.

Sheila's warning had been: Under no circumstances should you demand to know the boy's name. Sharon had heard of women who really lost it at times like this, confronted the boy, the boy's parents, made every kind of hellish scene. Best way in the world, Sheila had said, to cause your daughter to never again confide in you. Sharon slid a hand under her hip. Though her fingernails dug painfully into the fabric of her chair, she kept her voice calm. "It goes without saying that a boy was involved."

Melanie's eyebrows lifted.

Sharon said, "Sweetheart, there are umpteen million teenage girls in this country who do things that they don't want their parents knowing about. Most of these things have to do with boys. If you'd stop looking at me as the police instead of someone who wants to help you, this will go a lot better for both of us."

Melanie looked as if she couldn't believe her ears. "You're not mad at me?"

Commander had scooted up closer to Sharon's chair. She leaned over and scratched the shepherd between the ears as she said to Melanie, "Of course not. Nor am I disappointed, nor do I feel that I must have failed you in some way." Her vision blurred. She couldn't help it. She said, "Certain things are part of growing up. My best gift to you now will be, if I can keep you from making mistakes that will haunt you for life."

Melanie's mouth twisted. "Oh, Mom. He made me . . ."

Sharon chewed her lower lip. She despised this boy,

whoever he was. *Hated* the little bastard. She said
softly, "Look, I'm not going to inquire about the details. If you want to tell me, sure. But we all have
inner battles to fight. How much you want to share is
up to you." She swiveled around, making room, and
patted the chair beside her. "Come on, sweetheart, sit
over here."

Melanie rose, her movements wooden, and sat with
her back touching Sharon's arm.

Sharon reached with both hands to massage her
daughter's shoulders. "Remember when you were little and I used to do this?"

Melanie lowered her head. Her neck was long, elegant, beautiful. A wonder, Sharon thought, that Rob
and I could produce a child so perfect. Melanie uttered a sob. "It hurt, Mom. God, it . . ."

Sharon pictured an identical experience in her own
life. Hurt? You bet it had. She threw her arms around
Melanie's neck and hugged her from behind. She
kissed her daughter's cheek as Melanie's shoulders
heaved. Sharon said, "Let's shower and change, Melanie. Eat breakfast in a restaurant, go shopping. Take
in a movie together." She stood and stepped toward
the house. "Come on, sweetheart. Hold your chin up
and have a look at the world. Last one dressed is a
rotten egg."

They dallied through Saks, Foley's, and Barney's
New York without buying anything, then went to see
Babe: Pig in the City at AMC's Preston Forest Twelve.
For once Melanie didn't flounce into her seat, mum-
bling that this was a movie for kids and that she was

plenty old enough to deal with R-rated. Sharon thought that the picture was out of this world and, during one of the cuter scenes, reached over and squeezed Melanie's hand. It thrilled her that Melanie was grinning from ear to ear in the darkness of the theater.

Later they had Frappuccinos at Starbuck's on Oak Lawn Avenue, and watched through the coffee shop's rear window as traffic whizzed back and forth on Turtle Creek Boulevard. Sharon wanted to ask Melanie about protection—God, the effect it could have on Melanie's life to become pregnant at her age—but didn't know how to approach the subject gently. The whole thing was such a delicate balance, the difference between offering loving advice and sticking her nose in where it had no business being. When Sharon had been in high school and had feared being pregnant herself, her own mother had handled the situation badly, screaming and throwing tearful fits, and Sharon had gone on a guilt trip that extended to this very day. Not with my own child, Sharon thought. She watched Melanie's profile, and followed her daughter's gaze as a Rolls cruised down Turtle Creek in the direction of Cedar Springs.

Finally Melanie said, as if reading her mother's mind, "It wasn't all Jacob's fault. It was as much mine as his."

Jacob, Sharon thought. The boy. The *man*-boy, taking advantage of Melanie's inexperience. Sharon despised him. Hated his freaking guts, even though she'd never met him. She said nothing.

"I sort of led him on," Melanie said.

Sharon was mute for an instant. God, she couldn't sit there like a rock. She managed, "You mean, intentionally led him on?"

Melanie's features set themselves in a mature look, that of a woman about to confess her transgressions. "I didn't start out to lead him on. I planned to go through with it, Mom. I meant to let him do it to me, and I told him that's what I wanted before he came over."

Sharon hated the words. Do it. *Do it,* much more to the point than the expressions of her own teenhood, such as "going all the way," which sounded as ridiculous now as twenty years ago. She said, "But when it came down to it, you changed your mind?"

Melanie vigorously shook her head. "No. I chickened out is more like it. I told him over the phone that I was ready. He thought that was the reason I went out in the car with him. By the time I tried to back out, Jacob was . . . you know, too worked up to stop. It wasn't his fault, Mom. Later he told me how sorry he was."

I'll just bet the little bastard was sorry, Sharon thought. Her smile of understanding felt frozen on her face. She said, "Melanie, did you . . . ?"

Melanie leaned back in relief, having gotten things off her chest. Her expression wasn't near as tragic as before, as if she enjoyed her mother's discomfort. Which would have been maddening as all get-out, if it hadn't been reminiscent of Sharon's own attitude at Melanie's age. Shocking adults and watching their reactions had been the trip of all trips.

Sharon stammered uncomfortably, "Did *he* . . . ?"

Melanie's chin tilted in understanding. "I'm not going to get pregnant, if that's what you're worried about." Her tone of voice was suddenly professional, as if she were the mother and Sharon the child.

Which is pretty much the norm these days, Sharon thought, the kids growing up at a rate that their parents couldn't have imagined. She's educating me, Sharon thought, holding my hand and leading me down the path to understanding. She said docilely, "He brought protection, then."

Melanie heaved a sigh. "No, Mom. I did. Trish knows a guy who works in a pharmacy after school."

Even as relief flooded over her, Sharon had a rush of anger. Melanie had now turned things around and placed her mother on the defensive. She's the reincarnation of me at her age. Sharon thought, which made the whole thing even more frustrating. She wondered how Sheila would feel about Trish's role in helping Melanie lose her virginity. Probably Sheila will take it a whole lot better than I am, Sharon thought. During Sharon's own adolescence, girls didn't confide in each other that they were considering having sex. Furthermore, once the deed was done, wild horses couldn't have drug the secret from their lips. Boys had liked to brag in those days, that much hadn't changed, but the idea that girls now openly discussed what once was taboo was a bit much to cope with. Sharon assumed a confidential tone. "Now that it's over, how do you feel about it?"

Melanie shrugged. "It hurt a lot. I wish I hadn't let it go that far. Aside from that, I don't know that it's all that big of a deal."

Not a big deal? Sharon thought. She watched Melanie. The child's lower lip quivered. Melanie talked a good game, but in truth she was grief-stricken. Somehow Sharon had to show her daughter that it wasn't the end of the world. That no one's life was ruined, that Melanie had merely experienced another turn in the road to adulthood. One helluva sharp turn, though, more like Dead Man's Curve. Sharon pretended not to notice Melanie's poorly hidden grief. She said, "Well, if you have any questions, I'm here for you."

Melanie relaxed in appreciation. "I know you are. And thanks. If I think of anything, it'll be cool to have you clue me in."

Melanie kept her composure for longer than Sharon expected. They locked gazes for an instant, Melanie's tough expression dissolving as Sharon opened her arms. Melanie bent near, buried her face in Sharon's shoulder, and sobbed for all she was worth.

"Let it out, sweetheart," Sharon said softly. "Best thing in the world for you."

Melanie raised her face, her tear-streaked skin glistening as she looked around the restaurant. "People are watching, Mom."

Sharon put her arms around her daughter's neck and hugged her tightly. "Know something, precious?" Sharon said. "I don't give a damn if they are."

They came home around five-thirty, with winter dusk fading into darkness. The phone-message light *blink-blink*ed like a distress signal at sea. Melanie went gloomily off to change while Sharon punched the playback button, and flopped down on the sofa to listen.

There were twelve messages in all. Sharon quickly fast-forwarded through the media calls—nine of them, including those from Andy Wade at the *Dallas Morning News*, the *National Enquirer*, the *Globe*, and a woman from CNN—and concentrated on the SOSs from Russ. He'd called three times, and there was real stress in his tone. Sharon drummed her fingers in guilt. Russ was like a father to her, or more to the point, like a big brother intent on keeping all the bullies away. Now she was letting him down. She punched in the D.C. area code, hesitated while she fished for her handwritten phone directory, called the State Plaza Hotel, and asked for Mr. Black's room. He answered on the second ring.

"It's me, boss," she said, settling back. "Returning your call."

"Calls, plural. An' don't play like you didn' get my messages before now. What's got into you, girl?"

Sharon felt like crying. "A lot has gotten into me. But know that I just walked in, and that all three of your calls were on the machine. I haven't been ducking you. I've just been out."

"Our client'll be glad to know that, sittin' in jail."

Sharon looked into the dining room, at the Christmas tree she'd decorated alone on the day before she'd gone to Washington. The stepladder on which Sharon had raised on tiptoes to affix the star was right where she'd left it. Visible past the dining room in the kitchen, her sterling silver punch bowl was upended by the sink in draining position. The bowl was exactly where it had been since Sharon had poured the punch down the drain after Melanie had flounced out of the house. Sharon winced. The whole thing had been an ugly scene. She said into the phone, "Sometimes there are more important things than clients."

"Tell that to Paul an' Mattie Ruth. They're fit to be tied."

She came within an inch of telling Russ how little she cared about the Benedicts' feelings, particularly *Paul* Benedict's, but instead said softly, "Russ, I can't tell you how sorry I am to let you down."

"Then get yourself back here and get to work. These reporters are drivin' me crazy."

Sharon glanced toward the answering machine. "They've been trying to do the same to me." She made her tone apologetic. "You know I'd never leave you in the lurch barring a national emergency. It's Melanie. I have to be with her. Whether I can come back to D.C., or when, I just can't say right now."

"The child injured?" Russ's tone was suddenly sympathetic and caring.

Which made it even harder for Sharon to say, "Not physically. It's a girl thing, boss. I have to help her get through a crisis. Everybody's got their priorities. The nation probably wouldn't understand this, but compared with Melanie's future, Will John Benedict's problems don't amount to a hill of beans to me."

Static sounded over the line as Russ paused for a beat of five. Finally he said, "I guess I understand."

"It's wonderful of you to say so, even if you don't. Look, boss, I know how tough this is going to be on you." She lowered her gaze to her lap. "If you'd like to take someone else on as second chair in the case, I'll step aside. At this rate I may have to anyway. I need to spend more time at home."

There was more silence. Finally Black said incredulously, "You'd quit me for good?"

Sharon was conscious of movement in the room, a presence behind her. She turned as Melanie stepped down from the hall into the living room. Melanie had changed into a pair of cutoffs.

Sharon said with a catch in her voice, "Of course I wouldn't quit you cold, not unless you wanted me to. I'm thinking of you, not myself. It's just that, you're on a complicated case up there and need all the help you can get. Help I can't offer right now. I'm sorry, Russ."

Black cleared his throat. "I'm not goin' off half-cocked on the spur of the moment. Hell, girl, I can handle things for a coupla days. They're not gonna consider bail for our man until Monday anyhow."

"Nice of you to give me a window. But I don't see how I can be finished here by then." Sharon watched her daughter sit on the sofa across the room. "I'll just have to let you know."

"Let's don't fly off the handle an' be makin' a decision this big, not without takin' the weekend," Black said. "Call me Sunday night." After a pause, he then said, "I want you in my corner, girl. I've had assistants over the years, but none as . . . well, you know what I'm sayin'."

"I do know," Sharon said gently, "And I will think hard on it. That you can count on. Thanks, boss." She hung up and looked sadly at the phone.

"Was that Mr. Black?" Melanie sat upright in interest, her gaze riveted on her mother.

Sharon shrugged. "Yes, sweetheart. It was him in person."

Melanie's eyes grew big and round. "You're not thinking about quitting your job."

"Not quitting completely. Just cutting back on my schedule so we can spend more time together. Wouldn't you like that?"

Melanie seemed thoughtful. "More time would be cool. But *all* of the time?"

Sharon laughed in spite of the seriousness of the situation. "You'd still have time for your friends, sweetheart. I don't plan to smother you."

"You know I wondered before I . . . did what I did, you know, with Jacob, how much different I was going to feel. It's surprising, Mom, but I don't feel much different at all. I'm still the same kid."

Not quite, Sharon thought sadly. Something about innocence lost. Melanie would never be *quite* the same again. Sharon said, "It's something to think about, the changes. But how does that affect whether I'm going to quit my job or not?"

The sudden maturity in Melanie's look was stunning. "I don't think it does affect you. But it's going to affect me a lot."

Sharon's mouth tightened. "Look, I don't want you to feel I'm going to act like a warden. I'm just going to be here for you more."

"That's not it at all. I know whatever you do will be for me, Mom. I don't act like I know that sometimes, but I do. It's just that, having a mother that's sort of famous, well, I like that. Gives me something for the other kids to be jealous of."

Sharon felt flattered, but apprehensive as well. "A lot of people would call it more like infamous. Lots of the causes I have to take up aren't popular with everyone by a long shot."

"Oh, I know it," Melanie said. "That's even cooler. Like these kids might say, hearing it from their parents, how can your mom sleep at night when she's defending this crook or that crook? That gives me a chance to say to those kids, you don't know what you're talking about."

Sharon supposed that Melanie and her friends discussed their parents a lot. During Sharon's own teenhood, most of the remarks about mothers and dads hadn't been particularly complimentary. The idea that her child would defend her to other kids gave Sharon goose bumps. She said, "I'll agree you might lose that one little edge. But I think having a parent to lean on a hundred percent of the time might more than make up the difference."

Melanie looked at her knees. "I'm sorry, Mom, but I guess I'd feel more like you were around to keep an eye on me. Like you didn't trust me."

Sharon took the last remark with a grain of salt. "You don't trust me," was a prime ploy for teenagers up to no good, and had been since the beginning of time. "Trust wouldn't have anything to do with it, sweetheart," Sharon said.

"I'd feel like it did, even if it didn't," Melanie said. "Besides, Mr. Black needs your help. I don't want you to desert him, Mom."

Oh, Jesus God, Sharon thought. "I don't want to, either, Melanie."

"I'm proud of you, that you're my mother. I'd like to be with you more, but I don't want you to stop doing what you do. I'd feel my whole life like, I'd ruined something for you."

Sharon felt tears coming on. She sat beside Melanie on the sofa and put her arm around her daughter's shoulders. She supposed that in the near future there'd be a lot of soul-searching for both of them.

Melanie said, "Go on back to Washington, Mom. I'll be fine. And I give you my word, Sheila won't have any more trouble with me."

Sharon crossed her ankles on the coffee table, leaned back against the cushions, and looked at the ceiling. "I don't think she will, either, sweetheart. It's just that, at the moment, I don't know what it is I'm going to do."

14

But Sharon should have known all along what she was going to do, and realized as much, as two days after New Year's, she stood at Reagan National and waited for a flight from L.A. to arrive. It was Melanie who'd made up her mother's mind during the two intimate weeks they'd spent together, the child showing knowledge far beyond her years. Having absentee parents for much of the time would be hard on an adolescent, but not as hard as knowing, until her dying day, that she'd held back her mother's career. Without Sheila in the wings, ready and willing to act as surrogate mom and taxi service, Sharon never could have continued in the practice of long-distance law. God love Sheila to death, Sharon thought as she paced back and forth beyond the security gates, peering occasionally down the walkways. There was a sign over the metal detectors reading, NO UNTICKETED PASSENGERS BEYOND THIS POINT. That's a marvelous skyjacker deterrent, Sharon thought, but it sure is a pain in the p'toot for nonterrorists who are meeting people from out of town. There were forty or fifty waiting along with Sharon, men in business suits and one tired-looking woman carrying an infant seat, all shuffling their feet in irritation. Sharon didn't blame them for being upset; she was more than a little p.o.'d herself. She raised herself on the balls of her feet and peered toward the arrival gates. Lyndon Gray and Olivia Welton approached at a fast clip, side by side.

At first glance the Brits looked like a London gentleman accompanied by his prim and proper country cousin, but Sharon knew better. Lyndon Gray was a tall brunette with the shoulders of a linebacker and the watchful gaze of a jungle cat, his eyes darting back and forth as he took in his surroundings, memorizing, categorizing. Even as Sharon smiled and waved, she noted that Gray's craggy features seemed just a hair older and wiser than when she'd first met him only a few months ago in California. Gray had been acting as chauffeur/cook/bodyguard to Darla Cowan and, as Darla's defense had progressed, Gray's Oriental partner Benny Yadaka had proved to be one of the bad guys. Sharon doubted if Lyndon Gray would ever be so fooled again. His social graces and impeccable manners aside, Gray looked exactly like what he was, a former British Secret Service agent in the investigation and protection business. Olivia Welton however, would stump the *What's My Line?* panel into conniptions.

She was dressed like a middle-aged nanny, complete with plum-colored pleated skirt and vest to match, spotless white blouse and black bow tie, her gray hair center-parted with sidecar bangs. A huge leather purse dangled by a strap around Mrs. Welton's forearm, and a near-angelic smile was plastered on her face. The nanny outfit, Sharon knew, disguised a lithe and muscular body toned by daily workouts, and the pleasant matronly expression was the same as Mrs. Welton would display while breaking a bad guy's arm.

The couple's luggage would contain the proper dress for any occasion in addition to a number of firearms. Lyndon Gray's weapon of choice was a 9-mm Ruger, while Mrs. Welton carried a .45 with a kick like a Shetland, and the pair traveled with a couple of palm-sized derringers as well. Gray was partial to nylon shoulder rigs while Olivia Welton holstered her weapons near the small of her back. Mrs. Welton was fluent in three languages, Lyndon Gray in four. Gray followed Welton past the metal detectors in courtly fashion. The couple approached, and Sharon held out both hands.

Gray took one of Sharon's hands while Welton gripped the other. Gray said, "A pleasure as always, Miss Hays."

Sharon felt as if a weight had lifted. "Not near the pleasure it is for me to see you two. I didn't think Darla would spare you."

"Nor did I." Gray fell in step with Welton, with Sharon in the middle, and the trio started down the concourse toward the baggage claim. Gray continued, "Normally she wouldn't, I fancy, but when Miss Cowan learned that the person requesting our assistance was you . . ."

Sharon quickened her pace. God, like keeping up with a couple of speedwalkers. She said, slightly breathlessly, "I'm in Darla's debt, then."

Gray chuckled. "I think Miss Cowan feels it's the other way around. She owes you her freedom."

"I don't know that that's a proper statement." Sharon passed under a sign and led the way onto the down escalator. "How is Darla making out?"

Gray ushered Welton onto the moving staircase and brought up the rear. Olivia Welton's expression was suddenly serious. "Miss Cowan's as well as can be expected. It may take years for the effects of what she went through to completely wear off. Her being such a public figure doesn't help."

Sharon looked up over her shoulder. "It makes things tougher. You should know up front, I'm afraid we've got a similar situation here with all the publicity."

Gray and Welton exchanged a glance. Mrs. Welton's angelic smile returned. "So we've heard, Miss Hays," she said. "And matters such as this are our specialty. Lyndon and I have discussed our roles thoroughly. And as for the media's hindrance of the congressman's defense, I can safely say you should fear no more."

Sharon had rented a blue Lincoln Town Car, which she'd left in the short-term parking near the terminal exit. She approached the rear of the vehicle with Gray on her left, Mrs. Welton on her right, and a skycap pulling a luggage cart along behind them. Sharon used the key to open the rear compartment, and the trio stood back while the skycap thunked the Brits' gear aboard—two medium-sized leather suitcases along with a steamer trunk large enough to hold a dead body or two. When it came time for the skycap to hoist the trunk from the cart, he tugged and wheezed like a cardiac patient. Lyndon Gray smiled grimly and bent to lend a hand. The temperature was in the twenties, the sky overcast. Sharon's breath fogged in the cold.

Mrs. Welton leaned near and said softly, "Is everything all right with you?"

Sharon started. "Why, yes. Why wouldn't it . . . ?"

"You seemed more concerned than normal. How is young Miss Hays?"

"Melanie?"

Olivia Welton nodded. "Lovely child." In California, Mrs. Welton had taken Melanie on a studio tour, and the pair had become thick as thieves.

One corner of Sharon's mouth bunched. "I don't think things have ever been better between Melanie and me since the day she was born."

"That's nice," Mrs. Welton said, looking as if she knew better, then changed to a more businesslike tone. "Will we be meeting the congressman today?"

Sharon briefly shook her head. "Ever since Will John made bail he's been laying low. Newspeople surround his condo and he can hardly stick his head outside. I thought we could meet with Russ and plan some strategy. Will John's arraignment is tomorrow, and there'll be plenty of time for you to talk to him after the hearing."

"How's the atmosphere around your hotel?"

Sharon scratched her jaw. "The same as at the congressman's condo, but we're coping. To pick up this rental car I ducked out the back way and walked two blocks to a hotel up the street. Gave them the slip for the time being, but I suspect they'll be out in force by the time we return."

Lyndon Gray slammed the trunk lid, tipped the skycap, and turned to the two women as the skycap tugged the cart back to the terminal. Gray said jovially, "I suppose we're ready to roll, ladies."

Sharon walked to the driver's door with the keys dangling from her hand. Her fingers were freezing. Gray followed her up and reached for the keys. "Allow me, miss."

Sharon stopped in her tracks, surprised. "I thought, since I know the way . . ."

Gray smiled, took the keys, and held the rear door open like Jeeves the butler. "I think I can get us there."

Sharon stepped toward the car. "You know Washington?"

"Was here a year and a half, a-servin' of 'er Majesty the Queen. During Nixon's time. The British government had more than a passing interest in Watergate happenings. I became quite familiar with keeping away from the local press then." He took Sharon's arm and ushered her into the car. "Not to fret, mum. When it comes to dodging newsies, I know roads in this town that angels fear to tread."

Lyndon Gray gazed thoughtfully out the window. "I don't suppose you've considered a plea bargain."

Russell Black was seated on the edge of the bed. He leaned forward and rested his forearms on his thighs. "Hell's bells, o' course we have. Our client says he didn' do it. We're obligated to take his position."

"Seems an incredibly weak position. Can we verify the part of his story where he goes out for drugs and sex toys?"

"That much, yeah. At least part of it. The sex shop employee remembers him. The drug dealer hadn' surfaced."

"And might not. And even if he comes forward, I've heard nothing that would have prevented your client from killing the young lady after he returned to the condo."

Sharon stood beside Mrs. Welton at the window, looking down. Far below on E Street, two mobile news units hugged the curb while cameramen and reporters milled about, huddled over, keeping as warm as possible. The area around Will John's condo in Georgetown was even worse; one couldn't drive within two blocks of the place without running into the media. Lyndon Gray had parked the Lincoln over at the Sate Department, and had led the women into the hotel basement through a tunnel that Sharon hadn't even known existed. Less than two hours in town, Gray and Welton were already earning their keep. Even Russ was showing respect, and there'd been no evidence of his usual snappishness with private investigators. Anthony Gear, Black's main man back in Dallas, had to go through a grilling session with Russ on every freaking thing. With Lyndon Gray and Olivia Welton, Sharon suspected that Black would be more inclined to take the British couple's word.

Gray turned from the window and sank down in a cushioned chair snugged up to a table. He folded his hands on the polished surface. "We can do all the obvious things, Mr. Black. Try to dig dirt on the young lady, though besmirching someone's character isn't the most tasteful of chores. But even should she turn out to be the tart of the century, I don't see that excuses her murder."

"We should canvass the condo neighborhood." Olivia Welton spoke softly and carefully, never taking her gaze from the street below.

There was a pause as the two men looked at Welton, at the slim straight back, the pleated folds of her skirt hanging down. Sharon tilted her head in curiosity.

Welton turned to face the room, her back to the glass. "Your client says that he left the condo and returned to find the girl murdered in bed. If the story's true, someone may have seen the killer coming or going."

"Or may have spied the congressman through the window," Gray said, "raising a knife over his head."

Welton showed the tiniest bit of irritation. "Those would be witnesses whom we don't need, then, wouldn't they? Do you have a better idea?"

"Not at present," Gray said. "As respects the victim's activities, I suppose we should begin with the roommate. I doubt she'll be eager to speak with us."

"I may have to mother her a bit." Welton's lips spread slowly into a smile.

"You do that well," Gray said, rising, "With everyone. We'll get what we can, Mr. Black. Of course it's up to you and Miss Hays to determine what is and isn't admissible in court."

Sharon and Russ exchanged a look. Gray sat back down and waited expectantly. Mrs. Welton leaned against the door frame and folded her arms. Gray said, "Am I missing something here?"

Sharon lifted, then dropped, her chin. "I doubt you

are, Mr. Gray. What is and isn't admissible doesn't matter at this point."

It was Gray and Welton's turn to look at each other. Mrs. Welton said, "That bad?"

"Worse," Sharon said. "With Will John Benedict insisting he didn't do it, our hands are sort of tied. The prosecution's case seems pretty airtight as we speak. Under normal circumstances I'd be asking our client to plea-bargain, but he won't hear of it. As of now, we simply have no defense. Unless we can uncover something to the effect that Will John's telling the truth, then trial or no, Will John's going to prison for a very long time."

Gray rubbed his forehead. "You could have said the same thing about Miss Cowan's defense at one time, Miss Hays." He smiled hopefully. "Darkest before the dawn, what?"

"With one exception," Sharon said. "I believed in Darla from day one. In Will John Benedict's case, I'm not really sure." She checked her watch. "We desperately need inspiration. Other than our client's word, we've seen nothing pointing evidence in our direction. While youall are nosing around, I'm going to see a guy. I don't know if he'll make a good witness, whether he's reliable, or anything about him other than what I've been told. But he may be the only grabbable straw that we have."

Mark C. Potter was a dull-looking man in a bland office with a view of the beltway. He wore a white shirt, black tie, and glasses in plastic frames. His hairline receded halfway back. He offered Sharon a vanilla wafer. The wafer tasted bland.

"What you propose can give me real problems." Potter touched manicured fingertips together.

Sharon tongued a piece of wafer from a jaw tooth. "That's not my intent. But there will be visibility for anyone connected to this case. It can't be avoided."

"That's the trouble. Twenty-three years in this town, my clients include names that everyone in the country would recognize. Yet I've never had my picture in the newspapers. I survive by being anonymous." Potter spoke with no discernible accent.

Sharon had a legal pad balanced on her thigh. She didn't have time to spar with this guy. She said, "For how long did you follow Congressman Benedict?"

Potter flashed the tiniest of smiles. "Follow? I prefer to say, 'Kept up with his activities.' "

Sharon lifted, then dropped her shoulders. "We can use whatever terminology you want. I just need the particulars."

Potter squirmed in his wooden, slatted-backed swivel chair. "I don't know as I'm comfortable discussing anything confidential."

Sharon rubbed a blank page with the end of her ballpoint. "Oh? Cas told me she gave you the green light."

"She did, I won't quarrel with that. But I'm not sure that even Mrs. Benedict has the right to disclose our business."

Sharon felt a tug of irritation. "The confidentiality privilege belongs to the client, Mr. Potter. Once the client waives it, well . . ."

Potter reached inside the box and withdrew another vanilla wafer. "I'm not a lawyer, but . . ."

"Well I *am* a lawyer. And Cas Benedict has waived the right."

Potter extended the box. "Wafer?"

Sharon jiggled her foot. "No, thank you."

"You didn't let me finish. Privilege matters in the courtroom only. If Mrs. Benedict allows it, you can subpoena me to testify, that much legalese I understand. But you can't force me to tell you anything right here, right now, when I'm not under oath. Off the witness stand the confidentiality of my files are my own prerogative. If you'd want to put on a witness when you didn't know what he was going to say . . ." Potter spread his hands.

Sharon expelled a sigh. "Touché, Mr. Potter. I can make trouble for you, and you can return the favor. Let's hope it doesn't come to that."

"Let's hope. But sometimes in my business, conflict is unavoidable. I'll give you an example. Three years ago I had a case where I followed a senator to a place where he wasn't supposed to be. Never mind where, the point is that the FBI was bird-dogging the guy as well, identified me, and I had the pleasure of appearing before a congressional committee. I pled confidentiality. Congress doesn't believe that anything is confidential where they're concerned, and I spent the balance of the hearings in jail for contempt. I protect my files, Miss Hays. Time in jail is temporary. To make revelations such as they were asking would destroy my reputation, translating to making me permanently kaput in this town."

Sharon regarded Potter with the same respect she'd show for the biggest cockroach in history. Doings in the nation's capital made her skin crawl. She said, "Let me ask you something."

Potter raised pale blond eyebrows.

"In the case you just described," Sharon said, "was the senator you were following charged with murder?"

"No." Potter's tone was flat, disinterested.

"And if he had been, and your testimony could have cleared him, would you still have refused to talk about it?"

"Yes."

"I find that incredible," Sharon said.

"Find it any way you want, Miss Hays. Politicians come and go around here. I don't. I'm permanent. I don't risk my permanency for any reason."

"Permanency and anonymity. Your keys to survival, right?"

Potter showed a smile that was practically a smirk. Five minutes alone with him, Sharon detested this guy.

She scooted her bottom forward and leaned back. "I can't do anything about your permanency. Your anonymity is a different story."

Potter's expression was suddenly grim. "I hope I'm not hearing a threat."

"You're not hearing an *empty* threat, sir. Do you know Rita Carboneau?"

"Only from afar. I use a nickname for her, but to tell you what it is could bring the feminist movement down on me."

"You'd be surprised how far across the room I stand from the femi-Nazis," Sharon said. "And I can probably fill in the blanks with regard to the nickname on my own, thank you. But necessity creates strange bedmates, and poor Rita's running short of dirt to dig on this case. Do you think she'd be interested in a private detective who's got some inside skinny he doesn't want to reveal?"

Potter's look was calculating, without anger, just a man considering his options.

"The truth is," Sharon said, "that I like Ms. Carboneau even less than you do. But if I need her I need her. She's a lot in the same position you are, in that what she writes in her column isn't under oath. Do I need her, sir?" She folded a page over in her legal pad and waited.

Potter spun his chair around and looked out the window, at traffic whizzing back and forth along the beltway. He turned back, picked up the box, and fished for a wafer. Sharon held her breath, hoping that he wouldn't offer her one.

Potter set the box down. "If I were to, possibly, speak in hypotheticals, could we keep my name out of it?"

"I don't think you'd have to be hypothetical, as in, suppose there was this congressman or something. As for keeping you out of it, I'll tell you what I told Cas. If you can give me names I can run down to use as witnesses, well, sure. If all I had was your word, then your word is what I'd have to put on the stand."

Potter seemed thoughtful. He stood, walked over to an upright hanging file, and withdrew a thick folder. He turned, retreated to sit, and thumbed through papers in the folder. "To help you there," he began, then cleared his throat and said, "To give you evidence, I'd have to tell you things that Mrs. Benedict doesn't know."

Sharon couldn't hide her surprise. "You mean you withhold information even from your clients?"

"Not on their case. What's their business is just that. But what isn't their business . . . Forget Hollywood, California, Miss Hays; Washington, D.C., is the infidelity capital of the world. Ninety-nine out of a hundred of my clients are wives, though why they want to know is beyond me, because they seldom do anything about it once they get the goods. I go about my business in a different manner than you'd think. I was a cop once, long ago. I learned that when there's a crime, the list of suspects is more often than not a group of people who've previously committed the identical crime. It works the same way when it comes to extra-marital screwing around."

Sharon couldn't help but be fascinated. Her gaze riveted on the file in Potter's hands, she said, "I don't know that I follow. That isn't the file on the Benedict case?"

"In the manner of speaking, but it's also the file on some other cases. Just as the same people are always robbing banks, liquor stores, whatever, the same people make a practice of dallying with other people's spouses. I find that when a woman comes to me, wants me to investigate her husband, in ninety-nine percent of the cases the other person involved is someone who's previously been involved with someone else's husband. Am I making myself clear?"

Sharon sighed as realization dawned. "I'm afraid

you are, Mr. Potter. You keep records on women who are prone to get involved with married men."

Potter waved a hand toward the hanging file. "For the most part, yes. There are a few homosexual men in my records, but you get the drift. So in the particular case, while I tell the client the name of the person her husband is sleeping with, I don't reveal the other men in that person's life. To do so would be giving trade secrets away. I don't do that. It isn't healthy from a business sense."

Sharon pictured the file Sally Pong had given her, the photo of Courtney Lee, the girl-and-her-dog pose. She said, "Then that file is on . . . ?"

Potter was matter-of-fact. "Courtney Lee, yes."

"You're saying, when Cas Benedict came to see you, that wasn't the first time Courtney's name had come up in one of your investigations?"

"No, it was the fifth." Potter thumbed through the file, *flop-flop-flop,* looked up, and grinned. "Three Democrats, two Republicans. The lady was bipartisan. Performing for Old Glory's sake."

During Sharon's first year in New York, a date had taken her to see Buddy Hackett at Radio City Music Hall. She'd thought the show vulgar and disgusting, the same feeling she now had listening to Mark C. Potter. She said almost spitefully, "Do you take videos, the whole bit?"

"Most certainly. I could arrange a private showing if you'd like."

"No, thank you," Sharon said. "I'd want these other men's names."

"Only if you'll protect your source."

"I'm a lawyer, Mr. Potter, not a reporter for the *Globe*. What I can offer is, you open up to me, I won't use you as a witness unless it's absolutely necessary. If you don't talk to me, and now, you'll be reading about yourself in Rita Carboneau's column before the week is out. Your choice, sir."

Potter testily brushed his lapel. "Sounds like a black-mail threat to me."

Sharon smiled. "Oh, it is. Make no mistake about it."

Potter dropped all pretense of being polite. "What is it you want, lady? I have things to do."

Sharon nodded toward the file. "A copy of that, for starters. Front to back. Then a rundown on your activities regarding my client, from day the first to day the last. Whereall you followed him and everything you saw."

"Everything? That could be quite R-rated."

"I'm over seventeen," Sharon said.

"That you are." Potter had calmed down, and Sharon wondered if his brief show of anger had been an act. For anyone to be in Potter's line of work, she thought, they'd have to be immune to insult. He dropped his file over in front of her with a dull *thump*. "It's all in there. My notes are transcribed, not only for the Benedict matter but for everyone with whom the young lady was involved. There are photos. There are dailies from the first time Mrs. Benedict contacted me, in November, I think, up until the night Miss Lee died."

Sharon hefted the file. It weighed a ton. Sleaze is heavy, Sharon thought. She said, "I'd like to cut through some preliminaries. Descriptions of how you followed Will John here and there until he made contact with Courtney, that wouldn't do me much good."

"Oh, there isn't any of that. I had Miss Lee identified as the woman with whom he was having an affair within an hour after Mrs. Benedict retained me."

Through her disgust, Sharon felt an odd admiration. "That fast?"

"It's the way we work. I employ one operative, a young woman who bartends at . . . at a place where a lot of politicos hang out. A bit heavy in the thighs, but a telephone voice to end all voices and a knack for making little alterations in her dialect. When I'm retained, the first step is to get my operative on the phone. In front of her she has a list of the people in those folders over there." Potter indicated the hanging files.

Sharon tilted her chin. "The women who . . . ?"

"Right. The ones with, let's say, a history around the Capitol Building. My operative calls the man we're investigating at his office. She tells the switchboard she's Jane Doe, the first name on the list. If the politician won't talk to Jane Doe, my operative waits ten minutes and calls back, using a slightly different accent, only this time she's Sally Smith, the second name. This goes on until, eventually, the guy comes to the phone. Whoever he's willing to talk to, that's the woman he's sleeping with."

"Sounds simple and efficient. If the other woman in the case isn't someone in your files, I suppose your work is then cut out for you."

"It would be." Potter intertwined his fingers behind

his head and leaned back in self-satisfaction. "But it never happens that way. If a woman's been playing around with a married congressman, president, whatever, she's played around before. With someone in this town, sometime. I have records on all these people, Miss Hays. Every single one."

Sharon spent the next half hour seated on Mark C. Potter's couch, going through the file he'd built on Courtney Lee. The folder was stuffed with letters, photos, written reports, and videocassettes. Sharon examined each item in turn, stacking the materials she wanted to copy or keep on her left, piling the discards on her right.

As she worked she was vaguely conscious of Potter going about his business. Or *lack* of business, since the detective spent most of his time with his feet on his desk, staring out the window. He had two phones, one the standard office setup complete with two lines and a hold button, the other a cell that he kept on his desk beside a paperweight. Potter let his voice mail take all incoming calls over his main line. Each time the cellphone *brrred,* however, he would grab the handset, turn his back, and speak in hushed tones into the mouthpiece. He had two such conversations while Sharon worked on the sofa, and during one of these he retreated to his reception area and closed the door.

Courtney had a history with a capital H, and Sharon was appalled. Jesus Christ, the girl had only worked in Washington since June, less than half a year before she died. Yet here she was in Potter's smut file, over and over. The first entry regarding Courtney had come during the summer, less than a month after she'd arrived in town, when she'd turned up at a party in Arlington as a member of a threesome. The couple with Courtney were a married southern senator in his forties and a twenty-one-year-old White House intern. According to Potter's report, the intern and the senator were an item and had brought Courtney along to introduce her around. Which hadn't taken long; Courtney had left the party early with a junior congressman from Hawaii. Since the married southern senator, not the Hawaiian, had been the target of Potter's investigation, Courtney's presence in the report ended when she left the party; she had at that point, however, become a part of Potter's file for future reference.

And the future hadn't been far away. Three days later Courtney and the Hawaiian congressman had turned up again, this time when they'd accompanied the senator and the intern on a weekend jaunt to Atlantic City. All-night gambling, the works. A parting at the airport, the senator and the congressman catching an early Sunday shuttle back to Reagan International, Courtney and the intern on a flight that left two hours later and landed at Washington–Baltimore. Courtney had become a regular in Potter's records after the Atlantic City trip, complete with trysts in out-of-the-way bars and motels in Virginia and Maryland. Will John Benedict had entered the picture as one of Courtney's escorts as far back as September, two months before Cas had hired Potter. At the time, however, Congressman Benedict's affair with Courtney Lee had been a mere footnote to a New York legislator's dallying with a waitress at Hooter's. There was another weekend trip in Courtney's resumé, this one only two weeks before her death, and this little sojourn had been a whirlwind overnighter into Manhattan. Once again the middle-aged southern senator, the Hawaiian guy (who Sharon had mentally dubbed Honolulu Harry by now), and the White House intern were involved. On this occasion, however, the women had changed partners. The intern had shared a room with the Hawaiian and Courtney had bedded down with the older man. Sharon laid the file aside and allowed her stomach to churn.

Sharon Hays had been there, and not that long ago. The players had been different—actors, producers, and New York stage show bankroll men instead of political hacks—but the stars-in-your-eyes syndrome had been pretty much the same. During her first months pursuing an acting career Sharon had pulled more than one stunt she wasn't proud of, and things had happened in the Big Apple that she hoped to God Melanie never learned about. Try as she might to zero in on the seamy side of Courtney Lee, Sharon couldn't help sympathizing. She let her gaze fall into her lap for a moment, then slowly looked up. From behind his desk, Mark C. Potter was watching her.

He said, "Is something wrong?"

Sharon expelled breath through her nose. "No, it's just . . . not that pretty a picture."

Potter toyed with a paperweight. "I don't know that it's much different from many pictures I run across."

Sharon slowly rotated her head from side to side. "All those young girls. Wasting their time with these . . ."

Potter rubbed his hands together. "Consider it as

what it is, a deal. The women get what they want, a brush with celebrity, a walk in the limelight, whatever. The men get what they want as well. So what's the harm?"

Spoken like a true porno dealer, Sharon thought. She patted the stack of photos, papers, and videotapes on her left. "I can copy these?"

Potter's look was wary. "Only if it helps keep my name out of it."

"I think with the information here I can drum up a few witnesses," Sharon said. "Which is a giant step toward keeping you anonymous. I expect resistance from these politicians, getting them to testify."

Potter blinked. "Massive resistance. As in lawyer after lawyer. I'm glad it's your concern and not mine."

Sharon thoughtfully poked her tongue into her inner cheek. "For you to remain totally anonymous in this, for you to have a *chance* to remain totally anonymous, there's another bump in the road."

Potter frowned. "Which is?"

"You telling me the story of what happened on the night Courtney was murdered. That's the most critical information you have, according to Cas Benedict." Sharon indicated the piles of data by each of her hips. "Anything about that night is pregnantly absent from all this."

"That's because I destroyed it all. After I gave Mrs. Benedict her copies. I knew it was information I was better off not having."

"So you wouldn't be dragged into the murder case, you destroyed information helpful to the suspect?"

Potter self-importantly inflated his chest. "That's the way I do things, take it or leave it."

Sharon sat back in wonderment. "You're a piece of work, Mr. Potter. I'm sure it won't bother you a bit for me to think so, but you are."

"Regrettably, not a skillful enough piece of work to keep it all from coming back to haunt me. Funny thing is, normally I wouldn't have been working when it happened. I charge double hours for holiday assignments. When Mrs. Benedict called me from Texas to say her husband was returning to Washington for a few days, that I should keep an eye on him, I was packing for a trip of my own. She almost missed me."

Well wouldn't it have been a shame if she had, Sharon thought. She wondered if Mark C. Potter had a mother somewhere in Hometown, U.S.A., or if he and a bunch of other sleazos danced around a Christmas tree fashioned from bones. She said, "I'd like you to detail the whole evening. Frankly our client has described certain things. I'd like to see if his description jibes with yours."

Potter's eyes grew mockingly round. "You'd doubt your client's word? In your business, that's probably prudent."

"What I doubt and what I don't doubt isn't relevant here, sir. Please tell me the story. Sometimes I may interrupt, to move you along, but don't leave anything out."

Potter slightly averted his gaze. "There's not that much to tell."

"That isn't my understanding, sir," Sharon said. "I suspect what I'm about to hear is a story that only you can tell, which translates to time for you on the witness stand. Tell it anyway, Mr. Potter. I'm not going to let you wiggle out."

Potter sighed in resignation. "I picked up on them at a party over in Maryland. Drove to a house over there, located Congressman Benedict's car and waited for him to appear."

"That checks with Will John's story, at least so far. But how did you know where he'd be at the time?" Sharon asked.

"I knew from the time his wife called from Texas that eventually he'd go to this gathering. It's the only reason a married man would return to Washington during the Christmas break. For insurance I'd installed a tracking device in his car, under the bumper. With Mrs. Benedict's permission, of course. So even if he hadn't gone to the party my dashboard monitor would have led me to him. Assuming he was driving his wife's Chrysler, which according to her he would be."

"I rode in that car," Sharon said, "on the night I met with Cas."

Potter offered a mirthless smile. "I know. You met Mrs. Benedict at Beggett's Pub, and she drove you to your hotel. My monitor was on that night as well."

Sharon leaned back, oddly impressed.

Potter continued. "He left the party early, and took the young lady to his Georgetown condo. Not the spot I would have chosen, had I been him, but that's where they went."

"Let's just say my client wasn't a veteran screwer around," Sharon said.

"Obviously. I, uh, observed them in the condo for

an hour or two. They spent time in the living room and then retreated to the downstairs guest room. That room doesn't have a window that's accessible from the outside of the house, Miss Hays. I can't give you a blow-by-blow of what occurred in there."

Deep Throat's got nothing on this guy, Sharon thought. "I can do without one," she said. "Rest assured I'm not in this for the titillation factor."

Potter seemed taken aback. He wet his lips. "The next thing that happened was odd. They came out of the guest room. He was dressed, she wasn't. She went to the door with him, and then he left."

So far Will John's story was right-on. Sharon said, "Left? Where did he go?"

"I got a good photo," Potter said, "of them at the door. She's quite naked in the picture."

Sharon patted the sofa in irritation. "I've seen the picture, sir, in this stack here. I hope you weren't so caught up in your photography that you forgot to follow him."

"No, but almost. His leaving caught me totally by surprise. I was hidden in some bushes near the front of the house, and had he taken the Chrysler I couldn't have reached my own car in time to put a tail on him. But he opened the garage and went inside, which gave me time to creep down the block to my Bronco."

"He took a different car?" Sharon dropped her hand to her side. "I wonder why he'd do that."

"As do I," Potter said. "The only thing I know for certain is, he did. A two-year-old Mercury, the car he normally drives to his office. Put me in a bind, Miss Hays. You see, I had no tracking device on the Merc and had to stay in eyesight. There were a couple of times I thought he'd made me."

Sharon made a note to ask Will John why he'd switched cars for the trip to the dope dealer and the sex shop. She could now list, in addition to the drug dealer and the smut peddler, Mark C. Potter as a witness. Oh, terrific, Sharon thought, it's a toss-up as to which of the three the jury will despise the most. She said, "Where did he go?"

"First he met a guy in a bar. They had some words."

"And exchanged some money for some cocaine," Sharon said. "Come on, Mr. Potter, don't tell me you're not up on the political drug suppliers around here."

"Of course I am. I didn't know that *you* were."

"Only to the extent that my client's clued me in. Did you see Will John buying the drugs."

"I was at the front, at the bar. I couldn't testify as to what went on back in the booth."

"Convenient for you that you couldn't, Mr. Potter. Keeps you from having to testify about the drug buy. When he and the man parted company, you kept on following him?"

"Yeah, I did. As he was leaving the bar with me a block behind him, my dashboard dinged."

Up to this point, Potter's story was so right-on with Will John's description of the events that Sharon had lost focus. It took a moment for Potter's words to sink in. She sat bolt upright. "Your what did what?"

"My dashboard . . . the monitor sounded. The tracking device, you know?"

Sharon's forehead tightened. "I thought you said Will John had switched cars."

"Exactly my point. My tracking device was still honed in on the Chrysler, back at the condo. That car was now in motion."

"You're saying that while Will John was out on a goody run, Courtney left the condo in the other car?"

"Someone did. I can't swear it was her, but two plus two."

"Jesus Christ," Sharon said.

"I couldn't be two places at once," Potter said, "and my assignment was to keep up with the congressman's whereabouts, so I stuck with him. He went to one of these adult places."

"A sex shop, yeah. We know about that."

"Do you know what he bought?"

"A vibrating dildo," Sharon said.

"I'm surprised he'd admit to it. Guy seemed really embarrassed, looking all around as he carried the sack out to his car."

"Wouldn't you be embarrassed in that situation?" Sharon asked, then thought it over and said, "On second thought, maybe you wouldn't. You followed him back to the condo then. Please tell me you also watched him dispose of the body. It can clear my client, assuming the jury believes you."

Potter showed a blank look.

"Well if she was dead when he returned to the condo," Sharon said, "and you have this photo of her bidding him good-bye as he left on his shopping trip, then he couldn't very well have killed her, could he?"

Potter licked his lips. "When he returned to the

condo, no one was there. Not her, no one. Dead *or* alive."

Sharon was stunned speechless.

"I watched him every step, Miss Hays. From the time he left the condo until he returned, he was never out of my sight. He pulled into his carport, got out, and looked frantically around the spot where the Chrysler had been parked. It was gone. Congressman Benedict ran inside the house, came back out, and stared up and down the street. This guy didn't know I was there and had no reason to pretend. He was scared out of his wits. He charged back inside and made a phone call. I watched him through the window. He fumbled with the receiver, dropped it on the floor. This guy was not faking."

Sharon picked up the stack of papers beside her, thumbed furiously through the pile until she located the photo of Will John leaving the condo, a bare-assed naked Courtney Lee smiling prettily at him through the door. She'd sent him on this trumped-up shopping trip to get rid of him, of that Sharon was certain, and, puppylike, Will John had trotted off to do her bidding. God, but Will John Benedict was a spineless . . . The longer she practiced criminal law the more Sharon came not to believe a word her clients told her, but Jesus Christ, this was the first time in history a client had told lies *implicating himself.* She held the picture in her lap and dropped the rest of the papers back onto the sofa. Watching Potter, she said, "I don't suppose we're lucky enough that you know who he called."

Potter smiled, enjoying himself. "I assume his father. That's who showed up next."

Sharon's lips parted. Seventy-five degrees inside
Potter's office, she was suddenly freezing to death. She
said, "His . . . ?"

"Paul Benedict. Come on, Miss Hays, I know you
know him."

Sharon wondered if the expression on her face
looked as stupid as she felt. Know him? *Know him?*
Well, sure, Mr. Potter, we were once so close he tried
to make me do the nasty with him. Know Paul Benedict? Are you kidding? Why, we're old buds.

"They had quite a row," Potter said. "Both out in
the yard and inside the house. A real dressing-down
the old man was giving him."

Sharon barely heard. Of *course* Paul Benedict, Sharon
Dodo, she thought. Will John, the nerd, had been
screaming for Daddy ever since the first time he'd
fallen off his tricycle. And Paul Benedict, professor
emeritus and all that crap, had enjoyed every minute
of turning his son into a worm. She said, "How long
did the father stay?"

"Couple of hours. Then he left. Drove off in a
hurry."

"And, of course, you don't have the slightest idea
where he went."

"I was paid to watch *Will John* Benedict. Other
than noting his fathers' presence at the scene, I had
no interest in the man."

Sharon's thoughts spun in a crazy quilt of colors. "I
assume you reported all this to Cas," she said.

"That's what I was paid to do."

Sharon watched her lap. She was deep in thought.

Potter leaned anxiously forward. "Going public with all this, getting my name in the newspapers, can ruin me in this town."

Sharon looked slowly up. Ending Mark C. Potter's career might not be the worst thing for the city of Washington. On the other hand, should Potter go out of business, there would always be a clone ready to crawl out of the woodwork. "I don't see many ways around it, sir," she said. "Having a client who's trying to cast suspicion on himself, that's a new one even on me. On the q.t., would you be willing to talk to the police?"

"I'd be willing to talk to anybody, to keep my name out of it."

"There's no guarantee, and having you tell your story to the prosecution could backfire. The case has become a political football. This U.S. Attorney has taken a position that Will John is guilty, and having one of these types admit in public he's made a mistake is close to impossible. What I'm saying is, it's a risk. Sally Pong and Cedric Hyde might very well listen to your story, pretend to believe you, then put every cop on the force on the case in an effort to discredit you. Once prosecutors go public with a theory, then who really committed the crime often becomes irrelevant to them."

"It would be worth a try," Potter said. "Nothing ventured, nothing gained."

"It's what could be lost that worries me," Sharon said. "In all due respect, sir, whether or not we'd be hurting your image isn't the most important thing to us. The question is whether holding you out as an ace in the hole is the proper strategy. It might be, it might not be. A lot hinges on Will John's attitude, once I confront him with what I've learned." Sharon gathered the stack of papers, stuffed them in her satchel, and prepared to rise. "I'll be in touch, Mr. Potter. Possibly to have you talk to Sally Pong, Cedric Hyde, and those two detectives on the case. The other possibility you won't like, but you may have to put on your testifying shoes."

15

Sharon didn't tell Russell Black what she'd learned right away, because she wanted to think things over. Convincing Russ that Paul Benedict hadn't been truthful would take some doing. She wanted to hit the entire Benedict clan, all at once, with Mark C. Potter's story, so that Paul, Will John, and Mattie Ruth wouldn't have time to put their heads together and concoct a new lie.

So she kept her mouth shut, spent a sleepless night tossing and turning, and the next morning held her silence through a two-hour meeting with Will John and Paul Benedict at the Georgetown condo. Russ decided that it would be better for him, Sharon, and the two investigators to go downtown alone, with Will John coming later in order to keep the defendant isolated from the media as much as possible. For once, Sharon couldn't disagree.

Russ leaned forward with intensity. He and Sharon were in springy French provincial armchairs, Paul Benedict on the sofa. Mattie Ruth was at the office and was to come later. Cas had excused herself and gone into the kitchen, leaving Will John alone at one end of the love seat. Alone as he always has been, Sharon thought. Lyndon Gray and Mrs. Welton were in the foyer, speaking in low tones.

Black said, "Now this thing this mornin' is nothin' but an arraignment. It's a formality. The law says you got a right to it, to have the charges read and all that, though the defense always waives readin' of the indictment, which is what we're goin' to do. In the overall scheme o' things, the trial, this mornin' means nothin'. The judge will continue your bail and the whole thing won't take over fifteen minutes or so. Piece o' cake.

"But it's also another appearance in front o' the public, keep that in mind. Everybody that's gonna be on the jury, if there is a jury trial, everybody that'll be on the panel will be watchin' on television. They know nothin' about the law, but they'll be formin' opinions. You been wronged. The whole lot o' you. Let it show." Black checked his watch. "We better be goin'. Paul, time your arrival for about fifteen minutes before the hearin' is to begin. That won't stop the press from buggin' you, but at least it'll cut down on their buggin' time." Black stood. Sharon hoisted up her satchel and came to her feet as well.

Russ stopped in the doorway, then fell into step beside Paul Benedict. The former law school prof wore a dark Armani suit. His steel gray hair was perfectly combed. He glanced at Sharon over his shoulder. She pointedly ignored him.

Will John was dressed in conservative gray. As he paused to let Sharon go in front of him he said softly,

"I can't tell you how glad I am that you and Mr. Black are here and on my side."

Sharon paused. Russ and Paul Benedict went on ahead. Gray and Mrs. Welton moved toward the exit.

Sharon turned to Will John and said in a whisper, "You may not be glad for long."

Will John's forehead wrinkled in puzzlement. "I'm not sure that I . . ."

They were, for the moment, alone. Sharon said, "If you don't stop lying to us, you won't be glad we're here at all."

"My God, Sharon, I didn't kill her. If you think I'm lying about that . . ."

"Not about that, no. Not only did you not kill her, you didn't even dispose of the body. Seems you left out a few things and added some others, such as that Courtney wasn't even here when you got back from your little errands and that you called your father and he showed up. Just little details like that. Things that I suspect Daddy told you to say."

Will John Benedict stared at her.

"For the moment," Sharon said, "you and I have a little secret. Your father can't keep you from going to prison under the circumstances, Will John. Only Russ and I can. Now. After this arraignment, you and I and Russ are going to have another meeting. And then you're going to tell us the truth, or Russ and I will be on the next thing smokin' back to Dallas." She took a step toward the foyer, then paused again. "Every bit of it, Will John. I'll find out if you tell another lie. And I wouldn't chance my finding out, if I were you, that wouldn't be good at all."

*   *   *

When they arrived at 500 Indiana Avenue, she allowed Lyndon Gray and Mrs. Welton to clear her a
path through the mob of reporters outside, hustle her
up two flights of stairs, and usher her into the courtroom. She stayed a few paces behind Russell Black
and went down the aisle with her head lowered in a
submissive attitude. It was a full half hour before Will
John's scheduled arraignment, yet Cedric Hyde and
Sally Pong were already at the prosecution table and
there were at least a hundred watchers seated in the
gallery. Sally Pong was in animated conversation with
Ginny Toledo and Isaac Brown, the D.C. detectives.
A swarthy man with jet black hair was bent over the
rail, speaking to Cedric Hyde in whispers, and Sharon
recognized Gregory Campisi from his pictures in the
newspapers and on television. Flanking the United
States Attorney for the District of Columbia were two
men in dark suits, probably FBI agents but possibly
AUSDA's from Campisi's staff. Strung out along the
second row like a summit meeting were Boots York,
Leonard Smith, and Mack Taylor, the Porter, Ragsdale & Jones lawyers who'd tried to bully the yokels
from Texas upon their arrival in D.C. Seated beside
Boots York was Wallace Burns, the politically connected, I'm-here-in-an-advisory-capacity-only black guy.
Democrats to the rescue, Sharon thought. Wallace
Burns attempted eye contact. Sharon kept walking and
ignored him. She went through the gate, moved in
alongside Russ, and thumped her satchel onto the defense table. Gray and Mrs. Welton sank watchfully
into chairs against the rail.

It was Sharon's first visit to D.C. criminal court, and the half-federal, half-local atmosphere was something else. The padded spectator's pews and beige pile carpet were a step up from most county facilities, but still a level down from what she'd seen in U.S. District Courtrooms. The judge's dais was dark wood, likely mahogany. Twin flags hung from gilt poles on either side of the bench, a Stars 'n Stripes and the blue-and-white banner of the District of Columbia. A shiny brass plaque affixed to the dais announced to one and all that the judge was named Wilson Whaley, and Sharon suspected that the defense had drawn the black bean in the courtroom assignment. Whaley, according to the bar association pictorial directory, was forty-four, a graduate of Columbia Law and a Bush appointee. According to Russ—who'd appeared sans Sharon for Will John's bail hearing while Cedric Hyde represented the people—the informal word on the judge was, "Look out." It was too hot inside the room, and in Dallas District Court Sharon would have removed her jacket and hung it over the back of her chair. She didn't think that going coatless in Wilson Whaley's court would be a good idea.

Sally Pong came over wearing a tight-fitting black suit and matching patent spike-heeled shoes. The suit had padded shoulders and showed her legs to good advantage without the slightest hint of cheesecake; if Sally Pong were to appear in front of a jury in that outfit, the male jurors would be appreciative and the women wouldn't be offended. Pong said hello to Sharon, then leaned over the table and extended her hand to Russell Black. "Sally Pong, sir," she said. Black scrambled to his feet, shook her hand, and mumbled his name.

Pong took a step back, folded her arms and stood with one foot slightly in front of the other. She glanced toward the two empty seats at the defense table. "I assume your client will be gracing us with his presence."

Black looked at the vacant chairs as well. "Will John's mama and daddy are bringin' him. Might be runnin' a little late, but he wouldn' miss it."

"A word to the wise, sir," Pong said. "This judge won't tolerate tardiness, something for both sides to keep in mind." She looked to Sharon. "We'd like to talk some stipulations to move the hearing along, Miss Hays."

Sharon's silence deferred to Russ. Black's eyebrow twitched. "Always open to savin' time, Miz Pong," he said.

"I'll assume you'll waive the reading of the indictment, then." Pong shrugged as if to say, no big deal.

Black folded his hands on the table. "Hell's bells, it was all printed in the newspapers the day after the bail hearin'. Who'd want to sit through all that again?"

"And will you do the same with probable cause?" Pong's tone was helpful. "We'd as soon not drag things out with a lot of testimony."

Black opened, then closed his mouth. Sharon softly drew breath. SOP in arraignments was to get things over with as quickly as possible so both sides could be on their merry way, so requests for the defense to waive probable cause evidence weren't unusual. In Will John Benedict's case, however, the press had printed innuendo after innuendo, much of which was

total baloney. Forcing the D.C. cops to testify as to
what they did and didn't have on the congressman,
right here and now, could set the record straight, and
also save a lot of grief when the same detectives took
the stand at trial. Sharon caught Russ's eye and jerked
her head toward the media section. She dug her toe
into her boss and mentor's ankle.

Black grinned at Pong. "Hate to sound uncoopera-
tive, but we'd just as soon you'd put your people on.
Most folks in this town an' around the country already
know the case front to back, but my memory idn so
good. Could be I'll learn somethin' that hadn been
on television."

Pong stiffened. "I suppose we're in for a long morning, then."

"I'm sure you can make it interestin'," Black said.
"The time'll go by before you know it."

"Mmm-hmm. Nice meeting you, Mr. Black," Pong
said haughtily. She turned on her heel and stalked
away.

Black winced, leaned over, and rubbed his ankle.
"That hurt like the blazes, girl."

Sharon scooted closer to the table and winked. "I
intended it to hurt, old boss," she said.

A short time later, Sharon twiddled her thumbs
while Russell Black paced back and forth in front of
the defense table. Both attorneys shot occasional glances
toward the rear of the courtroom. Still no Will John
Benedict, no Paul Benedict or Mattie Ruth, no Cas,
and no word from any of them. After Sally Pong's
conference with Sharon and Russ, the pretty Oriental

had returned to confer with Toledo and Brown, the
D.C. detectives. Now the meeting was over, and both
prosecutors watched the rear of the courtroom as well.
The detectives were hunched over in their seats, going
over their notes in anticipation of having to testify.
Cedric Hyde wore a look of triumph on his face. He
whispered something to Sally Pong. She nodded and
smiled. Someone in the spectator section muffled a
cough.

Sharon dug into her satchel, produced a notepad,
and scribbled two phone numbers. She tore off the
page, signaled to Lyndon Gray and, when the Englishman got up from his seat at the rail and bent
near, handed him the slip of paper. She said softly,
"The top number is Will John Benedict's condo and
the bottom number is the cell phone in Paul Benedict's car. Go find a phone in the corridor and call
both places. I've got to believe they're stuck in traffic
or have had an accident or something."

Gray nodded and headed off, nodding slightly to
Mrs. Welton as he passed her chair and went through
the gate. Mrs. Welton wore a brown pleated dress with
a white ruffled collar. She frowned at Sharon. Sharon
spread her hands in frustration. Lyndon Gray had
made it halfway up the aisle when the bailiff marched
in, stood at attention, and bawled at the top of his
lungs, "Awwwl *rise.*" Gray paused and slipped onto
the end of a row of onlookers.

The gallery came to its feet with a creak of wood
and a whisper of nylon. Russell Black stopped pacing
and faced the front. Sharon got up in a hurry. Then

the door behind the bench popped open and the judge hustled in.

Wilson Whaley was a short man with black hair combed over bald spots, and walked in a near goose step as his robe swirled around his calves. He had an abbreviated mustache and a pinched-together mouth, and Sharon thought immediately of Hitler. She wondered if the judge's hair was dyed, and decided that it probably was. Whaley jogged up three short steps and ascended to his throne. The bailiff bellowed, "*Beee* seated." The rustle of lawyers and spectators retaking their seats was like a collective sigh.

Whaley's eyes moved rapidly back and forth in his head as he surveyed the courtroom. He looked like a lizard seated on a rock, and Sharon halfway expected his tongue to dart in and out. Good Lord, she thought, what have we gotten into here? She glanced over her shoulder. When she'd defended Darla Cowan in California, all the judges and lawyers had been camera-conscious. Here in Washington, however, the TV people weren't permitted past the courtroom entry. A sketch artist was seated in the media section, a slender young guy with longish hair. He watched the judge and worked his pencil with flowing strokes.

Sharon turned back to the front as Judge Whaley snapped open a folder and read loudly, "The court calls Cause Number 99-CR-70448, the People of the District of Columbia versus William John Benedict, hearing on arraignment. Are both sides ready?" He closed the folder and placed one hand over the knuckles of the other.

Pong and Hyde popped up on the prosecution side

as the detectives continued to study their notes. Hyde squared his posture and said, "The people are ready, Your Honor." Judge Whaley turned his glare on the defense table.

Sharon couldn't remember ever having felt ill at ease in the courtroom in her life, but also couldn't recall ever beginning a hearing without her client by her side. She stood, certain that her ears had turned red, and hoped against hope that Russell Black could think of something brilliant to tell the judge.

Black did his best. "Russell Black, representin' the defendant." He folded his hands over his belly. "An' I'd like to introduce my associate, Miss Sharon Hays here."

Sharon wondered if she should dip into a curtsy. She considered inching sideways to stand in front of the vacant seat on her right, to cover up Will John's absence. God, maybe the judge wouldn't notice.

"I see you, Mr. Black," Whaley snapped. "And I see Miss Hays, she of Hollywood fame." His mustache wiggled as he pursed his lips. "And while we're all impressed to have these famous faces here, who I don't see is your client."

Black's Adam's apple bobbed up and down as he swallowed, hard. His smile seemed plastered on. "Seems the congressman's . . . been detained."

Cedric Hyde didn't let Black get away with it. He said loudly, facing the bench, "The *defendant* Your Honor. The people will object to any murder indictee receiving special treatment simply because of the job he happens to hold." He put clenched fists at his waist and glanced at Pong, who nodded encouragement.

"As will the Court, Mr. Hyde." Whaley indignantly tugged on the sleeve of his robe. "Mr. Black, I don't think it's possible that your client doesn't realize the seriousness of what is going on here. Do you?"

" 'Course not, Your Honor." Black sounded unsure, even lame. "But no way would he not be here unless somethin' happened."

Whaley smirked. "Something is *about* to happen, sir. I don't know how they do things in Texas, but Washington is a city steeped in tradition. One of which is, if a criminal defendant fails to appear, we call his name three times on the courthouse steps and then issue a warrant. And forfeit bail. Mr. Tirelli."

The bailiff stepped up to stand before the bench. He was a man in his fifties with graying hair and a slightly stooped posture. Whaley wrote something down, folded over a piece of paper, and handed it over the top of his dais.

"To the steps, Mr. Tirelli," Whaley said. "Call for Mr. William John Benedict, three times. If he doesn't appear, turn the bench warrant over to the marshals."

Sharon stood helpless, thinking, are they really going to do this? Yelling three times from the courthouse steps, sure, that was buried in the statutes right beside ducking stools and stocks on the town square, but everywhere else in the world the tradition had gone the way of the horse and buggy. Apparently in D.C., they still went through the motions. She halfway expected Wilson Whaley to reach under his chair and don a powdered wig. For pity's sake, if the defendant had skipped, did they expect the guy to come running up, huffing and puffing, when the bailiff called his name? Of all the . . .

The bailiff nodded to the judge, turned, and marched through the gate toward the exit. Sharon watched him go, and looked toward the rear. She expelled breath as the door swung inward and Cas Benedict came in. The bailiff stopped in his tracks and looked to the judge, as if inquiring what to do next.

Something was terribly wrong. Cas's hair was disheveled and she was dressed in jeans, a baggy sweater, and dirty white Nikes; no way would Cas appear in public without being perfectly coiffed barring one helluvan emergency. Her cheeks were pale. Sharon took a step toward the gallery, planning to meet Cas halfway, but Lyndon Gray was way ahead of her. The big Englishman was already near the back, and bent his head to listen as Cas talked to him in excited whispers. Gray turned toward the front and met Sharon's gaze. His lips were parted in shock. He came down through the gate and murmured something to Russell Black.

Judge Whaley banged his gavel. "What's causing this disturbance? Mr. Black, if you . . . ?"

Black held a hand, palm out, in the direction of the judge. Distress flooded the older lawyer's features. Sharon hurried over to stand between Russ and the Englishman. "What is it, boss?" Sharon said.

Black looked down at the carpet.

Sharon turned anxiously to Lyndon Gray.

The Brit slowly shook his head. "It's Congressman Benedict, Miss Hays. Something's . . . according to Mrs. Benedict, they think it's a suicide."

16

Sharon's face was numb, partly from shock and partly from the cold. Another front had blown in, this one threatening snow, sleet, and icy roads. The scene in front of the Benedicts' Georgetown condo was like something out of *Gorky Park,* policemen in clumsy thick overcoats lumbering in and out, reporters taking notes, fumbling with their ballpoints through heavy gloves. The minicam operators stood poised and stiff, like people made from boards. Everywhere there was the wind, rustling leafless branches and turning lips a purplish blue.

The crime scene and emergency medical units had come and gone, going through the motions, and any moment the cops would take down their yellow tape and leave the scene. Sally Pong, Cedric Hyde, and the two D.C. detectives had stopped by, more to verify that the subject of their investigation was really dead than for any other reason. They'd treat Will John's death as an open-and-shut suicide, and Sharon could practically hear the sighs of relief echoing from Capitol Hill. Paul Benedict had briefly addressed the reporters to tell them, yes, Will John Benedict had apparently killed himself, and to ask them to show some compassion for the family. When her former law prof had gone into his personal grief, his loss, Sharon had felt like puking on the ground. She'd watched the EMTs roll the shrouded body down the walk to an ambulance, load the gurney into the rear, and drive away.

Now she stood on the lawn near the sidewalk, with Lyndon Gray and Mrs. Welton on either side. Mrs. Welton wore a linen coat over her pleated dress, and seemed immune to the cold. Paul Benedict's dark blue Mercedes sat across the street, motor running, heater on. Russ was in back with Cas, consoling her. Mattie Ruth sat in the front passenger seat with Paul Benedict behind the wheel. He'd joined the others after his statement to the press, and had invited Sharon to share in the warmth inside the car. She'd declined. If her choice was to occupy the same space with Paul Benedict, she'd rather freeze.

A black Lincoln stretch pulled to the curb. Boots York and Wallace Burns got out and came over. Burns wore a muffler at his throat and York had a ski cap pulled down over his ears. Burns nodded hello to Sharon. "Is it true? Is he really . . . ?" There were splotches on his chocolate-colored cheeks.

She shoved her hands deep into her overcoat pockets and nodded sadly. "He's gone."

"Jesus." Burns turned to York. "Jesus, Boots, he's . . ."

York's nose was red and dripping. "Nasty business. Nasty. Uh, Miss Hays?" He stepped forward.

Sharon turned to face the managing partner of Porter,

Ragsdale & Jones's Washington office, a guy freezing to death, wearing a hijacker's hat, his nose running like a five year old's.

"Has anyone made a statement?" York asked. He indicated the knot of reporters.

"Yes, sir, they have. Paul Benedict spoke to them a minute ago."

"Ah, Paul. He'd know what to say."

"Yes, sir," Sharon said. "He certainly would."

Burns surveyed the scene. "There's not much for us to do here, then."

"Doesn't appear that there is," York said. Burns started back to the car. York hesitated, then leaned closer to Sharon. "Could you give our condolences?"

Sharon expelled foggy breath. "Oh? What condolences?"

York stared at her.

Sharon let it out. "You heard me. Will John's dead. That's sad for him, but I don't know anyone else who seems to give a damn. For everybody who's been holding their breath over this case, including you and the holy-assed Democratic Party, things couldn't have worked out any better. You've checked out the scene, Mr. York. You can now notify all those frigging politicians that the nation won't learn they've been playing around with girls the age of their daughters after all. Tell them they can breathe easier. But condolences? I'd as soon you'd spare me the bullshit, okay?"

Sharon didn't really have the stomach for it, but spent some time in the first-floor guest room along with Welton and Gray after the cops and reporters had gone. The wall and carpet in one corner was spattered with Will John's blood. According to the story Cas had told the police, the congressman had excused himself shortly after his lawyers had departed on their way to the courthouse. Cas and Paul Benedict had remained in the sitting room. Moments later they'd heard the gunshot, then hurried down the corridor to find Will John crumpled in the corner. A pistol had been on the floor beside his hip. There was a hole in the plaster where the crime scene people had dug a bullet out of the wall. The CSUs hadn't bothered to mark the spot where the body had lain.

Sharon bent from the waist to study the wall. The hole was twice again the size of a silver dollar. "Pretty big bullet, wouldn't you think?" Sharon looked over her shoulder at Lyndon Gray.

Gray nodded agreement. "It's no twenty-two, mum."

"Give you odds it's a nine-millimeter." Sharon straightened and turned to him.

"If you can deduce that," Gray said, "from the size of that digging, you're a better detective than I."

"I'm merely adding two and two. It was a nine-millimeter that put the holes in Courtney Lee's face. Are you up on your forensics, Mr. Gray?"

"In an amateurish sort of way, miss. That's more Olivia's department. She had training in L.A., on the force."

Mrs. Welton came over from beside the bed. Her chin was tilted in curiosity.

Sharon smiled hopefully. "Did your schooling include blood spatter evidence?"

Mrs. Welton was matter-of-fact. "Some. It wasn't my specialty."

"I dabbled in it," Sharon said, "when I was a prosecutor in Dallas. Forget powder burns. Any forensic reports on Will John will be buried so deep we'll never see them. But is it possible to tell from blood spatter how far the gun was from a shooting victim?"

Mrs. Welton was dubious. "Blood spatter is generally used in analyzing knife attacks, Miss Hays. The caliber weapon would be a factor. It's true that the further away from the victim the lower the speed of the projectile on entry, which could affect the distance the body fluids would splash about, but . . . well, we'd be talking an educated guess at the most favorable."

Sharon smiled at her. "Which, knowing you, means plus or minus a millimeter or so."

Mrs. Welton blushed. "You're too kind, mum."

Gray folded his arms. "I'm not sure I follow. The congressman was charged with a grisly homicide. Suicide is a natural conclusion under the circumstances."

"*Too* natural," Sharon said. "And natural except for one thing. Will John didn't commit the murder. They had the perfect alibi concocted, which yesterday was handed to me on a silver platter. We were going to get Will John acquitted and everyone was going to go their merry way. Courtney Lee wasn't Will John's exclusive property by a long shot. No telling how many politicos are wiping sweat from their foreheads, right now."

"Are the police aware of this alibi?" Gray asked.

Sharon vigorously shook her head. "Three people knew about it that I'm aware of, Cas Benedict, me, and this private detective. You and Mrs. Welton make five. I suspect Paul Benedict knew, and possibly Mattie Ruth."

"Which could create motive to murder the congressman?" Gray regarded Sharon as if he expected her to sprout wings and fly away.

"Possibly not, Mr. Gray. But all that coupled with what I see here make suicide fishy as all get-out."

Gray spread his hands. "I see a room. A blood-spattered wall. A bullet hole."

"And the forest, and the trees," Sharon said. "Mrs. Welton, how many suicides did you investigate when you were an L.A. cop?"

"A few," Olivia Welton said.

"Okay, and in how many of those cases did the guy stand in the corner and blow his brains out?"

Mrs. Welton looked thoughtful. "The bath is the favorite place."

"Exactly," Sharon said. "For wrist slashings, pill overdoses, and self-inflicted gunshot wounds right?" She pointed to a closed door. "There's a guest bath right in there."

Gray continued to be skeptical. "The usual place, yes. But that doesn't prove . . ."

"Bear with me, Mr. Gray. You, too, Mrs. Welton, I'm not going to start screaming and attack you or anything." She walked over to the corner, near the spot where Will John would have stood in order to drench the wall in blood and brain matter when he shot himself. "I'm five-nine, nearly five-eleven in heels. When Will John and I dated in law school I used to wear flats so I wouldn't be taller than he. So make him five-ten. Picture this five-ten guy standing here blowing his brains out. Now, look at the bullet hole in the wall."

They looked. The place where the CSUs had dug out the bullet was at the level of Sharon's breastbone. Gray said, with little conviction, "The victim's skull could have deflected its path."

"Some," Sharon said. "But a foot and a half? A nine-millimeter is capable of blowing a hole in an elephant, folks." She raised her hand, formed a pistol with a thumb and forefinger, and aimed downward at the side of her head. "He'd have to be a contortionist. No way." She relaxed her arm and walked back to stand between the two Brits. "There's more," Sharon said. "And this is something you'd never get before a jury in a million years. Will John Benedict didn't have the guts to kill himself. That's not showing much respect for the dearly departed, is it? But a spade is a spade, what can I tell you?"

17

Sharon blinked in wonderment as Mrs. Welton produced a tape measure from her handbag and, with Lyndon Gray holding one end and calling out the measurements, began to plot the height of the various blood splotches and the distance from the topmost spatter to the spot where the body had lain. The things this pair can come up with, Sharon thought. Who would think to carry a tape measure around, just in case? She left the Brits hard at work and went into the living room.

Will John had been dead for mere hours, yet the atmosphere by his fireplace was hardly a wake. Paul Benedict sat on the Early American sofa, chatting calmly with Russell Black. This bozo just lost his son, Sharon thought, yet acts as if he's talking football scores. Black himself looked uneasy and just a bit incredulous, his gaze darting back and forth between Paul Benedict and his U.S. Senator wife. At least *Mattie Ruth* Benedict's grief was real; she sat across the room from Black and her husband, her eyes red from crying and her makeup streaked. She looked helplessly at Sharon; Sharon felt a surge of sympathy and placed a hand on the senator's shoulder. Mattie Ruth sniffled and blew her nose.

Paul Benedict was saying, "I suppose transporting the body back to Baytown would be the best. We have a family plot in Austin, but Will's constituency would expect the funeral there."

His constituency? Sharon thought. His freaking *constituency?* What about his mother, you . . . ?

Mattie Ruth was near hysterics. "I want him buried in Austin, Paul."

"Oh? A memorial service in Baytown then, perhaps. At least that."

"I'm going to bury my son where he'll be near me forever," Mattie Ruth said, twisting a handkerchief. "And to hell with Baytown, his constituency, and everyone else in the world."

"He is a public figure, Mattie," Paul Benedict said. "Which gives us obligations to others than ourselves."

Russell Black's chin lifted in surprise. Can't believe this guy, old boss? Sharon thought. Well, I can. She pictured her talk with Sheila Winston, and Sheila's opinion that Paul Benedict was a one-of-a-kind psychopath who viewed people only as a means to an end. Including his own son? Sharon thought. You bet, Sheila would have told her. The only death this man would grieve would be his own.

Mattie Ruth sobbed and rubbed her eyes. Paul Benedict's look at his wife was one of . . . disgust, Sharon thought, that's the only word for it. Jesus H. Christ in a candy store, Sharon thought, Mattie Ruth's grief over the death of her son *embarrasses* the guy. Sharon narrowed her eyes and glared at her former law school prof. He blandly met her gaze.

He killed his own child, Sharon thought.

At that instant she knew. And not only did she know, Paul Benedict *knew* that she knew, and understanding passed between the two of them.

Prove it, his look said.

You bet I will, her look said back.

Paul Benedict calmly turned to Russell Black, and asked the older lawyer if he'd mind helping with the arrangements.

"Do what I can." Black's tone was unsure; he hadn't missed the exchange between Sharon and Will John Benedict's father. He threw Sharon a curious glance. She concentrated on something in the far corner of the room.

An idea came to her. "How is Cas dealing with it?"

Paul Benedict stiffened. His gaze rested warily on Sharon Hays.

Mattie Ruth looked toward the staircase in the corridor. "She's taken to her room."

Sharon stepped toward the exit. "I should go to her."

Paul Benedict shot up as if stuck with a pin, stepped forward, and blocked her path. "I don't know that Cassandra is up to company at the moment." He seemed determined; Sharon could talk to Cas after Paul Benedict had rehearsed her, not before.

Sharon harked back to her acting days, and slowly softened the area around her eyes. It was the identical look she'd once used off-Broadway, in a play called *Hester's Farm,* when her character's father had died and she'd managed some crocodile tears for an audience of fifteen or so. "I realize that it's a terrible blow to Cas," she said. "But for her to be alone at a time like this?" She gently touched Paul Benedict's arm and smiled up at him. *I never should have left the stage,* she thought. "I'll go to her while Russ helps you with the arrangements," she said. She exchanged a sympathetic look with Black, then returned her attention to Paul Benedict. "Believe me," she said, "we feel your pain. We want to bear as much of it as we can." *Bill Clinton and me,* Sharon thought. She stepped quickly around Paul Benedict, hurried through the doorway, and mounted the stairs. As she went up she chanced a look over her shoulder. Her former teacher seemed rooted in place, the hatred in his eyes enough to kill.

The grieving widow was in fact painting her toenails. As Sharon entered the bedroom without knocking, Cas gasped as if in terror and almost dropped the polish. She was seated on the four-poster king-size, wearing a pale blue shortie nightgown, one leg bent at the knee, her foot resting on a towel, cotton balls between her toes. Her jaw slackened into the same shocked expression she'd worn when she'd hurried into the courtroom. *Not a half-bad actress herself,* Sharon thought. Cas's voice quavered in just the right tearful pitch. "I thought it might keep my mind off of . . ."

Sharon sat in a cushioned armchair and crossed her legs. The bedroom carpet was rose-colored, the drapes pink lace. In an Early American style cabinet was a big screen television. Sharon folded her arms and jiggled her foot.

"I can't believe he's . . ." Cas capped the bottle and gently placed the polish on the nightstand. The tufted bedspread was snow white. Her toenails were pale pink.

"I can't, either," Sharon said. "The police aren't necessarily buying the suicide story, Cas." She remained deadpan and hoped that her nose didn't grow.

Cas's eyes widened. "Why? Why wouldn't they?"

"There are things that make the medical examiner wonder. We have to be certain we're all in sync as to exactly what happened."

"What could make them wonder? Will John's been despondent ever since . . . I suppose he couldn't bear the thought of . . ." Cas fumbled for words.

"What thought? The thought of being acquitted? I spoke with your detective yesterday."

"Oh? Mark?"

Sharon studied Cas, the slightly averted gaze. Time to drop the pretenses, Sharon thought. "I don't mean Bulldog Drummond, Cassandra," she said. "And you know already what the detective had to say. What I'm not certain of, what changed youall's plans?"

Cas tried her best. Her expression tragic, she said, "Yes, everything's changed now. My entire life's going to be different."

"Not *your* plans. *Youall's* plans, plural, as we say in the quaint rural areas of the Lone Star State. Your plans and your father-in-law's. Paul Benedict's going down, count on it. The only question in my mind is, are you going down as well? I don't think Mattie Ruth is part of the plot, though I don't understand how youall pulled it off without her being in on it. Paul Benedict is the one-in-a-million father who could murder his son without blinking. Mattie Ruth, conscienceless politician that she is, is still a mother. She'd have no part of it." Sharon was reverting to her days as a prosecutor, grilling the suspect like a pro, throwing in supposition as if it were an established fact.

Cas recoiled as if slapped. "Surely you don't think that I would . . ."

"Oh, hell, Cas, except by marriage you're not even part of the family. I can't think of a single reason why you wouldn't, if you thought it could do away with a nasty problem. And Will John's problem was as nasty as they come."

Cas sat up straighter, like a schoolgirl caught cheating, determined to deny to the bitter end. "He shot *himself*, Sharon. We were in the parlor and heard the gunshot."

Sharon chewed her inner cheek. "I heard the story you told. And you charged down the hall to the guest room in a panic, right?"

"That is what I said."

"Yes, you did. And found the body where?"

Cas stared at her. Cas's lips parted. She closed her mouth.

"By the bed, right?" Sharon said. "In between the dresser and the bathroom door."

"If you say."

"I don't say. *You* said. Where was the body, Cas?"

"Right there, close to the . . ." Cas caught herself. Her facial muscles relaxed as realization dawned.

"Right, Cas," Sharon said. "The body wasn't anywhere near the bed. Was there much blood?"

Cas stared. She started to say something, then closed her mouth.

"So now that we've established that you never personally saw the body at all," Sharon said, "why don't you tell me what really happened?"

Cas hung her feet over the side of the bed and hugged herself. "God, Sharon. It's over. Why do you even care?"

"Pick a reason. I was representing a client, and even though he's dead I'd like to see his innocence established for one thing. For another . . . hey, old schoolmate, you might not like this one."

"That's not a bit funny."

"No, it isn't. The other night you were going to tell me something about Paul Benedict, then changed your mind and drove off in a cloud of dust."

Cas looked toward the dresser. "What makes you think that I was going to tell you anything about him?"

"Oh, come off it. You asked me if my problems with the Benedicts had anything to do with Paul."

"Maybe I was only guessing."

"And maybe pigs fly. I have a story about Professor Paul, too. Want to swap?"

Cas's expression was suddenly petulant. "I already know you had an affair with him."

Sharon was stunned speechless. She looked up at the ceiling. "Is that what he told you?"

"You weren't the only law student throwing herself at him," Cas said. "Don't worry, it's never really affected my opinion of you one way or the other. You were never exactly Miss Perfect."

"How the hell would you know that? You talked to me one time, total."

"I heard things. Think what you want about me, Sharon, I never slept around for my grades."

"Slept . . ." Sharon propped an elbow on her thigh and rested her chin in the palm of her hand. "Jesus Christ, is that what you meant?"

"What I meant when?"

"The other night. When you asked if my problem had anything to do with Paul Benedict."

"That could have been what I was talking about."

"Well, now hear this," Sharon said. "Not that I care what you think, but my having an affair with Paul Benedict is too absurd for even you to believe in. He tried to rape me and in the process beat the crap out of me. That's not my idea of a hot romance. Is it yours?"

Cas's teeth clenched in hatred. "You're making that up."

"Why on earth would I make something like that . . . ?" Sharon trailed off. Her expression softened. She felt pity. "My God, you've been sleeping with your father-in-law, haven't you?"

Cas stood up from the bed. "I don't have to listen to this. Not from you."

"I don't think it matters who you hear it from, Cas. You know the truth, and so do I. And while you're all dressed up for the funeral like Jackie O, that won't change what has happened. You got together with Paul Benedict to kill the girl because she was putting your meal ticket's political career in danger. But why Will John? It seems like a lot of trouble to go to, murder Courtney Lee, frame your husband, then conveniently have that private detective as an alibi witness. That was going to get him acquitted. You'd gotten away with it, scot-free. We were going to get Will John off and you were going to be on your merry way, possibly even eventually into the White House. So, why kill the guy just when you'd pulled it off? It seems to me you were headed for sunny seas, full speed ahead."

Cas marched to the door and opened it. "I think you'd better go."

Sharon breathed through her nose. She stood. "For now I will. But don't think you're through with this. Why, Cas?"

"You're only guessing."

Sharon went over and stood in the doorway. Cas's nose was a foot from her own. "I was only guessing," Sharon said. "Not anymore. You and Paul Benedict have handled the mechanics pretty well. But it's your motive for killing Will John that'll screw you up. You just wait and see."

18

Sharon sat in the Lincoln Town Car with the heater running, tiny snowflakes drifting down and melting on the windshield. She unfolded a slip of paper and checked Mrs. Welton's directions once more. This was the place, had to be, a two-story garden apartment house with trees lining the sidewalk and a courtyard pool, twenty-five minutes from downtown D.C., in a middle-class neighborhood of Arlington. Steam rose from the heated pool. A volleyball net flapped in the wind. Sharon buttoned her jacket up to her throat, got out, and approached the building. She thrust her hands deep in her pockets and hunched her shoulders. The breeze wafted up her skirt and chilled her legs.

Number 283 was upstairs overlooking the courtyard. Sharon pressed the buzzer and waited on the landing. She let a couple of minutes pass, then pressed the buzzer a second time. The handle rattled and the door opened inward the length of a chain lock. A pretty brown-haired girl looked out. Her lips were curved in a natural smile and there was some baby fat in her cheeks. Sharon thought immediately of Ashley Judd.

Sharon stepped closer to the opening. "Miss Rudolph? Melissa?"

The girl had a soft voice, barely audible over the wind. "Yes?"

"I'm Sharon Hays."

"I know who you are. I've seen your picture." The young woman made no move to open the door.

Sharon shivered, perhaps a bit more than necessary. "Look, it's freezing out here, could we . . . ?"

"Those two people here a couple of days ago. They said they worked for you."

"Yes. Mrs. Welton and Mr. Gray. They said you wouldn't talk to them."

"I'm not a rude person," Melissa Rudolph said. "It's just that I . . ."

"You were a witness for the District of Columbia. It's understandable that Miss Pong and Mr. Hyde didn't want you talking to us. If you'd have been my witness I would have told you the same thing. But I think you'd have to agree that the circumstances have changed now."

"You mean, since there won't be a trial?"

"Exactly. My client's no longer around for them to try. Can I come in?"

"Gee." Melissa Rudolph looked past Sharon. "I don't know if I'm supposed to."

Sharon tried to smile. God, it was as if her mouth were frozen in place. "It certainly can't hurt the people's case now, can it?"

There was a give-in kind of uncertainty in Melissa Rudolph's expression. "I don't suppose it can. That guy and that woman. They're British, right?"

"As British as they come. And if you don't open that door right now, you may come out this spring and find me melted on your porch in a puddle. I'm turning into an icicle out here."

The door closed. The chain lock rattled. Then the door opened and Melissa Rudolph stepped aside. Sharon stepped across the threshold. Warmth flooded over her. She vigorously massaged her face. God, her nose might break off if she touched it.

The apartment was done in Modern College Student, beanbag chairs, a cast-off faded cloth sofa, a kitchen table from a garage sale. On the table were an open three-ring binder, a couple of ballpoints, and a book entitled *Advanced Calculus*. "Math was my weakest subject," Sharon said.

Melissa Rudolph wore jeans, cloth sneakers, and a U.S. Naval Academy sweatshirt over a blouse with a white collar. "It's my major." She sat down on the sofa. "Look, I have finals coming."

"Oh? Back home, those are before Christmas." Sharon waited for an invitation to sit. None came. She sank down into one of the beanbags. BBs, or whatever stuffing was inside the plastic, scrunched under her bottom.

"I know. Courtney went to S.M.U. before she moved up here. Here our semesters aren't over till the end of January."

"I won't keep you for long. I've got a couple of questions."

Melissa Rudolph wriggled nervously. "Mrs. Hays, I . . ."

"Sharon, and I'm not married. It's Miss. And I'll

call you Melissa, if it's all right. It's probably nice for
you to chat with someone from close to home. I lived
in New York once, and it was a relief to run into a
Texan occasionally among all those Yankees."

Melissa looked vacantly toward the window. "I'll be
back in Texas in a couple of weeks. My father wants
me to transfer someplace closer to home, after what's
happened."

"I can't say that I blame him," Sharon said. "Did
you and Courtney go out a lot together, or were you
like ships passing in the night? I had two roommates
in my single days. One was pretty close to me, but I
barely knew the other one." She didn't add that she'd
had a third roommate, Rob, though her time living
with Melanie's father had been pretty well publicized.

Melissa drew up her legs and sat on her feet. "Oh,
we did stuff together. Not much at night. My boyfriend's at Annapolis."

"So I understand. Courtney didn't date any college guys?"

Melissa seemed distant for a moment. "It's odd you
should ask."

"Why so? Don't college girls normally date college guys?"

"It's just that, ever since this happened, really a lot
right after Courtney died, a lot of newspaper people
called. All they wanted to know about was her going
with this congressman and that. All of it made her
sound so sleazy, when she really wasn't. You're the
first one who's asked if she ever went with any regular people."

"Well, did she?" Sharon asked.

Melissa looked down at her lap, then slowly back up. "Growing up and everything, Courtney Lee was the most sheltered chick in Baytown. And that means like, *really* sheltered. You ever been to Baytown?

"No. But I can imagine."

"Right. Wildest crowd there doesn't get home until after dark. Her mom wouldn't even let her date until junior year. And then it was like, the preacher's son or somebody. Even when she was at S.M.U. she didn't go out that much. I guess coming to Washington made her sort of like, wild."

Just like a young lady moving to New York to take up acting, Sharon thought. Someone I used to know. She remembered her purpose in being here, and said, "Melissa, other than Will John Benedict, did you meet anyone else Courtney was . . . that she saw socially?"

"A few. Most of it I really didn't want to know about. There at the last, the last month or so, it was like she was a completely different person. All these older guys. I called one of her dates 'sir' one time. I don't know who it pissed off the most, him or her."

"Will John wasn't her oldest suitor, then?"

"God, no. One of the youngest."

Sharon spoke slowly and carefully, measuring her words. "Melissa, did you . . . ever meet Will John Benedict's father?"

It was as if Melissa Rudolph had been slapped. She actually recoiled.

"Believe me, I'm not any kind of voyeur," Sharon said. "It's very important, or I wouldn't be asking."

Melissa's mouth twisted, as if she felt ill. "My Lord,

this is so *sick*. I just don't want her remembered like
she was at the end. Not by anybody."

"I won't have her remembered like that," Sharon
said. "Listen, I'm certain Will John Benedict didn't
kill Courtney. Wouldn't you like to see the proper
people punished for it?"

"You're the first one I've heard that from. To tell
the truth I didn't think he did it, either. He just
seemed like such a wuss."

"A good analysis," Sharon said. "Will John was as
out of it as you say Courtney was when she was
younger. His father taught in law school. Do you
know him?"

Melissa seemed near panic. "My God, he's about
sixty. He's almost as old as my *grandfather.*"

Sharon sat calmly back in the beanbag chair. "You
have met him, then."

"Please don't let this out, Mrs. Hays."

"Sharon. Miss. I'm not about to let anything out.
My only purpose is to see that the right people get
what they deserve. Trust me."

"Man." Melissa's eyes widened in wonderment.
"Man, you're sure a different kind of lawyer than
my father."

"Oh? How?"

"Daddy says, getting on a personal level with clients
is a mistake. Once the case is over, it's over."

Sharon thought about it. Was she wrong in doing
this? "Your father's right, in most instances. But I
became personally involved in this case many years
before any of this happened." She forged her most
encouraging look. "You loved Courtney, Melissa, I

can tell that with half an eye. I never knew her, but I'll tell you something. The more I learn about her, the more I can relate. Now help me put the demons away. Did you know Will John's father?"

Melissa's features tightened in thought. She expelled a sigh. "Not really know. Met is more like it."

"I don't know if anyone really knows this man. If you spent five minutes with him, you probably know him as well as his own wife."

"I saw him once, as I came in from school. He was sitting right here in this living room and I thought, What's this old man doing here? It's the only time I saw him with my own two eyes. What I know is just what Courtney told me."

"I'll need to know what Courtney said to you about him," Sharon said. "But first, did you tell any of this to the police?"

"I wouldn't. I'd never. It's bad enough Courtney being, you know, dead. But I wouldn't tell this story on her even if she was alive."

Sharon thought about her own childhood, and about some conversations she'd had with Sheila Winston. She said to Melissa, "You were a real friend to her, and that's something rare. Courtney and her father weren't particularly close, were they?"

"She wanted to be close to her dad. When we were like, in grammar school she was dying to hang out with him more. But he spent all his time working. Courtney practically never saw him."

Which reminded Sharon of another child she knew. Melanie Hays.

"Why do you want to know about Courtney and her father?" Melissa said.

"Something you learn in psychology, about young women who fixate on older men. Something about, searching for a father figure. So Courtney was seeing Will John Benedict *and* his father?"

"Really sick, huh? Most people wouldn't believe it."

"You're right about that," Sharon said. "But it so happens, you're speaking to one of the people in the world who *would* believe it. Let me guess. Courtney was out with Will John someplace and they just happened to bump into Daddy Paul."

Melissa lowered her gaze. "At a restaurant. Then the first time the old man called her, he said he wanted to talk to her about her relationship with his son. Even Courtney said it never entered her mind that he might want to hit on her himself."

"Did Courtney say," Sharon began, then licked her lips and said, "Did Paul Benedict . . . force himself on Courtney?"

"No. I'll tell you something, Mrs. Hays. Sharon. By this time Courtney had gotten into ludes, coke, hey, she wasn't the same person as when she came to Washington. She acted like, doing it with this old man was way cool."

"Odd as this sounds," Sharon said, "it's better that she cooperated. If she'd resisted she could have gotten hurt."

"You mean like, physically?"

"I mean like, physically. So how long was Courtney seeing both of them?"

"Couple of months. And there were other guys. I just hate making Courtney sound like a slut."

Sharon said tenderly, "She wasn't a slut, Melissa. She was inexperienced, the type the Paul Benedicts of this world prey on. Did Will John Benedict know that Courtney was seeing his father?"

"Gee, this gets sicker and sicker."

Sharon had a surge of sadness. Sheila's slant had been: Paul Benedict likes to brag about his conquests, particularly to his son. Puts the boy in his place. Sharon made her tone matter-of-fact. "Will John knew about it, then?"

"Worse than that," Melissa said. "Courtney told me Will John would want a blow-by-blow of what happened between her and Paul Benedict and then, vice-versa. The old man would want a blow-by-blow of what happened with Will John."

"As if the two of them were comparing each other's performance?"

"Kind of like that."

"Melissa, would it surprise you to learn that Paul Benedict killed Courtney?"

Melissa looked vacantly thoughtful. "No. From what she told me, the old man was more capable of it."

"He's more capable of violence," Sharon said. "That you can bank on."

"I'll tell you something I never even told Courtney. If she hadn't died, I wasn't going to live with her after this semester. I just couldn't deal with it. I was hiding the whole thing from my boyfriend, everybody."

Sharon watched the pretty young woman. "I've got

to level with you. I'm probably going to ask you to tell this whole thing to the police."

Melissa's vacant expression vanished, replaced by a look of fear. "Won't that make them mad, that I didn't tell them before? Those two detectives scared the shit out of me."

"That's part of their job," Sharon said. "If they do give you any grief, you just leave them to me. For Courtney's real killer to be punished, though, you're going to have to tell them."

"Would Courtney's parents have to know the whole story?"

"They might. The option is for Paul Benedict to get away with murder. He's gotten away with everything else."

"How will my telling stop him? I didn't see who killed her."

"Nor did anyone else that I know of. It's all circumstantial, but there's a lot of it. Your story along with a tale this detective has to tell could get the ball rolling. Paul Benedict didn't only kill Courtney Lee. If I'm right about this, he killed his son as well. He has an accomplice, Will John Benedict's wife, but she's as much a pawn as everyone else Paul Benedict comes in contact with. I need your help, Melissa. So does Courtney."

Melissa looked toward the table where her books lay. "I'm going to be in great shape for finals. When do I have to give you my answer?"

Sharon struggled to her feet from her position low in the beanbag chair. She almost stumbled, but righted herself. "I'll make a bargain with you. In addition to your story I have some other evidence to show the police, and I want to be certain this private detective doesn't back out on me. Unless I get my ducks in a row I won't be calling on you."

"I don't know which way I'm hoping," Melissa said. "Neither way will be too cool for me."

"I hear you." Sharon stepped toward the door. "I'll be in touch. And good luck on the old exams. Dead Week certainly wasn't my favorite time in college." She reached for the handle, to turn the knob.

Melissa said, "Sharon?"

Sharon turned back to her.

Melissa said, "Courtney wasn't bad. Know that, okay?"

Sharon was suddenly hoarse. "You heard what I said earlier. I don't believe she was."

"She got caught up in Washington, is all," Melissa said. "In a lot of ways I'm glad my father's making me move closer to home. If I keep living here, this town might eventually do something to me."

Sharon pulled into a convenience store on her way back to the city, and stood in freezing weather to use the pay phone. Sheila answered on the third ring. Sharon said, "Hi, there. My daughter around?" Though she tried to remain calm, she was certain her tone was urgent.

There were a few seconds of silence. The two single mothers had always shared a weird sort of ESP. Sheila finally said, "Sure, hold on."

There was a rattle over the line, more silence, then another rattle. Melanie said, "Mom?"

"I love you, sweetheart," Sharon said.

"I love you, too, mom. The TV Says Mr. Benedict committed suicide."

Sharon watched her own breath fog. "Yes." She held the phone for five seconds without saying anything.

Melanie asked, "Is that all, Mom?"

"I suppose it is," Sharon said. "Sometimes things happen that make me feel as if I have to talk to you, just to tell you how much I love you. You'd have to be a mother, sweetheart. See you in a couple of days, okay?"

19

Neither Sally Pong nor Cedric Hyde seemed interested in opening up an investigation into Will John Benedict's death. Sharon knew why they weren't interested, but thought it wouldn't be politic to say so. She asked them, "Won't you at least look at Mrs. Welton's report?"

"What's the purpose?" Hyde said. "You're a defense team with an agenda. Not to say your report would be biased, but . . ." He was hunched over his desk in round-shouldered posture. Pong sat prim and erect across from Hyde, as did Sharon. Lyndon Gray and Olivia Welton were in straight-backed chairs that Hyde had dragged in from the corridor. Gray's chair was halfway into the hall. Sharon wondered if Cedric Hyde's office was even smaller than the one she'd occupied as a prosecutor with the Dallas D.A. About a toss-up, Sharon thought.

She said, "Biased or unbiased, it's all we've got. I saw your Crime Scene Unit in action, Mr. Hyde. A lick and a promise is giving them the benefit."

"It's an open-and-shut suicide, Miss Hays," Hyde said. "Given what Congressman Benedict was facing;

hey, men have shot themselves for a whole lot less. Under the circumstances I'm surprised the CSU responded at all."

"Whether they *responded* or not is open to debate," Sharon said. "They were on the scene in body, that I'll grant you." She extended her arm over the back of her chair. Mrs. Welton handed over two copies of her report, neatly typed on a word processor in the USDA's law library. Sharon dropped one copy in front of Hyde, and gave the other to Sally Pong.

Hyde made no move to pick up the report. Pong glanced at her copy, read the heading, and dropped the pages into her lap.

"I can see I've got you mesmerized," Sharon said. "The blood spatter indicates that Will John Benedict was shot from at least five feet away. The bullet passed through his head on a downward trajectory."

"We're not really forensics people," Pong said. "And unless I'm mistaken, neither are your investigators."

"They were in the British Secret Service, and Mrs. Welton did a considerable stint with the Los Angeles Police Department."

Hyde looked to Mrs. Welton—who smiled at the prosecutor and adjusted the hem of her pleated skirt—then said to Sharon, "Oh? As what?"

Sharon didn't know. She threw Mrs. Welton a questioning glance.

"Four years in robbery, two in homicide, sir," Mrs. Welton said.

"And none as a criminalist, right?" Hyde exchanged a triumphant look with Sally Pong.

"Not officially," Mrs. Welton said.

"Let me put it this way, Mrs. Welton," Hyde said. "Could you get on the witness stand and qualify as an expert?"

Mrs. Welton lowered her lashes in defeat. "Not really, sir."

Hyde spread his hands. "I rest my case."

Sharon's face was getting warm. "Well I don't rest mine. Not yet."

Pong picked up her copy of the report and thumbed through some pages. "Even if we accepted everything that's in here, you're forgetting the two witnesses. Congressman Benedict's wife and Congressman Benedict's father. How do you propose to get around that?"

"Cas Benedict's already admitted to me that she didn't even see the body."

Hyde sat up straighter in interest. "That could be a start. Would she admit as much to our detectives?"

Sharon chewed her lower lip. As much as she hated to admit it, Hyde had a point. "I doubt it," Sharon said.

"So we'd have a swearing match between you and Paul Benedict," Pong said. "Who, I might add, is pretty well respected in this town."

"By everyone except the people who know him," Sharon said.

Hyde thumped his desk with an air of finality. "Let's get real here, Miss Hays. You're asking us to believe that Will John Benedict's own father killed him, even though this congressman had every reason to commit suicide. What would be the father's motive? Trying to make any jury believe that someone could kill their own son is no piece of cake to begin with. Without evidence of motive it would be impossible."

"I don't know his motive yet, but I'm going to. Let me ask you this. What kind of a father sleeps with his son's wife?"

Pong waved a hand as if batting mosquitos. "Yeah, right. And under questioning they're both going to say, sure, we've been doing the nasty for years."

Sharon refused to be rattled, though it took a lot of effort. "Of course they're not going to say that. I've been in a few courtrooms, folks. I know what you have to prove, and if all I had was my own version of what someone told me I wouldn't be sitting here."

Hyde and Pong regarded each other. Thus far they'd been having a ball, trashing Sharon's theories. If she really had evidence to force them into action, it could rain on their parade.

"For one thing," Sharon said, "I have a witness whose testimony proves that Will John Benedict didn't murder Courtney Lee."

Hyde's brows moved closer together in a frown. "If you have that, why didn't we see such evidence while we were investigating the killing?"

Sharon decided that diplomacy wouldn't work any longer. "You would have, and in short order if we were still fighting that war. I didn't speak to the witness myself until the day before the arraignment. I was thinking of the best time to play the card, whether at trial or beforehand."

"If you'd brought us something irrefutable," Hyde said, "there wouldn't have been any trial."

"We're both in the game, Mr. Hyde, on opposite

sides of the fence. You might have dropped the charges, sure, if you thought you couldn't contradict my evidence, but if you thought you could, then I'd have been exposing my hand. Right? Even now, with Will John no longer among the living, for the U.S. Attorney's office to admit they were wrong would be a bitter pill."

"One we've swallowed before." Hyde grabbed his armrests and hoisted himself halfway up.

"Sure, if someone holds your mouth closed and strokes your throat, the same way I give medicine to my German shepherd. If they leave the pill and a glass of water on your nightstand, the pill gets flushed. Come on, why are we sparring here?"

Hyde sank slowly back down. "Okay, why are we? Who is this person?"

Sharon looked over her shoulder at Gray and Welton. Both shrugged. Nothing ventured . . . Sharon turned back to Cedric Hyde. "Mark C. Potter," Sharon said.

"Jesus," Hyde said, then said, "Jesus" again before adding, "What's Mark the Shark got to do with this?"

"Cas Benedict hired him to shadow her husband. On the night of the murder, Mark C. Potter was with Will John every step of the way."

Hyde looked to Sally Pong for help. Pong's dark eyes brightened in interest. "That was your mystery witness? So Paul Benedict and Cassandra plotted to murder this intern and frame Will John Benedict, then conveniently sent this private detective along as an *alibi witness*? Your story is getting queerer and queerer, Alice."

"That it is, until you think about it," Sharon said. "They didn't want Will John convicted, only charged. He was their political meal ticket. The plot was simple, really. The young lady needed removing. Will John was fooling around with her, that was documented. So once your office gets on the scent and secures an indictment, ta-*taaa*, they produce Mr. Potter out of the woodwork and get Will John acquitted. They knew once that happened, you'd continue to point the finger in Will John's direction and never look for the real killer."

Hyde thumped the table in indignation. "That's not showing much respect for the U.S. Attorney for the District of Columbia."

Sharon gazed steadily at the prosecutor. "No, it isn't," Sharon said.

Sally Pong was all at once analytical. "That was an awfully brutal killing. Not the mark of a sane person."

"You're assuming that Paul Benedict is sane," Sharon said.

"Yes, but a bludgeoning *and* a shooting?"

"One committed in rage," Sharon said, "the other after the fact, to make certain the girl was dead. Also to point more fingers at Will John as the killer. You'll find that the nine-millimeter used to kill the girl and the one with which Will John supposedly shot himself are one and the same."

Pong and Hyde twisted around a bit. Sharon had struck a nerve.

Sharon slowly shook her head. "You're wanting me to open up to you, yet you're keeping secrets? My, my. It was the same weapon, wasn't it?"

Hyde said, rather sheepishly, "Appears to be. Our lab people say that deflection could account for the downward trajectory."

"Perhaps, if Will John's skull were made of steel. A nine-millimeter passes though bone as if it were paper." Sharon did her best to sound sympathetic, to keep the contempt out of her voice. "Look, Mr. Hyde. Miss Pong. I know that finding out Will John Benedict was innocent all along will give the D.C. prosecutor's office a black eye of sorts, but wouldn't it be worth it to convict the right person?"

Hyde leaned thoughtfully back and touched his fingertips together. "I don't have a great deal of faith in your main witness. Mark Potter's given us grief before, numerous times. Once even stood in contempt of Congress and still wouldn't talk. What makes you think he'll open up now?"

"Congress only had jail to threaten him with. I threatened him with public exposure. Jail doesn't hurt a man in his profession. Newspaper publicity can be fatal to him." Sharon assumed a pleading attitude. "Come on. Won't you at least listen to what he has to say?"

Hyde looked at Pong. Pong shuffled papers in her lap. Finally, Hyde said, "Get Detectives Brown and Toledo on the phone, Sally. If we're going to make fools of ourselves, we may as well include those two. Why should we bear the U.S. Attorney's wrath on our own?"

Sharon left Lyndon Gray and Mrs. Welton to wait in Hyde's office while Sally Pong scared up the two detectives, excused herself, drove to the State Plaza Hotel, and went to her room. She'd made careful notes on her conversation with Mark C. Potter and wanted to take them along to any meeting in case Potter's story should change. If Cedric Hyde didn't trust Potter, Sharon trusted him even less, and she'd only had one visit with the man. Potter had had a day to think things over and would know that Will John had allegedly committed suicide; for all Sharon knew, Will John's death had altered the entire picture where Potter was concerned.

Her legal pad was in the nightstand, right where she'd left it. She dropped the pad into her satchel, made a quick inventory of the satchel's contents, and dropped a miniature tape recorder in on top of the legal pad. She'd tried recording conversations before. Normally the satchel muffled sound to the point that whatever came out on the tape was unintelligible, but she had no time for a better plan; she'd do her best to put whatever Potter had to say on record. She turned from the bed. Her message light flashed.

Sharon hesitated. She didn't have any time to return calls. But what if it was Sheila? What if something had happened to Melanie? She sighed, picked up the phone, and brought up her voice mail. Russell Black, three times. In the last message, there was an unmistakable edge in his voice. She scribbled the number he'd left on a pad beside the phone.

She'd ducked out on Russ and taken Gray and Welton along, right after her confrontation with Cas Benedict at the condo. Her excuse had been lame, something nebulous about having matters to clear up, and she could tell at the time that Russ hadn't been fooled. She'd wanted to clue her boss and mentor in, right then and there, as to what she was up to, but Paul Benedict had been there staring daggers over Russ's shoulder. Russ had agreed to help Paul and Mattie Ruth with the arrangements. Sharon suspected that Will John's funeral plans were the last thing on Paul Benedict's mind.

She'd never before seen the phone number Russ had left, of that she was certain. She glanced toward the door, feeling time slipping away, then picked up the receiver and punched in the number. Mattie Ruth's cracked alto answered on the second ring.

Sharon very nearly hung up. After several seconds' pause, she said, "It's Sharon Hays, Mrs. Benedict. Russ called me and left this number."

Mattie Ruth's tone was still edged in grief. "He's been calling all over for you, Sharon. Where have you been?"

Sharon thought fast. Whatever story she came up with would probably sound just as lame as her excuse for leaving the condo. She looked down at her feet. "There are legal matters to clear up, ma'am. The court record has to be purged and Will John's case closed. It's a lot of red tape, which I'm sure you aren't interested in at a time like this, but believe me it's necessary."

Mattie Ruth seemed to accept the story. "I'll get Russell," she said. There was a rattle over the line, thirty seconds of silence, then a second rattle, and Russ Black said, "Where you been, girl?"

"First, where are you, boss? This phone number isn't on our list."

"We're at Paul and Mattie Ruth's place, in California."

Sharon held the phone away, stared at the receiver in puzzlement, then jammed the phone against her ear and said incredulously, *"Where?"*

"Just a minute." There was a rubbing noise, likely Black placing his palm over the mouthpiece, then Black said something that was faint and far away. Then he said, his tone now clear as a bell, "Kalorama. K-A—"

"I know how to spell it, boss, Kalorama is an upscale neighborhood on the outskirts of Georgetown. Sort of the Highland Park of Washington." Highland Park was the Beverly Hills of Dallas. Russ would get the point.

Black said, "Yeah, the area's similar. None of which explains what you're up to."

"Are Paul and Mattie Ruth Benedict both there in the room with you?"

"Along with their daughter-in-law. What's—"

"I don't have any time, Russ. What I'm about to say is for your ears only. You'll have to fake it with the Benedicts, okay?"

Sharon listened to a faint crackling noise. Black said, "I'm listenin'."

"I told Mattie Ruth that I was clearing up Will John's court case, getting a final dismissal or something. It's a story she'll buy. She's not a lawyer, and the tale is partially true, the record does have to be cleared at some point. Paul Benedict will know better, but he won't be able to challenge you in front of his wife. Paul Benedict killed Courtney Lee. And Will John."

"Huh? You been smokin' somethin' funny?"

"You're not playacting real well, boss, for the benefit of your audience. And no, I haven't been smoking anything. Look, I have to go. I'll be out of pocket for another couple of hours. Give me the address where you are." Sharon readied a pen over the pad by the phone.

Black told her to hold on, then, his voice faint, asked Mattie Ruth for her address. He repeated the address to Sharon. She wrote it down.

"I'll be there as soon as I can. Go right on with the funeral arrangements as if nothing was wrong."

"Sharon . . ."

"You'll have to bear with me, old boss. For now, there's nothing more I can say."

20

There were too many to fit inside a single government four-door sedan, so Lyndon Gray and Mrs. Welton got in with Cedric Hyde and Sally Pong while Sharon rode with the cops. She sat in the front passenger seat as Detective Ginny Toledo drove. Detective Isaac Brown hunkered dead-center in back, looking cramped and uncomfortable. Sharon wondered briefly where the enormous black cop shopped for his clothes. Brown would be tough to fit; his waist was a thirty-two, thirty-four at the most, but anything that would accommodate his shoulders would have to come from the Big & Tall.

As they cruised down wide Pennsylvania Avenue with the Capitol Building dead ahead, Isaac Brown said gruffly, "At least we're doing one thing right. Crashing in on the guy."

Sharon threw a curious glance over her shoulder. "No one called to be certain Mr. Potter is in? I could have, I've got his number."

"It would be a waste of time." Toledo steered into the center lane, passed a slow-moving bobtail, then wheeled back curbside. "You'll have to take our word for it, Miss Hays. We've been dealing with Mark the Shark for years."

"Guy's got forty-seven different kinds of caller IDs," Brown said. "Plus two or three different phone numbers. If you're not somebody he wants to talk to, he just don't answer. Even if we do the deal where our call comes up 'Anonymous' on his screen, he won't answer that."

"Just so long as he recalls the story he told me the other day." Sharon looked up at the Capitol dome. Toledo made a right turn in front of the reflecting pool.

Brown said, "He won't."

Sharon wriggled testily in her seat. "You hope he won't, is what you mean."

Toledo looked in the rearview and exchanged a look with Brown. Toledo ran her little finger along her lower lip. "We'll talk out of school here, Miss Hays. About Sally Pong and Cedric Hyde, you're right. They want this case to go away. Anything that might embarrass them, show they charged the wrong man, they'd just as soon avoid. To Ike and me, it makes no difference if we're working on the Will John Benedict case or a murdered hooker in the Southeast Sector. Our paychecks are the same, either way. But Mark Potter is a royal pain, the type we'd all be better off staying away from."

"Give you an example," Brown said. "Two, three years ago I ran across Potter, who just happened to be following this senator who just happened to be buying dope from a dealer who we just happened to know had killed this guy. Potter gave me a load of information that could have convicted this dealer, but we would've had to have him testify. Potter wouldn't come forward, no way, and we had to drop the case. In Potter's mind, there's no Number Two. Only him, Number One."

"I could see that," Sharon said. "He opened up to me only after I threatened to have Rita Carboneau put him in her column."

"Yeah," Brown said, "and five'll get you ten he's talked to Carboneau since you've seen him. He's made her a deal to drop a tidbit or two her way, inside stuff about some politician in his file, in return for her not printing anything about Mark. With Will John Benedict dead, Potter's not going to give us the time of day."

Sharon sighed in disappointment. "If you're right, Paul Benedict might've gotten away with murder. Two murders. Listen, if this Potter is that slippery, what makes you think he's in? He might be making it a point to be gone for the day. He knows good and well I'll be calling on him."

"He's in," Toledo said.

"You sound awfully certain of that," Sharon said.

Toledo had circled the Capitol, and now headed out Independence Avenue toward the western side of the beltway. "We have to take measures with this man. We have, let's call them friends, who work in the same building. Potter's car is in the lot and his office light is on."

"You keep that close of a tab?" Sharon couldn't believe it.

"With Mark the Shark it's a good idea," Toledo

said. Potter's lice. I've got nothing against his profession, if you want to call it that, but he takes either side of the street. Soaks the poor women for information about their husbands, then sells the same information to people like Rita Carboneau. There is nothing Potter won't do for a buck. For years he's been our Moriarity. Ours, the FBI's, everyone in D.C. law enforcement."

"Oh," Sharon said.

"Huh?" Brown leaned forward and put his head in between the two women. "Our what?"

Toledo gave Sharon a knowing wink. "Moriarity, Ike," Toledo said. "Arthur Conan Doyle. Moriarity was Sherlock Holmes's nemesis."

Brown scratched his head. "Arthur who?"

Sharon softly laughed. "She could have said, 'Our Jerry Jones.' The owner of the Dallas Cowboys."

"Oh," Brown said, "Yeah, Potter's a really bad guy."

"I think that was the point," Sharon said. "One way or the other, Detective Brown. You get the Jerry Jones connection, huh?"

It was after five and getting dark when Sharon entered Mark C. Potter's building to find Gray, Welton, Pong, and Hyde waiting in the corridor. Detective Toledo following close on Sharon's heels. Isaac Brown brought up the rear, slouching in, and relaxed in a corner close to the elevators. Sharon thought that Brown looked right at home, as if he leaned against a lot of walls. Many policemen did. Cedric Hyde thumbed the elevator button, stood back, and folded his arms. The whole gang piled into the car and rode up to Potter's floor.

Most of the offices in the building were closed for the day; Potter's door was the only one with light showing through. Toledo knocked softly, waited, then tried the handle. The handle turned easily with a click; Toledo opened the portal like an usher and stood aside.

Potter's reception area was brightly lit but silent; the heating unit made a soft hissing sound. Garish orange cloth chairs sat beside a hideous green sofa, and on an end table was a pile of magazines. God, like a doctor's office, Sharon thought. She had yet to see a visitor in Potter's office, and wondered who would take the time to thumb through the magazines to begin with; she imagined that Potter's customers were for the most part incognito, and hurried in and out wearing dark sunglasses with scarves tied over their heads. The prosecutors and the detectives fidgeted about. Sharon nodded to Lyndon Gray, and indicated the half-open entry to Potter's inner sanctum. The big Englishman shouldered his way through, then halted just inside. "Olivia," he said. "Come here, please. I'd be careful not to touch anything, ladies and gentlemen."

A cold knot formed in the pit of Sharon's stomach and stayed there.

Mrs. Welton went in Potter's office and stood beside Gray. She reached in her handbag, brought out a camera, and there was a sudden flash as she took a picture. Then the detectives were in Potter's office as well, with Hyde and Pong following close behind. Sally

Pong said, her voice an octave higher than normal, "Christ Almighty."

Sharon sighed in resignation. She went resolutely through the doorway to join the group, three men and three women in a semicircle, holding a meeting with a dead man.

Mark C. Potter had passed from this life in the saddle, or in his case on the phone, with a file open in front of him and a box of vanilla wafers at his elbow. He'd been using the cellular; the instrument lay catawampus with its antenna extended and the light on Potter's answering machine *blink-blink-blinking* on the credenza. Three photos were face-up at the front of the file folder; from Sharon's upside-down angle, the naked man and woman in the pictures looked odd. Potter was slumped forward in his chair with his head resting on his blotter pad, turned onto its right cheek. There was a small round hole dead-center in his forehead. No nine-millimeter this one, Sharon thought.

Mrs. Welton walked quickly to one side and photographed the body from a different angle, then crossed over to stand directly behind Potter and aim her camera at his back.

Cedric Hyde said stiffly, "Stop that."

The camera flashed a third time. Mrs. Welton stepped forward, lifted, then dropped Potter's arm. His hand flopped down on the desk, loose as a goose. "Rigor's come and gone, Lyndon," Mrs. Welton said.

Gray bent from the waist and studied the corpse's head. "Blood's completely dried as well. Been at least some hours, eh? Check the times on those answering machine messages."

Mrs. Welton turned to the credenza and reached for the playback button.

Hyde said, furiously now, "Dammit, I said stop that."

Welton depressed the button, and fast-forwarded through several calls. The tape was full, and the computerized female voice announced that the last message had come in at 10:46 A.M.

Just about the time we were in the courtroom, Sharon thought. And just about the time Will John died. She stepped forward and said quickly, "Small caliber, Mr. Gray. Probably a twenty-two, no more than a twenty-five. Make a note of that."

Sally Pong snapped to. She strode quickly to stand between Sharon and the body. Cedric Hyde went around the desk and shooed Mrs. Welton away. Welton went to the end of the desk and stood with her head cocked in an inquisitive angle. Sharon suspected that if she were to give the order, the Brits would draw pistols, hold the others at bay, and finish their inspection of the crime scene.

Sharon said softly, "Not now, Mrs. Welton. Mr. Gray. I'd love to, but no."

Both Brits relaxed and looked disappointed.

Sally Pong spoke with authority. "Secure the crime scene, detectives. All civilians out in the hall."

Sharon looked from Welton to Gray, then back again. "I think she means us," Sharon said.

Brown and Toledo stepped in front of the desk, doing their jobs, neither seeming particularly enthusiastic about it.

Sally Pong extended a hand in Welton's direction. "I'll have that camera now."

Welton calmly dropped the camera into her handbag. "In all respect, mum. I wouldn't try to take it."

Pong turned furiously to Isaac Brown. "We'll have that camera, Detective," Pong said.

The big cop seemed amused. "Can't do that, Miss Pong. Against regs. We can secure the scene, but the regs say nothing about taking personal property from civilians. I don't see how we could stretch it, that the camera was potential evidence. It wasn't even in the room when the murder happened." He glanced at the corpse.

Welton took her cue and stepped quickly to the doorway. "We've been ordered off the scene, Lyndon."

Gray politely cleared his throat. "That we have. Good day, people," He joined Welton, and the two went out through the reception area.

Cedric Hyde stepped up and pointed at Sharon. "I'm holding you personally responsible for those pictures."

Sharon put on her innocent face. "Responsible how, sir?"

"That they don't fall into the wrong hands."

"Oh, come on, Mr. Hyde. They're pictures of a body. Your own Crime Scene Unit will take the same photos. How can they possibly be any different?"

"That's not what I mean, Miss Hays," Hyde said. "The photos will show the exact position of the victim. Something only the killer can know."

Sharon looked to Pong, who stared defiantly back, then returned her attention to Hyde. "We have no intention of turning them over to the newspapers, if that's what you're getting at. In fact, so long as the investigation proceeds at a rapid clip, I doubt you'll hear from us again."

Hyde placed his hands at his waist. "I resent that implication."

Sharon stood her ground. "What implication is that?"

"That we'd be less than diligent."

Sharon nodded toward the victim, Mark C. Potter, dead with a half smile on his face. "Let's face it," Sharon said. "Mr. Potter wasn't Mr. Popularity around the beltway. I'm standing here without a shred of evidence, but I know who killed him. Not who pulled the trigger, possibly, but who's responsible. And so do you."

Pong butted in. "With this particular victim there could be any number of suspects. Hundreds. Even thousands."

"Exactly my point. He talks to me. He's Will John Benedict's alibi witness. I made the mistake of telling Will John that I'd visited with Mr. Potter, and I'm sure he relayed the information to his wife and Dear Old Dad. Will John turns up dead, and now so does this guy. Two plus two."

"Can equal five," Pong said. "Can equal anything. Until we do a thorough rundown, we just don't know."

"And your thorough rundown might take years," Sharon said. "Which is why we're going to, us and our investigators along with anyone else we can think of, be behind you fanning your bottoms. This won't go away, folks. If you're thinking about sweeping this under the rug, filing the case under 'Unsolved Mysteries' of the day, forget it."

Isaac Brown uncomfortably cleared his throat. Ginny Toledo gazed at Sharon with respect.

Cedric Hyde's voice quavered, like that of a man who was under pressure. "We have no more to say until our lab people can go over the scene."

"And wait for orders," Sharon said. "Until you find out how deeply Mr. Gregory Campisi wants you to bury this thing."

"That's an accusation. You're saying the U.S. Attorney for the District of Columbia would impede a murder investigation?"

"The duly appointed," Sharon said. "He'll do whatever the Democratic Party wants. You live in Coverup City, Mr. Hyde. You know it, and so do I. Will John Benedict's dead, but his case isn't. And won't be, if I can see to it."

Hyde seemed on the verge of apoplexy. "I've already said, civilians out in the hall. You hang around until the CSUs arrive. Then I can have the detectives take you back."

Sharon looked contemptuously around the room. "Don't bother with that. We have the cab fare. Unless we're under arrest, my investigators and I will go it alone." She stepped toward the exit, then stopped and turned. "And I wouldn't try arresting us, Mr. Hyde. We're not material witnesses to anything. And Rita Carboneau's slant on why you were keeping us under lock and key? That's something your supervisors wouldn't like to read."

* * *

Sharon and the Brits rode in virtual silence to the parking lot at 500 Indiana, and likewise had little to say on the drive to Washington's exclusive Kalorama section in the rented Lincoln Town Car. Mrs. Welton sat in the front passenger seat with her hands folded in her lap while Lyndon Gray drove. Sharon watched the scenery through the backseat side window. Gray remarked as they passed DuPont Circle that there'd been some new construction on the circle since his time in D.C. with the British Secret Service. Sharon said that was interesting without really meaning it. Mrs. Welton remained silent, apparently busy with her thoughts.

The Benedicts' Washington residence was a mammoth Tudor structure with a fountain in front and a circular drive. Twin blue Mercedeses were parked near the fountain; Sharon stopped in front of a red brick porch and killed the engine. She stared in silence as the Lincoln's headlights illuminated a giant maple tree that grew at the side of the house. The wind had come up; the branches quivered and rattled. Snowflakes whirled around the maple's trunk like confetti. The automatic sentinel extinguished the Lincoln's headlamps.

She'd performed with a fair amount of bravado at Mark C. Potter's office, enough to cause the USDA not to drag his feet on finding Potter's killer—or at least to see that the police *pretended* to investigate, even if their hearts weren't in it—but the reality was that Paul Benedict had likely won. When Sharon had grilled Cas Benedict in her bedroom, Cas's responses had been in the form of body language. Her expressions, tone of voice, and demeanor had said that Sharon had struck a nerve, but in truth the merry widow hadn't revealed a thing that would be useful in a courtroom. Melissa Rudolph's testimony would show only that Paul Benedict had been carrying on an affair with Courtney Lee. Father and son passing a female intern back and forth might be juicy tabloid material, but was next to worthless as evidence in a murder trial. Without Mark C. Potter to place Paul Benedict on the scene after Courtney's disappearance from the condo, in response to Will John's phone call, there was no case. Will John would have a grand funeral at which the Benedict clan could gather and grieve for all the world to see, and then Paul and Mattie Ruth could continue hand in hand through the corridors of political power. What the future held for Cas Benedict, Sharon hadn't the slightest. She imagined that Paul Benedict would store his former daughter-in-law away, somewhere down in Texas, where she could stand ready to service him at his will.

Lyndon Gray pushed open his door and stepped out on the circular drive. The Benedict porch was bathed in light from a flood lamp. "Getting colder, I think," Gray said. "Be ready for a numbing blast of air, ladies."

Sharon reached for the backseat handle. "Thanks for the warning, Mr. Gray. And I'll button up my coat, thank you. But to tell the truth, in my present sate of mind I doubt I'll feel a thing."

A uniformed maid opened the thick oak front door and led the way through an entry hall the size of the

Astrodome. The floor was polished hardwood, and down the center of the corridor ran a row of ten-foot Persian rugs. They skirted a floating staircase and headed for the rear of the house. The maid's starched apron swished and her shoes made little squeaking noises. Sharon followed close, with Gray and Welton on her heels.

They went through a living room featuring a walnut grand piano and a bearskin rug, and entered a study with floor-to-ceiling bookcases on either side. Rolling ladders were attached to the bookcases, which were filled with D.C. statutes, red-bound copies of the U.S. Code, and every research volume known to the legal profession. Sharon imagined that Paul Benedict's law library had cost a fortune. Straight ahead past two computer work stations was a seating area, chairs and sofas clustered around a rough-hewn coffee table. Paul Benedict and Russ Black occupied two of the chairs, and Mattie Ruth Benedict was on the sofa. Cas Benedict, wearing pleated slacks and a white blouse, was leaned back in a recliner with her feet up. The maid led the newcomers to the seating area, excused herself, and left the way she'd come. Sharon felt suddenly all alone.

Black, ever the gentleman, climbed to his feet. "You get your business accomplished?"

Sharon was stumped for an instant. Business? Oh, yeah, business, the cover story she'd made up for Russ to tell. She said, "The case against Will John is dismissed, boss." She mentally crossed her fingers.

Paul Benedict rose as well. "Can I get you some refreshment?" He wore a silk smoking jacket along

with a muffler, and confidently returned Sharon's gaze.
He reached for a dinner bell.

Sharon deadpanned it. At that instant her hate for
Paul Benedict tightened her throat. This was a man
who'd gone through life taking women as he pleased—
including by force—cheating on his wife, screwing his
daughter-in-law, and now had murdered his son. And
was going to get away with all of it, and continue to
live the Good Life. "No, thank you," Sharon said.

Mattie Ruth had calmed down, though her eyes
were slightly bloodshot from crying. "Russell has been
invaluable, Sharon. There's a memorial service here
in Washington, another in Baytown the day after. Funeral at the First Methodist in downtown Austin,
burial in the North Austin Cemetery in the family
plot. My son would be pleased."

Sharon lowered her lashes. "I'm sure he would, Mrs.
Benedict." She looked up. Cas watched her from the
recliner, not saying anything. The two locked gazes
for an instant. Cas looked down at her lap.

"An' it's time for us to be goin'," Black said. He
bent, took Mattie Ruth's hands in his own. "I'll be
prayin' for the both of you, Mattie."

Mattie Ruth hoisted herself up to her feet and
kissed Russell Black on the cheek. "Will John would
be beholden to ya. You comin' by tomorrow?"

"Got an early flight out. Things at the office. I'll be
seein' youall in Austin, day of the funeral."

Paul Benedict stepped grandly forward. "We'll see
you out, then. Come on, Mattie. Cassandra." He extended a hand toward the recliner. Cas accepted,
gripped Paul Benedict's hand, and pulled herself up.

Her index finger brushed her father-in-law's palm. Sharon didn't miss the gesture. The flesh at the nape of her neck quivered and crawled.

As Welton and Gray prepared to usher Russell Black and Mattie Ruth to the exit, Sharon stepped quickly up and stopped them. She said to Black, "I'll need to take a minute, boss. Something for Professor Benedict and Cassandra. Their ears only."

Paul and Cas Benedict exchanged a nervous glance. Mattie Ruth's forehead tightened in alarm.

Sharon fondly squeezed the senator's arm. "Just some legal business, Mrs. Benedict, nothing for you to worry yourself over." She smiled at Russ. "Just some papers, boss, someone needs to sign. I'll join youall out front in a minute."

Mattie Ruth seemed to accept the lie, and allowed Russ to take her arm and lead her out of the library. The U.S. Senator from Texas was all at once just another grief-stricken mother, her regal posture slumping. As she went through the doorway she leaned her head on Russ's shoulder. Welton and Gray followed; Gray threw Sharon a look over his shoulder. Did she need him? Sharon answered with an imperceptible shake of her head. The foursome disappeared into the corridor, leaving Sharon, Paul, and Cas alone. Just us, the gruesome threesome, Sharon thought. She faced the two. Cas dropped Paul Benedict's hand as if it were red hot.

Paul Benedict had the look of a trapped man. "What is it, Miss Hays? There can't possibly be anything for me or Cassandra to sign. I also doubt there were any pressing matters for you at the courthouse this afternoon. I suspect you've been stirring up trouble."

Sharon had acted on impulse, without a plan. Now that she had these two alone, she didn't know what to say. She squared her posture. "To sign? No, that was a ruse. Unless it's a handwritten confession, of course. You folks interested?" She smiled.

Cas Benedict's lips parted. She looked terrified. A pulse jumped in Paul Benedict's forehead. "Cassandra has already told me about your ridiculous accusations this afternoon," he said. "I don't know where you get your opinions, Miss Hays, but if you have no proof you should keep them to yourself."

Sharon had had about enough. She pictured Will John Benedict, and a sudden realization came to her. "Good for him," she said. "It won't help him much at this point, but jolly good for him."

Cas looked to Paul Benedict in confusion. The ex-law professor showed puzzlement of his own. "Good for who?" he said.

"Why, Will John, of course. For once in his life he stood up to you, didn't he? It got him killed, but good for him."

Paul Benedict put an arm around Cas. "The woman has no shame, Cassandra. My son not in his grave as yet, and she . . ." He trailed off.

Sharon looked behind her, toward the exit, then faced the couple once more. "Put a sock in it, professor. We're all alone here, just the three of us. I'm not wearing a wire, though I'm not about to strip down in front of a sleazo like you to prove it. But it's the only answer. You had the perfect plan to kill Courtney

Lee and shut her up. There are men in Congress who will be ever grateful to you. Then you talked Will John into taking the fall, and had Potter the Public Eye all ready to give him an alibi and let all of you off the hook. That should be the ultimate ego trip for you, that you could bully your son into faking guilt to murder to protect you. Will John had no reason on earth to commit suicide, because you'd convinced him he'd be acquitted and could go merrily on his way to the White House eventually. In fact, once the prosecutors heard Potter's story, they probably would have dropped the charges. So what happened to screw up your plans, professor? For some reason Will John was going to expose you, otherwise you wouldn't have killed him. The fact that he was your flesh and blood didn't mean beans to you, did it? Did Will John find out you were screwing his wife? Your own daughter-in-law? God, you are so . . . fucking . . . *sick* . . ."

Paul Benedict remained expressionless, but Cas was feeling the pressure. Her chin sagged.

Sharon zeroed in on Cas. "Come on, old school chum, what happened? Did Will John find out by accident, or did you rub it in his face in order to put him down? It could be either one."

Cas's face rearranged itself like Play-Doh. Her expression was all at once petulant, like a schoolgirl's. "That's coming from one who slept around for her law school grades, of course." She looked to Paul Benedict for support.

Benedict averted his gaze to the far wall.

Sharon sucked in breath. Ten years she'd been waiting. She showed Paul Benedict a broad grin. "What's this, professor, no comeback? Cas has already relayed your lie to me, that I slept with you voluntarily back in law school. I'll bet she forgot to mention that when she was describing our little chat this afternoon. You and I both know it's a bare-faced freaking lie, but whatever turns you on."

Cas looked up at Paul "Don't let the bitch talk to you that way, darling."

In spite of the seriousness of the moment, Sharon nearly laughed out loud. "Darling? *Darling?* That just takes the cake." She put her nose an inch from Cas's nose, and pointed at Paul Benedict. "He tried to rape me, Cassandra, and in the process beat me half unconscious and crushed my septum. Which he paid to have repaired, which accounts for my current goddesslike countenance, haven't you noticed? And yes, after that he made law school life easier for me, but not for any so-called sexual favors. He did it to keep my mouth shut, and I've regretted accepting his offer ever since. If I could go back and put this bastard in jail where he belongs, I'd give up law school, my career, and would have been glad to work as a waitress to this very day. If I had, Will John would still be standing here."

Cas's eyes grew big and round. She looked up. "Paul," she said softly.

Benedict tried his best. "I think you'd better leave now, Miss Hays."

Sharon was staring at Cassandra Mason Benedict.

Paul Benedict said, more sternly this time, "Miss Hays, I said—"

"Jesus Christ, Cassandra." Sharon felt a sudden

tightness in her chest. "Jesus Christ," she said again. "He talked you into killing Potter, didn't he?"

Cas sagged visibly. She loosened her grip on Paul Benedict's arm.

"Of course," Sharon said, "that's the only way it could be. Once he decided Will John had to go, then Potter became the only link between him and Court-ney Lee. No wonder you didn't see Will John's body, Cas. While the naughty professor here was murdering his son, you were out by the beltway, shooting Potter. I'll say this for you, Cassandra, your victim was the more despicable of the two." She looked to Benedict, then to Cassandra, and back again. My God, what a woman will do for her man, huh?"

Paul Benedict's face twisted in anger. He pointed to the exit. "Out. Out, Miss Hays. You have no proof of what you're saying, so go. Leave us in peace."

"Don't worry." Sharon took a step as if to leave, then stopped in her tracks. She turned back. "Potter could do more than just place you at Will John's condo, couldn't he? Sure, no way could those two jog-gers have mistaken Will John for you, even in the dark, because there's too much difference in age. But Potter could pass for Will John, at least closely enough to confuse the witnesses. Potter was about as sleazy as you are, and you paid him to dispose of the body and then concoct the lie to tell me. Not half bad, even for a maniac. But you've forgotten one link, professor. Potter wasn't the only link between you and Courtney, was he?"

Benedict's expression softened. He chewed his lower lip as realization dawned.

Cas showed terror. "What's she saying, Paul?"

"Why, the roommate," Sharon said. "Melissa Rudolph. Don't even think about killing her, professor, because as soon as I leave here I'm getting her on the phone."

Benedict put on a front. "Kill? What's wrong with you, Miss Hays? I haven't killed anyone and I'm not going to. This is too ridiculous for words."

Sharon and Paul Benedict stared at each other. The air crackled between them.

Cas said softly, "What roommate, Paul?"

Air came out of Sharon's lungs in a gasp. She looked on Cas with pity. "Jesus Christ," Sharon said. "You poor dear. Do you think you're the only female this bastard has been fucking? He's sick, Cassandra, and has hit on every woman his son's ever been interested in. That's why he tried to rape me, years ago, and that's why he's been doing it with you. And that's why he was screwing Courtney Lee. God, she was young enough to be his freaking *granddaughter*."

Cas gaped at Paul in disbelief. "Courtney?" she said. *"Courtney?"*

"Oh, Jesus," Sharon said. "He told you he was protecting Will John and his political career, didn't he? Don't you know by now, Cassandra? The only thing this bastard is interested in protecting is himself."

From far in the background, Russell Black said, "Sharon?"

Sharon turned. Her boss and mentor had reentered the library and stood halfway between her and the hallway.

"Come on, Sharon. We're waitin' out here."

"Coming, old boss," Sharon said. "I was just saying good-bye." She smiled at Paul and Cassandra Benedict. Cas seemed as if she were gasping for breath. Sharon said, "I so enjoyed our little talk, folks. And good luck in the future. You two have a lot to look forward to, you know?"

21

Russell Black was as mad as Sharon had ever seen him. "We're in the defense business, girl," he said. "Not the accusin' business. And accusin' a man like Paul Benedict is about as crazy as anything I ever heard of."

They were in the elevator at the State Plaza Hotel, going up. Black had fumed in silence on the ride back from the Benedict home, but as soon as Lyndon Gray had dropped them off in front and Mrs. Welton had ridden with Gray to the hotel parking lot, the older lawyer had descended on Sharon like a ton of bricks. She'd answered him thus far with a series of yes sirs and no sirs, and felt as if she might have to bite her tongue if the barrage went on much longer. When Russell Black was wound up, he could show the widest of ornery streaks.

Black stood with his head down and his hands thrust into his pockets, facing the door as the light flashed on each passing level. " 'Fore we got this case, I didn' even know you and the Benedicts were acquainted. I don't know what Paul did to get on the wrong side o' you, but it couldn' be enough to go

callin' him a killer. That was his boy, Sharon. His flesh
and blood.''

Sharon leaned a shoulder against the wall. The bell
dinged and the doors slid open. She stalked past Black
without a word and headed for her room.

Black came out in the corridor. "I'm not finished,
young lady."

Sharon planted her toe, closed her eyes, and whirled
around. "Yes you are, boss. Right now. Yes you are."
She opened her eyes and a tear rolled down her cheek.

Black gaped at her. She'd stunned him speechless.
Finally he managed, "What's got into you?"

Sharon walked closer. She respected Russell Black
more than anyone. She absolutely hated crossing him.
But she had to make him understand. She regarded
her boss and mentor thoughtfully. "What makes you
think you know him?"

Black seemed puzzled. "We go back a quarter of
a century."

"As acquaintants. You've worked a case or two
with him. That doesn't mean you know him. He did
it, Russ." She turned and started down the hall.

Black followed after her, matching her stride for
stride. "What makes you think you do?"

Sharon kept her head down and continued on.
"Do what?"

"Know him. Outside o' class, I made it a point *not*
to know any of my professors."

Sharon almost laughed. "So did I. This acquaintance
was forced on me one night. Come on, boss, don't
make me elaborate."

"It's not my nature to pry," Black said. "But in this

instance I feel like I have to. The man just lost his son, Sharon."

Sharon paused, took another step, then stopped and uttered a long sigh. "Don't make me, Russ."

Black stood in the hallway. "Don't make you what?"

Sharon gave a little shrug. "Make me go on and on about it. I have no proof. For all practical purposes you may as well be right. If he did it, he's gotten away with it. So it's over. I got some pleasure out of confronting him, that I'll confess. But why belabor the point?"

"Why not belabor it?" Black said. "You've thrown one helluva kink in any relationship we might of had with that family."

"*You* might've had. I never had. I never wanted to have. As far as I'm concerned you and Paul Benedict can become fishing buddies if that's your bag, but include me out. Permanently. I have to go to bed, boss." She continued on.

Black watched her go. There was worry in his voice. "This idn like you, Sharon."

She stopped a final time. "No, it isn't, and I'm glad you know it. If I can be so against someone, there must be ample reason. Ever think about that?"

Black nervously cleared his throat.

Sharon said, "What's done is done, and life goes on, I learned that when I was much younger than I am now. Good night, boss. My emotions don't run away with me, not ever. If I hate someone there's a reason. Just give me credit, okay?"

* * *

Sharon burst into tears as she entered her room.
She couldn't hold back any longer. She pitched face-
down on the bed like a teenager and pounded the
mattress. In seconds, the bedspread was wet with
tears.

She'd spent nearly a decade trying to erase Paul
Benedict's image from her mind; the attack on that
horrible night in Austin, the cover-up, her own feelings of guilt, but sometimes when she was alone that
dreadful period in her life came back to haunt her.
And now in one short week, through no fault of her
own, the past had come roaring up to slap her in the
face. And he'd won again. The bastard had won.
The . . . fucking . . . *bastard* had . . .

She sat up, trembling, and hugged herself. Be calm,
she thought. She eyed the phone, wondering if Sheila
was still awake. Sheila would talk to her, make her
feel better. Calm? Sharon Hays wondered if she'd ever
be calm again, for the rest of her life.

As she stared at the telephone, it rang.

At first the noise didn't get through to her. What's
that ringing sound? she thought. She dug in her purse
for a Kleenex. She blew her nose.

The phone rang again.

It's him, she thought. Paul Benedict, calling to taunt
her. He'd laugh at her, an insane hollow chuckle that
would echo in her ears until the end of time. Until
she lay right down and . . .

The phone rang a third time.

Answer it, she thought. No, on second thought,
don't answer it. Let the freaking phone ring off the
wall, she didn't want to talk to anyone, maybe not

ever again. She would sit here until the phone stopped ringing. Until whoever was bothering her had gone away.

She let out a gasp which was almost a sob and grabbed up the receiver. She put the phone to her ear and tightly shut her eyes. "Hello?" Her voice sounded faint and far away.

"Sharon?" The homespun drawl and rich female tenor were unmistakable.

Sharon gazed wildly around the room, as if searching for help where there was none. "This is Sharon," she finally said.

"It's Mattie Ruth Benedict. Can we talk?"

Sharon tried to compose herself. The task was impossible. She beat her fist against her thigh. "Yes?"

"First of all, is Russell there with you?"

Russell? Russell who? Oh, yes, Russell. "No, he isn't," Sharon said.

"Good. I wouldn't want him to hear this. I really wouldn't want anybody to hear this, but I'm afraid I need a lawyer. I started to call the police, but I read somewhere I'm not supposed to talk to them without my attorney. I don't trust any Washington lawyers, never have, so I'm callin' you."

A short time earlier, Mattie Ruth Benedict had been grief-stricken, sobbing out of control. Now she was oddly calm. She sounded almost like a robot. As if she was in shock.

Sharon's chin tilted in curiosity. "What's wrong, Mrs. Benedict?"

"I suppose you'd better drop by the house, Sharon. As quick as you can. I can't give the details and I'm not sure if I remember them all clearly myself. But you know my husband? And my daughter-in-law?"

Sharon gripped the receiver until her knuckles were white. "Cassandra and . . . Paul. Yes, I know them."

"Well they're layin' here dead, Sharon. And I'm pretty sure I killed them both. Please come by. Do. And I'll be beholden if you won't waste any time."

22

The upstairs study in the Benedicts' Kalorama mansion overlooked a rose garden covered in snow. A floodlight illuminated the garden, a patch of stark white lawn, and a greenhouse roof; the background scenery faded away into midnight darkness. Sharon wondered why she wasn't tired at this hour. She turned away from the window as she made up her mind.

Cassandra Mason Benedict wore the same white blouse and pleated slacks she'd had on earlier; if it hadn't been for the body's sprawled-out position and Cas's expression of death, the splashes of red across the front of the blouse might have been something she'd spilled. Her eyelids were at half-mast. One of the bullets had penetrated just below her left breast. Sharon wondered idly how long it had taken for her heart to stop pumping.

Paul Benedict had dressed to go out since Sharon had seen him; in place of the smoking jacket and muffler was a navy blazer over a red vest. He sat behind his desk, and if it hadn't been for the small hole in the center of his forehead he might've been napping.

His head was back against the high cushion of his swivel chair. Sharon walked around and gave her old law prof a push from behind. His head sagged limply forward, his chin resting on his chest. There was no exit wound, no red stain on the leather upholstery. So the bullet was still rattling around in there among the legal theories, textbook civil remedies, moral indiscretions, and evil plans. Sharon grimly smiled.

"We shouldn't be touching things, miss," Lyndon Gray said. "You're already in enough hot water with the locals, I fear."

Sharon watched them, the proper British couple standing side by side in the doorway. She'd caught them in their hotel rooms before they'd undressed for bed; Gray wore a dark suit and Mrs. Welton was in her nanny costume. "I believe Miss Hays may have something else in mind, Lyndon," Mrs. Welton said. She looked impassively at one corpse, then at the other.

Sharon's smile remained in place. She came pensively around the desk, went between Welton and Gray, then paused in the exit. "I'll only be a minute, folks," she said. "Secure the scene, or whatever it is that they say."

Mattie Ruth Benedict was in the downstairs den, seated on a stool, leaning on the magnificent grand piano. She wore pale blue lounging pajamas. A bourbon on the rocks sat before her on a coaster; Sharon had poured a stiff one, and noted with some satisfaction that Mattie Ruth had managed to get about half of the liquor down. The senator's face was an expressionless mask, her eyes staring vacantly at nothing. Sharon stepped over the bearskin rug, came up close to Mattie Ruth, and leaned one hip against the edge of the piano. "By the numbers, Senator," she said. "One more time."

Mattie Ruth turned calmly to her. "The details won't matter once everything comes out in the wash. Idn't it enough that I did it?"

Sharon said tenderly, "It's not enough for me. Please, Senator, one more time. We're trying to put things in perspective here."

Mattie Ruth was in another world, detached, as if she were the audience and the room were a stage. Sharon wished that Sheila were here. Mattie Ruth said in a monotone, "Paul gave me a sedative. He told me that he was takin' Cassandra home and he'd be back in a little bit."

"What kind of sedative?" The lawyer in Sharon came out; she was thinking defenses, under the influence, things like that.

"A prescription, I don't know the name. But I didn' swallow the stuff."

"He didn't watch you take it?"

Mattie Ruth shook her head. "He left a glass of water and two tablets on the nightstand, put on his vest and blazer and said good-bye. I intended to take it, I really did, but I wanted a few moments alone. I'd just lost my boy today, Sharon. I didn't want a damned sleeping pill to muddle his memory, not until I'd thought awhile."

Sharon tenderly put a hand on Mattie Ruth's forearm.

Mattie Ruth took a breath, remembering. "I didn't

go to eavesdrop, either. In fact when I heard these voices, at first I thought I was havin' a hallucination. A séance. I even called Will John's name." Her lips tightened into a bloodless line. "An intercom we had installed a year ago. So that if Paul was in the study and I was in the bedroom, I wouldn't have to go down the hall to roust him. He did a lot of briefin' in there. Evidently we'd left it on."

Mattie Ruth took a sip of whiskey, shuddered slightly, placed the glass back on the coaster. "When I realized what I was hearin' I got out of bed to shut the intercom off. Then I heard Cas's voice. Dammit, Sharon, why did I have to hear that? I stood there beside that bedroom speaker and it was like my world was endin'. Forty years I've been married to a man I didn't even know."

Sharon watched her. She wondered how Mattie Ruth could possibly not have known. Politics and power had blinded this woman for all these years. Sharon went around, sat on the piano stool, and poised her fingers as if ready to give a concert. She didn't say anything.

"They were arguin'. My husband and my daughter-in-law, like lovers. What the hell, they *were* lovers. Lovers and murderers. God in heaven . . ."

Sharon watched a row of glistening piano keys. "I know about all of the story, Senator. They killed Courtney Lee, and Will John, and a detective named Mark C. Potter."

Mattie Ruth looked incredulous. "You knew?"

"I had no proof." Sharon helplessly shrugged. A tear formed, blurring her vision.

"Did you know my husband was sleepin' with that . . . *teenager*?"

"I knew. Tonight I confronted them with it. Cas hadn't known until tonight."

"That's what she was tearin' into him about," Mattie Ruth said. "They weren't sorry my son was dead, or about anything else they'd done. My daughter-in-law was mad because my husband had been playin' around with an intern and she didn' know it."

The women sat in silence. Sharon depressed a black key, played a single note. B-flat.

"I don't have much memory of shootin' 'em," Mattie Ruth said. "That pistol was in a drawer, Paul got it for me several years ago." She indicated the pearl-handled derringer that lay on the piano. A twenty-five. Sharon wondered idly if it was the same weapon Cas had used to kill Potter. She doubted that it was.

"I sort of remember takin' the gun and some bullets from the drawer, and walkin' down the corridor to the study. I do remember clear as a bell the look on Paul's face when I came in the study. He was about to think up another lie, Sharon. It was in his eyes. He knew he was caught, and he was concoctin' a story to tell his way out of it. If I hadn't shot him, right then and there, he probably would have pulled the wool over my eyes one more time.

"And Cassandra," Mattie Ruth said, "seemed resigned to it. I'll give her the benefit and believe she saw it comin' and thought she deserved it. I shot her in the chest. She just looked down as if to say, well, here it is, and then collapsed on the floor. I had to reload to shoot her twice more. Other than on the practice range it's the only time I've fired the damned thing. I'd almost forgotten how to reload." Mattie Ruth picked up the tumbler of whiskey and stared at the amber liquid. "It's the woman in me, Sharon. Instinct older than whatever makes us want to be so goddamned equal these days. Everything was Paul's fault, yet I took it out on the other woman more than on him."

Sharon watched as Mattie Ruth took a stiff glug of whiskey. "I'm finished, Sharon. Let's call the police now," the senator said.

Sharon said, pensively, "Are you sure you want to do that?"

"Damn him." Mattie Ruth squeezed her glass so hard that it seemed the heavy tumbler might break. "*Damn him.* Everything could have been so perfect for us all."

Sharon considered the last part wishful thinking. Things could never be perfect in a family that dysfunctional. Never, never, never. Odd as it seemed, she felt a strange bond with Mattie Ruth Benedict at that moment. Two women decades apart in age; both, however, harmed by the same man in a way that could never be quite repaired. Sharon said, "Senator Benedict, look at me."

Mattie Ruth swiveled her head. She started to speak, but something in Sharon's tone stopped her. The United States Senator from Texas watched in silence.

Sharon said, "I want you to listen carefully. There is the law and there is justice, and they're often two entirely different things. I'm about to tell you something I've never told another living soul. I killed a man once. Never mind who, when or why. But it was justice, and under the same circumstances I'd kill him again. I'm not a bit sorry, and that's the same situation you should be in right now. There is nothing for you to be ashamed of, and you should never feel that way."

Mattie Ruth's voice strengthened, regaining some of its natural resonance. "I don't know that I should, either, child. They killed my son. If the police had your attitude, it would be a lot better for me right now."

"The police deal in a different vein. And you're right, they wouldn't be so forgiving. In this instance you should cultivate your own forgiveness, not that I believe any is necessary. Judge your own actions and live with yourself. You don't owe anyone anything, Senator, not over what happened tonight. If anything, the world owes you."

Mattie Ruth showed a regretful curiosity. "What are you sayin', Sharon Hays?"

"I'm saying that we're not calling anyone at the moment. You should sleep on it. If you feel tomorrow that you should contact the police, then that's to-morrow."

"Those two bodies in my upstairs study aren't gonna disappear."

Sharon stepped away from the piano. "Oh, yes, they are. You sit right there and finish your whiskey, Senator. The rest you should leave up to me."

*   *   *

Sharon reentered the study to find Lyndon Gray and Mrs. Welton watching the bodies like detached spectators. Gray said, "How is the senator holding up?"

Sharon went over to the desk and studied Paul Benedict. She said, "As well as could be expected."

"Given the circumstances," Gray said, "a jury shouldn't be too harsh with the lady."

"If there is any jury. Mr. Gray, when you landed at the airport you told me you knew roads in this town that angels fear to tread. You think you can remember any of them?"

Gray's jaw tightened in anticipation. "It's been two decades, mum. But I might muddle through."

Sharon looked at Paul Benedict, then went over and straddled Cas Benedict's body. She looked to Mrs. Welton, then zeroed in on Lyndon Gray once more. "I hope you've kept up your conditioning, Mr. Gray. Mr. Benedict might weigh a bit. But hoist him up, please. We might strain ourselves, but I believe Mrs. Welton and I can handle Cassandra on our own."

Sharon knew they were in Maryland only because she'd seen the sign when they'd crossed over the border, but she couldn't have found her way back to Washington if her life depended on it. On the way out Gray had taken a zigzag path in Cas Benedict's Chrysler and it had been all that Sharon, driving her rented Lincoln, could do to keep Gray's taillights in view. They were in a wooded area a mile or so from the nearest traveled road. Twin ruts led into the forest. The Lincoln sat ten feet behind the Chrysler. Gray had carried Paul Benedict from the Chrysler's trunk and set him behind the wheel while Sharon and Mrs. Welton had lugged Cas around to the other side and deposited her in the passenger seat. Sharon was out of breath and a strand of hair clung wetly to her forehead. Neither Mrs. Welton nor Lyndon Gray seemed to be breathing hard.

Gray said earnestly, "Be certain, Miss Hays. There will be no backing out once the deed is done."

"I'm not giving this one a second thought," Sharon said. "We're doing the right thing. I doubt there will be consequences, where we're concerned. We've given Mattie Ruth an opportunity to make it all go away. If she makes the right choice, she'll live with it."

Gray spoke with finality. "The die is cast, then. Olivia?"

Mrs. Welton gave the corpses in the front seat a professional once-over. She said, "the woman will be the victim, the man the suicide. You have the senator's derringer?'

Gray produced the pearl-handled weapon from beneath the folds of his coat. Mrs. Welton took the pistol and held it gingerly by the barrel. Both Brits wore thin rubber gloves. Mrs. Welton dug in her handbag and came up with what looked like two empty bullet jackets. The first was too big. The second fit snugly into the derringer.

Sharon looked to Gray in curiosity.

He said, "It's loaded with a thin paper wad which will disintegrate when the weapon is fired. Leaves a nice powder burn."

As Sharon watched, Mrs. Welton placed the barrel

of the derringer over the hole in Paul Benedict's forehead, eared back the hammer, and pulled the trigger.
There was a pop like a firecracker, echoing through
the wintry stillness.

"Good show," Gray said.

"Instant suicide," Mrs. Welton said.

Sharon stood by with her breath fogging. "You two
have disposed of a body or so, haven't you?"

Welton and Gray exchanged a look. Gray smiled.
"We might have to eliminate you if we answered that,
Miss Hays," the Englishman said.

23

The next morning Sharon sat beside Russell Black in the tourist cabin of a 757 at Reagan National, and waited for takeoff. The engines throbbed and the wings vibrated. Black silently read the morning paper. Visible through the window, the sun shone brightly. The Potomac's banks were covered in melting snow. The Capitol Dome towered in the background.

Sharon had slept very little. On the ride to the airport, Black had apologized for last night's tirade. Tiffs between Sharon Hays and her boss and mentor seldom lasted very long. She'd called Sheila from a pay phone by the boarding gate. Sheila would bring Melanie and meet Sharon's flight at DFW. Sharon couldn't wait to see her daughter. She would hug the teenager's neck until Melanie pulled away in embarrassment.

She'd scanned the morning paper, front to back, and tuned in the morning reports both on CNN and the local D.C. channels. Not a word about two bodies discovered in a car over in Maryland, identified or otherwise. Someone would run across the Chrysler parked in the woods eventually, no doubt about that. Sharon had called Mattie Ruth Benedict just as the 6 A.M.

news was over, and had asked the senator what she planned to do. Mattie Ruth was undecided. Sharon had suggested that Mattie Ruth phone the police and have her husband listed as a missing person.

The police and prosecutors would dismiss Paul and Cas Benedict's deaths as a murder/suicide. If Mattie Ruth kept her silence, that would be that as far as any investigation was concerned. Politically Mattie Ruth would become the perfect sympathetic figure, and Sharon was certain that Wallace Burns and the guys at Porter, Ragsdale & Jones wouldn't miss the opportunity to build the tragedy into a windfall for the Party. Mattie Ruth would survive. In a year or two, Will John and Paul Benedict would be sad footnotes in Mattie's Ruth's career. Who knows? Sharon thought. More power to her, the old gal might even be president someday. Sharon's conscience was clear. Paul Benedict, the dreadful night in Austin, the feelings of guilt she'd felt for a decade, she at long last was certain she could put it all behind her.

The jets rumbled to life and the 757 streamed down the runway. In seconds the airliner lifted off, banked, and roared through a curtain of low-flying clouds. Within a quarter of a minute Sharon's head dropped back against the cushions, and she drifted into the most peaceful slumber she'd had in years.